Metamancer

Skeltouch Saga, Book 1

William I. Zard

Cover art by Matt Stawicki

Zmancy Books, First Printing June 2023

ISBN: 979-8-9886631-8-8

LCCN: 2023942010

Contents

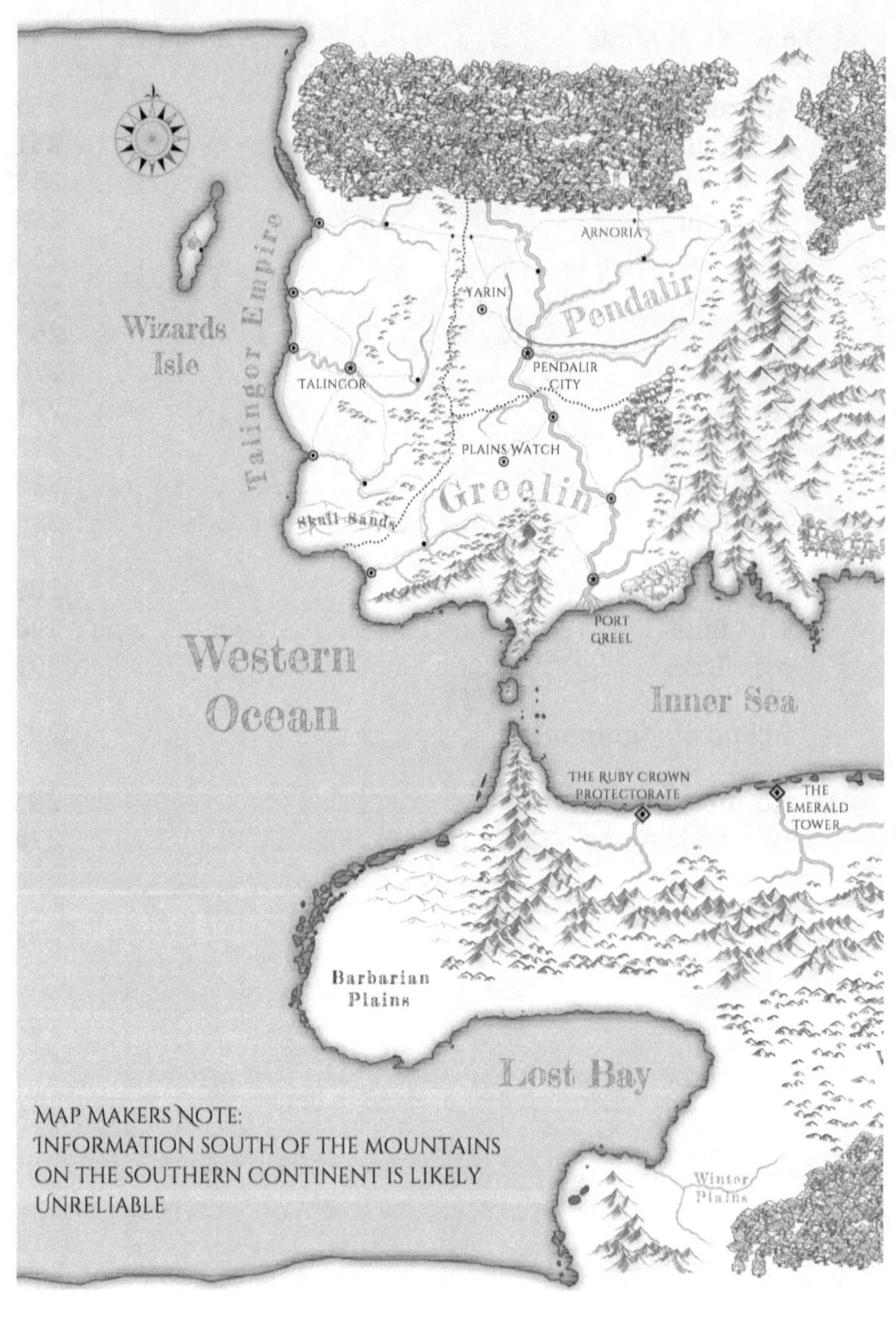

Wizards
Isle
Talingor Empire
ARNORIA
YARIN
Pendalir
PENDALIR
CITY
TALINGOR
PLAINS WATCH
Greelin
Skull Sands
PORT
GREEL
Western
Ocean
Inner Sea
THE RUBY CROWN
PROTECTORATE
THE
EMERALD
TOWER
Barbarian
Plains
Lost Bay
Winter
Plains
MAP MAKERS NOTE:
INFORMATION SOUTH OF THE MOUNTAINS
ON THE SOUTHERN CONTINENT IS LIKELY
UNRELIABLE

Prologue

1 Basket

Long, dark, silky hair fluttered in front of the woman's still-beautiful face, shadowing it faintly in the light of the rising gibbous moon.

Dust on her dark-brown cloak and mud on the hem of her charcoal-gray traveling dress were signs of a long journey. The cloak and dress were bulky and nondescript, neither particularly high quality nor so worn and faded as to seem unusual. Similar garments were sometimes worn by well-off peasant women with a need to travel or by wives or daughters of merchants of modest means. Her clothes were so ordinary that they flirted with seeming deliberately inconspicuous. On a night with less moonlight than this, she wouldn't be visible without a torch. Even with the bright moon, a casual observer would likely overlook her entirely if she raised her hood.

Right now, the hood of her cloak was down, revealing a face that was as unreadable as a blank tombstone. She was beautiful enough to lighten a man's heart with her smile, but the fine creases at the corners of her eyes made it clear that she was no maiden and looked young for her age. Her hair was slightly too black and contained no gray, except at the very base of her hair where it met her scalp. She wore no makeup and had no jewelry. Most decent men would view her favorably and be glad of her smile without getting any inappropriate ideas.

Her eyes were a pale bluish gray and yet could not be forgotten easily. Her stare was unnerving and intense with a driven look. There was nobody on the road at this time of night, and her vantage above the road ensured that she would see anyone approaching in time to raise her hood and melt into the darkness. She was a ways off the road on the far side of an old, broken-topped hickory snag that stood atop a small hillock. The night was unusually silent, and the smell of the season's first snow hovered in the air. From here, she could see the manor and the lights in its windows.

Those lights had come on slightly before dusk about an hour ago. The man who held the lordship over this manor was due back in about an hour if the pattern held, and normally two hours after that the lights would go out as he and his wife went to sleep.

The night was cold enough that timing was important. It was a five-minute walk to the front door of the manor, and two minutes should be left for the setup, then another two to position herself in the garden nearby. Give it ten minutes to be safe. She would take up a position out of the range of torchlight but close enough to observe and take action in an emergency. If all went as planned, she would never need to reveal herself.

She bent down to check a basket by her feet, resting in the lee of the snag out of the wind. After a little rearranging and a few soft words in an ancient language from a far away land, she settled down to wait, noting the position of the moon as it rose over the town on the eastern horizon. In a few days, the moon would be full, but the light was not important to her. She also noted with satisfaction that high, thin clouds had begun to show a faint ring around the moon. Soon there would be snow, which was more important. The silence was deathly, but she didn't mind as it made approaching travelers easy to pick out. Nothing to do but wait.

Some time later, when the clouds had become a uniform, transparent veil across the moon, the woman glanced up and noted its position above the horizon. With a small nod, she raised her hood, picked up the basket, and descended from the hillock. The filtered moonlight made everything look flat with no distinct shadows, only dark areas and light areas. She moved steadily but did not appear to hurry. It was a traveling pace, though travelers at night, especially women, were uncommon out here on the fringe of the kingdom.

As she approached the entrance to the property associated with the manor, she came to two life-size white marble statues of griffons. The statues faced each other across the road, each a mirror of the other. The lion-like rear portion seated, the eagle-headed front raised up, feathered wings extended vertically behind. The taloned foot nearest her was planted on the ground, and the far foot was raised at a ninety-degree angle with talons spread and facing her. Each statue gazed away from the manor, their gazes intersecting a hundred paces away. She carefully stepped off the road just before that point and passed to the right of the statues before returning to the road. Her hood hid a subtle smirk. This was not the first time she had seen this type of statue, and she seemed amused to find them so easily circumvented.

Beyond the statues, tall trees flanked the road. They'd been planted many generations ago and were at twenty foot intervals. Their branches still held a few dried leaves that rustled just once, shifting in air currents that only they could sense. The woman's step made no audible sound either, though she didn't seem to be taking any particular precautions. Silence reigned as she approached the large wrought iron gate that was the only entry to the inner grounds and the demesne.

Gates this far from town were always locked. Bandits and goblins were rare but not unheard of. She gestured once and then pushed lightly on the gate. It swung open silently. Stepping inside, she rested her basket on the ground and shut the gate. The latch snapped into place without a sound.

She picked up the basket again and moved at a steady, unhurried pace along the road around the far side of the decorative pond and up the front steps of the manor entrance. The gardens were clearly well cared for, but the flowers had been taken by frost weeks earlier. Ice rimmed the edges of the pond, but the center still reflected the branches of leafless cherry trees along the far side.

At the top of the steps, the woman paused. She did not seem uncertain in any way, but this was a significant moment, a point of no return. Carefully, she placed the basket on the steps and folded back a layer of cloth, pausing again to reach down and stroke the cheek of the infant she had just revealed with her gloved hand. The gesture was heartfelt but somehow seemed out of place and slightly awkward. She did not repeat it, instead withdrawing a strip of paper-like white bark from her cloak and tucking it into the side of the basket. After leaving the note, she stood upright and paused, listening.

As if on cue, the faint sounds of a horse trotting up the tree-lined path became audible. The woman smiled. Her timing was perfect. She moved carefully off into the garden and ducked inside the cover of a well-manicured blue-needle tree, ignoring the prickles of the needles and the jabs of the branches. Somehow, not a single twig snapped, and the branches were entirely still by the time the rider reached the gate.

His mount was a tall, broad-chested gray stallion, almost the size of a draft horse but with none of the sluggishness. The man and his horse were unarmored, though they certainly looked as if they ought to be. He wore a long-sword at his left hip in a finely made but well-worn leather scabbard. The hilt of the sword was simple and well polished from use. He wore a dark-green wool coat with lapels and cuffs embroidered in a lighter-colored thread that glinted slightly. His pants were brownish and well cut, neither baggy nor tightly fit. He pulled a key from his coat pocket and stuck it in the lock. When it turned freely, he froze and stood listening. It was a full five minutes before he moved.

In the shadows of the blue needle tree, the woman's brow creased. There could be no doubt that he remembered locking the gate. He waited with unusual patience. As the minutes ticked by, her lips became a thin, tight line. Her jaw began to clench, and her eye's flickered to the babe on the doorstep several times.

Eventually, he pushed the gate open, and it produced the usual loud squeal. Only then was the depth of the preceding silence truly evident. A light flickered and then became steady behind the door to the manor house. The sounds of the manor door being unbolted followed suit. The man uttered a single "tssk" sound as if vexed by the results of the noisy gate and mounted his horse with the fluid grace of a man who had ridden more miles than could be counted. After mounting, he paused briefly, going suddenly stock still at the precise moment of silence just before the manor door opened. Hearing nothing, he moved forward, drawing his sword with his right hand while guiding his horse with his left. The unsheathing of his sword took a fraction of a second, and the man's focus on the garden and his surroundings never wavered.

There was no sign of nervousness as he barked out in a tone of command, "Look sharp! The gate was unlocked!"

The door stopped halfway open and a woman's voice gasped and fell silent. The woman who opened the door did not shrink back, instead listening with a care that resembled the man's. He had stopped near to the manor door and was listening intently, peering at all the dark shadows.

As the man's piercing gaze moved toward the blue needle tree with its heavily shadowed inner branches, the woman gasped again and called out, "Jared, a basket!"

"Stand clear, Madeline! Remember what happened to Lyle! It could be a snake as easily as a gift!" The man dismounted and began to cautiously walk closer to the steps, with his blade leading low, pointed directly at the basket.

There was an imperceptible shift in the shadows within the needle tree, and the man paused, clearly sensing something but unable to pinpoint its direction. He looked back toward the basket and hesitated again. The man licked his lips and unconsciously rubbed the back of his neck. It was a nervous gesture that seemed wholly at odds with his bearing and the steadiness of his blade.

The covering on the basket shifted, revealing a small white foot that popped out of one end. A second later a choking cry came from the basket.

Madeline's demeanor softened, and she jibed her husband, "For a snake it sure has cute toes. Besides, the days of asps in fruit baskets are supposed to be behind us, remember? That's why we moved to the middle of nowhere, isn't it?"

Jared looked around briefly and muttered, "A snake would be easier." Louder, he said, "Still, the gate was unlocked, and I would like to know how that happened."

"So would I," Madeline replied as she stooped to pick the baby out of the basket. Her voice maintained a level tone, but it was clear what her theory about the unlocked gate was. As she cradled the child in her arms, the child began to quiet down. Jared came closer and then leaned down to retrieve a scrap of paper-like tree bark. After a quick glance, he started to put it down and then held it up to the light streaming from the lantern inside the door to the house. His eyebrows shot up, and he frowned thoughtfully.

"Yes, dear? His name, I assume?"

"Hrmph. Yes, his name alright, an odd name..." He peered out into the night toward the still-open front gate. "I better shut the gate," he grumbled, and with that Jared strode off the steps slowly, still watching all around, his sword drawn and ready. The closing and locking of the gate was the usual creaky, noisy affair, which somehow seemed offensively loud tonight though otherwise uneventful.

While she waited on the steps, Madeline kept one eye on the garden and rocked gently while she spoke softly to the sleeping child in reassuring tones, covering his head using the cloth from the basket to shield him from the cold night air.

As Jared crossed the garden, he sheathed his sword, retrieved his horse, and looked up the steps. "Where's Al?"

"Cindy's still recovering from giving birth. I let him go to her. You'll manage. You know how to rub down a horse... after you tell me."

"Tell you what?"

"His name."

"Oh, the note says 'Sal Lehan,' but I don't trust it."

"Why?"

"It looks strange, not sure why though." He paused, left his horse, and brought the note to her. She freed her right hand and accepted the note, backing into the light from the doorway to read it. Almost immediately, her eyebrows shot up, and she squinted at the paper as if remembering something.

"Yes, I don't trust it either."

"Why?"

"Because it's a fake. The writing is very sloppy, as if the author was untrained and could barely write. It's very convincing in that respect. But the letters are all written in ancient modes. Only a scholar would know those forms."

"Hmm. Might be interesting to see if that peasant traveler I saw yesterday still has her basket tomorrow. The woman that I mentioned two days ago..."

"The one you said gave you a creepy feeling for no apparent reason at all? Yes, indeed it might, but somehow I suspect that she will have vanished without a trace. It's cold, and there's a storm coming. No way we can investigate tonight and maybe not for a day or two depending on how bad the storm is. Interesting coincidence."

The woman in the dark dress and cloak under the blue needle tree allowed herself a chagrined smirk but remained silent and perfectly still otherwise.

"Hrmph."

"The good news is I now believe you did lock the gate," Madeline said with a winsome smile. Their eyes met for a moment, and there was an unspoken recognition, two minds thinking alike. When she spoke, Madeline's voice was relaxed and carried just a tiny bit further. "When you finish with Storm, we can discuss what to call him. I don't think we have anymore to fear tonight. This sort of thing wouldn't be a short-term ploy. I'm confident that the child is just a child."

"No, probably not tonight," Jared said with an emphasis on the last word. He didn't sound at all pleased, nor did he sound entirely convinced. He walked back to his horse as his wife dropped the paper-bark in the basket and picked it up, setting it down inside the door before pulling the door shut.

"Come on, Storm," Jared said gruffly to his horse in a voice that carried through the courtyard. "You need to be rubbed down, and I need to think." With a heavy sigh, he led his horse around the corner toward the stables. The sound of the barn door soon creaked from afar in the night.

Patiently, the woman in the dark cloak waited among the branches of the blue needle tree. She never moved or even twitched, blinking only when necessary to maintain clear vision. The breeze rustled the leaves in the garden occasionally, sending some skittering noisily across the paving stones between the gate and the front steps of the house. Still she waited.

After a while a very slight sound near the gate caught her attention. Jared had been kneeling in the shadows to the left of the gate long enough for his foot to go to sleep, forcing him to shift his weight. He had silently crept up along the outer wall. From his current position, any attempt to open or scale the gate would be easily intercepted. He had returned and eluded her notice. A slight twitch at the corner of her mouth betrayed her irritation. Such a thing had not happened to her in a very long time. For a full twenty minutes, he did not move again, and she waited. Time was not a problem for her.

Suddenly, he stood up, sighed, brushed the leaves off his knees, walked to the house, and then went back around toward the barn. It wasn't until ten minutes later that she heard his footsteps, the barn door closing, and then the sound of a smaller door. The garden was silent once more, and still she waited with the patience of a stone. Over the next two hours, the occasional breezes became a steady wind from the northwest. The darkness was total. The moon had become completely obscured, and the garden was shrouded in shadows so thick they seemed alive.

Eventually, the last light in the manor house went out, and the first flakes began to fall. The woman waited an hour after that. In the dead of night, she came out of hiding. Nothing but icy wind swirling with snow and shadow was visible beyond twenty feet. She walked with a limp now, one leg impaired from over four hours of immobility. A strong gust whipped her hood back briefly as she quietly opened the gate and soundlessly shut it behind her.

Once she reached the tree-lined lane outside, she began to move more quickly, purposefully toward town. She only stopped once. She ascended the hillock overlooking the manor and faced it for several minutes in silence. The manor lights were all out, the landscape was dark, and so was the sky. There was nothing to see through the swirling snow, yet still she looked intently as if searching. For a while her gaze softened, her attention focused elsewhere. Finally, nodding to herself, she descended and turned toward town, striding confidently down the pitch-black road.

1 Faux Pas

1.1 Pancakes

The dry air in the chamber was dustless. Even the finest grains of dust had settled ages ago. The skeletal figures standing in the room never moved. Twenty rows of twenty-five. The dust on the floor was undisturbed. No vermin. Good. Their swords were without rust. No moisture. Good. Each eye socket flickered faintly. None had fallen. All standing as commanded until another command was given. Good. On to the next chamber, only one hundred such rooms to go, almost done...

Madeline stood, holding her infant son Zachary in her left arm and looking down on her adopted son Johnny with concern as he murmured in his sleep. This was new. As far as she knew he had slept soundly every night since his arrival on their doorstep. With her free hand she reached out to wake him.

Johnny woke reluctantly as his mother shook his shoulder. He rolled over, mumbling something that sounded like "not done." He obviously wanted to go back to sleep, but Madeline had other ideas. The baron's wife was coming to visit, and Madeline had a busy morning ahead of her.

"Come on, sleepy-head. Wake up," she said gently. "I'm making pancakes. You don't want to miss pancakes, do you?"

"Pancakes!" Johnny exclaimed and bounced out of bed, all signs of sleepiness fading before the prospect of pancakes and the syrup that always accompanied them.

Madeline smiled to herself and hoisted her infant son into a more comfortable position before following Johnny toward the kitchen. "Pancakes always work like a charm, don't they, Zachary?" she cooed as she entered the kitchen. She set Zachary down in a bassinet on the kitchen table and then placed a skillet over the fire.

1.2 Dragon Tree

Christina D'Arnor, Madeline D'Abrac, and Madeline's housemaid Cindy relaxed in wooden lawn chairs under the shade of a tree near Madeline's manor. Christina's visits were irregular and often hastily planned. The baron's wife didn't feel bound by the need to consider other people's schedules, so more than a day's notice was rare. Good relations with the baron were important, so Madeline always welcomed her and her daughter Caroline graciously. Living in the manor outside of town, Johnny's only nearby playmate was Cindy's son Derek. Thus, he and Derek were always happy to see Caroline, even though she was almost two years younger.

Christina wore a cobalt-blue silk dress with a corset and several layers of petticoats. This was once fashionable, but the height of style had moved on from what it was ten years ago when Christina left the capitol to marry Baron D'Arnor on the outskirts of the kingdom. Few people out here could afford such frippery. Only Madeline was wealthy enough to own a similar wardrobe, yet she wore a comfortable sun dress with a light, floral pattern. The only hint of her wealth was a bit of lace around the edges. Cindy wore her usual plain, green dress. Although she didn't realize she was doing it, Cindy smoothed the front of her dress every few minutes.

The three women were as varied in age as they were in appearance, with nearly a decade between each. Christina, the youngest, was in her early thirties. She had rich, dark-brown hair tied up in a fancy, complicated style that allowed a few locks to dangle and attract attention. She was vain, but she enjoyed food, and Caroline was her fourth child, so she struggled to maintain her figure. The corset often made her light-headed.

Madeline's hair was a straight, pale blonde that she wore in a long, comfortably loose braid down her back. Her natural hair color effectively hid the gray hairs that had begun to creep in, and it just looked slightly paler than when she was young. She had married later in life but was recovering well from giving birth to her first son, Zachary, a few months ago. Ironically, she could have worn Christina's outfit in relative comfort without the corset.

Cindy, who was in her early fifties, was the oldest of the three. Her hair had been straight and black when she was young, but now it was half gray, and she wore it tightly bound up in a single neat bun secured with a simple wooden hairpin. She had never been slim, and now her age showed in her figure as well as her hair. Though her hairstyle appeared severe, her expression was usually pleasant and her smile always warm. Cindy had missed most of her youth caring for her many younger siblings and then lost more years barely surviving as scullery maid in the capitol. By the time she had been hired into a better position and an easier life as a lady's maid for Madeline, Cindy had become resigned to her fate as a spinster. It wasn't until the trip north from the capitol with Madeline and Jared seven years ago that she encountered her husband Al, and they were pleasantly surprised by Derek's arrival soon after.

"Can you believe summer is already starting?" Christina said, fanning herself.

"This warmth is such a relief after the cold winter," Cindy responded and then unconsciously smoothed her dress yet again.

"Quite an excellent day for mint tea," Madeline added.

Simultaneously, they all sipped their iced mint tea, and for a while they silently watched the children play in the open grassy field in front of them. Madeline's infant son, Zachary, dozed in a covered bassinet between her and Cindy.

Johnny and Derek streaked across the open grass brandishing wooden swords and shields. On the opposite side of the field Caroline stood by a tree and shrieked as they approached, calling out for someone to save her. The boys skidded to a halt as they neared her, raising their shields. Fending off some imaginary force. Then they darted in and slapped the tree with their swords, telling Caroline to run.

With a shriek, Caroline took off across the field running at top speed, her shrieking punctuated with the rhythm of her stride, enjoying the use of her high-pitched vocal cords as only a four and a half year old can. The boys fanned out, flanking the tree from either side, alternately one raising his shield to fend off attack while the other darted in to slap at the tree. Derek, who was the stronger of the two, struck the tree, and his wooden sword cracked in half. Johnny jumped over to his side, and they both raised their shields together. Then Johnny dove in, spearing the tree and knocking off a flake of bark.

Meanwhile, Caroline reached the far side of the field, made a right-hand turn, and headed for the women, still shrieking until she reached the safety of the shade tree. Zachary woke and started to cry, but Cindy was quick to settle him with a soft word and some attention.

"They saved me from the dragon!" Caroline proclaimed upon arrival and flopped down unceremoniously into the grass in front of them out of breath. Though the tree was less than a hundred yards away, it was a long run for her young legs. By now the boys were heading toward the women as well, holding up the flake of bark from the tree.

"Dragon scale!" they proclaimed in unison as they returned.

"It can go on my shield to protect against dragon fire," Derek proclaimed.

"Nuh uhn! I'm the one who knocked it off. I had to rescue you when your sword broke," Johnny countered.

"But I'm the biggest and strongest. I should get it. The sword only broke 'cause I hit harder than you do."

"All right, you two, hand over the dragon scale," Madeline said, ending the argument before it grew any further. "Cindy, why don't you take this dragon scale back over to the tree and assess the damage? As for you two dragon slayers, you had better hope that tree doesn't rot because of your antics."

"Aw mom, we were just having fun."

"And they saved me from the dragon!" Caroline added seriously in their defense.

"Dragons or no, it's nap time," Madeline said and began herding the children inside. Cindy started for the tree, and Christina poured herself some more tea. Once the boys were inside, Derek protested that he didn't want to take a nap.

"Then you have guard duty. You can sit over there in the corner and watch them," Madeline decided. "Make sure no dragons come to eat them." Within minutes however, all three were sleeping peacefully.

1.3 Dreamtime

A room full of boxes. Valuable boxes. Boxes on shelves. Open each one. A disembodied hand. See it move. Good. Next box.... Now a different type of box. Each is set in an alcove, each with a glass side. Hovering in each, a pair of eyeballs. All are watching. All are tracking movement. Good.

A stone room built inside a larger room. Symbols on every wall. Many symbols on the door. A surge, tingling, exciting. The door is opened. Warriors standing at at-

Madeline paused as she entered the room to wake the children. They were all sleeping, even Derek, but Johnny was murmuring in his sleep again, clearly dreaming. Madeline tsk'ed softly to herself. A chagrined look came over her face and then a thoughtful one. As she watched, his dreaming seemed to subside. A moment later she puffed once as if making a tough decision, shook her head, and put on her cheerful voice.

"Wake up, sleepy heads," she lilted cheerfully. Derek startled awake and looked around frantically.

"Oooh no! I fell asleep on guard duty!" he exclaimed, clearly distraught.

"Don't worry. This room is a safe place, magically protected by spells from a powerful wizard," Madeline responded quickly

"You're making it up!" he accused her.

"And can you prove that?"

"Well... no," Derek said, becoming uncertain.

"And it is true that nothing hurt you, right?"

"Well... yeah."

"So maybe it is protected then?"

"Yah ok, but does that mean it's always been protected, or did the wizard just put the spell on it today?"

boys were leaving, and Cindy was washing their dishes already. Not wanting to be left behind, Caroline quickly bussed her dishes too.

By the time Caroline caught up with the boys, they had made their way through the main building of the manor and out the large wooden doors at the front. They were already asking Madeline if they could get their wooden swords and go play.

"Aww, come on, Ma. Can't we? I promise we won't hurt the tree again," Johnny pleaded.

"Can't we what?" asked Caroline as she caught her breath.

"Play swords," Derek answered solemnly, clearly already perceiving that the answer would be no.

"Yes! And I can be the princess again!" Caroline said happily.

"I'm afraid not, my dear. We shall be leaving as soon as our carriage arrives," Christina clarified, speaking to Caroline without even a glance at the other two children. Even as she said this, the sound of a carriage approaching became evident.

"Karl's driving too fast again," Madeline noted, listening to the sound.

"He better be! This is the third time he's been late this week. If he smells like ale again, he's fired!" Christina said vehemently.

The carriage came into sight, bouncing along behind the swiftly trotting horses. It was an enclosed coach style, black with metal-shod wooden wheels. The body of the coach was supported and somewhat insulated from the bumpy road by a pair of leaf springs over each axle. Even in the capital city that was relatively rare; out here it was entirely out of place. More importantly, nobody out here really knew much about driving anything more than a farm wagon, and so the baron and his wife regularly fired their drivers. Today, the driver had made a serious error. He was driving with one door swinging and banging, the glass of the window long since gone.

"The oaf!" Christina cursed as Karl's latest and probably last mistake as a driver for her became apparent.

"Oh no" Madeline said in a much quieter voice as if realizing what was about to happen.

The oncoming coach had distracted the children from their play requests. The noise of the coach was clearly louder than normal, and the coach was going faster than usual. Both women and all three kids were watching the racing coach as it came through the front gate without slowing. Karl pulled back on the reigns, but neither horse was responding. They had been worked up to a level of excitement that was not so easily quelled.

After passing through the gate, the lane ended in a circular drive that traveled around a decorative pond, and naturally the horses changed their course to follow it to their right. The force of the turn was too great however, and the carriage tilted up on two wheels. As it did so, Karl was thrown from his seat, but his boot laces on his left boot caught on the decorative iron filigrees alongside the driver's seat. The coach might yet have righted itself, but with Karl's weight hanging off the side it was hopelessly overbalanced. With a horrendous crash, the coach toppled onto its side.

The horses screamed, stumbled, and fell over one another. The top of the coach broke away as it hit the ground and flipped end over end, landing in the pond. The main body of the coach collapsed like a box and came off of the chassis. As everything came to a stop, neither of the horses was able to rise, one clearly injured and the other constrained by the harnesses and rigging that held it to the remains of the carriage.

Even before the coach came to rest, Madeline issued a single command to the children to stay there with Christina, lifted her floral sundress, and ran toward the accident scene. Christina, who had been preparing to launch into an angry tirade to scold the driver about the coach door, now stood frozen with her mouth open in stunned disbelief.

As Madeline approached, she raised her hand once. By the time she reached the accident scene, the horses had quieted and were lying against each other with their nostrils flaring wildly but not struggling. She immediately went to Karl's body, but it was jerking spasmodically, and she just stopped and looked down, putting her hand over her mouth. Then she turned and called to Christina, "Take the kids in the house. Tell Cindy to find Al."

Christina just stood there in shock, not reacting to Madeline's words but at that moment Cindy appeared at the front door. Cindy's eyes went wide, and quickly her gaze went from the accident scene to the children and then to Christina. As she began to move to gather the children, her lips pursed tightly, and if anyone had been watching her it would have been obvious that she felt she was gathering four children, not three. All eyes were on Karl's body, which now lied still and unmoving, his head and shoulders hidden under the wreckage of the coach.

As Cindy reached Christina and the three children, Christina gasped, "He wrecked it."

Cindy's face hardened and went white. In a tight, firm voice she said, "Christina! We need to get the children inside. NOW!"

The tone of Cindy's voice got through to Christina, and she began to turn with a haughty look. However, as she saw Cindy's face she thought better of whatever rebuke she had been about to utter and instead picked up Caroline and headed for the double doors at the front of the manor. Cindy took Johnny and Derek's hand. When she tugged on Derek's hand, he turned away to follow, but Johnny stumbled backward, unable to take his eyes off the scene. Cindy released his hand, gently cupped her hand around the top of his head, and turned him away. Once his gaze was broken, Johnny took her hand and followed, but he kept looking backward every few steps.

Cindy led the boys in through the large, thick double doors at the front of the manor. Christina was standing with Caroline beside her just inside the front door. Caroline was holding Christina's hand with one hand and sucking the thumb of her other hand. Since the manor was designed to be defensible against attack, the entryway was bare stone with no furniture and walls pierced by half a dozen arrow slits. There was nowhere to sit, and the accident scene was still visible through the open main doors.

"The waiting room by the main hall," Cindy said in a no-nonsense voice and Caroline immediately began to follow. Christina lost her grip on Caroline's hand. Caroline, Cindy, and the boys all left the entryway before Christina could object, and thus Christina was forced to follow.

Upon entering the waiting room, Cindy turned to Christina and started to speak, but Christina spoke first. "I'll watch the children here... You go fetch your husband." she said in a prim and proper tone of dismissal.

Cindy's jaw clenched just briefly, and tersely she replied, "Of course M'Lady." After a pause that was ever so slightly longer than proper, she turned and left.

1.5 Funeral

Karl's funeral was held near sunset two days later in the town cemetery. His casket was only briefly opened during the portion of the ceremony in which the family paid their respects. The ceremony did not attract a very large crowd, but Madeline, Jared, Christina, and the baron were all in attendance. Karl's wife Rhielda and six-year-old son Dillon were seated at the front of a group of about twenty people.

Johnny and Derek sat next to each other with Madeline and Cindy on either side. Madeline was holding Zachary in her arms. Both boys were silent and somber, reflecting the mood of the surrounding adults. As the service progressed, Johnny stared distractedly off away from the casket. At the finish of the service, which was timed to coincide with the setting of the sun, he was still not paying attention. As people started to stand to leave, Derek nudged him in the ribs.

"Ow, what was that for?" Johnny said slightly too loudly.

"You weren't paying attention. It's time to leave," Derek explained in a hushed and somewhat embarrassed whisper.

"Oops, sorry," Johnny whispered back as the two of them received stares from the adults.

As they were filing out of the cemetery, Derek leaned close and asked Johnny, "What were you thinking about? I saw your face. You looked like you were looking right through the people in front of us."

"I was thinking about the crash," Johnny said. After a pause, he explained further, "I saw things I don't understand. Some things happened, and I feel like I should understand, but I don't"

"Yeah, I suppose we'll never know why he lost control of the horses."

"Not that. The horses probably got out of control because he pushed them."

"Then what?"

"Remember how the horses were right after the crash? They were panicked and trapped by the coach. They were kicking and screaming... Then my mother went to them, and they calmed down."

"Well, they probably knew she was going to help them. Horses are pretty smart, you know."

"Possibly..."

"You spent the entire funeral thinking about the horses? It's sad that one of them broke a leg. My dad says that a horse with a broken leg has to be killed, but really it was Karl's service, John. You should think about him some." One of the adults who had become friends with Karl and often drank with him at the tavern nodded, approving of Derek's advice.

Not noticing the audience, Johnny continued, "Oh, I thought a lot about Karl too. I really don't like walking over the spot he died. It makes me feel all weird inside. It was very strange seeing him die. One moment he was alive, and then the coach fell on him. I think he was still alive for a while after that, but then he changed. I don't know how to describe it, but after that he was dead."

"I suppose that was when his leg stopped kicking," Derek replied somberly, looking off toward the sunset thoughtfully.

Johnny shook his head and opened his mouth to reply, but he was interrupted by the adult behind them who had been listening. "You kids are unfortunate to have witnessed such a death. I'm sure Karl's spirit would want you to be at peace and not worry about his death. I got to know him in the short time since he moved here from the east. I probably knew him better than anyone, and he was a very nice man. It's a wonder he would have to run so far from anyone. He told me about his religion and I'm not religious myself, but if there's anything to his religion, he's in a better place for sure now."

"Who are you?" Johnny blurted out. Then realizing his rudeness he added, "Sorry."

"It's ok. I should have introduced myself before butting in. My name's Ryan. I'm the hostler for the Pig's Eye, and Karl was a friend. I got him the job driving the baron's coach. A good job at that," Ryan said with a slight touch of pride mixed with obvious guilt. The Pig's Eye was the recently rebuilt inn at the center of town, a place Johnny had seen from the outside but never entered.

There was a short, awkward silence, and then Madeline interrupted, "There was no way to know it would end like this, Ryan. Everyone should have a friend like you. Come on, Johnny. We need to offer our condolences. You should say something nice to Dillon." With that she shifted Zachary to her other arm and led Johnny away. Cindy took Derek's hand and followed.

Rhielda was standing by a hay wagon with Dillon at her side, her face wet from crying. The wagon was a local custom for this town, where the family of the deceased were always given a ride to and from the cemetery. Ryan had offered a few words and taken his place at the driver's seat, and people were one by one offering condolences in the fading light. The baron and his wife were the first to offer condolences and rode off on their horse immediately, with Christina looking impatient and the baron looking slightly apologetic.

Jared and Madeline allowed others to go first, knowing that folks would remain to hear what they said, and thus Rhielda and Dillon would drive away from a waving crowd rather than a lonely, empty cemetery. In the few years since the D'Abracs had moved here, this had been a regular pattern, with the D'Abracs regularly being the polar opposite of the D'Arnors in their treatment of the common folk.

Most folks in the town understood that this was a contrast cultivated by Madeline, and that the baron himself was often acting in appeasement of his wife, who came from a powerful duchy in the south of the kingdom and was not thrilled with her politically arranged marriage.

The joke occasionally whispered around town was that the king had sent the D'Abracs to apologize for sending the D'Arnors. It was almost fully dark by the time Madeline, Jared, and Johnny's turn came.

Jared spoke first to Rhielda, "I've seen many folks die in military service, and your husband's death, while not one of gallant battle, was one that I believe reflected his good heart, his concern for his family and for proper conduct of his job. It is unfortunate that he was delayed by a peddler haggling over the price of the cloth you asked him to buy. His haste to make up the time lost and remain in good standing with his employer surely was born of a concern for his family and a personal pride in his work. Although he was not a soldier, I count men with such an attitude at the top of the ranks when they are fighting under me. Your family has suffered a great loss this week, but I see the potential for great gains standing by your side." Turning to Dillon, he said, "Young man, yours is the task of living up to your father's good heart and sincerity. Surely you'll miss your father, but when you do you should take the void you feel there and fill it with the knowledge of the things you have done that would make him proud. I am sure there have been many already, and there will be many more to come. Honor your father's memory by continuing as he would have wanted you to, and you will know peace in time."

The crowd murmured in appreciation, and both Rhielda and Dillon looked like a cloud had been lifted from their faces.

Madeline spoke next and said simply, "Truly, we are saddened by your loss. Since it happened on our property and we bore witness to it, we are also touched by it. Please let us know if there is anything you need, and feel free to bring Dillon by if you need someone to care for him during the day. I'm sure he would be an excellent playmate for Johnny and Derek." She glanced at Cindy, who nodded in agreement. Then she prodded Johnny, who realized suddenly he was expected to speak.

Johnny glanced at his father, envying the beautiful speech he had given but didn't know what to say. After a pause he blurted out, "I'm sorry your dad is dead. Perhaps his spirit will become one of the powerful ghost warriors."

Johnny had said it with sincerity, hoping to cheer up Dillon, but Dillon was now frowning at him as if he didn't understand, and Rhielda had fixed him with a baleful stare. Madeline gasped slightly, and there was an awkward silence. A few people in the assembled crowd started to murmur, and it didn't sound like the murmurs after his father's speech.

Johnny looked at his father, and his father was staring at him with his mouth half open as if he had no idea what to say. A red flush began to creep in to Johnny's face and neck, and he started to open his mouth, but before he could say anything his mother cut him off.

"Our apologies, I think he's still a bit young and doesn't fully understand death yet," Madeline said to Rhielda and Dillon. With that she pulled Johnny back to her side, and it was clear that he should say nothing further. The murmur of the crowd lightened as people observed Johnny's confusion and accepted Madeline's explanation.

Rhielda and Dillon climbed aboard the hay wagon. As the wagon departed, Dillon and Rhielda stared back at Johnny, and their faces seemed clouded with doubt again. Johnny's face was very sad. He hadn't meant to make anyone unhappy, and apparently nobody liked what he had said. His mother handed Zachary to Jared while she mounted. After returning Zachary to Madeline, Jared helped Johnny up and then mounted himself so that Johnny was seated in front of him. As they rode away, the crowd dispersed.

1.6 Questions

The ride back from the funeral was quiet and slow with no talking. Johnny sat in front of his mother on the horse, his face somber and confused. Jared rode close behind, scanning ahead to the sides and occasionally looking behind. His manner was not nervous or afraid. His alertness was habitual and instinctive, done without conscious thought. Riding to the west out of town, they soon came to the familiar cap nut tree lined lane.[1] As they passed in front of and then between the griffon statues that marked the formal entrance onto the D'Abrac's land, Johnny shivered and looked at the statues as if they were ready to pounce. He always did this, but when asked why he could only explain, "I don't think they like me." The statues never moved, and clearly they were only stone, yet they were such a detailed and unblemished work that one could easily imagine them as sentient.

When the D'Abracs moved to the area, they adopted the ancient manor to the west of town as their own. The locals claimed it was the home of the baron who had originally attempted to settle in this area and failed. The ancient manor was considered haunted, but the D'Abracs had carefully inspected the ruins and found no sign of magical curses or creatures of the living death.

Their habitation of the old manor was originally greeted with suspicion. Most folk in town were expecting them to go crazy, become reclusive or be consumed by the ghosts. When they remained engaged and even active in helping the town, the people soon came to trust them. Soon, it was rumored that Sir D'Abrac's reputation as a warrior had scared away the ghosts, or even that he had fought the ghosts and won. Most people seemed to think that they had cleansed a blemish from the town.

While no ghosts had ever been battled, what Madeline and Jared did find within the decayed fortifications were signs of a battle some hundred or so years previous. The primary signs of this battle were a few remains of soldiers that had been left unburied. The most prominent of these was on the front steps of the manor. This sight was probably the origin of the rumor that it was haunted. The dozen or so former soldiers found in this condition were all from the same side of the battle and universally wore the rotted remains of similar leather armor and held rusted

---

[1] If "cap nut" doesn't instantly lead you to think of a particular type of tree, you may wish to check out the appendix.

18

short swords. The swords all bore an identical heraldic mark of a rising falcon and falling stars on the pommel. Madeline had reached the conclusion that they were defenders of the previous baron and that the attackers were probably human bandits or a rival baron because bodies of the attackers were not left behind. There was no evidence of this being a place lost to goblins or other monsters, since such creatures always abandoned their dead.

Unfortunately, there was little history available for the area. Many records from that time had been lost when the kingship changed houses seventy years ago. The victors had sought to obliterate the memory of their predecessors, and in one infamous incident an overly ardent supporter of the new regime had started a fire in the capital library. Miraculously, the fire was controlled, but many of the more recent historical accounts and property documents were lost. The records for the north lands were almost all destroyed, and several savvy families managed to lay claim to larger areas than they had previously controlled. This area however was essentially undeveloped at the time. The previous barony had been short-lived, and thus the area went unclaimed. Later, as fur and other trade increased over time and a town sprang up, the crown felt the need to ensure that it was properly protected and of course properly taxed. The D'Arnor Barony was established to oversee this.

The original property line for the ancient manor had been marked with a fortified wall ten feet high and four feet thick. This probably was only intended as a casual deterrent because this area had never to anyone's recollection been populated heavily enough to support a force large enough to properly defend several miles of wall. It was a mystery why the wall had been built in the first place. Most of the wall still stood today but was falling down in places.

The D'Abracs had elected not to undertake the repair of such an obviously useless fortification and instead had removed the wall to either side of the road for a hundred feet in either direction to make the entrance to the property more welcoming. Despite their imposing visage, the griffon statues, which had flanked the original entrance, were left in place both because they were too massive to move easily and because the beauty of their detailed sculpture, in a pure milky white stone of unknown origin, was such that it seemed unthinkable to destroy them.

After passing between the statues, the D'Abracs moved steadily up the cap nut tree lane and to the manor gate. They unlocked it, and it opened with its familiar squeal. Jared and Madeline considered the squeak and squeal of the gate a security feature, so it was never oiled. Inside the gate, Jared turned his horse sideways and looked at Madeline then at Johnny and then back again. Madeline nodded just once, and Jared dismounted, helped Johnny down, and then silently received Zachary from Madeline. Holding Zachary in one arm, he offered her help down as well. Madeline was entirely competent on a horse and had spent many a long day in the saddle. She had no such need of help, but Jared always offered, and Madeline always accepted with a smile.

Jared handed Zachary back, relocked the gate, and lead both horses to the barn. Madeline led Johnny in through the front door. Al was their hostler and Cindy their maid, but they had been given the night off so that they could raise a toast to Karl with his friends at the inn. Funerals were a formal affair, and the attendance of nobility was not unexpected, but it would have been highly unusual for Baron D'Arnor, or Sir D'Abrac to have shown up at the Pig's Eye for the remembrance toast.

Johnny went with Madeline quietly, as she led him to the kitchen where she set Zachary in a bassinet. The kitchen was a familiar place, and it put Johnny more at ease. "Are you thirsty?" Madeline asked him.

"Yes."

"Do you want water or milk?"

"Water, please."

Madeline selected a sturdy earthenware mug and poured some water into it from a copper vessel. The water vessel was always on the counter and seemingly never went empty, though Johnny knew that was because Cindy filled it from the well out back twice a day.

Madeline brought the water over to Johnny and sat down on the other side of the table from him, pushing it across.

"Thank you," Johnny said in an unusually polite voice. Clearly he expected that now she would tell him he was in trouble.

"How do you feel about the funeral?" she asked instead.

"It was nice, I suppose," he said. She sat silently, observing him for a while. About halfway through his glass of water he stopped and asked, "Am I in trouble?"

"No, but you said something that may have upset some people today."

"I'm sorry. I just wanted to make Dillon feel better. Why did everyone get upset?"

Madeline paused for a moment and then replied, "Because they didn't understand what you meant. Do you remember what you said?"

"Yes."

"Can you repeat it?"

Johnny stared at his water, and then admitted, "I don't want to."

"Why?"

"I don't want you to be upset"

"I won't be as long as you help me understand what you mean, ok?"

"OK." After a pause he continued, "I said 'I'm sorry your dad is dead. Perhaps his spirit will become one of the powerful ghost warriors.'"

"I understand the first part about you being sorry. That was a very nice thing to say, but can you tell me what you mean by 'powerful ghost warrior?'"

"One of the ones that you can see through. They are a group and have a leader, I think. They have armor and swords too, but you can see through that too. And they have candle flames in their eyes too. They are the most valuable ones." Johnny had become somewhat excited as he said this but suddenly stopped noticing his mother's very still face. It was a little too still. In a more subdued voice he asked, "What's wrong?"

Madeline's face had momentarily become a mask of self-control. After a second she seemed to relax and replied, "Nothing, sweetie. You just described a very scary monster. Don't monsters like that scare you?"

Johnny paused, never having considered this possibility. "No," he replied.

Madeline pondered this for a moment and then asked, "Who told you about such a monster?"

"Nobody," Johnny said, clearly beginning to suspect that now he really was in trouble.

"Did you see one?"

"Kinda."

"Where?"

"I dreamed about them."

Madeline's hand unconsciously smoothed the front of her dress as she stared off to the side.

"And you weren't scared? They sound very fearsome."

"No, they weren't chasing me. They were waiting for something, I think."

"What?"

"I don't know."

"Have you told anyone else about this dream?"

"No."

"That's good," Madeline said and looked back at Johnny with

a genuine smile of relief. "Please don't tell anyone. I think if you do, you will scare people very badly. Do you understand?"

"Yes. I don't want to scare anyone. I won't tell anybody."

"And please tell me if you have this dream again."

"Ok."

"Johnny?"

"Yes?"

"Thank you for being honest. Are you ready for bed?"

"Yes."

With that, she led him up to bed, tucked him in, kissed him, and turned out the lantern just as she had so many times before. Things seemed to return to normal, but as she left the room Madeline paused and looked back into the darkened room for a moment, which she had never done before.

1.7 Discussion

"I know it's a bad sign, but we can't just abandon him."

"Deluding ourselves will only result in tragedy. You know that. You can't deny the implications of his dreams."

"I can keep an eye on him. It might be better to play along until we know more about what has influenced him in this way."

Jared turned and peered out the window overlooking the front entry to the manor, and after a while he turned back and said, "And how much are you willing to gamble on that? Our lives? Our home? Our family?" His voice began to rise as he finished.

Madeline motioned for him to be quiet and nodded in the direction of Johnny's bedroom. "Jared, he *is* part of our family. Either way may harm our family."

"A partial loss guaranteed or a risk of losing it all." Jared sighed and turned back toward the window.

"Any action or inaction presents risk to all. Think about it, Jared. Why did you hesitate to slash the basket to pieces on that first night? We know what danger an unwelcome basket can hold. Why did you hesitate?"

Turning back from the window, Jared faced his wife as she sat on the edge of their bed. She was beautiful in her long, pale-blue silk night dress with a light-golden-yellow hem. The hem seemed to match her hair as the light from the fireplace flickered, but Jared just stared at her as if she had asked him why he might wear a sword when hunting goblins.

"Obviously, I didn't know what sort of trouble might come from the basket. An incendiary trap might have killed us both if I did that. A basket snake is only one possible problem. You know that I'm not so silly as to just hack at something without knowing what it is!" Jared looked puzzled and slightly offended by the question.

"Of course, I know you wouldn't, dear. You are a very seasoned veteran of many battles and adventures, and you have learned caution. You have always had very good instincts for when to attack and when to observe. This is one of the reasons we have survived so much and one of the reasons I love you and feel safe with you.

"However, your instincts begin to falter when it comes to long-term decisions. You are a man of action in the end, as is every skilled warrior. On the other hand, I have been trained to take a longer view, and in the bigger picture we are still in exactly the same position as you were that night. We don't know what Johnny is. He could be the next nefarious necromancer to start a war and kill thousands of innocents, or he could be with us to hide him from someone who wants him to do that. We might be serving as hosts or as camouflage, and we might be watched in either case.

"It's clear from his dream that there is some connection to the necromantic arts about Johnny, but the nature of that connection I cannot say. I am trained, but I am among the least of the grad-uates. I am barely worthy of my title, skating by on my one true talent rather than a general aptitude. Together, we have made a fabulous team, but we must not lose sight of the fact that our famous exploits are not because of my strength. Your skill and our close teamwork and no small share of luck have allowed us to persevere against the odds.

"In the larger picture, we are still unable to know if any of us are watched or forgotten. If we allow him to be harmed or abandoned, we may face retribution from a Wizard, Adept or even a Master. Our sneak attack against Nazh was fairly lucky. If we face a true Necromancer who is ready for us and seeking us, we won't stand a chance. We are mildly famous back in the capitol, but we are not nearly as powerful in real life as in the bard's songs. A Wizard or Adept who is ready and expecting battle will have no more trouble with us than you have with an average goblin.

"So as much as either one of us would happily kill a necromancer or evil wizard before his rise to power to save the lives of many, we don't know if Johnny is such a necromancer. The same talent for affecting souls that allows necromancers to control the undead is also the key to all forms of healing magic. He could grow up to save many lives, and even if he is a future threat we don't know that we would survive any abandonment of him."

Jared sighed heavily. "I feel so trapped."

"That's because we are," Madeline continued. "But we must wait and observe and determine who has trapped us and why before we decide if we want to break out of the trap and how. Come to bed. We had a long and stressful day. Sleep always helps, and sitting here talking about it is just wasting time."

"How can we just do nothing? What about Morposersus or whatever his name is, the one the townsfolk call 'The Wizard of the North?' Should we seek him out?"

"His name is Morphosius dear. Definitely not. I am far beneath his notice. He would be unlikely to even give me the time of day, and I'm happy to be below his concern. He's on the Wizard's Council, and a Master of Mutamancy, few if any wizards are more powerful. He's never actually been caught doing anything truly forbidden, but rumors abound. Folks who have dealings with him seem to have accidents a tad bit too frequently as well. If you think politics in the capital city are frightful, just imagine the same politicians, none of them fools and all of them with untold magical powers at their disposal. That will give you a fair picture of the Wizard's Council."

"I see. I just hope we aren't raising Johnny just for him to become the next necromancer like Nazh or some other sort of evil wizard. I'd hate to have to hunt him down or turn him over to an executioner. I'd also hate to have the blood of innocents on our hands if he grows up to start a war or kill hundreds of people."

"That would be terrible, but we must wait, watch, and do what's necessary. He may turn out just fine too. He might not even become a wizard. Tonight we do nothing, but soon I think it shall be our time to visit the monks. That may be a way to gain some understanding of the situation, and this seems serious enough." With that, Jared nodded and with another heavy sigh banked the fire, put out the lantern, and got into bed.

Out in the hall, Johnny approached his parents' room, unable to sleep. About three feet before he reached the door, he stopped, standing stock still when he heard his father say, "I just hope we aren't raising Johnny just for him to become the next necromancer..."

Johnny stood pale and shaking in the hall, then he heard his mother's reply. Johnny mouthed the words he had heard over and over. "Hunt me down? Blood on his hands?... a wizard? A necromancer? What is a necromancer?" Many minutes later after his father was snoring, he quietly crept back to his room, cold, confused, and afraid for the first time ever in his life.

1.8 Mystics

The heavy bronze doors were emblazoned with a copper and gold sun-flare design. The wall at the back of the Room of Waiting into which the doors were set was of simple and smooth yet unpolished granite. The stone had the distinctive dark cast with occasional white or rare gold flecks that marked it as being from the baron's quarry, though very likely mined long before the baron had established his lordship in the area. This temple had stood for many generations, always bypassed by wars and conflicts as a place that had been chosen specifically because it had little or no strategic value. The presence of the sect of monks well-trained in martial arts also had a dissuading effect on those who might claim it for one reason or another.

An even more effective protection was that the monks all took a vow of poverty and charity. Nobody cared to steal from them or conquer them because the costs would be high and the rewards meager at best. Only the doors to the inner sanctum showed any real gold leaf at all. Their order favored light yellow with gold and silver thread, but the thread was not true gold, only an imitation. The inner sanctum admitted none who were not of the order, but the sect had its occasional defectors, and all reports were that the doors were the only thing of value in the place.

The room just inside the entrance to the public areas of the temple was cool despite the heat of the day outside, and the stillness of the place had an aura of great peace and power. Jared D'Abrac sipped the water that the monks had given him while they waited. Madeline's water remained untouched on the stone bench next to her as she fidgeted absently with a button on her blouse, staring at the doors through which the Al' Helios had taken Johnny.

"I asked the wrong question," she breathed quietly. "All my training and I've asked the wrong question. Silas would be so disappointed in me for that."

"The answer will be of value. Don't fret that you haven't maximized it," Jared whispered soothingly. "We will know more than before we came here. That will be good enough."

"The stories of the ages are rife with the tales of those who asked careless questions of mystics and demons only to be led astray by the answer they thought they understood. We must think carefully on the answers we get today."

"Yes, of course, dear. That is always true."

"It's because I care for him. I asked with my heart not with my head." Madeline sighed and fell silent beside her husband, and they waited. Jared sipped his water again, and put his arm around his wife. She still fidgeted with her blouse and occasionally bit her lip, lost in thought, but she leaned against Jared allowing herself to be comforted.

Time in the room of waiting stood still and was both infinite and then seemed to have been nothing when the doors to the sanctum creaked and opened outward. The Al Helios led a small boy out into the room of waiting. The boy pulled free of the ascetic's hand and ran to Madeline with a carefree smile. Silently, he climbed into Madeline's lap and nestled in as she put her arm around him.

"Did you have a good time?" she asked.

"Uh-huh," Johnny replied, nodding. "He's a very nice man. I like him. He showed me where he prays, and then I felt tired, so he let me take a nap. Then we came back out here."

The Al' Helios smiled warmly at Johnny and then cleared his throat. "Johnny was a very good boy." After a slight pause, he turned to Jared D'Abrac and began speaking in a formal, ritualistic manner.

"One question my order allows thee, as they do any who come peacefully to our door. You have chosen the single question you judge to be most important. I have sought the answer to your question in communion with the higher powers. The answer must only be heard by the one who asked the question. You may then share the answer as you so choose. Come with me to receive your answer." The Al' Helios beckoned to Jared and gestured toward a small wooden door in the side of the chamber opposite the waiting benches.

Jared gave Madeline's hand a squeeze and rose, reaching over to ruffle Johnny's hair playfully, producing a giggle. Then, all business, he turned to follow the ascetic into the antechamber. As he went, his left arm flailed slightly as he tried to rest his hand on his sword hilt, out of habit. No weapons were allowed past the monastery gates. Never comfortable unarmed, Jared sighed and went into the antechamber closing the door behind him.

The antechamber was spare and unadorned with no furnishings. The only feature was a small, raised platform on which the Al' Helios stood and faced him. Formally intoning the Ritual of the Answer, he spoke without hesitation in a flat monotone devoid of any emotion. His manner was identical to the Ritual of the Question several hours earlier.

"Sir Jared D'Abrac, knight of the Kingdom of Pendalir and former commander in the king's Royal Army, you have on this day asked me a question. It is the duty of my position in our order to provide you with a truthful answer to one question, one time in this life. After the answer is given, you will be asked to leave our monastery never to return. If you attempt to return for any purpose, we will consider your life forfeit and use deadly force, if necessary, to prevent your re-entry to our sacred grounds. Do you understand the consequences of receiving your answer?"

"Yes, I do," Jared replied firmly and without hesitation.

"Then I will give you your answer. Do not interrupt or ask questions. I will not stop, and I will not repeat myself. This is the only time I will speak this answer. Listen well."

"Your question was, 'Is he possessed or a carrier for a necromantic soul other than his own?' As you asked this question, you gestured in the general direction of the boy who you call Johnny, and so I answer the question in reference to the boy. The answer has been sought and is as follows.

"The boy who you call Johnny is not possessed by any being alive or dead, and does not carry in his body or his essence any other soul. This answer I have been instructed to give you, and no further questions may you ask."

Stepping off the stone platform, the Al' Helios said in a warm, friendly tone that indicated the ceremony was over, "Normally, the monks escort you out of the monastery immediately, but I have instructed them to let you tarry in the courtyard so that you and your wife may leave the monastery together."

At that moment, a monk, clad in loose-fitting silver and gold-trimmed pants and tunic opened a door on the far side of the antechamber. Sunlight streamed in around him as he beckoned.

Jared went outside into a small courtyard where twenty monks stood quietly on either side, each holding a wooden staff. Each monk was still as a statue with the staff held in the hand furthest from the temple exit and nearest the exit from the monastery. One end of each staff was planted on the ground next to the monk's foot. Their demeanor was that of a ritualistic guard and entirely non-threatening, but none of the monks wore the novice garb. These monks were well-prepared for individuals who were dis-pleased with their answer.

Soon thereafter, Johnny was ushered into the courtyard and silently came over to hold Jared's hand. Several minutes later, Madeline was brought out into the courtyard. She was biting her lip again and joined Jared and Johnny, once again lost in thought. Almost immediately their horses were brought, already saddled. Once they had led their horses out of the monastery, they were given their packs, and Jared's sword was returned. The entire escort out of the monastery was done in silence with neither the monks nor the D'Abracs speaking. After they had mounted, one of the monks gasped. His eyes went wide as he looked back at the gate. A flurry of sideways glances and small movements indicated that the other monks were unsettled too.

The Al' Helios now stood at the gate, obviously in violation of custom. Before any others could speak, he said, "Take care in the education of the boy you call Johnny. He is very special indeed."

Several other monks gasped, and the attendant who had accompanied the Al' Helios looked like he was going to have an apoplexy, but the Al' Helios turned and walked back into the monastery as calmly as if this were part of the normal ritual. As he did so, the entire honor guard of monks seemed to regain its composure and filed in behind him. The attendant gave a long, unreadable look to the Jared and Madeline and then shut the gate in silence.

The D'Abrac family rode with Jared leading the way and Johnny riding in the saddle in front of Madeline. They needed to press on to return home before dusk, and so they kept a brisk pace and did not speak until they were back in the manor and Johnny was asleep in his bed. Jared knew they would talk before they went to bed, so he went to his study and sat in his reading chair. Madeline had gone up to the bedrooms to tuck Johnny in, and they obviously wouldn't want to talk about their answers where he might overhear. Johnny had behaved strangely the day after the funeral.

Shortly, Madeline arrived, bringing with her a pair of wine glasses. She handed one to Jared and kept one for herself. After a moment she asked, "You asked the question we agreed upon?"

"Of course," Jared replied, startled.

"Good, what did you get for an answer?"

Jared sipped the red liquid in his glass and raised his eyebrows. "You opened the last bottle from Pendalir City?"

"Yes, today was a once-in-a-lifetime day. It seemed appropriate. We have received a truthful answer to one question one time in this lifetime" she said, echoing the ritualistic tone that the Al' Helios had used.

"True enough, I suppose," Jared said and savored another sip of his wine.

"Your answer?" Madeline prompted with impatience creeping into her voice.

Jared recited his answer verbatim and took another sip.

"Any being alive or dead? He used those exact words?" Madeline's brow furrowed, and the wine glass in her hand tipped precariously close to spilling.

"Yes, exactly those words. Believe it or not, I kept my mouth shut and listened," Jared said with a smirk and sipped his wine again. After a moment, he volunteered, "Seemed pretty definitive to me."

"Very clear, actually. I've never heard of a mystic giving a straight answer before this." She paused and sipped from her glass, and in doing so righted it just before any of the extremely expensive wine spilled. "My answer was very clear as well."

"What question did you ask?"

Madeline made a face as if her wine had gone sour. "A very stupid question, I fear." Jared simply sipped his wine, so she continued, "I asked, 'Is he destined for a life of evil Necromancy?'"

"What's so bad about that question?"

"It's too specific, too similar to yours, and worse yet can be answered with a yes or a no. The answer gives us no leads on where we might get more information. You can't research the word no or go ask it questions. I should have stuck to my original question about the boy's mother. As I walked in, I had the sudden fear that his mother would be inconsequential or dead and that I wouldn't learn anything useful."

"You could be right. At least you did learn something... I presume he did answer 'No?'"

"Yes, and then he added, 'He is not destined to conquer the world or lead armies of undead.'"

"Very solicitous of him really. It could be that these monks aren't as cryptic as everyone claims they are," Jared said.

"He was making fun of me. When I asked my question, his facade cracked slightly. He was surprised and, if I'm not mistaken, relieved. Clearly he knew something and was afraid I would ask it."

"Ah, and you are mad at yourself for not reading his mind."

Madeline smirked. "That, of course, would be a useless attempt even if I were skilled enough to cast such a spell on ordinary folk. The Al' Helios is far from ordinary. Not to mention that it would go against our agreement that I should not perform magic near Johnny."

"And so you have done the best you were able. The answers were positive, and the boy is clear of Necromancy at least. Perhaps we need not fear a more inclusive education for the boy."

"Have you forgotten what the Al' Helios said as we left?"

"Take care in his education? Perhaps he means we should be sure not to leave anything out?"

"Unlikely. He clearly thought we would get the wrong impression from our answers. The obvious implication of our answers is that there is nothing special about the boy. I'd say it is much more likely he was afraid we would become complacent. Clearly there is something special about the boy, and we have missed our opportunity to learn it."

"Hmm, odd that he would be so helpful. Maybe it's something good."

"I'm afraid you have no idea how odd it was." Madeline sighed and finished her glass of wine. "All my research on their order and the ritualistic way in which their answers are given indicate that the monks of Helios must never answer a second question. I'd bet my staff that the prohibition includes unasked questions."

"Well, history has to be made sometime. Maybe they are lightening up."

"More likely by sunrise there will be a new Al' Helios."

"He'd be forced to step down?"

"Do you remember what they said about our lives if we attempt to return?"

"They are forfeit."

"I doubt the strictures for the monks are less than the strictures on the non-believers."

"Oh. Hmm. I see. I hope that's not true." Jared frowned and put down his wine glass. His thirst didn't seem to matter now. Madeline sighed heavily and left the room. There was little doubt as to what she believed to be true.

———————

The attendant to the Al' Helios paused after shutting the gate and then rushed back to his master's side. After they were alone, back in the temple, he asked, "I don't understand what happened today. You broke our two most sacred vows. Why?"

The Al' Helios turned his old leathery face and hairless head to regard the assistant intently. He smoothed his yellow and gold robes as he composed his answer. After a long pause, he said, "You will in time. After you have performed the rite of the answer many times, you will come to understand that some who come before you are like thistle-down on the wind. They are inconsequential and passing through this life. Most of these have no effect, never sprouting into anything more than a simple thistle plant. They never do more than produce more thistle down. Occasionally, more important people arrive. The weight of their questions and the effect our answers may have on the world is of more consequence than just who gets a thistle thorn stuck in their foot.

"Today, the weight of the entire world bore down on me. We are just one small monastery. Our religion, our service, and our prayers are holy and important, but it would be wrong of us to place ourselves before the fate of the world. This you must remember."

The attendant considered the response for several minutes, and the Al' Helios waited patiently. When the attendant spoke, he was hesitant. "You speak of me giving the rite of the Answer. I am flattered you think I will someday ascend to your position."

"I think not. I know. I am naming you my successor."

"But that is reserved for your final hours! How can you break yet another of our laws on this day?"

"I would not name you my successor if I did not have full faith that you knew our laws in detail. Part of the law is the penalty for breaking it."

The attendant gaped. "But that means..."

"Yes," said the old, bald man as he faced his long-time attendant. Slowly he began to disrobe. When he was naked, he folded the robes and handed them to the new Al' Helios. "You should not don these until the stroke of midnight. You will find me by the alter in the morning. Remember this day well. Speak not of what I have just told you. You, too, will bear the weight of the world before your term is ended. The things I have learned today must not return to the knowledge of man, and no living necromancer must disturb my rest with questions about this day. Thus, I lay my final charge and my eternal trust upon you to only give the most cryptic answers possible about this day and about me, should you be asked." And with that, the old, bald, and naked man opened the door of the sanctum for the last time.

2 Young Guards

2.1 Wall

"I'll be a bandit instead," said Johnny.

"There's no bandit in this story," Caroline complained.

"Come on, Johnny. The story is that the evil wizard has taken the princess hostage in the tower. Even I know that that's not the same as a bandit," complained Derek.

"I don't want to be a wizard!" Johnny shouted violently at the top of his lungs.

Surprised and stunned, both Caroline and Derek looked at each other, and then Caroline's face began to wrinkle. Derek and Johnny quickly glanced at each other and simultaneously said, "Don't cry, Caroline!"

"Johnny didn't mean to frighten you," Derek added.

Caroline's expression froze, and she seemed undecided whether she ought to be re-assured. A small tear crept out of the corner of her eye and ran partway down her cheek. Even though Caroline was almost seven years old now, she still threw tantrums to get her way with her older playmates. As annoying as this was, playmates were hard to come by. There were only two noble families in town, most peasants would hesitate to mingle with nobility, and the D'Abracs lived outside town.

"Honestly, I'm sorry. I didn't mean it. Let's go exploring instead. You can lead us this time," Johnny offered.

Caroline hesitated a moment, and then her face brightened, the tears and tantrum forgotten. "I lead?"

"Yes, and we will follow wherever you go," added Derek.

Johnny opened his mouth to say something to Derek, but noticing Caroline watching him carefully he shut it again.

"Ok, then follow me!" Caroline said happily, starting off across the yard toward the fields. After a moment, Johnny and Derek grabbed their wooden shields and swords and followed her. She led them out to the near edge of the field, turned around, marched back the way they came, and then did a circle, happily checking to be sure they were following all the while.

One time when Caroline wasn't looking and starting to get out ahead, Johnny whispered to Derek, "Wherever she goes?"

"I'm not the one who almost made her cry."

There wasn't much that Johnny could say to that, so for a half hour they marched around the yard in circles, and figure eights, clockwise and counterclockwise, and then in random squiggly lines across the yard, sometimes slow, sometimes almost running. Finally, unable to endure the boredom any longer, Johnny spoke up, "Where is our fearless leader leading us, I wonder?"

The sarcasm wasn't lost on Caroline, who looked back, narrowed her eyes, and headed back out toward the fields. Johnny and Derek followed, but this time Caroline didn't zigzag, and when she got to the near edge of the turnip fields she just kept going. Johnny and Derek slowed and began to protest, but Caroline was moving quickly and wasn't paying any attention to them.

"We aren't supposed to go into the fields," Johnny called.

"I don't think she heard you," Derek said.

"She did."

"She's not stopping"

"I know."

"What do we do?"

"Keep your promise and follow her. I certainly don't want to be the one to tell Mom that we let her go out into the fields alone. Do you?"

"Yeah, that wouldn't be good, would it?"

The boys headed out after Caroline, hurrying to catch up. Despite being almost two years younger and only six years old, Caroline had a good head start. The three of them were halfway across the field before the boys caught up. When they did, Johnny put a hand on Caroline's shoulder and forced her to slow down. She turned around and said, "What's the matter? Are the big brave warriors afraid of the turnips?"

She kept marching across the field, and Johnny protested, but nothing short of bodily force was going to stop Caroline now. Muddy shoes and straying outside their boundary were one thing, but a muddy dress and breeches from a struggle would really go over very badly. Also, there was still a chance they would get back before they were missed. Shoes were not so hard to clean.

As they got to the far side of the field, they also came to the north wall. The wall was three times their height and four feet thick. The side facing them was made of weathered gray granite and feldspar blocks. It ran east to west and protected the fields from the wild lands outside. Most of the wall was intact, but a couple dozen feet to the left was a section where the inside face of the wall had crumbled and tumbled inward, but the outer face still held.

Caroline stopped, and all three of them considered the wall. They had never been this far, and curiosity began to take over. "Hey, I bet we could climb up onto the wall where it's crumbled," said Derek.

"Yeah, probably," Johnny said indecisively, obviously wanting to and knowing that they probably shouldn't.

Caroline, however, started for the crumbled section immediately and was climbing up, and soon all three of them were standing atop the wall.

"I never knew there was a walk way up here," said Derek.

"Of course there is. What good would a wall be if you can't stand on it and shoot arrows?"

"Not much, I guess."

"I'm your leader, and our mission is to find an arrow," announced Caroline.

"Hey, yeah, that would be cool," said Johnny, and Derek nodded emphatically. For several minutes they walked along the wall, looking for an arrow from the past battles they imagined must have been fought on these walls. Mostly they found loamy leaves and half rotten twigs piled in the corners of the walls, and soon they grew tired of the search.

2.2 Combat

"What's that sound?" asked Caroline.

They listened, and soon enough there was a hoarse guttural shouting sound that cut off suddenly. They looked at each other in amazement.

"I don't like it..." Caroline said in a plaintive tone.

"No, it doesn't sound like anything good. We should go back now. We are probably already in enough trouble as it is," said Johnny.

"What is that?" Derek shouted and pointed through one of the crenelations on the outside of the wall. Caroline and Johnny each ran to the neighboring viewpoint, and they all gasped at what they saw next. The land outside the wall was covered by a hundred yards of field that was halfway grown over with bushes and scrub. Beyond that distance, the forest was full and lush and unbroken for miles. Fighting its way through tangled brush toward them was a four and a half foot tall creature. It had a vaguely human face but with a bulbous nose, pointy ears, and an under-bitten jaw. Protruding up from the jaw were two tusks, one sharp, one broken. The figure was dressed in heavy leather armor and wearing a simple skullcap-style helmet made of dented bronze. It was hacking bushes out of the way with a short sword and looking back over its shoulder every other swipe. Almost instantly three similar figures broke out of the forest. All were heading straight for the wall.

"Goblins!" Derek exclaimed in a excited whisper.

"Oh, not good..." Johnny moved to Caroline as fast as he could but didn't get there in time. A high-pitched squeal of terror split the air for a second before Johnny could clamp his hand over Caroline's mouth.

"Relax, they can't get up here," Derek said and looked back out over the wall. Johnny shushed Caroline, motioned for her to stay down, and went over to Derek.

"Suddenly I really *don't* want to find an arrow," Johnny said, motioning for his friend to move away from where he was staring out over the wall, but Derek was pointing again. When Johnny looked out once more, he could only see three of the four monsters, but he could also see eight men on horseback had emerged from the forest.

His father was in the lead accompanied by a man wearing a greenish cloak with a longbow. The man with the longbow withdrew an arrow from a half empty quiver and knocked it to his bow, ready to shoot. The goblins were sheltering behind whatever bushes they could find to avoid the man with the longbow. This kept them separated, unable to cooperate. Johnny spotted a fourth goblin lying in the tall grass with a feathered arrow protruding from the back of its neck.

The men fanned out, flanking the creatures and trapping them against the wall. They advanced slowly, closing the trap relentlessly. They did not appear to see the children peering down from atop the wall. As the men drew closer, three of them, including Sir D'Abrac, dismounted and drew their weapons. All three of them did so with a calm, cool confidence that could only come from years of practice. The one on the left was of medium height but heavily muscled and swung a largish hammer in one hand as if it were a toy. On the other arm he carried a large round shield, and he wore a mismatched set of plate armor and no helmet. The one on the right was taller, wiry, and advanced with a spear. He was protected only by relatively light leather armor. In the center, Sir D'Abrac was in full plate armor with a long sword and shield.

The goblins all had mismatched leather armor, some studded, some plain, much of it in need of repair. For weapons, they all had varying styles of ill-kept, rust-spotted, short swords. Each goblin had an identical leather-covered shield with a wolf tail and some feathers dangling from the bottom. The shields all seemed new and in good repair.

The muscular warrior on the left got to his goblin first and waded in with a backhand hammer stroke from left to right. His opponent dodged the blow and then moved to stab with a speed that seemed surprising for a creature as stocky as a goblin. The shield arm however had followed the hammer, and the goblin's blow clanged against the shield which the warrior then used to push the sword arm out to the left. The overbalanced goblin stumbled to its right and began to raise its wooden shield.

The warrior had not lost his balance and stepped toward the goblin, reversing his previous strike into a powerful forehand that came down on the outer edge of the goblin's shield. The goblin, prepared for a blow in the center of the shield, had tensed and pushed out, but the actual blow torqued the shield around, encouraging the very motion that the goblin had started. The result was that the goblin's shield arm rotated painfully out to one side, while his sword arm was still out to the other side from his failed strike. Neither arm could return quickly enough to parry the warrior's kick. Teeth and blood scattered, and the goblin could only stagger backward. Its dazed reflexes were nowhere near fast enough for the skull-crushing overhand blow that followed.

"Cool," whispered Derek.

On the right, the man with the spear faced off with the second goblin, spear point held low. There was a short series of spear jabs and shield blocks exchanged, and the goblin's position shifted, putting him on the outside of the circle. It was clear that the man with the spear was faster and more cunning. At one point, the thrust of his spear missed initially, but the side of the leaf shaped point slashed the goblin's thigh when the man swiped the tip sideways on the return stroke. Clearly loosing, the goblin turned and ran at the first opportunity. The goblin probably thought he was about to escape the encircling humans, but this was exactly what the man with the spear had been waiting for. With a lightning-quick, fluid motion, he reversed his grip and threw the spear so hard that it ran right through the goblin's thigh. The goblin fell and tried to roll over, but the spear got in his way, and he howled in agony. The wiry man was already on him and ended it efficiently with a dagger stroke to the back of the goblin's neck.

"Nice..." said Johnny, appreciating the way that the man with the spear had obviously anticipated the goblin's behavior.

In the center, the final goblin made a desperate headlong charge, perhaps thinking to catch the knight off-guard. The knight simply sidestepped lightly despite his full armor, and the goblin rushed by. Sir D'Abrac continued to move away from the goblin, and gestured with his sword toward the man in the greenish cloak, who was already drawing his bow. The goblin recovered from his charge, and at the moment when he was turning toward the knight to try again an arrow took him in the side of the neck. He staggered, dropped his weapon, and grasped at the shaft. Another arrow soon followed, this one sinking deep into the unarmored armpit of the arm that was grasping at the first shaft. The goblin's eyes went wide, and he fell forward, landing face down in the grass.

Silence fell upon the brushy field, and Johnny, Derek, and Caroline just stood there peering over the wall with their mouths open. Each battle had been quick and decisive. The goblins hadn't stood a chance. They had heard stories of battles against goblins and other creatures, but now they had witnessed a real one.

The moment of awe was broken when Sir D'Abrac looked straight up at them as if he had known they were there the whole time, and yelled, "Son, I don't know what you are doing up there, but I expect you and your friends will be back at the house by the time I get there and ready to explain. Do you understand?"

"Yes, Dad," Johnny yelled back, knowing that he was already caught and there was no sense in hiding now. The three children looked at each other, sighed, and began to make their way back to the manor.

On the way back, Derek admitted, "I know we will be in really big trouble, but almost any punishment is worth having seen that."

"Yes, but just don't say that to my dad, ok? We are probably already grounded until we join the guard," replied Johnny.

"Of course not. I'm not that dumb. Besides, I don't think we can be grounded for seven years..."

"You won't tell them I was leader, will you?" asked Caroline, turning to look back and almost slipping in the mud of the turnip field.

"It's best if none of us blames anyone else. Besides, the truth is we all wanted to climb the wall."

With that pact, they returned to the manor to await their chastisement.

2.3 Change

When Johnny, Derek, and Caroline got back, they entered via in the kitchen door. They were met by Madeline D'Abrac, who was standing in front of the fireplace with her hands on her hips. The look on her face said clearly they were in trouble with her as well.

"Hi, Mom!" Johnny tried to sound cheerful and act as if nothing were amiss.

"Don't 'Hi Mom' me, young man," she responded in a tone that left no question where things stood. "I just sent Cindy to the barn to search for you, and here you come in the kitchen door. Your shoes are all muddy. You know you aren't supposed to go out into the fields."

"Yes, Mom," Johnny replied meekly.

Just then Cindy entered saying, "I don't see them any... Oh, there they are. I see they've been in the fields." The tone of her voice went from near panic, to relief and then to verdict as her eyes bored into Derek, who squirmed but said nothing.

Caroline, seeing the attention focused on the two boys, began to speak and cry at the same time. "It was... (sniff) my fault. (sniff) They let me lead, and now Johnny's dad is mad at us."

"His dad?" Cindy said and looked at Madeline.

Madeline, just looked at Johnny, and said "Well?"

"Um, well, we kinda saw him fight some goblins."

"WHAT!?" both women said in unison.

"Don't worry. We were safe on top of the wall."

"WHERE!?"

"We had climbed up on the wall to look for arrows, but then we saw the goblins on the outside. Then Dad and some other men arrived and killed them. The goblins didn't stand a chance. There was a guy with a bow and a guy with a spear too."

"And a guy with a hammer and shield. It was really cool!" Derek added, clearly forgetting that they were in trouble.

Johnny winced but nodded and finished, "But we were on the wall, and there was no danger."

"This time," said a deeper voice from the doorway to the kitchen. Sir D'Abrac was standing there, still in his armor.

"Please see to Caroline. I'm going to talk to these two would-be warriors in the study." Madeline looked at him with eyebrows raised, and he added, "Boys, go to the study and wait for me."

Johnny and Derek did as they were told, and soon Sir D'Abrac entered the study. For a full thirty seconds he regarded them in silence, but neither of them were foolish enough to interrupt him. He cleared his throat, and Johnny and Derek braced themselves himself for a tirade. Surely they had gone too far this time.

"You boys are getting older."

Johnny and Derek looked at each other. This was not what they expected.

"You fancy yourselves as warriors, yet you can't even follow a simple order to stay close to the manor. You act as children still, and perhaps it's because we continue to treat you as children." He paused and looked at them sternly before continuing, "Today you witnessed what it means to be undisciplined. Those goblins were childish, much as you are. They probably knew that they shouldn't come this far west, yet they did anyway. They were looking for coin or provisions or whatever they might rob from the corpses of towns folk they encountered. They were tempted by something they wanted, and it cost them their lives. This is not so very different from your temptation to look for arrowheads atop the wall."

Johnny and Derek both studied their feet. This was more like what they expected. The words stung all the more in that they were so obviously true. Warriors needed discipline, and they had failed to do what they knew they ought to. They should have stopped Caroline rather than allowing her to lead them away from the safety of the manor. Childishly, they had accepted the excuse to disobey the rules laid down by their parents.

"The two of you will soon be young men, and young men do not roam the fields idly. We must begin preparing the two of you for adulthood. There is much work to be done."

Johnny, still looking down, closed his eyes, anticipating the list of chores to be long and potentially permanent. What better way to keep him out of trouble than to keep him busy? Derek looked up, puzzled.

"The two of you need to begin to train."

Johnny's head snapped up, and Derek's jaw dropped open.

"Henceforth, you will tend to chores assigned by Cindy in the morning and calisthenics and exercise supervised by Al before lunch. Then in the afternoon your mother will begin to teach you horsemanship. In the early evening I will return to train you in combat techniques, and after dinner you will learn your letters."

"What about Caroline?" Johnny asked.

"I doubt she'll be visiting again once Christina hears of this."

"I see." After a pause Johnny spoke again, "Dad, aren't you mad at us?"

"Son, I'm disappointed, and it's a shame I can't rely on you. I suppose your failing is partly my fault. I haven't taught you responsibility yet. To become a man and a warrior, you must always take full responsibility for your actions and their consequences, especially where those actions might hurt others. So far, you've only learned to play. We shall be fixing that henceforth, and on any occasion when you don't complete your chores in the morning, you will complete them in the afternoon instead of training. If you don't try hard with Al or you don't abide my instruction or that of your mother, you'll spend more time with Cindy. I am confident of her ability to occupy idle hands."

"We won't disappoint you!" Derek proclaimed. And Johnny quickly agreed

"Good, now go have some supper and prepare for bed. Cindy is already making a list, and you need to be up at dawn."

"Dawn?" Johnny asked.

"Sleeping in is for children, cripples, and old folks. I sincerely

hope you won't be sleeping in any time in the next fifty years."
With that, they were dismissed.

The next day, Cindy's tasks included scrubbing the kitchen floor, drawing water from the well, and polishing silver. Al's 'calisthenics' included mucking out stalls, followed by foot-races and learning to chop wood with an ax. Horsemanship included feeding the horses, rubbing them down, and lessons and quizzes on their anatomy. Madeline explained that in a few weeks ponies would be added to the stable, and riding would not begin until then.

Finally, the part of the day that the boys had most anticipated arrived. Out behind the kitchen, the boys awaited the arrival of Johnny's father.

"What kind of sword do you think he'll give us?" Derek asked

"A short, wooden one I expect," Johnny replied.

"I thought he didn't like our wooden swords."

"He doesn't. They are little more than sticks. I think the ones he gives us will be the proper size and weight, but we aren't big enough to handle a full long sword yet, so we will probably get a short sword and buckler."

"I'm bigger than you. Maybe he'll give me a long sword."

"By two inches."

"And twenty pounds."

"Of flab."

"Muscle!"

"Who won all the races?"

"Yeah, well who finished their stall first? Looked like you couldn't even lift a horse turd."

Before Johnny could reply, Sir D'Abrac emerged from the barn and began to head their way. He was carrying no weapons at all. Johnny and Derek looked at each other and then back at Sir D'Abrac.

"Where are the swords?" Johnny blurted out.

Jared D'Abrac smiled, having fully anticipated the question. "You are not yet ready to wield a sword. A sword is not a common weapon, and you must learn the basic techniques with the most common weapons first. Only once you understand the use of a weapon are you prepared to fight against it with any other weapon. And before you can hope to control any weapon, you must control yourself and your movements completely. It does no good to have a perfect swing or know a series of strikes if you stand too far or too close to your opponent to use them or lose your balance. A knowledge of parry and thrust and slash and strike will leave you helpless against the reach of a pole arm or spear if you have no knowledge of these. Do you understand?"

"Yes," they both replied obediently but with obvious disappointment.

"What is the most common weapon?"

"Spear?" offered Derek.

"Club?" Suggested Johnny

"Nope, the most common weapon of all is the fist. Before you learn to wield any other weapon, you must learn to throw, block, and avoid punches and kicks."

Both boys sighed, even more disappointed than before.

"Do you remember how Stark felled the first goblin yesterday?"

"Yeah, he blocked, struck, and then kicked, and finished with a massive blow," Derek said, enthusiastically emphasizing the word "massive."

"And which move defeated the goblin?"

"The kick," Johnny said.

"So do you now see the importance of the basics? Stark was able to kick the goblin senseless because he had good balance and had spent many long hard hours practicing kicking and punching.

If you can't even do these simple things, the sword and shield will only be a danger to you, giving you false confidence, the same confidence that the goblin had." Jared D'Abrac gave the boys a long, serious look.

"I see," said Johnny, and Derek nodded too.

"One more thing before we begin. What I teach you, and what you may later learn in the guard, are methods of inflicting serious injury. Once you learn these, you must not get into fist fights or any other type of fight with each other or with other children. This is serious business and not a game. Real fighting is life and death. Do you recall how the goblin I faced died?"

"He rushed you, and then he got shot," Johnny said immediately.

"Yes, and in all combat there is always a chance of a slip or your opponent surprising you. Every opponent might kill you or do serious harm. You must treat every opponent with full respect. If there is an easy way to win the fight, you must take it without hesitation. The goblin had come out from the bushes. When he charged, he lost control of his position and allowed me to remove myself such that he was standing alone and undefended.

"If I had rushed back in, I probably could have defeated him easily, but there's always a chance that I would slip, my sword might break, or that the goblin would have some surprise tactic and catch me off-guard. Real combat is not about honor or fairness. Honor and fairness have their place before and after combat. Combat is about not dying and about killing or disabling your opponent before they do the same to you. In real combat, there is only one rule: live. You must practice all forms of combat as if the fight were real. You don't want to practice anything fake or weak, or that is what you will do in combat, and surely you will be hurt. Are you ready to begin?"

"Yes," they said in unison.

And with that their training began. Punching bags of grain were suspended in the barn. They did some stretching, then they got quick introductions to punching, kicking, and some simple footwork.

When they finished, Derek said, "Man! I never knew kicking and footwork were so hard."

"Yah, but you throw a really good punch! I'm glad we haven't gotten into a fight in the last year. You'd knock me out."

"Only if I catch you. You won all the races."

"True, now it's time to learn to read and write."

"Ugh, I just want to rest."

"Yeah, but just think how lucky you are. Most common folk never get to learn letters. Being able to read and write guarantees that you can always find a job with a merchant or a skilled job for nobility, a job that won't break your back every day."

"Nobles like you?"

Shocked, Johnny paused and considered Derek for a moment. "You're my friend. I'd certainly help you if you needed it, but it would be kinda weird to have you work for me."

"We had better get to your mom before she gets mad," Derek said, looking a bit embarrassed and starting toward the kitchen.

Johnny stood there for a moment, a puzzled look on his face, and then followed.

The chores and exercise in the morning changed little over the next few years, except that learning to swim was added once a week in place of calisthenics. By the age of fifteen they had trained the basics in unarmed fighting, then with clubs, then the staff, then spears, and then daggers, the longbow, and finally short sword and buckler. Derek prevailed at unarmed combat and clubs, while Johnny's speed allowed him success with the staff and the spear. He also had talent for the longbow that quickly exceeded Derek, but when the sword and buckler came, Derek was once again superior initially, for he was now four inches taller and thirty-five pounds heavier. However, with practice, Johnny's skill and wit began to show, and it almost became a fair fight again.

Sir D'Abrac decided that Johnny would likely be best suited to the ranger corps, and so on some weekends Corporal Zandar of the ranger corps took them both into the woods and taught them how to stalk quietly through the grass, brush, and leaves. They also learned how to track animals and how to survive in the woods. As predicted, Johnny excelled at woodcraft. Eventually Derek, who struggled with woodcraft, especially moving silently, stopped participating in woodcraft lessons. As the years passed, Derek grew tall strong and sturdy, while Johnny became wiry and quick.

It was a sunny afternoon in late summer before their sixteenth birthdays. Next year they would be joining the guard. The sun had come out after morning rains, and humidity rose from the drying ground around them, promising a hot, sweaty afternoon of training. Derek and Johnny stood at attention in the yard, awaiting Sir D'Abrac's customary approach and declaration of the focus of the day's training schedule. Usually, they stood for no more than a few minutes, but it had been ten minutes today, and the sun was hot. A rivulet of sweat crept down Johnny's forehead and got caught in his eyebrow. Soon, another ran unimpeded down his left temple. Minutes ticked by, and a faint breeze stirred, the cooling effect barely noticeable, but it was enough to cause his tunic to flutter and then stick to his sweaty back.

Neither Johnny nor Derek moved from the spot. They occasionally flexed their calf muscles and never locked their knees to keep circulation flowing without undo motion, as they had been taught. There had been tests of their patience like this before. They knew that to move or to talk would mean a day primarily consisting of calisthenics and labor rather than training. On a hot day like this, neither of them wanted that, and so they remained standing as a half hour came and went.

Finally, after both boys were drenched in sweat, and Derek's face was beginning to redden, there was an unfamiliar clanking sound and the sound of metal shifting on metal. This was unusual, but neither boy moved. Presently Sir Jared D'Abrac stepped out of the barn in full plate armor, sword belted to his waist, and shield upon his arm. His visor was down, and the red horsehair plume upon his helm swayed across his back as he strode toward them. The sun glinted off of his polished armor in a hundred places, and despite their best efforts the boys did blink a few times as he approached.

"Young men," the knight began, and despite the heat both boys stood slightly taller, and Derek inhaled as goosebumps formed on his arms. Both boys could guess what was coming next. "I have trained you for the better part of seven years, almost half of your lives. You have become skilled with weapons and physically fit. Your minds have become disciplined and your determination steadfast. You now understand the importance of adherence to rules laid down by your elders and your superiors. Disobedience and the disregard for rules that preceded the start of your training is but a distant memory, nearly forgotten. Now, I have every confidence that you will not be involved in such an incident again. Come into the barn out of the sun. Drink some water and cool down. Today, in my estimation, you are ready to carry a real sword."

With that, the knight beckoned with a gleaming hand and turned toward the cool darkness of the barn. Both boys looked at each other and grinned as they followed. "Our own swords!"

Derek barely breathed, and Johnny nodded enthusiastically as they passed into the shade. While the boys drank and splashed themselves with water, Sir D'Abrac removed his helm, shield, and gauntlets.

Sir D'Abrac opened the gate of a stall, stepped inside briefly, and returned with two swords and a dagger. One sword was four feet long with a cross guard slightly under a foot wide and a grip big enough for two hands. The other was a little less than a foot shorter but also much lighter. Both had an S-shaped cross guard a burgundy leather sheath and a swirled metal ball as a pommel.

Sir D'Abrac solemnly presented the larger sword to Derek and said, "This sword will require you to use both hands and no shield for the time being, but you are still growing, and I expect that with time you will become strong enough that you'll have the option of using this with a shield or axe in shorter fights. If you prefer the two-handed style, you may want a longer, more forceful weapon some day, but this sword was crafted by a master in Pendalir City and should be a good, versatile general-purpose blade for the rest of your life. It's not so large as to require an entire open joust field to swing it, yet it should still have enough heft to it to allow you to take advantage of your size and strength."

"Wow... Thanks... " Derek barely breathed, eyes locked on the sword.

Then he turned to his son, holding the remaining two weapons. "Johnny, watching you develop has shown that you require a different sort of weapon than Derek. You will never match him in size or strength. Speed and cunning are your allies. Also, with your woodcraft I expect you are likely to find a position in the ranger corps. Therefore, this sword, which is shorter and half the weight, will suit you best. It also will be far less likely to tangle in tree branches or bushes if you find combat on the trail or from a horse. Should you find yourself in one-on-one combat, this parrying dagger should be better for you than trying to maneuver a heavy shield. You've done fine against Derek with sword and shield, but doing well against a boy in training will not be the same as an experienced warrior. Your shield moves too slow, and a light, fast dagger will provide you with more options. If you can't block the blow with your dagger, you should endeavor not to be where that blow is aimed when it arrives.

"Like Derek's sword, this is made by the same master, but it is also a compromise. It is suitable both for cutting and thrusting, and your future preferences may take you in the direction of a more thrusting or fencing-style rapier or a more utilitarian short sword and buckler. Perhaps once you are a ranger you shall eschew swordplay altogether for archery, since you show great skill there. In that case, you might retain this sword so as not to be helpless when a combatant closes the gap."

"Thank you, Father," Johnny said, accepting the sword and dagger with a smile.

"You may draw them from their sheath, and we will discuss how to properly sharpen and care for your swords, but be careful and do *not* swing them yet. They are new and very sharp."

Both boys drew their swords from their sheaths and for several minutes simply admired the blades both of which were hollow ground on the edge with a broad fuller running to within a third of the tip where it tapered out and the blade's cross-section became hexagonal. Both cross pieces had hoops to protect the wielder's hands and wire-wrapped leather grips. The leather had a surface like fine sandpaper. Sir D'Abrac watched quietly, a knowing smile on his face and the memory of his first sword in his heart.

"What type of leather is this?" Johnny asked.

"It's a special type of shark skin. The smith who makes these swords buys skins that come from a small shark found in the warm islands off the southern coast. It's rough enough to always give a good grip but won't wear the skin off your hand like a larger shark's skin would. His name is Master Pyree, and the mark upon the cross piece is his. You will find that the blades are strong and stiff yet light and unlikely to snap. They are both good for cutting but also good for piercing through chain mail, or in Derek's case he should even be able to puncture lightweight plate armor if he gets a solid thrust. The three of us are likely the only residents of the north country to have swords of this quality.

"Do not sell these swords for any price. If you do, you may never wield their equal again. They happen to be the last swords made by Master Pyree before his retirement. You have the honor of wielding his final works."

Sir D'Abrac paused, and the boys solemnly nodded their agreement.

"Although Pyree swords are less prone to rust than most, you must still learn to protect and care for your sword appropriately..."

2.4 Joining

A little over a year after Johnny and Derek received their swords, they stood outside the western town gate in the late summer morning. The dew was heavy and the air just slightly chilly. The chill was a faint hint that the season would soon pass into fall, but as yet, it had no bite and was far from frost. Both of them were clad in light leather armor, had their swords belted to their hips and were carrying a large sack of clothes and personal effects that would be their only possessions for the next two years. The light was coming into the sky, but the gate was not yet open. The town had three gates, an east gate that led down to the river, a west gate to the farmlands, and the D'Abrac manor. The south gate opened to the south road. Produce came in the west gate, some fish and water came in the east gate, and traders from the capital, Pendalir City, came and went via the south gate. All the gates normally opened at dawn.

"I wonder what the delay is," Johnny said.

"No idea, but I wish they would get on with opening it. I can't wait to finally be a guard," Derek replied.

"Don't forget we have two years of being a recruit first."

"Yes, but with your father's training we'll be the top of the class for sure. Then I can become a great warrior like your Pa. I'll become a knight and have lands, and my family will have a noble name, just like yours!" Johnny had heard this plan many times and nodded ascent but did not comment.

"There it is. I hear them unbolting it now!" Derek nearly shouted. Several loud clunking noises followed, and the boys stepped back as the gate split down the middle and opened outward.

Despite their eagerness, the boys had to wait another minute or two for several farm wagons to exit the gate on their way out to the fields. On the inside of the wooden palisade to either side of the gate, there was a stone structure with a pair of arrow slits. On the town side there was a door. The dual guard houses served to reinforce the gate and were the beginning of the baron's plan to surround the town with a stone wall. The guard on duty was a friend of Jared's, so they passed through with just a wave despite their swords.

Johnny and Derek proceeded down the wide lane, the north side of which was another wooden palisade wall surrounding the guard compound and separating it from the rest of the town. To their right were a variety of shops and houses, most made of timber or timber and plaster. The street itself was paved with uneven cobblestones, but the alleys were packed dirt. They passed a dozen folks, some of whom recognized them and waved. Finally, they came to the gated entrance to the guard compound on the left.

The guard at the compound's gate, called to them, "Better run! The entrance tourney is about to begin on the practice field to the right."

Derek and Johnny could see a half-dozen boys their own age lined up, and a sergeant was walking down the line, inspecting. Almost another dozen were lined up near the barracks. As the sergeant finished with a red-haired boy and moved on to the next in the line, the red-haired boy grabbed his pack and walked over to a scale by the barracks where he was weighed and his height measured. A corporal wrote something on a piece of paper that was tacked to a board he was holding, and then the red-haired recruit was inserted into the middle of the lineup by the barracks.

Johnny and Derek hurried over to the end of the line and stood at attention the way his father had taught them, just before the sergeant finished with the last recruit. The sergeant stared at them for a moment, looking them up and down. He noted their swords with a grimace. "I suppose you think that just because you're a noble with a D' before your name you can just show up any time you like."

"The west gate was late opening. We came in as soon as we were able... sir."

"Boy, if you're lying to me, you'll not be admitted to the guard in this year or any year after. Dishonesty is not tolerated in the guard. I don't care if you're the crown prince or a homeless beggar. You must be truthful, and you must show up on time. Now I'll ask you one time and one time only. Why are you late?"

The sergeant moved closer to Johnny until he was looking down at Johnny. This left Johnny staring straight at the sergeant's chin.

"The west gate was late opening, sir!" Johnny's responded instantly.

"Well, you've definitely got backbone." The sergeant backed up, peered at Johnny, and then looked at Derek. "You got the same story?"

"Yes, sir," Derek replied respectfully.

"I see. Well, someone's in trouble, and I hope for your sake it's the gate guard, not you. I see you have brought your own weapons as required. Do you each have five changes of clothes?"

"Yes, sir," they replied in unison.

"And you're both over sixteen years of age?"

"Yes, sir!" In unison again.

The sergeant chuckled. "I see your old man's been pre-training you and your friend. This year should have an interesting crop of recruits. Do me a favor. Try to remember that some of these boys have never done more than swing their sword at innocent hay bales. Don't hurt any of the ones who've had no training. Go get weighed in." He gestured toward the scales.

"Yes, sir," Derek replied.

"I understand, sir," Johnny replied, and then asked, "Does this mean that some of them have had some training already?"

The corner of the sergeant's mouth twitched as if he wanted to smile, and then he said, "Apparently your dad forgot to teach you that recruits don't ask questions. I gave you an order. Go get weighed in... NOW."

Johnny blushed and replied "Yes, sir!" He and Derek headed for the scales.

After they were weighed and measured, Derek was placed at the far left end of the line and Johnny near the middle. It had become clear that they were being lined up by some combination of height and weight, and the left-hand side was bigger and heavier by far than the right-hand side. To Johnny's right was the red-haired recruit and to his left was Dillon.

While they waited in line, Johnny turned to the red-haired boy. "Hi, I'm Johnny. What's your name?"

Before the red-haired boy could respond, Dillon said, "Careful, spook boy wants to know your name."

Irritated, Johnny turned to Dillon and said, "What?"

"Careful, Red. Give him your name, and he'll curse your dad too," Dillon continued.

"Dillon, what are you talking about? I never cursed your dad."

"You wished him a restless undeath as a ghost warrior, but I guess for a spook who hides with his coward father in the ghost keep it's normal."

"Coward? My dad's a knight! I've seen him decimate goblins right outside our wall!"

"Oh, he beats up on goblins! Great, anyone can do that. How come he doesn't participate in elf raids? My stepdad has been on dozens of raids. People actually get killed on elf raids."

The line had mostly dissolved, and the recruits began to form a circle around Dillon and Johnny. They smelled a fight brewing. Johnny was still shocked but was beginning to turn to face Dillon fully. Before Johnny replied, Derek put a hand on Dillon's shoulder and turned him around. "I think you need to calm down, Dillon. You shouldn't be saying those things."

Dillon pushed Derek's hand away and said, "Ah, like father like son, he gets his peasant friends to do his fighting." Several boys who had closed in and now stood next to Dillon guffawed at the remark. Dillon soaked it up.

"THAT will be ENOUGH of THAT!" roared the sergeant. "Get back in line!" The recruits resumed their former positions and stood facing the sergeant.

"I turn my back for a minute, and I find you recruits circling for a common barroom style brawl? I've never in twenty years of service have seen something this disgraceful. Don't start pointing. You all left the line. You all encouraged it, and as of right now if I ever see one of you strike another outside of sparing you're out for good. We are building a cohesive fighting force. You will be brothers in arms, and you will need to trust each other with your lives! Whatever grudges or petty disagreements you had before you walked through that gate must be left behind. If you can't leave it behind, back out the gate you go. Am I clear?"

Without thinking, Johnny and Derek replied in unison, "Yes,

sir!" Dillon and several of the others snickered quietly. Johnny began to blush. The sergeant glared at the line. Seconds ticked by, and the sergeant kept glaring.

Eventually the red-haired recruit meekly said, "Yes, sir." One by one the others followed suit as the sergeant glared directly at them.

"Am I CLEAR?"

"Yes, sir," was repeated by several recruits immediately. The rest replied soon after.

"AM I CLEAR?"

All the recruits replied in unison, "Yes, sir!"

"Good. Don't forget it even once. Now, unbelt your swords and hold them in front of you."

The recruits did as they were told, and two second-year recruits began collecting the steel weapons from the recruits and replacing them in turn with a medium-length wooden practice sword. The practice swords were about the same length as Johnny's sword but had an extra long hilt that might allow assistance from a second hand.

"The steel weapons you were required to bring for your entry into the guard will be returned to you if you successfully graduate to the second year of the program one year from now. Until then, you train with wooden weapons for your own safety."

Soon after, a ranking tournament was arranged with a round-robin format. By lunch, it was already clear that Johnny, Derek, Dillon, and the red-haired recruit whose name was Thomas were the only real contenders. They were all undefeated, and simple observation showed that only they had any concept of footwork, balance, or striking techniques. Thomas's footwork was rudimentary, and several of his wins had come with close calls. The other three had made such short work of their opponents that it was hard to make a comparison.

After lunch, Thomas immediately went up against Dillon.

Though he started off with one surprisingly quick swing that nearly caught Dillon off guard, Thomas soon stumbled and was defeated. Watching to the side, Johnny and Derek smiled at each other with confident looks on their faces. Short though as it was, the match had still lasted long enough that both contestants had revealed weaknesses. An hour or so later, Johnny and Derek had dispatched Thomas with ease, and the much anticipated matchup of Derek vs Dillon was next.

Dillon knew he was at a severe size disadvantage and kept dodging back from Derek's heavy but controlled and measured strokes. The dance continued with Derek pursuing Dillon round the enclosure, taking the occasional swing. Dillon's strategy to let Derek tire himself out soon became evident, and Derek pressed harder, occasionally forcing Dillon to block before dodging back. Derek was confident that if his opponent had to work too he could easily last as long, and so this continued for several minutes. Then on one block Derek's wooden sword, which had endured the abuse of Derek's arms that were as big as some other recruit's legs, cracked, and the tip flew into the crowd, striking Thomas in the leg.

Thomas went down with a scream, and Derek turned toward Thomas to apologize when a solid stinging blow landed on his sword arm, and a triumphant shout from Dillon announced the source of the pain.

Derek then turned to the sergeant and said, "But the sword broke!"

Without hesitation the sergeant said, "And you lost your concentration, then you died. Match to Dillon. Good patience on his part paid off." He turned to one of the second years assisting with the tourney. "Rory, find our large and most unlucky dead friend a new practice sword."

Dillon whooped again, and Derek sighed. "You're right." He rubbed his arm and took a seat.

Soon after Johnny and Derek faced off. Having sparred so many times, they both knew that with both of them constrained to a light, short weapon Derek could neither use force of blow nor reach of his weapon to compensate for Johnny's speed. Johnny did win, though Derek put up a good fight for almost five minutes. His strength did still give some superior force to his strikes, and their blades whistled and hummed faster and clacked louder than anything seen thus far. By the end the look on Dillon's face was grim. The last few novices put on lackluster performances, and then the final match between Johnny and Dillon began.

Early on, they circled each other cautiously, and Dillon, tried taunting Johnny by whispering "Spook" and then "Coward's Son." After that taunt, the grim, confident look that crossed Johnny's face almost caused Dillon to stumble.

Sensing the miss step, Johnny flashed in with a series of slashes in sequence that ended with his wooden blade whistling inches past Dillon's nose. Dillon blinked, startled, and Johnny smiled grimly, feinting one way and then coming hard the other way again. His blade whistled just short of striking Dillon. Over and over, flurry after flurry beat Dillon but missed on the final strike. Soon it became obvious that Johnny could have struck home on any of the combinations.

Dillon's face was no longer just red with exertion but also flush with embarrassment. He began to make wild counterattacks, which Johnny parried and riposted, repeatedly missing by just inches. Dillon began to tire, yet Johnny seemed faster and lighter on his feet than ever. Dillon's swings began to become heavy and wild. He was panting hard after fifteen minutes of continual taunting and humiliation. Finally, on one wild swing by Dillon, Johnny turned his blade and struck near the base of Dillon's sword. Dillon's sword flew from his exhausted hand, and Dillon stumbled after it. Instantly Johnny sidestepped, whipped his sword around the other way, and spanked Dillon on the buttocks with the flat of the blade, winning the match.

Many recruits, including several second years who stopped to watch, cheered and congratulated Johnny while Dillon's friends, including Thomas, consoled him. The second years adjusted the final rankings on the barracks wall nearby. Johnny first, then Dillon, Derek, and Thomas.

The sergeant announced, "This concludes our monthly ranking tournament. We will hold a similar tournament each month. Placements from the previous three months will determine which of you are in the lower third of the class and not on track to graduate to the second year of the program. Please be sure that all practice swords are returned to the racks." Then he looked at Johnny and Dillon. "You two, come with me. The three of us need to talk." From his tone, there was no question who was going to be doing the talking and who was going to be doing the listening.

2.5 Drunk

"Well, we're finally recruits now and at the top of the list! We should celebrate!" Derek said as they entered their barracks somewhat ahead of the other new recruits. "My dad gave me several coppers, so let's go down to the Pig's Eye and get some ale. Now that we're recruits, they'll finally serve us!"

"True, I hadn't thought of that," said Johnny. "Ok, I suppose now is as good a time as any to learn about ale. Let's go."

"Learn about ale? Hah! That's a good one. You make it sound like reading a book. Come on. This is supposed to be fun!" And with that they set their excess uniforms in their trunks and were leaving just as the others were coming in.

When they got to the Pig's Eye, it was slightly before dinnertime, and the common room was only a third full. The bar was empty. Johnny started to head for a table, but Derek grinned and pulled him toward the bar. "Now we can sit over here."

"Ok, but I'm hungry. We need to eat something too. Do they serve food at the bar?" Johnny asked.

At that point the bartender spoke up, "Ale goes just fine and proper with a bowl of stew and a slice of bread, my lads. And eating food will improve your stomach for the ale too. Food is certainly what I suggest, given that it's your first time at the bar."

"Sounds good to me!" Derek said emphatically. Food always sounded good to Derek.

The bartender nodded to Johnny and asked, "Which division did you get recruited into?"

"Rangers. And he's in the infantry," Johnny said, pointing his thumb at Derek.

"Figured that by his size. I'll get that food now," the bartender said and headed for the kitchen.

They sat and looked out over the tables from their new vantage point across the common room. "Nice to sit up high where we can see everything," Johnny commented.

"Sure is," Derek replied with a grin.

Several other recruits having had a similar idea entered the bar. Derek waved, but they took up seats at the far end of the bar.

"That's not very friendly of them," Derek said.

"We're unpopular because they know we kicked their butts. We've been trained by my father for years already, and most of them are still playing with swords. In his quarters, the sergeant told Dillon and I that we need to stop our bickering now. He said both of our individual fighting skills were good enough to graduate first year already, but we will serve out the full year to ensure that we demonstrate the ability to work as a team. I'm supposed to mentor Dillon. I don't think he liked that. After Dillon left, the sergeant said my graduation test is to get Dillon to like it. He says he expects me to become a leader, and he doesn't want to see me embarrass anyone else the way I did today. He's right, of course. Today I made it very difficult for Dillon and I to work together. I should have just beat him on the first pass."

"Yup, John, you and him don't get along, but you're the smartest guy I know. I'm sure you'll find a way to work it out. As far as the fighting's concerned, this is going to be an easy-peasy ride thanks to your dad. Dillon won't be so lucky next time. It's going to be me and you straight through from here."

The bartender, who had just arrived with their food, corrected him, "Ayup, that'll be the challenge for the two of you. You two will be tempted to slack off. Nobles always have that challenge."

"He's the nobleman," Derek said, pointing at Johnny. "My dad's just a stableman."

"That may be true, son, but Sir D'Abrac is a rare noble indeed. He takes keen interest in the welfare of the common folks. Now the baron's rightly our lord, and he does kep' us safe from the elves to the north and more importantly from them goblins to the east, but he don't seem to have a thought for what happens to the common folk so long as enough of 'em volunteer for his guard and the rest pay their taxes. Sir D'Abrac has helped out more than a few folk around here, and you, young sir, are the one he's done the most for."

"I do appreciate his teaching us to fight, but it doesn't seem that special. I was there when he was already training John here. I just got to tag along."

The bartender looked at Derek seriously and after a pause said, "Mind yourself, young man. Common folk don't have time to spend teaching their children very much, cause they gots to work all day long. The main difference 'tween a noble and a commoner is not so much their blood but the fact they have money and time to train their young'uns. They start earlier, eat better, and that allows 'em to grow stronger, learn more, and become better fight-ers, or become better at business or politics or whatever else they choose. They also can afford proper equipment. The other lads you're training with barely scraped together enough coin to buy a sword. Any old sword, whereas, I'd bet that you two have fine, well-made blades from Pendalir City, hmm? Yes, I think I hit the mark from your expressions..."

They both nodded, and the barkeeper said to Derek, "You, young lad, are halfway to becoming a noble yourself... if you don't squander it relaxing on 'easy-peasy' street. You'll need to keep working hard to continue to improve even when the going seems easy."

"If you say so," Derek replied, but he didn't seem convinced. Other patrons were calling for ale, so the bartender left them, and they dug into the stew, dipping the bread and drinking the ale. At first, they sipped the ale tentatively, discovering that besides being foamy on top it was somewhat bitter, but soon they were drinking freely. By the end of their meal they had each ordered a second one. They talked about the day's events, how easy the other recruits were, and their prospects for the future. More ale was ordered, and the talk drifted inexorably back to reminiscences of their training with Sir D'Abrac and then their childhood.

Early in their dinner, they were interrupted by a sudden query from behind. "You two aresh new recroosh?"

Johnny and Derek looked at each other quizzically as they turned to face the speaker, not understanding the question. The speaker was an old semi-retired tailor who sometimes still did some work for Cindy and Madeline D'Abrac but mostly spent his time in the pub these days. Nonetheless, Johnny and Derek had met him several times.

"I'm sorry. What was the question, Master Tirin?" Johnny replied, addressing him as his status as a master craftsman of the Tailor's Guild required.

"I ashked if you two jusht joined the guard... on account of your position at the b... bar."

"Yup, we sure did!" Derek replied enthusiastically.

"Good, go kill some elves," Master Tirin said in a surprisingly clear if slightly too loud voice. A few folks stopped talking and glanced over. But when they saw Master Tirin, they quickly returned to their previous conversations. Master Tirin didn't notice any of this and continued emphatically. "Those blood shucking elves took my son from me... " At this point Master Tirin burped, swallowed, made a face, then continued as if nothing had happened. "Jusht after the baron discovered that they were hoarding the woods... That was twenty yearsh ago today!"

"Certainly, we'll get the ones who killed your son, and we'll get their friends too," said Johnny, not at all surprised by this. Tirin's story was well known by almost anyone who spent more than a week in the small town of Arnoria, which wasn't big enough for two inns, and Master Tirin was almost always in the pub by afternoon every day. His shop didn't open till almost noon, and often closed by three. If there were any other tailors in town, he'd have been out of business long ago.

"Goodsh! Hero'sh son might just do it too! Some day I'd like to see a dead elf inshtead of reports that the elfsh have been cleared from here or chased to there. We shertainly get to see enough dead or wounded guardshmen. We ought to get to see at leasht one dead elf now and then. I shay."

He peered into his empty beer stein and blinked. Then he looked up and said, "Needsh more beeeer." He abruptly headed toward the middle of the bar where the bartender was chatting with another customer.

Looking after him, Derek said, "Heh, he sure is far gone tonight."

Johnny nodded thoughtfully, and they resumed eating and drinking. They talked of what it might be like to catch an elf for a while then drifted to reminiscing about the goblins they witnessed from the wall and gossip about Caroline, who had not been allowed to play with them since. They ordered again and briefly they dwelt on how pretty she was now, but then they somehow wound up talking about the accident with the coach.

"I'll shtill never figure out why he was driving so fasht," Derek said.

"Hard to say. I still remember seeing his soul dishappear," Johnny said.

"Yup, that's what hupp'ins, but you can't see it... silly."

"I dunno... I felt something weird there for a while after. I also remember my mom doin' somethun' to the horses."

"And I remember you caused a fush at the funeral too," Derek said and laughed, but his laugh was interrupted by a burp.

"I was young. It was because of those stupid dreamsh I had."

"Dreams?"

Johnny's eyes got a glazed look as he remembered. "I dreamed of skeletons and zombies... all standing, waiting in rows... twenty deep, twenty-five wide". Johnny was interrupted briefly by the crash of a mug behind the bar and the innkeeper's subsequent profane oaths as he bent down to pick up the pieces.

"There were hands in boxes, and eye's that floated in glass boxes, too."

"That's a seriously meshed up dream, Johnny."

"The most powerful ones are the warriors you can see through... but they have their own leader."

"I tink you're jusht making stuff up..." Then Derek had a revelation and said, "I tink you're drunsh!"

"You mean drunk... yes... I think we both are," Johnny said seriously.

"I think both of you lads need to go home and sleep it off," said the innkeeper, collecting their steins and plates. Soon he had them ushered out onto the street. After what seemed like an epic journey, including Johnny throwing up on the front step of the bookbinder's shop, they made it back to the barracks. There they passed out until morning, which came far faster than Johnny wished it would.

2.6 Baron

An unctuous butler ushered Sir Jared D'Abrac into the baron's study. Baron D'Arnor was seated at a massive, ornately decorated wood desk reading a large book with a gold embossed leather cover. He was in his late forties with dark hair, a long face, soft facial features, and a short, upturned nose. Despite his soft looking face, he was a capable warrior and still in fighting shape. When he looked up from the book, his steel-gray eyes were hard and calculating.

The baron gently closed his book as Jared approached. Gesturing at the book on his desk, the baron said, "Such a hard thing to find decent books on elves. I've nearly read this one to pieces... I should get it rebound some time. Yet it's so hard to let it out of my grasp for that long." Jared opened his mouth, but the baron plowed on unconcerned, "With it being so very rare, if I do get it rebound perhaps I should lend it to you. You seem interested in elves. Or at least that's the only thing you seem to visit me to talk about. This is another of those chats, right? No wife this time? Ah, let me guess. It's because your adopted son has just joined the guard, isn't it?"

Jared unclenched his jaw and began to reply at length. "Yes..." But the baron only interrupted him.

"Now that your son is involved, that changes everything, or so it seems to you. Alas, Jared, while you have the finest combat skills in the region, perhaps in the country, and you could probably inspire a thousand men on the battlefield, you are as helpless as a babe in swaddling when it comes to politics. That's more or less how you wound up out here. Another time you went to see someone without your wife as I recall, right?"

Grimacing, Jared tried again, and this time the baron let him speak. "People are getting hurt, sometimes killed, and you are spreading fear and ignorance needlessly," Jared said.

The baron clucked his tongue and sighed. "You were doing well there till that last bit... There *is* a need. Look at how this town has changed since it started fighting the elves. This town is twenty times bigger, one hundred times stronger, and a thousand times more prosperous than when I first got here."

"You mean a thousand times more profitable."

"That too, of course, the same thing in then end. Take the inn, for example. It's twice the original size after it burned down twelve years ago, and it is full every evening. Now, when traders visit, they and their guards have a place to stay, and a place to get a drink. It makes the trip up here much more attractive. There's a full wooden palisade, seventy-six guardsmen to defend the city, and twenty-nine rangers to watch the wilderness around the town. When I got here, goblin raids out of the east threatened the village several times a year. Now, because of your patrol and the men I lend you, it's been two years since goblins have shown their faces, and half a dozen since they've done any real harm. We are building a stone wall longer and surrounding more of the town than any other in the region. It is almost a quarter complete."

"A wall we don't need and twenty-nine rangers to harass the elves needlessly."

"There you go with that word again. The common folk aren't soldiers. You try to think of them as such, but they don't do things out of a sense of duty, and unless motivated most of them only do barely enough to buy drinks at the tavern. Without fear, without an enemy, they are doomed to mediocrity. Sure, one or two might learn to soar, but most *need* motivation. They *need* a tangible reason to band together."

"A reason to pay your taxes."

"Progress isn't free. In return, they get security, and they get to be their own region rather than the outskirts of some larger region that couldn't care less about them. The taxes pay for a wall, and the guards, the roads in town, and the bridge outside of town.

"Yet you would have me declare peace on the poor, timid, tree-loving elves and take all that away from the good people of the town. Now, you think the fact you have a son in the guard now gives you leverage? Quite the reverse, actually. Corporal Zander and the sergeant know the nature of this conflict and back me one hundred percent. You look shocked... Did you really think my top two commanders wouldn't be in on it? They know which side their bread is buttered on too, so our deal stands. The ghost keep is yours so long as you keep your mouth shut, and if I hear any reports of your kid spreading elf sympathy, we know who's going into the forest sooner rather than later. Got it?"

The baron paused, but Jared didn't seem to have an answer, so the baron asked, "Unless of course you'd like to take me up on my other offer?"

"Never. My oaths are to the crown, and I highly doubt they approve of your charade."

"Think about what you've seen over the last seventeen years that you've been here... How many areas have grown this fast?"

"That growth can't continue. In another ten years you would become a rival to the duke. You know that's not wise."

"Well, Jared, you do have a shred of point there. It would be pretty politically inconvenient to be fielding a bigger force than the duke, wouldn't it? I shall have to think on what to do about that, won't I? A force that size would almost be worthy of your command too, and with you in charge, your reputation and fame would make the game with the elves unnecessary. Don't tell me it's not temping you..."

"Not in the least," Jared growled through clenched teeth.

"Very well then, please show yourself out. I'd hate for this to get to the point where you might say something like what forced you to move out here. I really don't know where you can go that's further from the capital than here, and that would leave us with a rather messy problem. Good evening, Sir Knight."

"Good evening, My Lord," Sir D'Abrac intoned with rigid formality and exited the way he came in.

2.7 Rise and Shine

"RISE WITH THE SUN!" bellowed the sergeant as he entered the barracks. A series of groans and yawns greeted him, and the sunrise streamed in through the door behind him.

"First lesson, recruits! Laziness gets you killed. When I wake you, you must hop out of bed and salute immediately. If you take ten minutes to wake up while an encampment is being overrun, you'll be dead!" Several recruits got the message, stood up, and saluted.

"Those of you who choose not to salute shall be first on the latrine duty list!"

Suddenly all but two were standing and saluting by their bunks. Johnny had tried to stand but fell back on his bunk holding his head as the room seemed to tilt out from under him. He briefly gave a puzzled look around the room as if he wondered how everyone else could remain standing under such conditions. He was hungover.

Derek was still asleep on his back.

Johnny began to try to stand, and the sergeant came over and pushed him back down. "You've already got latrine duty, son. Let's not make it worse by falling and splitting open that skull. Just sit for now." Johnny sat, and saluted weakly, and then held his head and looked at his toes. Several of the recruits snickered.

The sergeant unclipped his canteen from his belt and emptied it onto Derek's head. Nothing happened, and suddenly nobody was giggling. The sergeant peered at Derek's still form for several seconds and began to swear. He wheeled on Johnny and accused him harshly, "You two were drinking last night!"

"Yes, sir," Johnny said, still looking down.

The sergeant puffed up as if to begin a tirade, but then paused. The room was so quiet a mouse would have seemed loud. Finally, sensing something was wrong, Johnny looked up at the sergeant. The hardness went out of the sergeant's expression, and he exhaled and squatted down beside Johnny. "Son, your friend threw up in his sleep last night and choked. He's dead."

Johnny's head whipped around, and he lost his balance. When he regained it, he gazed at Derek's motionless form for half a minute. When the truth hit him, he screamed, "NOOOOOOOO!!!!"

He looked back at the sergeant with pleading eyes. Almost immediately, his balance gave out, and he fell off his bunk, landing on his hands and knees, throwing up all over the sergeant's boots.

Johnny wiped his mouth, mumbled an apology, and then reached over and shook Derek's shoulder. "Wake up. You have to wake up," Johnny repeated this several times, shaking harder and harder.

The sergeant reached down and stopped him on the fourth shake. "That won't help. He's gone."

Johnny stared at the still, unmoving face of his only true friend for several seconds, and then collapsed, weeping uncontrollably.

The sergeant released a long sigh laden with heavy experience and turned to the nearest two recruits. "Help him get to the medic," he ordered them in the weary yet still commanding voice. Then he pointed to a short blond recruit with curly hair. "You were last to salute. Fetch me a rag and then clean this floor up. And also make sure no one touches the body or any of his stuff until his parents arrive."

2.8 Latrine

Johnny stowed the mop and bucket in the corner of the latrine and sighed with a look of weariness on his face. For two weeks, he had found himself on repeated latrine duty. Given the things he had done, he deserved it, but that didn't make it any less smelly and unpleasant.

As Johnny exited the latrine and headed for the barracks, Dillon and Thomas watched from across the yard. "He may be a lordling and lives in the old spook's keep, but I do feel sorry for him. Derek dying like that was really terrible," Thomas said with a sigh.

Dillon smirked. "Yeah, but if he keeps mouthing off to the sergeant, we won't have to worry about him. I heard the sergeant complaining that with Johnny always on latrine duty, he's having trouble figuring out how to punish other recruits who step out of line."

"Maybe," Thomas replied. Dillon was looking away from him and didn't see the distasteful smirk Thomas directed at the back of his head. "He's awfully good with weapons. I hear they can't find any second year to beat him either."

"Lord of the Latrine," Dillon said. "That's what we'll call him." Dillon was smiling wolfishly, clearly pleased with his new epithet.

"Not for long I bet," Thomas said.

"Why not? He's only been getting worse. It's like he thinks he shouldn't have to be a recruit. Stupid lordling thinks he's better than the rest of us."

"He is."

"At swords perhaps, but he has no discipline. He's not a good soldier."

"He had plenty of discipline when he got here. I think he just can't deal with Derek dying. I figure he's about ready to quit. We'll see if he comes back after our first weekend off."

"Now wouldn't that be a shame," Dillon said sarcastically.

"Yes, it would. I'd rather have his sword with me than any other on a scouting mission," Thomas said and walked away toward the mess hall.

Dillon started to reply but then stopped, mouth half-open, and just watched Thomas walk away for a moment. He grunted sourly and followed, glancing back at the barracks.

3 Elf

3.1 Bindery

Johnny stepped inside Percy's Book Shop and squinted into the dim interior. The smell of books resembled the smell of his father's library, though it was somewhat stronger and sharper.

"How can I help you, lad?" a quiet but deep voice inquired. As his eyes adjusted, Johnny found he was being addressed by a short, wide man about fifty years of age.

"I've come to offer myself as your apprentice," Johnny said without hesitation.

"Oh, have you now?" Master Percy said skeptically. "I am overdue for taking one on, but why on earth would I want a flunking recruit from the ranger corps as a book binder's apprentice."

"I'm flunking because I don't want to be there anymore. Everything there reminds me of Derek, his hopes and dreams, our friendship, and the way I imagined things would be."

"Quitting the guard won't bring him back, you know."

"Yes, but every time I'm in a practice session, I get angry. I nearly forgot myself and landed a killing blow on one of the second years with live steel. I worry that if I keep swinging a sword one day I won't remember to stop, so I need a more peaceful occupation, one that doesn't remind me of the pain and loss."

"Hmm, you can read and write?"

"Yes, my mother taught me that in the evenings."

"And you realize that you can't quit being an apprentice the way you can quit being a recruit. Their program is designed to weed out the ones who can't take it. And perhaps you should be weeded out if you can't recover from the loss of a friend. Apprenticeship is different. The reason a master takes on an apprentice is economic. It's a binding agreement, and you are expected to work for one thousand days of satisfactory work before you are released. No other master of any other guild will have you, and I can get the guard to flog you or jail you if you refuse to work. Any day on which you don't put in a full day of work is not counted, though I may grant reductions in your term or count partial days at my discretion, typically as a reward for good work. Also, you should know that one day a week neither of us works, and those days do not count. As such, you will normally be committed to work for me for somewhere between three and four years."

"I understand, and once I have worked my thousand days I become a journeyman and can seek employment with you or abroad."

"Yes, though I must warn you that you will be seeking abroad. While free labor in exchange for room and board is attractive, this small town will not support a living wage for more than one of us."

"That is just fine with me. When can I begin?"

"First you must quit the guard."

"I already did."

"You have a letter of dismissal?"

Johnny dropped his bag and opened the top, withdrawing a somewhat wrinkled roll of parchment.

Master Percy looked it over. "OK. Seems you're serious about this. Come back at noon, and I'll have the magistrate here to witness your induction. You have till then to change your mind or not."

3.2 Why

Once the magistrate finished binding Johnny to Master Percy as an apprentice, he went straight to the pub for lunch and told everyone the news about the new apprentice. From there the rumor spread like wildfire. Despite timing his apprenticeship to coincide with the release of recruits to their first day off, Johnny was chagrined to find that his parents already knew of his decision when he returned to their manor for dinner.

His mother had prepared a veritable feast, probably in an attempt to raise everyone's mood, but the atmosphere at dinner was anything but festive. Johnny sat to his father's right side as usual, but Jared D'Abrac never seemed to have cause to look his way. At one point he announced his decision, and things just got quieter and more awkward. Johnny went up to his room immediately after finishing his plate and asking to be excused.

Up in his room, Johnny went to stand and peer out the window into the darkness. He heard his father's boots on the stairs and sighed but did not turn. He knew what was coming. This was the moment he most dreaded. The sound of the boots stopped at his door and the hinge squeaked just faintly, as the door swung to admit his father. Then nothing. Just silence.

After a long minute, Johnny turned from looking at the fields bathed in moonlight and the forest beyond to find his father leaning one massive shoulder against the door frame, arms crossed in front of his chest, weight on one leg, the other crossed over and toe pointing to the ground. The lantern by the door guttered, and the shadows played across the lines in his face, making him look older and more tired than he'd ever looked before.

"Why?"

Johnny looked down at his boots then up at the ceiling and then gathering his resolve, looked straight at his Dad. "Because I don't want to kill anyone."

Jared sighed, and automatically began his oft repeated cate-chism regarding the nature of combat and the need for good men of steel to stand in opposition of those who might do evil, and the monsters that threaten all mankind.

Johnny cut him off before he got two words out. "Yes, I know that one by heart, Dad, but that's not what I mean." Johnny paused, and Jared waited for him to explain.

"They have been putting me up against the top second years because they are afraid to let the new recruits spar with me. We both know I have the skill to spar safely with anyone, it's not like I can't control my blade. That's not the problem. Whenever I spar, I remember all those good fun times with Derek, and I get upset... angry, really... angry that he's gone. I want someone to blame, I want someone to pay for it, but there's no one... no one except the person in front of me and the sword in my hand."

"Son, this is a difficult time, but you should do breathing exer-cises and clear your mind."

"I have, Dad. It works until I'm swinging the sword, and then it just wells up in me. I marked Therry, one of the second years, two days ago."

"Son, that's not good. You *must* retain control. Losing your composure and wounding a sparing partner can ruin everything, and in a real fight it can leave you vulnerable. I'm sure he'll re-cover and be fine. A little nick on the arm or leg is actually a beneficial thing to experience before your first battle. It was a small mark, wasn't it?"

"I marked his neck."

Jared D'Abrac sucked air through his teeth and was clearly taken aback.

"He'll live. It was low on the muscle, but I almost didn't stop, and I don't want that to happen again. I almost took him away from his family and his pals. I don't want that. It would hurt them as much or more than losing Derek hurt me. I have to stop.

I have to get away from it. In any case, they would have had
to kick me out soon enough anyway. After that, nobody wants to
have anything to do with me. I crossed a line there... I don't think
there's any going back."

Jared D'Abrac squinted slightly, and pursed his lips as he considered his son for a long moment. Then he relaxed and made a
tsk sound. "Well, you might be right about that in the short term,
but much can be mended over time with earnest reform. I wish
you had talked to me about this first, son, but you've made your
decision, and not for bad reasons. I was prepared to buy out your
contract with Master Percy, but maybe I shouldn't do that. Decisions have consequences, and this is possibly a better way to learn
that than at the wrong end of a sword. You'll get no buyout from
me. Don't ask for it in two weeks when you're bored with books.
Once you've become a journeyman, I'll help you with whatever
path you want to pursue from there. Now you have to live with
the decision you made."

"Yes, I do," Johny said quietly, and he turned to resume staring
out the window, thinking.

3.3 Alfyra

With the sun just about to peek over the horizon and the cool
morning air heavy with dew, Johnny quietly opened the kitchen
door that led out toward the fields. Nobody else in the manor
was up yet. Johnny briefly looked back at the note he had left for
his mother on the kitchen table, a note that let her know that he
wanted to have time to think, to relax, and that he would be back
by evening. He adjusted his belt pouches and quietly closed the
door.

Johnny scaled the wall where it had partly crumbled on the
north side of the manor. This allowed him to avoid the rusty gate
at the manor entrance that would squeak loudly and risk waking

his parents. Once atop the wall, he looked back at the manor. All was silent; nobody had noticed his departure.

He looked outward at the field where his father had fought the goblins. For several minutes he just stared at the fields, and a tear crept down his cheek. "I need to get out of here, away from the memories," he mumbled.

After wiping his cheek and adjusting his sword belt, bow, and quiver, he carefully lowered himself over the edge of the wall. Once he was fully extended down the face of the wall, he was only about four feet from the ground. Kicking off from the wall slightly, he released his grip and landed in the grass outside the wall. After a brief teeter, he managed to avoid an ungraceful end to his descent and then quickly looked around. There was nothing but dewdrops and a couple of birds flying over the trees to observe his landing. Johnny visibly relaxed. Now there was no chance he would be seen and called back by his parents. A hundred yards later, he disappeared into the forest, his trail through the dew already evaporating as the sun rose and began to warm the day.

Soon, he found the woodcutter's trail and carefully followed that west for several hours until he came to a split in the trail near mid-morning. This was the furthest point he'd ever reached on this trail, having never started as early. Usually he turned back here, but the day was beautiful, and it wasn't even noon. He patted his pouch containing lunch and a large snack for late afternoon. He was well supplied to remain out until dusk. One side of the trail led south and likely out of the forest and onto the great north road in short order, and the other led deeper into the forest and northwards. He checked his weapons and took a drink from his canteen. He considered both directions, for a long moment.

The sun was warm, the sky was blue, and a few leaves were showing a hint of color indicating that it was near the beginning of fall. The peace and calm of the surrounding woods beckoned.

Johnny headed north in spite of the danger of elves. Along the northern trail, he studiously practiced all the stealth techniques that Corporal Zander had taught him during the weekends before he joined the guard. Several times he came around a bend or over a rise and spied wildlife unaware of his presence. The first was a flock of turkeys. He had heard them scratching and scraping and was able to watch them wandering up the trail toward him. After a minute, his weight shifted just slightly and a branch cracked under his heel. The formerly noisy turkeys went silent in an instant, and slipped off the trail. Johnny made no other sound, but the turkeys had vanished by the time he moved again.

The next interesting find was a small group of deer that had bedded down for the day a few yards off the trail. Johnny quietly stalked along the trail. If he had bothered to take his bow off his shoulder, he could have had an easy dinner of venison. Proving himself against their twitching ears was more important. The deer flies were not fooled by his stealth and discovered him as he approached, but not once did he react to their bites.

After nearly a half an hour, the deer were behind him, unaware of his passage through the area, and his movements became swifter. A few hundred yards later, he shooed the last of the flies and took off his wool shirt, revealing a sweat-soaked undershirt. After a glance around, he left the trail and headed for a grove of needle trees that looked cooler. Corporal Zandar had taught him that this type of needle tree usually grew near water, so a pond or spring was likely to be nearby.

As he entered the grove, he got the inexplicable feeling that he was not alone, and he began to sneak quietly. Near the center of the grove there was a spring, but that was not the thing that caught his eye. Lying on the soft needles under the trees was the most beautiful woman he had ever seen. She had been swimming and inexplicably had not dressed herself before falling asleep in the warmth of a small pool of sunlight. She had lightly and evenly tanned skin probably from time spent outdoors. Loose-flowing, bright-red hair that was somewhere between wavy and curly cascaded down her shoulders and across her bare breasts.

Her face was beautifully formed with fine features and unusually high cheekbones. Her expression was one of infinite peace. Johnny watched motionlessly, entranced by her beauty, but did not approach. Some inner instinct held him back. Something wasn't right. His weight shifted slightly yet again, and the tiniest twig snapped, this time under his big toe. It was a faint sound, nothing any normal person would have noticed.

With fluid grace and blinding speed, she rolled to her feet, picked up the bow, fit an arrow to the string, and drew before Johnny could blink. There were no signs of sleepy lethargy; she was instantly alert. Now that she was standing, her pointed ears shown through her hair. She seemed completely unaware of her nakedness.

Johnny's head swam. He knew she was death. She would surely kill him if anything he had been told about elves was true. The only drawings he had seen of elves had been male warriors, so he had not expected a female elf, but certainly elves had to have women too. What he saw now so closely resembled the drawings he had seen with fine high cheek bones, almond-shaped eyes, thin nose, and pointed ears. There was only one thing she could be... yet something was wrong. Slowly, it dawned on him that she could have killed him several times over already, and yet she had not. She just circled him. As she moved, she made no sound. It wasn't that her footfalls were soft. She actually made no sound at all, at least none that Johnny could detect.

Even so, she seemed to be moving without effort, flowing from one foot to the next with a fluid grace like nothing Johnny had seen. Even Corporal Zander would look clumsy beside her. After she completed her circle, she paused and then laughed. As she did so, her jade-green eyes sparkled with merriment. The sound of her laughter was like the tinkling of bells and the gurgling of a stream combined. She had obviously discerned his folly. His bow was still over his shoulder, and his sword still in its sheath. He was helpless against her bow.

He waited for her to end it, but she just smiled and lowered her bow. She said something in a musical language, and when he didn't respond she paused, obviously thinking. Meanwhile, as his panic subsided, he began to become aware of her nakedness again. She noticed him looking and giggled merrily as if he had just told a wonderful joke. She turned around to give him a better look at all sides. There was nothing for Johnny to do but blush and look away. She seemed to find this even more amusing.

For a while, Johnny just waited. Mostly he was looking away but occasionally stealing glances that betrayed a total confusion of wonder and worry. As the novelty wore thin, and the minutes stretched on, his manner became resigned. Increasingly, he simply watched her, waiting for some inevitably painful or humiliating resolution. She was standing in her personal sunbeam again where she had started, her hair looking like liquid fire.

She motioned at his belt, and when Johnny didn't respond she motioned again, pointing to her hip and then pantomiming throwing something aside. When he didn't respond immediately to her second gesture, a hardness crept into her eyes, and she put both hands on the bow and arrow again. Luckily, Johnny caught on, and with slow, careful movements he slowly unbuckled his belt and let his pouches, dagger, and sword fall to the ground.

Then at her pantomimed suggestion, he carefully lifted his bow from his shoulder. He was very careful to only grasp the bow by the tip, a position from which he could never hope to draw it quickly. Once it was free, he discarded the bow and his quiver of arrows too. Through all this it remained clear that to do otherwise would have been instant death from the beautiful elf maiden's bow. At her insistence, he moved away from his weapons and pouches, toward the water until she was between him and his equipment. Not sure what else to do, Johnny simply complied.

Suddenly, his stomach growled. He blushed furiously. She giggled again, smiled, danced over to where she had been sun-bathing, and took something out of a tooled leather pouch that had been almost perfectly camouflaged lying on the tree needles. It was about the size of a large cookie. She broke it in half, and handed him half, and nibbled on the other half.

As she handed it to him, her hand brushed his. He realized that he had just done what no other man in his town had ever done; he had touched a live elf. The question now was if he would live to tell anyone about it. He nibbled the piece she had given him. As he tasted it, surprise crept across his face. The cookie was good. It tasted like several types of fruit mixed with spices that would have cost a fortune. Soon he realized it was extremely filling. He suspected it was also probably very nutritious. He couldn't imagine tiring of the taste, and it was small, compact, and lightweight.

As he marveled at it, she watched him. When he looked up, she just smiled. Then she uttered two syllables. Clumsily, he tried to repeat what she said and pointed to the food. She smiled and nodded. Nodding seemed to have the same meaning at least. As he finished it, he decided that she must not want to kill him. How-ever, he noted that she did keep the bow within reach at all times as if concerned about his motives. A light breeze stirred, blowing at the back of his neck. She was downwind, and her nose wrin-kled in a way that was very cute, and she looked thoughtful for a moment then rose from where she had seated herself in front of the spot where he was still standing. She beckoned for him to follow and turned and began to walk.

He realized that this could be his chance to get away. Some-thing in him couldn't leave though. Society had lied to him, told him that elves were evil and ferocious, not beautiful and friendly.

He began to wonder if there were other lies. This might be his only chance to find out more about elves. Besides, she was beautiful, and a part of him just wanted to watch her graceful movements endlessly. He had always been curious to a fault, and so he followed. He began to hesitate as he realized where she was going.

She was heading for the spring. Momentarily he wondered if she just wanted a drink. That was quickly answered when she got to the edge of the water. She set the bow down and dove in. She came up in the center of the spring and laughed merrily while beckoning to him.

He shook his head and indicated his clothing. She just looked puzzled and beckoned. He suddenly got the impression that if he didn't follow suit she would probably get out and might decide he was still hostile. He had two options. Either join her or pick up the bow and become the first recruit in history to take an elf alone. He would be a legend in his town, and his father would be immensely proud. Then he realized what he was thinking. She had spared his life a million times already, and she had fed him. He could not respond to such kind and friendly gestures with violence. He might be able to pick up the bow, but in his heart he knew he could never fire it. So he joined her.

After he disrobed, he followed her example and dove in. He screamed as he came up. The water was ice-cold! She laughed merrily and swam a circle around him. He treaded water for a while, unsure what to do. Suddenly she dove. For a second he thought she might swim to the edge and leave him. As he watched through the crystal clear water, she headed to the bottom, which had blotches of blue near the center. She reached the center and then came up. She surfaced very close to him and handed him a fist-sized rock. It was blue with silver streaks in it. When he realized what it was, he nearly forgot to tread water. The chunk of turquoise she had handed him was worth a fortune. Then she headed for shore, beckoning for him to follow.

He followed her to shore still griping the turquoise and glad to get out of the cold water. She appeared to be cold too. She dried herself off with a small piece of cloth and dressed herself in a strange sort of mottled and patched leathers. He followed suit after she handed him the cloth. After he finished dressing, he realized that she had been watching him, but she showed no sign of it now.

As soon as he finished, she said something in Elvish and beckoned him to come over to her. As he approached, she began drawing pictures in the sand. The pictures were of trees and a stick figure walking among them. He had no idea what she meant, so she took her hand, gestured at the surrounding woods, and made a walking motion across her hand with her fingers and pointed at him.

After a moment he said, "Why am I walking in the woods?"

She stared blankly at him, not understanding his words. Hoping he had interpreted correctly, he shrugged and motioned with his hand at the trees around him and smiled. She cocked her head in wonder as if the idea of a human enjoying the woods had never occurred to her. Then her face lit up with joy, and she smiled warmly at him. Next he pointed toward her and then vaguely out to the woods and put fingers at the top of his ears to mimic pointy elf ears. Then he made a mock bow and arrow motion and then as if he had been shot, followed by a puzzled shrug. This was his way of asking why elves hunted humans. Johnny fidgeted as she puzzled out his meaning, hoping he had not gone too far, but he had been unable to stop himself. Nothing about the war with the elves made sense anymore.

Suddenly, his meaning dawned on her and her eyes went wide, shocked. Vehemently she shook her head no, and through a series of pantomimes indicated that humans attacked them, not them attacking humans. They looked at each other, puzzled and worried that maybe communication was not successful, but then something dawned on her. She held up a hand indicating he should wait. She patted one tree fondly then another and another until lovingly caressing and hugging a fourth, which happened to be the largest in the grove. Then accusingly she pointed at him and followed with an axe chopping motion as if felling the tree and scowled at him.

"Oh, we're cutting down special trees!" Johnny immediately pointed at himself and shook his head clarifying that he never did that, which was true enough if one didn't count branches for firewood. She nodded solemnly and then pointed at him and then out vaguely to the south in a circular motion. He didn't, but some humans did. Johnny nodded sadly.

After a long, slightly awkward pause, Johnny pointed to himself and said "John." She smiled, bowed her head slightly, then pointed to herself and said "Alfyra." He imitated her nod and smiled too. She motioned to the forest around them and seated herself at the base of a tree. Not knowing what else to do, he copied her and chose the nearest tree to her. For a while, they relaxed and merely listened to the woodland sounds observing the squirrels, the birds, and the insects going about their daily business. It was a precious, shared peacefulness bordering on meditation, and it thoroughly relaxed them both more than any pantomimed conversation could.

Eventually, Johnny sighed, breaking the silence and pointing at the sun, which was now well past noon. She nodded, understanding immediately, and quickly moved to a patch of exposed sandy soil near the spring. She drew a sun in the sand pointing to the sun above, and then a moon and another sun. Then she motioned toward the surrounding glade. Johnny shook his head and added six more moons and suns. She seemed disappointed but eventually nodded. They each gathered their things. He donned his sword, quiver, and bow without worry.

She spoke an Elvish word followed by his name and nodded again. He smiled , waved, and said, "Bye, Alfyra." With a brief hesitation, she copied his wave and smiled. He turned, began to walk, then looked back, but she was already gone. She disappeared even faster and more quietly than the turkeys.

After retracing his steps from the morning for a while, he smiled and spoke to the woods and empty air, unable to contain himself, "I went skinny-dipping with an elven maid prettier than any woman in town. I even have a date with her in a week. The guard would execute me for treason for either of those. I am truly a fool." He smiled for a moment and then said, "Wait till I tell..."

Suddenly his smile disappeared. His brow furrowed, and he sighed. There was no one he could share this with.

Derek was gone.

3.4 Stones

The dry, dusty back room of Master Percy's shop was a place of stillness, except for the occasional pop and billow of a small oil-paper window reacting to the wind outside. There was a yellowness to the light at all times due to the paper window, but with the afternoon sun low in the sky and shining directly on the window, the room was bathed in a distinctly golden glow. A few dust particles near the window danced in the light above Johnny's head as he studiously and efficiently copied a decaying manual on swordfighting technique.

The manual was one of many from the guard Academy archives that had recently been commissioned for rebinding where possible and recopying when necessary. This one had been chewed by rodents and thus had to be recopied. Since few recruits could read, the manual consisted mostly of drawings and diagrams, but since this was the twentieth copy of this particular volume that needed to be made, and his father had made him read this manual since he was twelve, Johnny already knew the missing text and diagrams by heart.

The stairs to the upper apartments creaked as Master Percy eased his bulk down from above, and Johnny's quill scratched slightly faster. Master Percy looked at the stack of old tomes and new tomes, quickly judging the day's progress, and smiled. With a sigh he said, "John, you're an embarrassingly quick study and a good worker too."

"Thanks," Johnny said, his quill never stopping.

"Your mother taught you well, and I'm very likely going to have great difficulty keeping you busy. Honestly, your apprenticeship is a fantastic boon, and my mother, rest her soul, always told me that when life sends you roses, you should share one with those around you."

"That's a beautiful sentiment," Johnny said absently as he turned the last page in the volume and continued writing.

"I'm converting your thousand work day apprenticeship to one thousand calendar days, and you still get every seventh day off so long as you continue to work hard."

Johnny stopped writing, set down the quill carefully, and turned around, smiling. "Thank you very much, Master Percy. That is most kind."

"You're welcome. It's a pleasure so far, and my sense is that this is going to be a very pleasant and profitable relationship. By the way, don't work past this point in the day when the light gets low. It's not good for the eyes. I made that mistake when I was young," he said, shifting his glasses on his nose.

Looking around, Johnny nodded. "Yes, of course. You're right. I get lost in my work, and the whole world disappears. It's soothing, but I should be careful." After a pause, Johnny continued, "Can I ask you a question?"

"Of course, what's on your mind?" Master Percy said, some concern creeping into his voice.

"I noticed a stones board and bowls on the shelf over there, but it has lots of dust on it. Do you play stones?"

Master Percy beamed a smile and said, "Yes, though not for several years now. Do you?"

"Yes, my mother taught me the basics. I can beat everyone I've played, except I've never been able to beat her."

"My, my, boy, you do have the most remarkable mother. Come, let's see how good you are." Master Percy lifted the wooden board and bowls full of black and white stones from the shelf and shifted several scrolls aside to set them on the table in the middle of the room.

Johnny respectfully took a seat with his back to the door, leaving the interior seat for his master.

"Very good, she taught you etiquette too. How many games would you say you've played?"

"I don't know, maybe a couple hundred?"

Master Percy's eyebrows shot up, and he stroked his chin and said, "Hmm, well then who knows what level you might be at. It sounds like your mother possibly knows what she's about, so let's play an even game with no compensation. You can take black. We'll see where that takes us."

They opened the lids on the bowls revealing black playing pieces in one and white pieces in the other. The black pieces were made from dark slate, and the white pieces from a fine white marble. Both types were a bit larger than a man's thumbnail and circular with a rounded top and bottom. Since he had the black pieces, Johnny played first. He placed his stone on an intersection near one corner of the nineteen by nineteen grid that was engraved onto the board.

The first dozen moves proceeded normally, each of them placing stones alternately on intersections with Master Percy humming and nodding approvingly. After Johnny's seventh move, the thirteenth of the game, Master Percy paused a moment and then played directly into a corner already containing one of Johnny's black stones. Johnny responded with the usual sequence immediately, and Master Percy paused to assess again and then proceeded. As the game drew to a close, Master Percy nodded in approval.

"Good game," he said. "You took care of your groups nicely but let me push you around a bit. Nonetheless, an entertaining game. I think we can play a three stone handicap next time."

"Yes, I think you are clearly stronger. Three stones should be interesting," Johnny replied.

3.5 Innkeeper

The innkeeper waddled down the narrow stairs, having assisted the final and most inebriated guest to his room. He was returning to the common room that he had just cleared to begin his cleaning. As he turned the corner, he let out a gasp, clutched his chest, and swallowed. Then he sighed as he recognized the intruder. "I sure wish you could knock or something," he said.

"That would require I stand outside where people can see me," replied the bald-headed intruder. His easy smile, comically long nose, big ears and pointed goatee made him seem harmless at first glance. It was strangely difficult to notice his brown robes or the snake-headed staff he carried.

"I know, but I can still wish, can't I?"

"If wishes were horses the beggars would ride. Any news? I'm in a hurry."

"You're always in a hurry," the innkeeper said with a sigh.

"Occupational hazard."

"I suppose it is. This time I do have news, so you'll be needing to tarry a bit tonight."

The bald man motioned to a booth in the far corner and said, "In which case I'll have a glass of the good stuff you keep in your office while you tell me the news."

"Eh? How... how do you know?"

"Do you really want to know?"

"I suppose I don't, do I?" For a very brief instant, a very dark grimace shown on his face, but almost instantly his expression was placid again, and with a sigh he disappeared into his office and returned with a glass of whiskey.

"Well?" the bald man said, gesturing with the as-yet-untasted whiskey.

The innkeeper paused, distracted by the sight of the whiskey in the man's glass approaching the edge and nearly slopping onto the table. Then the innkeeper said, "Sorry. What?"

"This stuff really that good? Hmm." The bald man sipped the whiskey, and his eyebrows shot up in surprise. "Wow, not bad at all. What's an inn keep doing with a bottle of stuff like this? It's probably worth as much as your entire ale stock. I'll give you some money, and you can have some brought in for me."

"My cousin who lives down south outside the capitol gave it to me as a gift just after my uncle died. He inherited my uncle's distillery where it was made. My uncle had become quite rich, even got an honorary title and a family name after the king tasted it too. Left it all to his son, who's more or less squandered the business and most of the fortune in a fruitless bid to win the affection of a baronet's daughter. This stuff is from my uncle's days. Nothing like it is made today. My cousin grew up a rich kid and had no appreciation for whiskey or for how to run a business. Unfortunately, rich uncles only leave you money when their sons aren't alive, so here I am, an innkeeper who owns, or rather used to own, an unopened fifty-year-old bottle of D'Atelier single malt whiskey."

"An aged bottle of D'Atelier. It seems I've abused my position more than I intended then. I'll compensate you for this one, as it was probably part of your retirement plan, and you've always been helpful. But first the news you mentioned?"

The innkeeper squinted and then said, "You didn't know I had it... You guessed!"

"Every innkeeper has something special tucked away. It's hardly a guess. The fun is in discovering what it is they have that they don't share with others. As I said, however, I'll compensate you. In fact, I'll pay you a fair price for the bottle as if it were unopened. I've been to Pendalir City and collected some whiskey over time myself. I was outbid on another bottle of D'Atelier once." He paused and sipped the whiskey. "Amazing stuff. Too bad most folks only trade it rather than actually drink it," he said, sipping the whiskey again. "Whiskey really was made to be consumed after all."

With that, the innkeeper relaxed some and seemed mollified.

"The news?"

"Right, sorry. So you told me to keep an ear out for any young lads or gals with strange dreams or who saw strange happenings, right?"

The bald man began to smile as if he knew and liked what he was about to hear next.

"I'd almost forgotten about that until a week ago. Two young recruits were drinking at the bar, nothing remarkable about that. The smaller one started telling his friend about nightmares he'd been having. People talk about bad dreams sometimes when they're drunk, probably happens once or twice a month, but this one seemed different. The lad was apparently describing a dream he'd had a long time ago, not a recent one. That's unusual, since few people remember dreams for very long. He described legions of skeletons and zombies. Shocked me so much I dropped a glass.

"He was so far into his ale at that point that my distraction didn't faze him at all though. He just went right on talking about it. His description was the second thing that seemed odd. They weren't chasing him or fighting. They were in storage or something. And as I listened I realized another thing was odd. I had assumed it was a bad dream, but he didn't sound like it scared him during the dream, but rather he was worried by the fact that he had such a dream. I don't think his friend took him seriously. They were both pretty sauced."

The bald man sat silently staring into the distance, and then asked, "Skeletons and zombies? Did he describe anything else? Did anyone else overhear this?"

"Yeah, ghostly warriors, disembodied hands, floating eyes kept in glass boxes too. Creepy stuff, things beyond what you hear about in children's stories. Thought that was odd too. The place was pretty full and as loud as usual. It was only by chance I overheard him while cleaning glasses. I doubt anyone else did."

The bald man smiled. "Good work. This is just exactly the sort of thing I wanted you to listen for. That's certainly an unusual dream. Who is he?"

"This is the part you're going to really like. It's Sir D'Abrac's kid, Johnny."

"Ah, that does make it interesting. You've done well. Today you've earned yourself three silvers."

The innkeeper started, smiled, and then looked worried. "What does it mean? Why is this so valuable to you?"

"It may or may not be valuable. I'm merely paying you for a job well done. Don't worry about the boy. It's unlikely I will have any reason to harm him. As I've said before, I believe in the power of both politics and dreams. I've paid similarly for dozens of such stories from various other folk, and mostly they turn out to be nothing. Being in the know and not being caught by surprise is what my game is all about. Knowledge is where the real power is. This story is definitely different from your average bad dream, and sometimes dreams portend events to come, so you've done your job well."

"No offense, but I hope this one's a dud. Legions of skeleton's can't be good for any of us."

"Good things happen, and bad things happen. I can't change the future. I just try to make sure that whichever one happens, I'm ahead of the game and either making a profit or avoiding a loss. Anything else I should know?"

"Yeah, two things. First, the kid he was drinking with, Derek, died in his sleep. Threw up in bed and inhaled his vomit that very night. Such a sad thing too. He was one of the good kids in town. Sure wish I'd cut them off sooner, but no way to know that such a thing would happen. He was the son of Sir D'Abrac's stableman." The innkeeper stared sadly out the window for while. "Poor kid... Johnny's quit the guard, I hear tell. Was his only ambition two weeks ago. He and Derek trained with his pa for years before they were eligible. They would have had bright futures, probably would have been placed with the second years immediately to keep the other first years from getting hurt..." He paused again and then continued, "Second, I think I know how long ago the kid had the dream."

"How's that?"

"Around a decade ago, shortly after I rebuilt her..." the innkeeper gestured outward at the rest of the inn. "...there was a tragic accident at the D'Abrac's. One of the coachmen for the D'Arnors overturned a carriage and got his head squished. He was rushing because he was late arriving to pick up Christina D'Arnor and her daughter Caroline at D'Abrac manor. According to Ryan, my hostler, the boy tried to console the coachman's son by telling him that his dad's spirit might become one of the 'powerful ghost warriors.' The D'Abracs smoothed things over, but people whispered about it for a week or more afterward."

"Ah, so this is old news. Still good to know the timing too however. An extra silver for your long memory. Anything else?"

"Nope, otherwise quiet."

"Good, here's your compensation for the bottle. That bottle is probably worth more than you realized. My losing bid on the last bottle I saw was ten platinum. The winning bid was twelve."

The innkeeper's jaw dropped as the bald man laid out a dozen platinum pieces on the table. That was enough to buy several inns. Enough to retire immediately. Then he squinted and looked up. "I can't use those you know."

"Yes, if an innkeeper were to present one of those, it would arouse great suspicion, wouldn't it? But you weren't going to sell the bottle anytime soon either, were you?"

"Well no, but..."

"So you can put these coins in a box and put it on the shelf where the bottle was. When you retire, I'll change them to gold for you."

"My retirement on your schedule only?"

"I wouldn't want to lose such a valuable helper so soon, though I can't really hold you hostage either. I suspect if you traveled down to Pendalir City with those, you would be able to find a way to exchange them there. If I gave you over 100 gold here and now, and you started spending it, people would begin to worry about where an innkeeper got such wealth. Keeping you safe from temptation is in both of our interests. Besides, I suspect you would have sold the bottle for less than a third of that."

"True... Ok. So life goes on, I suppose."

"For now, it does with a hard cash pension ensuring your retirement instead of a bottle that could get broken."

"Also true. I suppose I can wait on my retirement a little longer, but I'm sure you'll understand that I won't necessarily want to remain here until I am too old to enjoy my retirement."

"Perfectly understandable. I'd expect you to stay another five or ten years at most. Then perhaps you can retire to Pendalir City and keep an ear out there for me instead. The bottle?"

"Right, of course!"

3.6 Friends

The fire and gold hints of autumn were just beginning to touch the upper leaves of the forest. The late-morning sun filtered down through the loose canopy of whirly seed, slate bark and cap nut trees. The sounds of squirrels harvesting cap nuts and the monotonous calling of a few remaining buzz-bugs up in the trees proclaimed the growing warmth of the day as a last vestigial breath of summer lingering in defiance of the inexorable approach of winter.

Across the forest floor and through the bushes, a deer trail meandered up the hill and out of sight. The trail wasn't well-marked. It was more of a barely perceptible crease in the undergrowth distinguished only by the occasional broken twig and disturbed leaf litter. It paralleled a wider dirt path at a distance of approximately fifty paces, but in contrast to the wide-open and well-lit path the deer trail was secluded and known only to deer and elves both of whom preferred its seclusion over the ease of travel found on the path.

Only a brief flicker of movement betrayed the arrival of the elf who was traveling along the deer trail today, and the fact that the movement was noticeable at all indicated that she believed nobody was around. Even so, she stood at the top of the hill completely motionless, just observing the trail as it descended the hill into the back side of a grove of needle trees. After several minutes of complete stillness, she began to descend the hill toward the grove. Her movements were smooth and fluid and absolutely quiet. Even moving as she was at a relaxed walk, her gait produced none of the up and down motion that instantly betrays the approach of the less graceful races. Her effortless gliding gait took her down the hill in a deceptively steady fashion. Watching her, one would never think she was moving quickly, but if one looked away and then looked back, the distance she covered would have been startling.

She paused just once on her way down the hill at an opening in the canopy near the side of a slanted outcropping of rock that jutted out from the hill. The shallow soil on top of the outcropping was insufficient for trees to grow and thus provided a small sunlit patch occupied only by tall grasses and a few wild flowers. As she paused, she plucked one of the longer seed stems from the grass and briefly chewed the bottom end for the pleasure of its slightly sweet pulp. After the end had been sucked dry of its minuscule treat, she brushed the finely bristled seed-tip across her cheek, closing her almond-shaped eyes as she enjoyed its tickling sensation. After her moment of indulgence ended, she awarded the stalk of grass a place of honor, threading it through her loose red-gold curls just above the point of her ear.

As she approached the needle tree grove, she slowed to a stop and cocked her head slightly, listening. She frowned and pursed her lips. After several minutes, she began to move into the grove dropping low into a crouch and stalking toward a large fallen tree just inside the grove. Upon entering the grove, she allowed herself a faint smile as she spotted Johnny. He was killing time aimlessly. He picked up a twig, broke it into small pieces, and tossed them away, then picked up several small needle tree cones and casually tossed them at random targets.

With a shake of her head and a look of mingled disgust and irritation, Alfyra soundlessly unlimbered her bow from across her shoulders, and knocked an arrow. Slow as a growing mushroom, she rose from behind the log, drawing her bow. Facing almost toward her but completely unaware, Johnny stretched and put his hands behind the back of his head and sighed.

ZZZZiiippttt! THONK!

Alfyra's arrow passed six inches below Johnny's left arm, and embedded itself in the trunk of a tree a few feet past him, quivering. Johnny jumped in surprise, froze for a split second, and then dived to his right side, rolling and coming up to a crouch. This would have been impressive except that he then fumbled for several seconds to draw his sword. Alfyra giggled loudly enough to be heard and hopped lightly over the log with a big grin on her face.

Johnny finally drew his sword and rose up off of one knee into a ready stance, sword in front of him and fear naked on his face.

Still fifty feet away, Alfyra smirked, and then her arms and bow moved so fast they seemed naught but a blur.

ZZZZiiippttt! THONK!

Her second arrow flew left of him by a large margin and split down the center of the shaft of the first arrow.

Johnny's eyes went wide, and the tip of his sword began to betray a nervous shake.

She laughed lightly and again, almost too fast for the eye to follow, drew an arrow, knocked it, and fired.

ZZZZiiippttt! THONK!

Her third shaft split the second and quivered in the same tree. She smiled and shrugged nonchalantly.

Johnny exhaled. A look of comprehension spread across his face. If she had wanted to shoot him, he would already be dead. Perhaps this was a normal thing for elves. He sheathed his sword, hand still shaking. She smiled and motioned for him to discard his weapons as he had done on their first encounter. Johnny hesitated and then complied, tossing his sword, his dagger, his quiver, and his bow over by the tree that sill had her arrow sticking out of it. She shouldered her bow and walked toward the sandy area they had previously used for drawing, beckoning him to come over.

By the time he got there, she had drawn a group of stick figures and was drawing a second group apart from it with the tip of her bow. She finished and spoke a few words in Elvish, pointing from one group then to him. Then she pointed at the other group and to herself, speaking a similar but slightly different Elvish phrase. When Johnny looked puzzled she paused for a while and then spoke awkwardly in the human language known as common tongue. Her speech was slow, halting, and unsure, as if remember a long forgotten lesson.

"You persons," she said, pointing from one group to him and then pointed at herself and then the other group of stick figures and said, "Persons," evidently not remembering the word "my."

Johnny nodded, and she continued by drawing violent X's between them, and Johnny nodded. Certainly their peoples were in conflict. With raised eyebrows and a look of disbelief pointed at him, she then pantomimed his antics with the needle tree cone throwing making a *paf* sound to simulate the sound of them landing and then *pop, pop* as she pantomimed him breaking twigs. Finally, she pointed at the two groups and then out into the forest all around them, ending with an expression that could only be interpreted as, "Are you an idiot?"

"Ah." Johnny said quietly as he recognized that she was scolding him for his carelessness. He nodded in agreement. "I understand. You're right. I should be more careful. It would be bad if we were discovered." She squinted and nodded, seeming satisfied that he'd understood but clearly not understanding all his words.

Johnny changed the topic by mimicking her elven words for "my people," and she corrected him several times until he improved. She smiled, and then they practiced the human common tongue equivalent until she got it reasonably correct. From there they taught each other a few basic words and phrases. Every few words she would pause to listen and then continue. Pausing to listen seemed to be second nature for her, but by the end of the day he had begun to feel the rhythm of it and knew when she was about to pause and that he should also listen for unwanted attention and not interrupt.

They ended by agreeing on a code. There was a rock near the center of the clearing that was pointed on one end and sat on a larger rock. They agreed to meet every week and that if the rock was pointing east she was hiding nearby waiting for him, and south if he was hiding nearby waiting for her. If the rock was pointing west, neither had arrived yet. If they had to leave before the other arrived, or if there was danger, they would point the rock north. If they saw the rock pointing north, they should be cautious, and if it was safe to do so point it west and try again next time. This way they didn't have to call out to each other or enter all the way into the clearing exposing themselves. The second person to arrive would make a bird call to announce their arrival. This was primarily arranged by Alfyra, and it took quite a while and lots of hand gestures. Once Johnny understood, he entirely approved of the precautions.

The fall was uncommonly warm and dry, and for over two months the weather cooperated, allowing them to meet every seventh day. Johnny learned to speak basic Elvish, and they refreshed Alfyra's prior lessons in the common speech favored by humans. Common was the only language humans spoke in the recently settled frontier areas like Arnoria. In the south, there were regional dialects, but the common speech was used by traders and merchants everywhere, so it prevailed in cities and larger towns or anywhere recently settled.

Language lessons remained a constant topic for them but not their only activity together. They often simply enjoyed the peace and harmony of the forest either by walking trails to the north away from town or quietly sitting back to back in a sort of listening forest meditation. Johnny discovered that she played stones and was much better than him at it. They rarely discussed their lives outside because bookbinding offered next to no excitement, and Alfyra's carefree life encountered no major difficulties. Her primary passion was discovering and mentally cataloging the individual living creatures and plants for as wide a diameter from the elven home as possible. She was able to recognize over one hundred individual deer, and countless trees flowers, squirrels, and many other living creatures Johnny hadn't even known existed.

Her companionship was a salve of tranquility. Slowly, the pain of Derek's death receded from Johnny's mind, not gone but no longer raw and uncontrollable.

3.7 Winter

A chill breeze stirred the boughs of the needle trees and brought occasional leaves tumbling in on the wind from the edges of the needle tree grove where the deciduous trees were now mostly barren. It had been eight weeks since their first meeting. Despite the bitter chill and the milky sky signaling the approach of a snowstorm, Johnny and Alfyra sat quietly staring at a game board full of black and white stones. Alfyra rubbed her cold nose and smiled patiently. Johnny on the other hand was hunched over the board reading out sequences, trying to find a move that would save his failing position.

They were so still and quiet that a squirrel trotted over with a cap nut in its mouth and buried it just three feet away. Alfyra watched it quietly as it busily patted down the tree needles. The ground was frozen, so the lump in the needles was still obvious, but the squirrel only knew that it was supposed to cover the cap nut as best it could and didn't seem to notice the poor job it had done. Johnny let out a big sigh and said, "I resign." The startled squirrel scampered back to the edge of the grove where it paused before climbing a cap nut tree nearby.

"Good game," Alfyra replied formally, and then in Elvish she asked, "Did you see the cutting move?"

"Yes," Johnny replied in Elvish as well. But then in the common tongue he elaborated, "I saw the cut, but I thought I could live anyway." Then in Elvish he continued, "This move surprised me, but at least I killed your corner before that."

"The large area on the right was more important than the corner," she said in the common tongue. "But you fought well," she added in Elvish. They had taken to alternating languages to ensure that they each got practice and learned the other's tongue fluently. They went over several other aspects of the game, Alfyra, the stronger player, pointing out places for improvement in Johnny's play.

A single flake of snow drifted down and landed on one of the black stones. It was the first snowflake of the season, and the bitingly cold wind from the north clearly indicated that soon there would be a significant snowstorm. Alfyra sighed and pointed at the flake, which was quickly melting onto the stone. "You know what this flake means?"

"It means I need to start heading back."

"Sadly, it means more than that. When there's snow on the ground, even I can't hide my tracks."

"What will we do?" Johnny blurted out. These visits had been his primary relief from the tedium of book binding, which he had nearly mastered, having already known how to read and write perfectly.

"We must wait for the snow to melt before returning. If you return, be sure it's after a melt, and mind the signal stone. I know that you only can come on a seventh day, so once weather improves I will be here on that day."

"And so will I," Johnny replied.

They looked across the board at each other for a while.

"I'm going to miss seeing you until then," Alfyra said softly.

"Yeah, me too. I wish winter wasn't so long..."

"Nonsense, it's only a few moons. That's no time at all... well, for an elf at least. I suppose it's harder as a human, but there really is no other choice."

"No, you're right of course. The last thing we want is bold, clear tracks in the snow leading here."

They started another game in defiance of the approaching weather and played a little longer, but their hearts weren't in it. When Alfyra was studying the board and didn't seem to be paying attention, Johnny was staring at her, as if save up the sight of her for the winter. Johnny resigned the game fairly early.

Wordlessly, they cleared the board and hid it in the tree hollow, carefully obscuring their tracks. Then when it was time to part, they stood there for a second, and then Alfyra took his hand and pulled. He bent, and she quickly and lightly kissed him on the cheek and then hugged him. "Don't worry. It really won't be that long, and I'll be here as soon as the snow is off the forest floor."

"I know. Let's hope for an early and warm spring," he said, hugging her back.

They parted smiling and waving. Johnny was halfway home when the snow began to accumulate on the ground.

4 Thief

4.1 Caroline

Master Percy startled at the sound of the bell above the door and looked up from the stones board as the baron's daughter Caroline entered.

"Not a bad time, I hope?" she asked.

Master Percy smiled his "for customers" smile and said, "No, not a bad time at all. Quite good timing, I'd say." He glanced at the board with a frown.

"Johnny misbehaving?" she said, smiling.

"Oh no, he's doing quite well. He's a quick study in every way."

"Not playing even handicap with the legendary Master Percy, is he?" she teased.

Master Percy smirked. "No, not anymore."

"Really?" Caroline looked truly shocked. "Perhaps we should have him play my father? He was lamenting the lack of players in the town just last night."

"No... definitely not. I don't think his Lordship would take well to lessons from an apprentice book binder. Six months ago I was giving a three-stone handicap to John, but that disaster..." Master Percy gestured to the board. "...was him giving me four stones. In another few months I fear no handicap of any sort will be able save me."

"Wow," she said, looking at Johnny speculatively, her smile slightly crooked as if a new thought were forming. Johnny shifted nervously until she looked back to Master Percy. Briskly she said, "Well then, enough about games. I've got a load of books for rebinding. We had a leak above the library again. We just fixed that section, but somehow it leaked. And of course it leaked on the baron's favorite books. Barry told him we need to bring a real crew up from Pendalir City to put a proper roof on it, but father insists on employing locals. If you ask me, no thatching will ever be reliable for more than a year..."

"Ah, well I'm sure your father has very good reasons for ignoring the advice of his seneschal. How bad was the leak this time?"

"Not too bad. Pretty much just onto one shelf containing books the baron uses regularly and some recent ledgers. We put the shelves under the newer roof specifically to avoid leaks of course. I think we should make the thatcher pay your fee. He said some sort of animal tried to make a nest or something up there, but that sounds like a lame excuse for lazy work to me. Most of the books I brought should just need a new binding due to splashing from the drip. A couple ledgers need a full recopy though, I'm sorry to say. I know those are the worst tedium possible, but there's no help for it."

"Usual ledger fee applies of course."

Caroline nodded absently as if she didn't care about the cost. "Oh, and the two books on elves are not readily replaceable. Barry wants restoration only if possible. Talk to him first if you think they need more. Father treasures those two dearly. He won't even let me read them, and he *will* notice if anything happens to them."

"Understood, let me look before you leave. I'm surprised Barry didn't come himself in that case."

"I was bored. Been snowed into in the keep for months now. There's so little to do in the winter. I had to get out... and I had to finally see if the boy who wanted to slay dragons and save princesses really had become a book binder," she said slightly louder than necessary.

"Stories are for children," Johnny said darkly and donned his cloak, leaving to fetch the books from the wagon.

"Sensitive, isn't he?" she said petulantly, staring at the closed door after he left.

"He never talks about it," Master Percy said solemnly.

"It was very sad," she sighed. "When I was young, I used to play with them. Derek was always kind. It was fun. Too bad that stupid coachman had to mess everything up. We only visited a few times after that. Mother hates wagons," she said bitterly, still looking at the door where Johnny exited, facing away from Master Percy, whose cheek twitched, and his eyes grew hard at her callous mention of the tragedy, but he said nothing, and his face was calm by the time she turned back to him.

As Johnny stepped out of the shop, it was a raw late-winter afternoon. There was still snow on the roof of the shop, but it was melting and dripping, not even forming icicles. The wind had shifted to the southwest. The big melt would come soon. Johnny stared for a moment off to the north in the direction of the glade where he and Alfyra had met weekly until the snow made it impossible for them to hide their tracks. After a sigh, he began unloading the wagon.

As he carefully wiped the muddy slush from his boots and set down the third and final load, Master Percy was examining a volume with a tooled-leather cover and gold leaf designs on the binding. "I can see why you don't want these volumes rebound. This one isn't too bad, but it looks like we will need to press and dry some pages on the other one. Just some mold prevention on this one, I think. How soon do you need these back?"

"Within the month should be fine," Caroline said, moving to stand in the open doorway, preventing it from being closed against the cold.

"Should be doable for all but the ledgers," Master Percy said, studiously ignoring the cold air flooding into his shop.

"Yeah, take your time on those. We only need them if the king's tax assessor comes in with a burr under his saddle."

"Very good. Would you like to share some warm tea before you go?"

"Tempting, but I'm looking for fresh air. Tea we have plenty of in the keep."

"Good day then, Miss Caroline."

"Yes, good day to you too, Master Percy," she said formally and then climbed up to her wagon seat. With a smile for Master Percy and a wink directed Johnny's way, she got the wagon moving with a few clucks and a snap of the reins. Soon she was under way, empty wagon rattling as she turned around in the square and long hair fluttering in the wind.

Shutting the door, Master Percy looked at the stones board. "Well, we both know you won this game. You know... it looked like Caroline was impressed by your stones skills."

"She's pretty, but she's turning into her mother. Not interested."

Master Percy smiled. "You're a perceptive young man. Best to get straight to work on the baron's books. Leave the one on elven history to me. The one on Elvish language you should treat with anti-mold powder immediately however. Make sure you get every page well treated."

"As you say," Johnny said, doing his best to hide the thrill running through his body at the thought of reading a text on Elvish language.

"Not sure why you're so excited, but have extra care with these two. Books like this are worth more than this shop to someone like the baron. Mess them up, and he's sure to seek a new book binder from the capital to replace us."

"Understood," Johnny said sincerely.

4.2 Imp

The creaking sound of the front door to the shop startled Johnny. He quickly and carefully closed the Elvish language book he was reading and placed it on top of its gold leaf and leather-bound twin in the box, ready for return to the baron. He had finished the baron's books way ahead of schedule and had taken to reading and rereading the volumes on elves whenever Master Percy was out and his work was finished. He quickly stood and went to greet Master Percy, putting some physical distance between himself and what he had been doing. Reading the book wasn't necessarily forbidden, but it also hadn't been explicitly permitted either.

"Still here?" Master Percy queried as Johnny opened the door from the back room.

"Yup, just finishing up."

"Heading to your folks place as usual? Nice that it rained the other day. At least you won't need to trek through the snow."

"Yeah, that's a relief for sure, just going to go upstairs to grab a few things from my room."

"Great, thanks for staying till I got back. Have a good time at your parent's place."

"No problem, enjoy the quiet while I'm gone."

"Heh, enjoy the quiet? You're practically a mouse anyway. Won't be much change. A hardworking and talented mouse though. Don't worry about me, son. Just be back bright and early when you're supposed to." Master Percy smiled warmly at him.

"Of course," Johnny said and smiled back.

Upstairs, Johnny belted on his sword and dagger as usual, grabbed his coat and left. Soon, Johnny was walking west into the setting sun heading home for dinner with his family.

The moonlight filtered faintly through the oiled paper window in Johnny's room above Master Percy's shop. All was quiet and still, the hour being late by some standards and very early by others. Suddenly, a tiny sliver of a moonbeam split the dark room as a pin-hole opened in the paper window. Several dust particles in its path sparkled quietly.

A moment later, the moonbeam faded as a fine dark smoke filtered in through the pinhole. A small cloud began to form on the window ledge. After about a minute the cloud coalesced into a solid form, and the moonbeam returned. The shape on the windowsill was about twelve inches tall and looked like a naked man with jet-black skin that reflected almost no light at all. It had pointy facial features, pointy ears, and leathery wings protruding from its back. Coal-like embers glowed where its eyes should have been, and small fangs peeked out from under its upper lip. The hands and feet were like those of a human, but with hawk like talons instead of fingernails.

It surveyed the room for a moment, its sight unhindered by the darkness. All was quiet except for Master Percy's slight snoring in another room nearby. With a flap of its wings, it glided across the room to the door. It made a small sound maybe as much as a mouse, as it landed and clung to the door handle. Slowly and carefully, it undid the latch with a faint click. For an entire minute it just hung there soundlessly. Then, with a light push against the door frame, it swung the door open about six inches.

There was a faint flutter as it flapped its wings several times, circling the room twice until it was near the ceiling. Then, converting its altitude to speed, it dived in a curving path, tucking its wings to pass through the narrow gap left by the opened door. Upon exit into the dark hall, it had to pull up immediately, doing a half loop to avoid crashing into the wall outside the door. At the apex of the loop, it spotted the stairs. With a quick flap, it rolled over and gently and silently glided down the stairs into the back room of the shop.

Still in flight and flapping occasionally, it circled silently around the perimeter of the shop twice, finally landing gently on a crate of books. The top two books sparkled faintly with gold decorations on the binding. The imp, taking great care to avoid contacting the soft leather with its razor-sharp talons, easily lifted the book, which was twice its own size. Holding the book high, the imp leaped from the crate to the ground.

Spread wings and deeply bent knees cushioned its landing, though the corner of the book almost touched the ground and there was a small thump despite the imp's efforts. It froze and listened for two full minutes to be sure no one had been disturbed by the noise. Once the imp was confident all was still well, it pranced lightly across the floor holding the book high until it got to the stairs. Each stair had to be mounted by placing the book on the stair and then hopping up. The book was placed with care and silence, but hopping up on each stair produced a small mouse-skitter sound of claws on wood. The imp paused to listen following each hop, but the tone of Master Percy's snoring never changed.

After the last stair was mounted, the imp once again raised the book high with both hands and scampered silently to the door of the room it originally entered. It had to pause to turn the book sideways to fit through the barely open door. Once back in the room, the imp deposited the book in the dust on the floor below the bed. The imp paused, considered its work, and then swept away some dust in front of the book as if it had been slid into place, also obscuring its own footprints in the process.

A pair of quick flaps and a gentle landing on the door handle caused the door to swing shut. The imp raised the latch just as it closed, re-locking the door. Though slightly louder than the unlocking, the sound echoed faintly and disappeared in the hall outside. Master Percy snored on without interruption.

The imp flew back up to the windowsill, and a moment later it began to boil away into a thin cloud of smoke, wafting back out through the pinhole. Soon, an imp's shadow was visible shading the oil paper window from the outside. The tiny moonbeam peeking through the pinhole disappeared suddenly as the hole in the paper window was obscured by something that looked very much like a bird dropping, and soon after the imp's shadow flapped its wings once and disappeared.

4.3 Book

A heavy pounding sound in the early dawn hours woke Master Percy. He sat up, blinked several times, and then stood up. He put his hand on the dresser for balance as he donned his slippers, and he took a robe from the hook by his bed. As he tied his robe together, there was more pounding on the front door of his shop. A profane oath and a query about what could be so important at this hour passed his lips, and as he worked his way down the stairs he invented a new policy on the spot, double fees for rest-day work.

As he reached the door, the pounding began again, and he yanked the door open. A cold rush of air ruffled papers on the desk nearby, and momentarily a well-dressed man with pepper gray hair and a beak like nose found himself pounding on thin air. A bored-looking guardsman stood behind him leaning on the wheel of one of the baron's wagons.

"Blazes, Barry, what on earth has got you in such a tizzy? The elves attacking, and you need a poetry book to fend them off or something?"

"Very sorry, Percy, but you know how impatient the baron can be, and this morning's not had a good start. I need the book on Elvish language back."

"Baron's got insomnia?"

"No, we actually need it," he paused, sighed, and continued in a low whisper. "Look, this morning the guard found an arrow stuck in the wood beam above the town gate, an arrow with a note wrapped round it. The note is written in elven script."

Master Percy's eyes went wide, and he let out a low whistle, "Ah, I see. Come in. Both volumes should be ready anyway. After I did some tricky repair work on the history one, I told Johnny to make sure he finished with those two first. They were both on the top of the box in the back room when I saw them a day or two ago. I think he's only just finishing up the ledgers at this point."

The baron's seneschal followed him into the shop, failing to properly wipe his boots and leaving a muddy trail. "Tricky? What sort of repair work?"

"Nothing too serious, but fancy leather like that requires an experienced hand. That is, if you want to avoid the much greater expense of completely reproducing a gold-leafed embossed cover."

"I smell an extra fee coming."

"Ah, here it is right here. No, wait that's the history one. The other... Oh, dear. It was here a couple of days ago. Johnny must have moved it for something. I'll check his work area."

The seneschal's face instantly grew grim. "Percy, if you've lost that book, you can't even begin to imagine the baron's wrath. This had better not take long." A moment later he huffed and said, "I don't need to watch you waddle around in a panic. I'll be waiting at the wagon outside. You have fifteen more minutes to find it. I made a point of telling Caroline to emphasize their value, and she assured me she did. There is no excuse for this! The time this is taking will have me in hot water already!"

Fifteen minutes later, the seneschal was mounting the wagon with the guard serving as his driver already at the reins when the door to the shop popped open. Covered in sweat and red in the face from exertion, Master Percy exclaimed, "Found it!" After gasping and pausing for breath, he heaved himself over to the wagon and handed over the fancy leather tome with gold inlay on the cover.

"Good. I was not looking forward to seeing you in the stocks in the town square, expelled from town, or worse. Given the terrible timing of this, I fear it might have come to that. I'm afraid the time I've been forced to waste will require me to report something of this indiscretion when I'm questioned as to the reason for my slowness in retrieving the book. I don't understand how you could be so careless."

Master Percy's face somehow went from beet red to pale white in a matter of seconds, and hastily he replied, "Twasn't me. I found clear evidence that my apprentice had taken liberties with it. Had it in his room for some reason. My *former* apprentice, that is! I assure you. Barred and banned by the guilds in this and all nearby towns, he will be. I promise you. His last name don't matter for something like this. I don't need this kind of trouble."

"I see, well that may be sufficient to save your skin. Especially given who he is, but I'd keep a mouse's profile for sure if I were you. I'll send for the rest of the books by the end of this week. Be sure it's all ready."

"Certainly. Certainly. You can be certain of it."

Master Percy's face darkened, and his expression went hard as the wagon drove away. "Practically treated him like a son, gave him days off and a shorter term, and this is how he repays me?" he muttered. The shop door slammed loudly behind him as he went back inside, causing a flock of pigeons on the roof to take flight.

4.4 Spring

The dawn had a sort of half-chill to it as Johnny took his now customary rear exit from his father's manor. Certainly the dead, brown winter grass had a light coating of frost, yet the air already seemed too warm for that. The frost would evaporate the moment the sun hit it for sure, and anyway his parents already knew he left this way to walk in the woods, so at this point his tracks were of no consequence.

As he traveled, Johnny found that some parts of the paths commonly used by woodcutters and trappers were still sodden from snow-melt and rain. He was forced to leave tracks in the mud in a few places. He had begun to worry about this, so he looked for a way to leave the path without a trace. Not far from where he customarily left the path onto a deer track he came to a dry stony section of trail next to a large wide tree. The tree had a thick, low branch hanging over the trail. He jumped up, caught the branch, and groped around for a better hold, almost slipping back down before he found a knot that allowed him a secure hold on the branch. Once he got a firm grip, did a pull-up, and got a leg up, he was soon sitting atop the branch, gasping for breath.

"Whoo! Bit out of shape after the winter," he panted to himself.

After a brief rest, he carefully removed his boots, almost falling when one popped free. Snapping a small twig nearby, he used it to clean as much mud as he could off of his boots and then after tying the laces together put them around his neck. Boots now stowed such that they wouldn't unbalance him, he carefully found his footing and stood upright on the six-inch wide-branch. He looked down, sighed, and had to sit back down again to dust mud off the branch where his boots had scraped against the bark.

"That would be a bit too obvious, wouldn't it?" he mused as he cleaned the mud off the branch.

Having mostly erased the muddy spot on the branch, he stood

again, wobbled, and then balanced his way to the trunk of the tree. From there, he walked out onto a branch extending away from the trail. Sitting down again, he replaced his boots on his feet and dropped lightly to the forest floor.

"Even a hound won't be able to follow that," he said with a smile. Soon, paralleling the path, he found the game trail that lead to the grove.

A short time later, he was stalking quietly along the trail approaching the grove. About one hundred feet away, he paused by a large rock, unmoving, just listening. The "pee-bee" birds, "peter-peter" birds and "cheer-up-cheery" birds were singing their songs, enthusiastically laying claim to territory to prepare for their spring nesting. A squirrel rustled through the leaves a few dozen yards away. A breeze clacked the leafless branches above against each other and then sighed through the needle tree boughs of the grove ahead.

After listening for several minutes Johnny crept forward again soundlessly. Just within the needle tree grove, he paused again, listening. This time a "need-her need-her" bird called, and somewhere in the distance a woodpecker drummed on a hollow branch. Needle tree boughs sighed in the breeze again. All normal peaceful sounds of the forest, no sign of disturbance.

Moving forward, Johnny spotted the signal rock that he and Alfyra used to indicate if one or the other of them was hiding nearby. The rock pointed west toward the spring at the side of the grove indicating that he was the first to arrive. Quietly, he crept over and turned it to point toward the south where the deer track entered the grove. After that, he hid inside a clump of some needle tree saplings and nestled down to wait. From here, he could see most of the grove. Only an elf purposely being quiet would be likely to arrive without him noticing.

A few minutes passed with the usual forest noises, and Johnny began to very slowly shift his weight to ensure adequate blood flow and prevent one foot or the other from going to sleep. After a half an hour of waiting, he heard a familiar feminine giggle just behind his left ear. When he turned to look, he was instantly greeted by a swift and light kiss on his cheek.

Alfyra danced away from him and into the center of the glade with a merry yet somehow still silent dance. Johnny just watched her for a moment, awed by her grace and beauty and wondering how it could be so much more than he remembered. The smile that grew on his face as he watched her was the purest kind, one that came from happiness that simply could not be contained under any circumstances.

As he joined her in the sun in the center of the glade, she observed his smile., "Wow... you really did miss me, didn't you?"

"More than I even realized until I saw you again."

She smiled just as genuinely and danced over to hug him tightly. "I missed you too!"

They hugged for a long moment and then separated. "Tell me about your winter," she said.

"Winter started out pretty boring. I still went into the woods occasionally, when it wasn't snowing on my day off. Winter is good for tracking animals, which was nice, but I also wanted to keep up the pattern so nobody would think twice in the spring when we could meet again. This way they just think I enjoy the forest, which is true of course. The hardest part was not letting my feet take me here just for memories."

Alfyra giggled and admitted, "I know."

"You do?"

She smiled impishly. "You went walking in the snow several times."

"How do you know that?"

"Once I spotted your track and followed you for a while. My brother Tindaliur shadowed you another time. Also, twice Sylian found your tracks and followed you. Human tracks in the snow are always investigated, both for fun and for security."

"Hmm, that's more than half the times I went out. Now I better understand why we can't meet in the winter."

She smiled at him and nodded. "Winter is boring. Tracking humans is a fine entertainment. The good news is that both of them were favorably impressed. They both reported back that you were unusually respectful and interested in the forest and its creatures. They were particularly pleased you found wolf tracks and didn't hunt the wolf. You actually have a nickname."

"They named me?"

"Yeah, some of the more interesting humans we encounter multiple times get names. You're known as 'Lone Observer,' but the human word 'observer' isn't quite right. We have several words that might be translated to 'observer.' This one implies a respectful, thoughtful observation."

"That's a little worrisome since we've been trying to keep these meetings secret."

"Don't worry. There are names for all the woodcutters and trappers, plus several of the more interesting warriors that your town sends. They especially like to laugh at the one they call 'Stalking Rudely.'"

"I wonder who that is."

"He seems to be the leader of the group of warriors who at least attempt to be stealthy."

"Oh. Oh dear. That must be Corporal Zander."

"Yeah, he's able to be quiet, but he hardly seems to see anything other than game to be hunted. He also likes to tell his followers that deer signs are actually from the passage of elves. That epithet is normally used to chastise elven youngsters who are not trying hard enough to learn the ways of the forest, the ones who learn the physical skills before developing true understanding of the forest."

"He taught me about the woods. That sounds pretty unfair."

"Yeah, but somehow you learned to see the forest and all its creatures, not just turkey deer and squirrels, shooting one every chance you get."

"Ok, but I don't want to become popular and have other elves following me for entertainment. That would be problematic for us."

"Yeah, you'll be fine as long as you stay south and west of this grove. It's just inside the corner of the area we monitor, and it is always skipped by our patrols because it's slightly out of the way and not important in any case. That is why it has been my special place to relax for the last few years. I am still within the area my father has requested we stay in, but there's little chance of any other elves bothering me here."

"Not important, even with the turquoise deposit exposed at the bottom of the spring?"

"True, that's the primary reason we made this landmark for the corner of the area, but there are several other better deposits, so nobody bothers with this one."

"Showing me the deposit was a test, wasn't it?"

"Yes, one you passed admirably. If you had brought friends back to exploit it, you would have never seen me again."

Johnny hesitated for a moment and then asked, "Do you think I could meet other elves? Since they aren't really violent or hunting humans like I was taught, and they have been favorably impressed, maybe we won't need to hide from them." Her face became pensive, and she drew away, her eyes downcast and uncomfortable. "What? What is it? What's wrong?"

She breathed deep, sighed, then looked up straight at him with intensity. "It's time. There's something I must tell you."

"Okay..."

"I'm not just any average elven girl. I'm the firstborn daughter of the overall leader of the Summer Elves."

"Oh... Oh my..."

"Yeah, our friendship... our *close* friendship could cause a lot of turmoil among the elves."

"Your father leads all the Summer Elves? All the way from here to the Western Ocean?" Johnny asked.

"Yes... wait. How do you know about that?" Alfyra asked, genuinely surprised.

"We got sidetracked, but I was going to tell you that the last bit of winter got interesting. The baron sent us some books to be rebound, two of which were about elves."

"The baron has books about elves?"

"Yup, and I read both of them several times each."

A thoughtful look crossed her face, and then she said, "Tell me what these books said."

Johnny explained about the baron's books on elves. He described the one on language and writing, and she was impressed with the number of words he had learned and that he had taught himself a little writing as well. Then he described the history book. He noted that it described Winter Elves east of the mountains and Summer Elves who lived west of the mountains. It also briefly mentioned Sea Elves who lived among the waves on the eastern shores of the continent.

Little was known about Sea Elves, but the principal difference between Summer Elves and Winter Elves was the structure of their society. Winter Elves had strict notions of rank and privilege, all of which could be earned by meritorious service to the elven nation. In contrast, Summer Elves didn't believe in privilege, rank, or really any obligations beyond an individual's obligation to adhere to a common agreement achieved via rational consensus and the obligation to speak only the truth during the discussions leading up to a consensus agreement. All elves were peaceful and avoided conflict with the other peaceful races, but were deadly foes of any perpetually violent races, such as the various types of goblinoids, hybrids, and giants.

As he described the history book, her brow furrowed, and her expression darkened.

"What's bothering you?" Johnny asked.

"If these are books the baron has read, he knows we are peaceful by nature. Why does he persist in sending soldiers into the woods to bother us?"

Johnny sighed. "I thought a lot about that. I'm afraid there is only one conclusion that makes any sense. The baron is a very bad man. An evil, greedy man. Whenever the elves wound a soldier or kill a soldier he makes a show of sympathy to the family and vows vengeance. He also vows to protect the town. Coincidentally, he also takes up a donation to buy swords or help build the wall etc." Johnny paused a moment. "I think he's intentionally sacrificing soldiers to scare the town and collect more money from the townsfolk. Certainly the workers building the wall seem less lazy for a few weeks after any such incident."

Alfyra just stood there for a long moment, her mouth slightly open, a look of horror on her face. Then she exclaimed, "That's HORRIBLE!" A bird startled and flew into a nearby tree. Johnny realized that this was the first time he'd ever heard her raise her voice or make any unintentional noise.

"I can only agree," Johnny said solemnly. "It makes me embarrassed to be a human."

Her face softened. "Don't be. It's not your fault. That's for sure. Long ago when I was still taking lessons as a youngster, they told us that humans are as varied as ice. Some are refined and beautiful in their nature, like a snowflake, others hard and inflexible as the surface of a pond in mid-winter. Still others are weak and fragile as the edge of the same pond in spring, and some are the deep, evil ice that forms inside your fingers and toes, killing you when it can.

"I remember thinking that this could hardly be true. It didn't make any sense at the time. Yet now I have found examples of both extremes. You, as my favorite most beautiful snowflake, tell me his people are held in thrall by a man who is like the killing cold of frostbite."

"Snowflake?"

She grinned impishly. "Yup, you're my snowflake" she said with a twinkle in her eye.

"I see..." Johnny said slowly. Clearly he'd just been nicknamed. "So I'm your snowflake? Then since you've been the light that has shown me the reality of both elves and my fellow humans, I guess you're my Sunshine," Johnny knew it was a lame and slightly cheesy nickname, but it was all he could think of on the spot. Alfyra didn't seem to notice.

"Sunshine? I like that one!" She smiled broadly and hugged him.

They discussed her winter next, but her winter was even less eventful than his. There wasn't much to tell beyond a few times trailing and spying on patrols or woodcutters she'd followed through the snow.

A bit later, when it was time to part and return to their homes, Alfyra said, "Well, I suppose since I don't want to melt my Snowflake in any inflamed passions among our people, I'll need to think of a way to introduce you to my family gently. We may need to be patient though. Timing is important."

"I understand. I hope the weather stays warm now. See you next week if there's no snow."

They hugged goodbye and silently crept out of the grove in different directions.

4.5 Tindaliur

Tindaliur, crown prince of the Summer Elves, smiled to himself as he stepped into the Eternal Glade. The council meeting had been short, less than a day. He leaned back on one of the ancestor trees, and his expression began to relax. A moment later, his cheek twitched as he remembered the heated debate in the meeting...

"Our tactics against the humans *are* appropriate based on our traditions. In that, I agree with the council," Nonirya said expansively, with a dramatic pause. "And *of course* our traditions are important," she continued, again with a dramatic pause, "but by what logic do we believe that those traditions were shaped by conditions like those we currently live in?"

Nonirya's question hung in the air before the Elven High Council. It was not a new question. The five members of the council sat arrayed in a semicircle. The council chamber was not very large, and its structure was disguised as a hill in the forest, so the atmosphere inside was always cool, damp, and earthy. The five members of the council considered the question respectfully for several minutes. Responding too quickly would be an affront to the speaker, an indication that the question was not taken seriously.

While she waited, Nonirya looked at each member in turn. In the center sat the elven king Telperios in his usual purple robes. To his left was the Wizardess Oranyil, Advisor. Left of her sat Sylidra, Treekeeper. To his right were Loftilan, Head Archer, and Faran, Tracker. Tindaliur, the crown prince, sat behind and to the right of his father. He was the Observer. The Observer was not normally allowed to speak unless one or more members recused themselves. Only in that case was he allowed to speak and cast a tie-breaking vote if one was required.

Since the question pertained to tradition, and Telperios was the oldest, he responded, "Although I have ruled less than ten percent of it, five millennia of tradition records hundreds of times when humans and elves have come into conflict. As I pointed out last time you petitioned us, two deaths in two decades is far from the worst our traditions have endured."

"And we still have no good clarity on the real motives for this recent aggression. We need more information," Oranyil added.

Nonirya replied after a period of reflection that was minimal at best. Her haste bordered on disrespect. "Their war cries were translated after their first attack."

The council members let her statement hang in the air, refusing to rush the discussion. Eventually, Faran replied, "This has been long-established, but the chant was clearly designed to enrage us. The idea of cutting down our ancestor trees is nearly the maximum vulgarity possible, yet of no apparent benefit to the humans. My scouts have listened to the conversations of countless human patrols since. We have not heard them mention this goal again."

"It is still a matter of shame that our archers were goaded into killing humans on the day of that initial attack. There is every possibility that our haste and anger on that day has fueled the continuance of the hostility," Loftilan added.

The mention of that relatively recent tragedy nineteen years ago led to an extended silence. Many minutes later, Nonirya spoke again, "Yet only five moons ago we lost one of our youths. Normally human passions fade with the seasons, but this has persisted for more than half a human generation."

In time, Sylidra replied, "This may be due to our lapses in vigilance. We have not always avoided killing where we might have. The incidents where we lost trees have led to human deaths. Greater vigilance and misdirection is required. We must work harder to keep them away from sacred spaces, lest the fire fueled by tragedy grow."

Telperios spoke again, "Sinsilyan was young and incautious. His death was tragic, but a result of impetuous youth not a manifestation of our policy. You may recall our extended discussion and the conclusion that while his mistake was tragic the freedom for youth to roam is critical to their development. My own daughter is affected by that decision not to raise the age of adventure to one hundred years. Do you think I would risk my own daughter if the situation were as dire as you propose?"

"No, of course you would not risk your own daughter," Nonirya replied after a much more respectful period for reflection.

"Do you have any new information for us, Nonirya?" Oranyil asked.

"Nothing further at this time."

Soon after, the council voted unanimously to remain vigilant and continue misdirecting the humans with illusion and woodcraft.

Slowly allowing the memory of the council meeting to fade, the elven prince unclenched his fists and exhaled. He made a mental note to himself to request leave from his duties for reflection and to strengthen his bond with the forest. These hot-blooded thoughts mustn't be allowed to distract him.

He massaged the fingernail marks on his palms and leaned against a tree near the edge of the grove. The massive cap nut tree held the spirit of his mother's mother, and it always brought him peace. He closed his eyes and let his other senses take over. He absorbed the sensations as they came to him.

His skin told him of the faint eddies in the air of the grove.
The sound and smell of leaves was ubiquitous.
He heard the soft calling of a dove off to the east.
The smell of the tree bark...
A chorus of tiny insects among the branches...
The warmth of a small shaft of sunlight during its journey from
   his ear across his face, heading for his chin...
The sound of a squirrel above and somewhat behind him...
The interrogatory song of a question bird as it foraged above...
The murmur of elven voices near the middle of the grove...
A faint breeze caressed his cheek...
The sound of a squirrel coming down the trunk of the tree...
Soft brush of the squirrel's tail on his cheek...
The squirrel climbing down his sleeve and then his pant leg...

The squirrel scampered off on her own business. For a while longer, he allowed his senses to drink deeply, but eventually he opened his eyes and noted that the shaft of sunlight had already fallen off his chin. The emerald afternoon light that filtered into the grove at noontime had deepened with the passing of the third quarter of the day. It was nearly time for the evening meal. He felt balanced once more and paused a moment to soak up a little more of the grove's peace before heading to the meal circle.

During this last momentary reverie, he noticed a flash of red-golden hair out of the corner of his eye as he turned. He made no attempt to look. He knew who it was and didn't want her to know that she had been seen returning. This sight caused most of his inner peace and balance to dart away like shadows fleeing a torch, and he sighed inwardly.

He had not mentioned that he perceived a pattern to his sister's forays into the forest to anyone last fall, but he worried others might notice. The fact that this was the first day on which one could likely avoid making tracks in snow and the fact that she rarely left in the same direction twice worried him greatly. She was concealing something. If she felt the need to conceal something, he worried what impact there might be when whatever it was inevitably came to light. She was still young by elven standards. He would have to speak with her, and she would not like his words. She wouldn't understand fully. She was very bright for her age, but she had not yet participated in the leadership of the clan. He doubted that she fully appreciated that appearances could have consequences.

4.6 Shouting

The spring sun was out, and a fresh breeze from the south ruffled Johnny's hair as he approached the western gate of town. The sound of the blacksmith's hammer was faintly audible ahead. The smith was probably mending hoes or plow blades for spring planting. As he entered town, Johnny smiled and waved at Thomas and Dillon, who apparently had guard duty today. Thomas waved back solemnly, all business, and Dillon made a snide remark disparaging cowards and quitters as he passed, but Johnny didn't care. He was in a good mood.

He had returned from visiting Alfyra just in time for dinner with his parents. Somehow even though it was just venison, rice and beans, dinner seemed like a feast. The news that his father would be away for a ten days traveling to Mountain Gate to bear witness to a land grant didn't faze him at all. The laws of Pendalir stated that any award of lands and title had to be witnessed by at least two nobles not blood related. The baron of course never wanted to leave town, so typically he sent Johnny's father in his place. Yet even the thought of his father traveling the dangerous road to the mountains could not dampen Johnny's spirits today. Alfyra had shown up as agreed last fall, and their time together had been wonderful. Nothing could get him down today.

Just inside the gate, Johnny turned right, following the palisade wall at a brisk walk. With a bounce in his stride, he turned down the second street on the left. His boots clopped on the cobblestones as he walked. Soon he came to the first intersection and a small square, where he turned toward Master Percy's shop at the far corner. As he approached, he noticed a sack on the ground by the front door. It was a green canvas sack with shoulder straps and two buckles to keep the top closed. It was a guardsman's sack, and it looked just like the one he had in his room. It was even worn on the top corner like his.

Curious, Johnny nudged the sack with his foot, and it seemed to be full of clothes. Why was a sack of clothes sitting outside Master Percy's door of all places? Maybe the owner had set it down and forgotten about it? He unbuckled it to see if he could learn something about the owner. It was clearly quite a few clothes, and someone would be very upset to have lost it.

As he opened it he gasped... those were *his* clothes. What was going on here? A quick inspection revealed that it was all of his clothes and other personal items that should have been safely up in his room. This made no sense at all. Slowly he shouldered his sack and opened the door to the shop.

"Hey, Master Percy, why..."

"GET OUT!!!" roared Master Percy, rising from his work table. "You ungrateful, thieving excuse for an apprentice! Get out and don't come back."

Johnny couldn't move. He couldn't think. This made no sense at all. "What? I don't understand..."

"You didn't think anyone would notice if you swiped the baron's book? Hmm? Well it certainly got noticed! Barry was here yesterday demanding the book. I almost couldn't find it. I don't know what you meant, hiding it under your bed like that! Were you hoping they would not notice it missing when the crate went back one book lighter? Hmm? I never would have thought you capable of it."

"But... But... I never hid anything under my bed... ever."

"Oh, so now you think you're going to lie your way out of this? I treated you almost as a son. Gave you days off, credited time for good work. You would have been journeyman in record time, and a damn good one too! But luckily your true colors showed before I made that mistake!"

"My true colors?"

"Do you realize that that was the baron's most *prized* book? That he relies on it and its companion volume for planning attacks on the elves? His seneschal threatened to put me in the stocks!" Master Percy was beet red, and his temples were sweating. He advanced toward the doorway, and Johnny backed out into the street.

"Don't come back, and don't expect any other guild to take you in. You're banned and barred from apprenticeship, and that's final." Master Percy slammed the door so hard the building shook.

Johnny just stood there for over a minute with his mouth open. He was stunned. His legs felt like lead, and his heart even heavier. He'd really liked Master Percy. He certainly would never have hurt him or stolen from him. And he had never had the book in his room, let alone stashed it under his bed.

Someone coughed, and Johnny looked up. Several passersby who had been staring at him suddenly had pressing business elsewhere and failed to meet his eye as they passed. One woman headed straight for Helga's shop. Helga was a seamstress and an incorrigible gossip. This was bad. Every one in town would think he was a thief soon enough.

Slowly, numbly, he turned back the way he had come and left for home. Partway there, he looked off to the left of the road at a grassy hillock with a rotting stump near the top. He looked toward the cap nut tree lined lane and the marble griffon statues guarding the entrance.

"What am I going to tell mother?" he wondered out loud.

After a pause, he ascended the small hill and set his sack against the far side of the stump, not caring if it got slightly dirty. Using his sack as a back rest, he sat down to think out of view of the road. Hours later, with the sun setting and the evening chill reminding him that winter might not have entirely given way to spring, he stood up, dusted off his sack and sighed. With a grim look, he started down the hill and onto the tree lined path, never even bothering to shoulder his sack.

4.7 Proposition

As he walked, Johnny was looking at the ground in front of him. He had walked to and from town a million times. His feet knew the way, so he let his thoughts wander, thinking about how very bad it was for him to have drawn public attention when he was visiting Alfyra every week. Maybe he would have to stop seeing her until things calmed down. If anyone in the town found out about Alfyra, he could be in real trouble.

He probably would have walked right into the man if he hadn't tripped. The trip was the minor sort where one regains their balance easily but look foolish. Naturally, Johnny looked around to see if anyone saw him.

As he looked up, the sun was in his eyes, a big ball of flame on the horizon. The oaks lining the road were spaced evenly about twenty feet apart at regular intervals. They had been planted over a hundred years ago and rose magnificently, their branches touching over the road. Ten oaks away was the gate to his father's keep where the road ended. The sun was showing through the iron bars of the manor gate. The sight was stunningly beautiful, but Johnny never noticed.

A couple dozen feet ahead, a figure stood in the middle of the road, silhouetted by the sunlight. Only a few details could be seen clearly. The figure wore a dark-brown velvet robe with a hood pulled up so that the face could not be seen. The edges of the sleeves and the hood had a border that was embroidered with four rows of spidery symbols that glowed as if written in molten metal. A staff with a serpent's head carved for its top was held in one hand, the bottom planted on the ground next to the figure's foot. The eyes on the staff glowed with a yellow light.

The instant he saw the figure in the road, Johnny's blood turned to ice, and his legs turned to jelly. He wanted to yell for help, but all he managed was a mouse-like squeak. He had not expected this. He lost his grip on his sack, and it fell from his arms. The sack never hit the ground. As it fell, the figure made a small gesture with its left hand. The gesture was insanely complex, but it was performed quickly and precisely as if the figure had done it more times than could be counted. The sack just floated in the air before Johnny.

There was no hope of denying who the figure was now. No imitator would have been able to do that. This was the real Wizard of the North. Johnny figured he was as good as dead. He had heard about the wizard and his human sacrifices but thought those were just tales to scare small children around the campfire and such. Now he was faced with the real thing.

The figure spoke, "Johnny...."

The voice was whisper soft but seemed to permeate the air and come from all directions and none. Then suddenly the figure sputtered and started giggling. Soon the Wizard of the North was laughing so hard he could barely stand, leaning on his ebony snake-headed staff with its intricate patterns of inlaid silver and gold for support.

Johnny began to feel as if life itself was picking on him. Not only was he facing public ridicule as a thief, barred from all apprenticeships, and in a treasonous romance with the daughter of the elven king, but now powerful wizards of myth and legend were playing practical jokes on him. His fear began to drain away replaced by a feeling of injustice.

Meanwhile, the wizard had recovered and removed his hood. Johnny had to work hard to keep from laughing. The wizard was really funny looking. He had a completely bald head, a beak-like nose, big ears that stuck straight out, and a small pointed beard. Johnny was sure life was picking on him now, just daring him to laugh and have the wizard fry him on the spot. Much to his own amazement, Johnny managed not to laugh.

The Wizard of the North spoke again, but this time his voice was as normal as any other man's, "Sorry, I haven't done that in a long time. You should have seen the look on your face." The wizard giggled and continued, "Oh, stop acting so scared. You don't really believe all those stories about me sacrificing demons to virgins and feeding goblins to small children, do you?"

"No... Umm, wait, did you say—"

"Good," the wizard cut him off in a tone that indicate that the matter was settled and would not be discussed further. "I have been watching you for quite some time. It's not every day that someone in this town falls in love with an elf."

Johnny staggered as if hit with a large object and his stomach turned watery. The wizard knew! If the wizard told anyone, Johnny would be in very deep trouble.

"And, no, I'm not going to turn you in. If I walked into your backward and unenlightened little town, they might well do something silly like try to burn me at the stake, and things would get very messy. Messes require clean-up and smoothing things out, discussions in the high council, inquiries, et cetera, et cetera. I just don't have time for that sort of thing. What I do have time for is to strike a deal with you."

Johnny's mouth opened and closed several times of its own accord. The wizard knew. Furthermore, he didn't seem to care that Johnny was meeting with an elf, but his mention of it put Johnny

in a tight place. This was a negotiating tactic, but were they negotiating? Eventually Johnny's managed to reply, "What do I have,
that you, the Wizard of the North, could possibly want?"

"Brains."

Johnny took an involuntary step backward.

"No, not like that, you ninny! I have been looking for an apprentice. You are the only person for many miles who has the
required intellect. However, what is more important to *you* is
that becoming my apprentice will ease, if not solve, most of your
pressing problems." The wizard sounded quite solicitous about
this, but Johnny didn't care. He didn't like the sound of this deal
at all. By mentioning Alfyra, the wizard was backing him into a
corner, offering both a stick and a carrot.

"Solve? Becoming an apprentice? Correct me if I'm wrong, but
didn't you just mention that they burn wizards around here?"

"Only when they catch us," he said with a smug little smile,
"and catching a wizard is quite tricky indeed. Not to mention
rather hazardous if one doesn't know what to do once they have
caught a wizard!" The wizard's bright-blue eyes twinkled as if
remembering some grand joke. "In any case, I have a room in my
tower where you can stay. You wouldn't have to come to town. All
your problems center on the prejudicial and unenlightened views
of the people in this pathetic little barony."

"But Alfyra..." Johnny couldn't leave her. If that had been
an option he would simply become a trader and leave town, yet
something in what the wizard was saying began to make sense,
and it scared him. Everything he had heard about the Wizard of
the North told him he should be sickened by the very idea of becoming his apprentice. Of course, he had been told similar things
about elves.

"She would be just as close. My tower is only a little further
from your romantic little grove than the town is. You would be
allowed to continue your weekly visits as long as your studies and

chores are complete, and you won't have to lie about where you went." The wizard smiled. Clearly, he had been ready for that one.

Johnny wondered how long the wizard had been watching him. Did he trust the wizard? No. He didn't want to become a wizard. Wizards were outcasts. Of course wizards were live outcasts, not dead traitors. He knew the wizard had him trapped. Just like in a stones game, he must ensure survival before fighting for profit. Yet he was unable to say yes. He knew that as a wizard he would never be welcome in his parents' house. His parents had killed a wizard once. After a long pause, Johnny responded with his most intelligent, "Umm..."

"Don't decide now. Take this." The wizard handed Johnny a silvery pendant. "If you decide to accept, come to my tower but remember to show this. The rumors about the forest around my tower are among the few true rumors."

"How do I find your tower?"

"That is another true rumor. Just turn left off the north trail where you've always been told not to go. That path really does lead to my tower," The wizard suddenly looked chagrined. "Oh, I almost forgot to introduce myself. My name is Morphosius. Please, don't ever call me the Wizard of the North. I can't stand that stupid name. For one thing, there are several Wizards who live north of me, and for another it sounds like a character in a campfire story for children."

Morphosius drew his staff across his body in a single smooth motion, and suddenly wasn't there anymore.

Johnny blinked and suddenly felt very tired. He wasn't entirely sure he hadn't imagined the whole thing. He looked at the pendant in his hand. It was about an inch and a half in diameter and appeared to be made of precious metal, either highly polished silver or perhaps platinum. In the center it had a finely detailed Caw Bird in flight attached to the outer ring at both wingtips and the tail. Caw birds were largish, black-feathered birds with pointed beaks known for showing up after battles and for stealing and eating baby birds, including chicks from chicken farmers. They were nuisance birds but also more intelligent than most birds.

The outer ring of the pendant contained twelve blood-red rubies, evenly spaced. Each gem was about an eighth of an inch across and sparkled brightly. Each ruby had a very small symbol inlaid on the center facet in a spidery script. The flip side was identical except for the bird in the center. One side was the top of the bird, the other the bottom showing the feet tucked under the belly in flight. Though the symbolism was decidedly odd, it had to be worth more than any single piece of jewelry Johnny had ever seen.

Quickly, he slipped it and its silver chain into his pocket and picked up his sack from where it was resting against a tree. He couldn't remember when it had come to rest there, but it also was in perfect condition, as if he hadn't used it as a pillow all day against a dirty rotten stump. The wizard sure was being nice, but even a demon can bring gifts. "In fact, in most stories they do just exactly that," Johnny said out loud as he reached the manor gate.

4.8 Mother

Johnny entered via the front door but was relieved that no one was there to greet him. He went straight up to his room. As soon as he got there, he put his sack into the closet, out of sight, and deposited the pendant in his desk drawer and closed it. As he turned to leave, he heard his mother's footsteps on the stairs. Momentarily, she was standing in the door to his room. The worried look on her face spoke volumes.

"You heard."

"I heard some gossip. Come to the kitchen. Let's talk."

"Ok."

Johnny followed her downstairs and sat down at the table in the kitchen.

"Are you thirsty?" she asked him.

"Yes."

"Do you want water or milk?"

"Water, please."

Madeline selected a sturdy earthenware mug and poured some water into it from a copper vessel.

As she handed him the mug, he said, "I wonder if this is the same mug."

"Possibly. We broke a few since then, but this is one of the old ones."

"What did you hear about me?"

"Nonsense, I thought, but you are home tonight unexpectedly, which worries me. What happened?"

"I wish I knew."

Madeline looked at him with the sadness of a mother who sees her child in pain, but she didn't rush him. After a while, he continued.

"When I left the shop, everything seemed fine. We wished each other well, and the parting seemed warm and genuine. When I arrived this morning, my clothes were outside the door, and he shouted me out of the shop." Johnny paused to take a sip of water. "A couple of weeks ago, the baron brought over several books including two prized volumes about elven history and language."

"This was all routine work. I finished it in half the allotted time... Well, except for the ledgers. I put those off, but they would have been done in time too.

"Having extra time, I pretended to be working, but I was reading the two volumes. I only ever did this downstairs at my desk. I knew that while I'm not exactly forbidden to read things I'm working on, the polite fiction is that bookbinders see nothing and remember nothing. For that reason, I didn't make it obvious that

I was reading the books, and I *always* put the books back where they belong when I was done. I'm one hundred percent certain I remember doing that the last time, because I did it quickly when the sound of Master Percy returning surprised me. There is one thing I don't understand. When he was yelling at me, Master Percy said the strangest thing. He claimed to have found one of the books hidden under my bed. This seems to be why he thinks I was trying to steal it."

Johnny took a sip of his water.

"Mom, in the entire time I've been at Master Percy's, I've never put *anything* under my bed. Never. Not even my shoes. Nothing."

The look on Madeline's face grew worried and introspective. The silence stretched.

"Mom, you believe me, don't you?"

"Of course, dear" she said after a pause that was just a fraction of a second too long. "Though it doesn't help that I had to retrieve my books from under your bed a dozen times when you were younger."

"But, Mom! I haven't done that in years! You know I stopped after you grounded me to do nothing but chores for a week," Johnny said, his voice raising in an aggrieved tone unique to children complaining to their parents.

"Yes, I know. But if not you, who? Does anyone else regularly visit Master Percy at his shop?"

"Just customers really. I think half the reason he took me on is that he was lonely, which also doesn't make sense. Why would he want to get rid of his only companionship? We certainly seemed to be friends as well as master and apprentice... until today," Johnny added sadly.

"So either Master Percy's suddenly gone mad, he's been threatened into expelling you, or someone snuck into his shop and put the volume under your bed..." she said, her voice trailing off.

"Or I'm lying," Johnny accused.

"I didn't say that."

"But you thought that!"

Madeline looked at Johnny for a long time, her expression not changing. Johnny pleaded. "Mom, I didn't do it," he pleaded.

"That's probably worse than if you had."

"What? I don't understand? What do you mean worse if I didn't steal it?"

"Because if you did do it, then life is simple. Your actions, while consequential due to the circumstances would not be all that bad. However, if you didn't do it and Master Percy hasn't snapped, then you are being used as a pawn in some sort of politics. That makes life very, very complicated. Do you know of anyone who would want to hurt you in this way?"

"Nah, only one I don't really get along with is Dillon. I can't imagine him pulling this off."

"No, certainly not him. Which means this isn't really about you. It must be something the baron is doing to your father and I."

"The baron? Why would he do this?"

"I don't know. It doesn't make sense. But again, if it's politics I hope it's him. Otherwise, it's someone very powerful, possibly someone from Pendalir City. If someone that far away has studied us carefully enough to find this way of hurting us, they are very skilled and the person paying them is very powerful."

"Why on earth would someone from down south care at all about anyone up here?"

"You know your father and I lived in Pendalir City early in our marriage. Your father is an excellent warrior but a hopeless politician. He... well, let's just say there was an incident that angered some folks. Initially, I hoped I could smooth things over, but after we found a fruit basket with a cobra hiding in it on our kitchen table, it became clear that the situation was out of hand. Following the incident, I convinced your father to retire as far from the capital as possible. This should have been sufficient. I don't really think that after all these years there would still be a grudge strong enough to justify this kind of subtlety, but I guess I have to consider it."

"I see," Johnny said simply.

"In any case, I think you should avoid town for a week or more minimum. The rumor mill might turn you into a target and create an incident more serious and more real, which is possibly what the person doing this would want."

"Or they want me not to go to town."

"Yes, but I think there is more risk if we're separated, so stay away from town, ok?"

"Ok, can I still go into the woods? I find it very calming, and I really need some peace and quiet to think now."

After a pause, she said, "Ok, but wait a few days at least, and try not to interact with anyone you run into out there any more than necessary."

Johnny nodded. They each sipped their water, silently thinking for a moment, and then the sound of small running feet broke the silence.

"Hey Mom, guess what I just heard from Al!" Zachary yelled as he ran into the kitchen. "Oh, hi Johnny, what are you doing here?"

Johnny opened his mouth to respond, but Madeline cut him off. "Never mind about Johnny. What did you hear from Al?"

"I heard they captured an elf!"

Madeline breathed a sigh of relief, but Johnny immediately asked.

"What did it look like?"

"Um. Well I don't know, but you can ask Al. I wasn't there."

"What was it wearing?"

"How should I know? Ask Al already. What has you so excited?"

"Sorry, I've had a hard day. Why did you come yelling when

you don't have the whole story?" Johnny asked, taking his tone down a notch.

"I don't know. I was excited. I wanted to tell Mom. I didn't know you were going to ask me all these questions."

Madeline interrupted diplomatically, "Johnny, if you want details, you should go find Al." Zach started to look smug, but then his mother turned to him and said, "And what have I told you about running in the house?"

"Sorry, Mom," Zach said.

"Just sorry?"

"I'm sorry. I won't do it again."

"Thank you. And Johnny..." But Johnny had already disappeared out the kitchen door and likely wasn't listening.

Johnny found Al in the stable, rubbing down a horse. As he entered, Al looked up and said, "Oh hey Johnny, what's you doin' here?"

"It's a bit of a story, but I heard something about a captured elf from Zach..."

"Yeah, 'pparently the patrols had set a trap. I guess it was the same sort of pit and net thingy that normally never does them any good at all, 'least from what I've heard previous to this. But this time, while they were building it, an elf was actually watching from a tree branch above them. Probably having a good laugh, I'd guess. Story I heard was that the moment the trap was complete that branch under the elf snapped, and he fell straight into the trap with all the guardsmen standing right there. Sounds mighty strange to me, but the guy tellin' was convinced it was true."

"He? a male elf?"

"Well, I guess I don't rightly know. I didn't see the elf myself. I just assumed it was a he. I don't imagine elves let their women do the fighting instead of men, though I don't know that they don't either. Never thought 'bout that, actually." Al's voice trailed off as if the thought were a major revelation.

"Did you hear anything about what it looked like?" After a second, Johnny added, "I've never seen one."

"No, though it would be interesting to see one, I agree. So much fuss and bother 'bout elves. Be nice to see what the fuss was all about, that's for sure. Story was that it went right on down to the baron's cells, though. Don't expect it will be out of there any time soon. Hey, I thought you gave up that guard stuff. You back midweek 'cause you've decided to return to the Guard? That might 'splain the crazy rumor I heard about Master Percy firing you."

"Ah, well that rumor is true. There's been a misunderstanding. I'm still trying to figure out how to clear it up, but I'll be home until things get sorted out."

"I see. They say you stole a book from the baron."

"I didn't, of course, but something happened that made Master Percy think I meant to. I don't even understand what happened... You said they took the elf to a cell. That means it's alive?"

"I presume so, not much point in locking up a dead elf."

"That's good," Johnny said emphatically. After a second he added, "I might still get to see it."

Al raised his eyebrows.

"Do you know who was guarding it?"

"Nope, not sure why you think I'd know that, but I'd be real careful about trying to go see it." Al stretched out the word real to emphasize it. "Sounds like you have 'nuff trouble already. Not the time to go showing interest in elves, if you ask me."

Johnny sighed heavily. "You're probably right about that. Thanks, Al, see you tomorrow."

"'Night, Johnny," Al said and went back to brushing the horse.

4.9 Brother

The next three days rained, and there was nothing for Johnny to do but hang around the house. It was hard not to mope. He spent some time doing chores and helping Al just to keep busy. Try as he might, he could not avoid his fear that somehow it was Alfyra who had been caught. He was always jumpy and tense and not very pleasant company. Several times he had to apologize for snapping at people. Luckily, they all assumed he was upset about the situation with Master Percy. And he would have been, but all he could think about was the possibility that Alfyra had been captured. He knew there was no reason to believe it was her. She was not the only elf in the woods. In fact, according to her, there were a few hundred elves, but he still could not stop his fear from gnawing at his gut.

On the morning of the sixth day after he was expelled by Master Percy, Johnny woke early. The sun was just barely causing a glow in the east, and the stars still shown clearly overhead. It was a cold day with a northwest wind that made the tree branches sway, but thankfully it was not rainy. He quietly dressed in a warm tunic and wool-lined breeches. He was ready to go before the sun made it over the horizon.

"Too soon," he whispered quietly to himself. "I don't want to make this trip seem any different from previous trips into the woods."

Now that he could go into the woods any time, he didn't want the established pattern to stand out. To disguise this trip, during which he hoped to meet Alfyra, he had spent the day before yesterday in the woods, even though there was no hope of meeting Alfyra.

Although he hadn't slept well, he was way too anxious to go back to bed, so he pulled a chair up to his window and spent the more than half of an hour watching the sun rise. He normally left just as the sun rose, and that pattern he would keep consistent so that this day seemed no different from any other, should his parents hear him leaving.

After leaving at the normal time, Johnny was extra careful to leave as few tracks as possible and made sure to move silently at all times. Tensions might be high among the elves too. At one point he heard someone coming up the trail. Absolutely silently, he ducked off the road and hid behind a fallen log. The man had jingling traps dangling from his pack and pelts of several large fur weasels hanging off one side, obviously too fresh to be packed away yet. The trapper passed by him, entirely unaware of his presence.

To further obscure his track, he also made some false turns onto other routes and then left the trail and doubled back wherever he could do so without leaving a trace. He hoped that even an elf would have trouble following his trail.

As he neared the grove, the sun was climbing well into the sky, and although it was still breezy the chill air had warmed considerably already. The previously clear sky now had small puffy clouds flying from west to east, as if they had somewhere important to be. Johnny watched them through the leafless branches above and paused to listen carefully but could hear little other than the sounds of the wind rustling leaves and whispering among the branches, some of which clacked together occasionally. The wind was shifting and would probably be out of the southwest soon. Johnny suspected it might rain before nightfall.

Sneaking up to the edge of the grove, Johnny got a view of the signal rock. Again it pointed to the spring, indicating he was first to arrive. This was the most common state; he often got here first, but part of him had been hoping she would already be here. Quietly, he adjusted the rock and selected a hiding place. They never used the same hiding place twice, since that would create a worn-in spot easily observed by others happening upon this glade, especially other elves. This time he silently climbed into the boughs of one of the pines to wait.

A few seconds after he got settled into the tree he heard a male voice above him say, "You move through the forest well for a human." It was in Elvish.

Johnny's blood froze, and his heart sank, but he kept an outwardly calm face and looked up to find that he had hidden himself ten feet below a male elf. He had to make a split second decision on how to respond. Responding in Elvish would raise questions, but feigning a lack of understanding without the expected fright or violence would also be suspicious. Given that he was not already shot through with arrows, the elf must want to talk, not fight, so on that guess he answered in Elvish, "Thank you."

"My sister claimed she had taught you our language, but I did not believe it was possible in such a short time as she described," he said quickly, possibly testing Johnny's ability to understand.

"She's a good teacher, I guess. Would you like to descend for a more comfortable conversation?" he said, again in Elvish.

The male elf's eyebrows shot up, impressed he understood or perhaps that he could reply so fluently. "For me there is little difference in comfort, but I have no cause to make you uncomfortable. You first of course."

When they were both on the ground Johnny said, "My name is Johnny D'Abrac."

The elf looked at him in surprise, then said, "Humans place great importance on the exchange of names. I had forgotten. My name is Tindaliur, first son and heir to Telperios, Steward of the Trees and Protector of the forests west of the mountains. I am honored to learn your name, Johnny D'Abrac."

"Since you mention your sister, you know that she and I were to meet here. Why have you come in her stead?" Johnny asked, some of his inner dread about the possible answers lending a slight urgency to his question despite his best efforts to remain calm.

"I sense you are worried about her, perhaps about her safety. This is good. Very good. It means you are indeed ignorant of the recent calamity, as she assured me you would be."

"I have heard rumors, but I know no details about the captured elf."

"Captured? Not killed? This is good news indeed!" He suddenly pursed his lips and whistled a distinctive bird-like whistle.

"Hi Johnny," Alfyra said, stepping out from behind a nearby needle leaf tree and smiling.

Johnny experienced a wave of relief that felt like an entire mountain had been lifted from his shoulders. He smiled, taking a step toward her, then realized he should be careful how he greeted her in front of her brother. His hesitation was unnecessary. She bounded over and hugged him just as enthusiastically as he had intended to hug her.

"It's fine, I told him all about you. He insisted that he be allowed to meet you independently though. His idea of a test I guess, but I knew you'd do just fine." she said. Johnny returned her hug, but he kept an eye on Tindaliur, who seemed to relax even further, much to Johnny's relief.

"Do not worry, Johnny D'Abrac," he said. "There was a time when I had a close friendship with a human. It's really not that uncommon from the elven perspective, though with so many more humans than elves it's likely very rare from your perspective. Sadly, for us it's an ephemeral thing, a wonderful sweetness with the salty bitter aftertaste when we inevitably outlive our human friends. At three hundred and twenty-three seasons, Alfyra is old enough to handle it now, I think." The tone of a protective older brother did ring through, but not in a menacing way.

"Tindaliur had noted my regular coming and going last fall,

and when he saw me returning again after the first snow melt he confronted me. Since we were already talking about you meeting others, I simply told him everything. He wanted to tell Father immediately, but I asked him to delay. He agreed on the condition that he be allowed to meet you."

Tindaliur nodded. "I'm satisfied that Alfyra has chosen well, and she is right that we may not want to introduce you right on the heels of Sylian's capture, so I will keep her secret for a while yet." He paused and then continued, "Until we meet again, Johnny D'Abrac."

"May it be under the boughs of a healthy forest," Johnny replied, using the response Alfyra had taught him.

Tindaliur smiled at him then at Alfyra and then left silently via a dear track out the back side of the grove.

After Tindaliur had left, Johnny turned to Alfyra and said, "Thank goodness it wasn't you. I was so worried. I've had the worst week of my life, and I wasn't able to get any good information. All I knew was that an elf had been captured."

"You sound very stressed. Was there more to it than just Sylian's capture?"

"Unfortunately, yes." Johnny told her of Master Percy's accusations, and his conversation with his mother, and how he was afraid to show too much interest in the elf in front of his mother and Al, yet he wasn't able to go into town to ask about the elf himself.

Alfyra listened quietly, her face growing long and concerned. When he finished, she said, "You must get your intelligence from your mother. I agree with her assessment. What do you plan to do about it?"

"Well, I don't have a lot of options. Master Percy is a well-respected senior guild master. There's no way any guild will have me now unless I move very far away, and even then I'd live in fear of the story reaching them. Furthermore, I suspect every guild master knows what it means when a young man is seeking apprentice work far from home. Even if I found work, it would be with someone who wanted to exploit me and didn't trust me."

"How typically human." Alfyra sighed. "I guess it's because your lives are so short that you don't have time to forgive each other."

"Maybe. Hey, you never told me your age. I heard your brother say three hundred and twenty-three seasons? Does that make you eighty years old?"

"Yes, this may sound old to you, but I'm very young from our point of view. My father has enjoyed two thousand three hundred and seventy-two seasons."

"Wow."

"So you can't be an apprentice in a guild. What will you do?"

"Well, financially I'm lucky. My parents have enough wealth that I probably don't need to do anything in particular for ten or twenty years at least, but I'm not sure if they've got enough to last my entire life unless I wanted to work hard at turning his lands into a profitable farm. My father is growing some crops now. Even so, I think he's still spending more than he makes. I suspect that if I live off of my parents without contributing and split the inheritance with Zach, it won't last more than a few years. I need to learn some trade on which I can survive or I'll be starving in my old age."

"It would be a terrible waste for someone as smart as you to get stuck farming. It's good, honest work, but it relies much more on physical labor and ceaseless endurance. Frankly, I was not sure book binding was much better for you."

"Yeah, originally I thought of binding as a way to get an infinite supply of free books to read, but the reality involves a lot more ledgers and duplicate copies of identical books than I had imagined."

"So what else?"

"Well, my sword-fighting skills would easily get me work as a merchant's guard, but I don't really want to do that. Other guards are likely to be dull company. From what I can tell, they mostly live to drink at taverns along whatever route the merchant takes. Also, it doesn't pay very well, it's dangerous, and I'd spend most of my time away from here." He looked up at her sincerely. "Away from you."

Alfyra nodded and smiled slightly, waiting for him to continue.

"Aside from farming, the primary non-guild jobs are groom, stable hand, barmaid, cook, wood cutter, fur trapper, and fighting with the guard. Grooms are poorly paid, and we only have one inn, which already has a groom. I'm not a pretty young girl, so barmaid is out. I could learn to cook, but again the inn and the D'Arnors already have cooks." Johnny paused and said, "I don't think I could work for the D'Arnor family anyway. Caroline and her brothers aren't too bad, but I'd surely get in trouble criticizing her mom or her dad.

"Being a trapper won't work either. I just can't imagine killing creatures for fur for a living. I know elves wear fur-lined coats in winter, but you also are respectful of the animals you kill and minimize what you need to take. Trappers are all about killing the maximum number possible just for money. I can't think like that. It makes me sick to my stomach. Of course woodcutter is out too for approximately the same reason."

"And..."

"And what?"

"And so what is the option you will take?"

"There's one more, but it scares me."

Alfyra waited patiently.

"I was offered a different type of apprenticeship."

Alfyra raised one eyebrow.

"Wizard's apprentice."

Alfyra's other eyebrow shot up briefly and then both crashed down into a worried frown. "Which wizard?" Alfyra asked very quietly.

"He said his name was Morphosius."

There was a drawn out silence and Alfyra's face was very still. "Tell me everything he said to you and how you met him."

Johnny related the story of Morphosius stopping him on the way home and his offer, then he showed her the amulet. She held it and turned it over in her hand several times, an unreadable expression on her face.

"What's wrong?" Johnny asked.

"Maybe nothing, maybe everything."

"What do you mean?"

"Wizards are tricky. They rarely mean exactly what you think said. It is said that the second most dangerous thing in the world is to meet a wizard."

"What's the most dangerous thing then?"

"To be friends with a wizard," she said seriously, "Morphosius built his tower a few years before your town's baron showed up. He claimed a small area without asking us, but aside from perverting that area with magical defenses he has not been a problem. It wasn't an area with ancestor trees, so we just ignored him, and so far he's ignored us. Other wizards in other parts of the northern forests usually seek to trade with us or otherwise establish peaceful relations. Morphosius is secretive and keeps to himself. It's worrisome, but he hasn't actually done anything problematic that we know of."

"So he's antisocial..."

"Maybe." Alfyra sighed heavily. "Problem is you might make a good wizard. You have the intellect for sure. I also suspect you have some innate talent."

"How would you know that?"

Alfyra didn't answer, but she held the amulet Morphosius had given him in the upturned palm of her left hand, and held her right hand over it. She wiggled her fingers in a rhythmic pattern and chanted something Johnny didn't understand for almost two minutes. The amulet was surrounded by a very faint blue nimbus for about thirty seconds after she finished.

"As I thought, it is magical," she said.

"You can cast magic spells?"

"Many elves know a little magic, and maybe as much as one in four of us have enough talent to learn a few of the simplest spells. However, it's very rare for elves to be strong in magic. Much rarer than for humans. I'm a lot stronger than average, but as you saw it took quite a long time for me to cast even that very simple detection. I only know of three elves on this side of the mountains who have been strong enough to actually become a Mage. The strongest is my father, who has even earned the rank of Wizard. Another was my teacher, and the third was exiled for pursuing forbidden magics."

"But how would you know if I had ability?"

"Anyone with talent will feel an affinity for any other person with magical talent. It's subtle, and if you haven't been trained you wouldn't know what it meant. Someone as weak as me would only feel it for someone who is very strong. This affinity may be part of why we became friends. You must have a substantial latent talent, because now that I'm thinking about it directly the affinity is quite clear to me.

"Would it then follow that someone strong can detect it more easily, so I can detect it even for someone weak like you?"

"Yes."

"That's faintly disturbing. I mean, I really did think we had something special, not just an affinity due to some strange talent."

"Of course, we do. The affinity just made it easy to start. You're not doomed to love every wizard or anything, especially once you are trained and can recognize the effect."

Johnny was speechless for a second. Then he said. "Love?"

Alfyra giggled. "Yes. You are in love with me, aren't you?"

After a moment Johnny said, "Yes, I suppose I am, though I'm afraid of what that means... Wait, is that what Tindaliur meant by 'close friendship?'"

"Yes, I didn't meet Tindaliur until my one hundred and twenty-ninth season. He was living with a human woman named Eleanor about fifty miles west of here. He took care of her till the very end. She lived almost to her eightieth birthday. I think he still misses her."

"How old is Tindaliur?"

"Eight hundred and thirteen seasons."

"Do you love me?"

"Of course I do! How could I not love a snowflake like you?" she said with a wink.

Johnny smiled and said, "I thought so, but it's really nice to hear you say it."

They sat there smiling at each other for a moment, and then Alfyra asked, "So are you going to become a wizard?"

"I don't know. I'm afraid that my parents would be very upset by this."

"Why? Do they think magic is evil? Magic is neither good nor bad."

"I don't know. They've never talked about magic really. The one or two times I asked a question about it they seemed nervous and changed the subject immediately. I got the feeling I shouldn't ask about it. Also..."

Johnny paused and licked his lips. The memory was painful, and the pain showed on his face. "Also I think they might have killed a wizard once."

Alfyra's expression was of pure surprise. "What makes you think that?"

Johnny told her about the conversation he overheard when he was young, and after she asked some questions he described the dreams he had about skeletal warriors and the incident at the funeral. For some reason he couldn't define he left out the details about trip to see the monks.

She pondered his tale for a moment. "I don't know what that means, but the killing of a necromancer might be understandable. Some necromancers are very evil. Although, Necromancy is also the talent required for healing. It sounds like the one they killed was evil. Did you hear a name?"

Johnny had not mentioned the necromancer's name when he related the story, but everything he overheard that night was burned into his brain. He could not forget any of it. "Nazh was the name they used."

"I have heard of him. He was a scourge. He raised an army of zombies and skeletons and attacked several towns southwest of here. So your father is the knight who killed Nazh? That's good. Nazh was an abomination. I can understand that they wouldn't want their kid to be a necromancer if that's all they knew of Necromancy, but I don't understand why they would be worried about you. That's kind of strange."

"Hmm, yeah, I never thought about it like that. I don't know."

They both were silent for a while. After a couple of minutes, by silent agreement, they moved to a sunny spot in the grassy area of the grove. For a long while they relaxed and meditated together, sitting with their backs touching as they had many times before, absorbing the natural sounds of the forest and letting its peace wash over them.

Finally, Johnny spoke, "I don't want to leave my parents, but if someone is trying to use me to hurt them maybe the best thing I can do for them is to disappear."

"I doubt they'd see it that way, but learning magic would be an excellent use of your talent. Now that the idea has come to us, I increasingly feel like it's something you were meant for. The idea just sounds right when I think about you."

"I don't really want to be a wizard, but I don't want to be a burden on my parents, and I suppose that if I become a wizard I'll be able to do pretty much anything I want from there."

"Maybe not anything, but certainly you'll have lots of options. Wizards can set up businesses, act as advisors to kings, or sell their services directly either to rich nobles or other wizards."

"I suppose that's what I should do. Even though I really don't want to be a wizard, it might be the best option left to me."

"Morphosius is not far. We would be able to visit."

Johnny smiled. "Yes. That's very important to me. I think that pretty much decides it."

"When will you go to the wizard's tower?"

"Tomorrow, I guess. I need to grab clothes and a few things. It's probably better to leave before my dad gets home. It will save him from fighting with the baron over the allegations Master Percy made."

They stood up and faced each other. Johnny said, "I should go home and pack my things. I don't know what lies in store for me now. I assume I'll have lots of work to do as a wizard's apprentice too. I hope we can at least continue to meet every seven days as before."

"Yes, you will need to take it seriously. That seems like a good plan. If you need to change the plan, leave a note in the tree hole we use to store the stones board and position the rock to point away from the spring if there is a message waiting. We can leave notes to work out new meetings if necessary. Now that Tindaliur has met you, we can worry slightly less about elves discovering us."

"Sounds good. I'll quit if Morphosius doesn't let me visit you. You're more important than anything to me now. I'm only interested in being a wizard if it means I can eventually be free, and we can spend whatever time we want together. If not, I'll find another way."

Alfyra smiled, and the pure joy of her smile made her indescribably beautiful to Johnny. "I love you, Johnny! I know you'll succeed," she said and hugged him tightly.

"I love you too," he said, and after a kiss that was finally something more than a light peck they parted and headed back to their respective homes. The sky had become gray, and the rain started before Johnny reached home, but his spirits were not dampened at all.

"This day in the forest seems to have done you some good," his mother noted when he returned.

"Yes, I think I finally managed to find some relief from my problems this time. I feel much better," he replied with a smile and then went up to his room to change out of his wet clothes.

5 Pledge

5.1 Goodbye

The lead gray sky slid by the open window slowly as Johnny dressed in the early dawn hours. He belted on his sword and dagger, slung his bow over his shoulder, and turned toward the window. He paused for several seconds, looking down across the yard and fields beyond and to the wall that surrounded his father's land. His expression was blank, his manner solemn. His eyes momentarily lost their focus as his attention turned inward to himself and his future then snapped back to the northwest horizon with resolution.

Quickly but quietly, he shut the window and turned to leave. As he turned, he discovered that his brother Zachary was standing in the doorway to his room regarding him. They stared at one another for a long moment.

"Where will you go?" Zach asked in a small voice.

"I don't know," Johnny lied.

"Will I see you again?"

Zach was six years younger than him, slightly older than the age at which their father had started training Johnny for the guard. "I hope so. Work hard and follow the rules better than I did. Try not to make any of my mistakes."

"When?" Zach said, ignoring the advice.

"When Dad can be proud of me again," Johnny said. He paused as if surprised he had said what he had said but then nodded as if to confirm it. "Don't tell Mom we had this chat?"

"You said follow the rules and don't make your mistakes, then you tell me to lie to Mom?"

Johnny smiled. "You're right. Don't tell her till she asks."

"Ok."

"Bye"

Zach trotted swiftly over, hugged his brother for several seconds, then let go. "Bye," he said before turning back down the hall toward his room.

Johnny stood there, unmoving and silent for almost a minute, his face flickering various conflicted emotions in rapid sequence. Finally, he closed his eyes, inhaled, and exhaled. When he opened them again, his face was calm and his gaze resolute.

5.2 Entry

Johnny followed the northern trail west of the road just as Morphosius had instructed, and all others had warned him not to. At first, it seemed a fairly normal path through the trees, but gradually the path descended into a bit of a small depression, or perhaps the land on either side of the path was rising, It was hard to tell which. As the sides of the depression became steep and treeless, it began to occur to Johnny that he would be unable to hide or maneuver should anyone else approach from in front or behind. Also, the path that was now more of a trench had begun to curve to the left so that it was impossible to see for more than a couple dozen yards in either direction. The gradual change had lulled him, and he had wandered into a vulnerable position.

Johnny paused and considered the situation for a moment, looking at the steep dirt walls on either side, then shrugged and continued. "He did invite me and told me to approach this way," Johnny said to reassure himself.

Perhaps another hundred yards later, the curving stopped, and the trench deepened further. He now stood in a narrow, dry ravine with solid rock rising on both sides. Johnny stared at the walls for a while. The rock walls appeared natural at first glance, but close attention to detail revealed that the stone was a bit too smooth in some places, and the walls rose too abruptly from the edge of the dirt path on which he traveled.

Directly ahead, whoever had constructed this path gave up on all pretense of naturalness. The ravine was blocked by a blank stone wall twenty-five-feet high. The wall was a single solid slab of granite, polished flat with no obvious joint where it met the ravine walls on either side. The final twenty feet of the path was paved with flat granite bricks. Johnny pondered this apparent dead end for a while.

"Hmm, a paved path must lead somewhere," Johnny murmured to himself. Not knowing what else to do, he approached the blank wall. As soon as he set foot on the paved section, the surface of the wall began to deform. Soon an arched molding suggestive of a doorway protruded from the wall. At he same time, text carved into the stone surface of the wall appeared.

"Maze of Morphosius"

Below that, it read, "Within, unwelcome visitors choose death."

Johnny put his hand against his chest where he could feel the medallion given to him by Morphosius under his shirt. "Well, I'm invited, so I suppose it's safe for me," he said. When he walked closer, the text disappeared and the area inside the arch melted away to reveal a ten-foot-long tunnel that ended at a T intersection. The wall at the intersection revealed glowing text as he approached.

"Direction matters not. Death awaits. Turn back now."

Johnny was confident that he was invited and that the sign didn't apply to him, so he entered despite the warning, choosing the left option arbitrarily. The tunnel was about six feet high and six feet wide. As he progressed, the passage became dark, and soon he was forced to go slowly, feeling his way along the walls. The tunnel twisted and turned several times but never branched.

Eventually it was too dark to see, and he began to fear that he had made a serious mistake. Even so, he pressed on slowly, buoyed by the thought that it wasn't possible to get lost as long as the tunnel didn't branch. If there were no choices, he could always leave by simply turning around. Luckily, it wasn't long before he began to detect light in the tunnel up ahead.

"Strange maze," Johnny murmured. As he moved forward, the dim light got stronger, and the passage finally branched offering him two options. To the left was a small four-foot-high tunnel that was only two feet wide. In this direction he could see an exit into daylight. The second option was to follow the present tunnel straight ahead back into darkness. The direction from which the light came was much smaller, uncomfortable and claustrophobic, but the light was more attractive than going back into darkness. Johnny went left, and after only twenty feet it opened out into a large open enclosure. The sky was visible above, and the ground ahead was rocky, barren dirt littered with small stones and various bones. Some of the bones were large, and at least one appeared to be part of a human jawbone.

Peering cautiously out of the small tunnel, Johnny noted that the enclosure only had two walls. One wall was a large flat cliff rising fifty feet above him and running about a hundred and fifty feet long. The other wall was a smooth semicircular solid-stone wall twenty-five feet high. At the center of the cliff there was a large ten-foot-high cave. Johnny's exit was near one end of the curved wall not far from where it joined the cliff, and he could not see into the cave. At the opposite end of the curved wall there appeared to be another four-foot-high, two-foot-wide tunnel. Ominously, the bones lying on the ground were mostly in the area between his tunnel and the large cave. There was a pervasive smell of animal excrement and rotting meat in the air.

Johnny cautiously considered the situation from within the apparent safety of his tunnel for a while. A breeze stirred and swirled the air around the enclosure. A moment later a deep growl emanated from the cave, followed by the sound of something large moving. Soon a massive bear standing seven feet tall at the shoulder came out of the cave, sniffing the air. This was no normal bear. Besides its massive size the bear also seemed to have, metallic armor plating embedded into its skin such that its red-brown fur only peeked out in a few places. Even its snout and forehead were armored.

The bear looked in his direction and then with frightening speed charged directly at him. Johnny immediately retreated back into the tunnel, only barely quick enough to avoid the swiping paw that the bear shoved into the tunnel reaching for him with long, sharp claws. The bear retracted its foreleg, stuck its head into the tunnel, and roared, but Johnny was already back in the larger tunnel by then.

"Let's see where else this tunnel leads. That doesn't seem like a good option," Johnny said to himself. He straightened his coat, his pack and the pouches on his belt before proceeding. The tunnel turned and twisted without branching for a while until he found himself back at the entrance where the wall now read, "Death awaits. Leave now."

Outside the maze, the sky was blue with fluffy clouds, and the angle of the sun meant it was just before noon. It was tempting to just return to the forest where the trees swayed softly in a spring breeze. He could hear bird calls.

Johnny sighed and then worked his way back to the bear's lair. Again peering out he said to himself, "Morphosius must be testing me." Though he didn't say it loudly, the bear evidently had good hearing and came charging out of the cave again, forcing Johnny to escape back into the maze.

Johnny noticed that the bear's shoulder had left a slight bloody mark on the wall this time. For several hours, Johnny baited the bear repeatedly. After the seventh or eighth time, the bear was slower to respond and didn't bother to stick its paw in the tunnel. Clearly the bear was getting tired. Johnny smiled and kept it up until he finally sat silently in the tunnel for over a half hour with no response, even if he uttered a word or tossed a stone. While he sat there, he studied the stone cliff that contained the bear's cave. It was rough with many outcroppings.

Then Johnny crept silently to the rough wall left of the bear's cave and began scaling it. About twenty feet up he began traversing across the cliff face. He was almost directly over the bear's cave resting on a small ledge about fifteen feet up when the bear ambled out of the cave. It sniffed the air several times, made a deep "huff" sound, and stared at the tunnel where Johnny had been appearing. After a few moments, it went back into its cave.

It took several minutes for Johnny's heart rate to stabilize. If the bear had looked up, it might have been able to reach him. His hands were threatening to start shaking from adrenaline, and climbing in that state could drop him right in front of the cave. Eventually, Johnny calmed himself and continued safely to the opposite side of the bear's cave. After climbing down, he left the wall and silently stalked his way to the other tunnel. Just as he crossed into the safety of the tunnel, a siren sounded for two seconds. The bear must have been rested by now, because it rushed out of the cave and spotted him. Again, it ran at him, and he was forced to retreat up the tunnel in haste. He was past the bear, but it seemed this tunnel was alarmed. There would be no going back.

After catching his breath, Johnny looked around and found that the tunnel widened out to the six-foot width and height almost immediately. It turned left fifty feet ahead of him. Cautiously, he followed the tunnel and peered around the corner. What he saw was apparently an exit from the maze, a doorway similar to the one he entered.

"More of a bear-trap than a maze," Johnny scoffed. "But it does seem designed to encourage people to just go away," he noted.

5.3 Council

Seagulls floated in the cool breeze above the small seaside town. The wind was rarely warm and never hot in the northern waters of the western ocean, even at this season. When they did come, warm winds typically presaged a major storm in this part of the ocean. Today, the sky was clear, and winds foretold calm weather ahead. The town was not very large and had the usual compliment of fishing boats and associated docks, but it was not a typical seaside town. Besides fishing docks, there was also a long dock suitable for larger ships.

Two ships were docked, one on either side. One was a large broad ship with three masts made for large, square sails. It was clearly a warship with a forward-facing, deck-mounted catapult and three ballistas on each side. The ship on the opposite side of the dock was almost as long but slimmer with only two masts bearing triangular green sails with a white eagle emblem. It had a somewhat larger swivel-mounted ballista fore and aft but no catapults. The larger, heavily armed ship was typical of the Greelin Navy, while the slimmer, faster ship was the mainstay of the Talingor Imperial Navy. In the harbor, another Greelin warship and two more Talingor schooners were anchored. Not coincidentally, the distance between the two groups was greater than the range of either type of weapon, but both had the dock well within range.

The presence of a long dock and naval contingents from two opposing nations was certainly unusual, but the thing that really made the town so unique was on the land, not the sea. A single well-traveled road led inland and up a hill from the town for about a half mile. This road ended at a large, walled complex containing several buildings and five towers. The wall around the complex was solid white marble appearing to be made from continuous solid stone with no joints or mortar. There was only one gate in or out, where the road reached the complex. The largest and most elegant central tower matched the outer wall both in terms of material and style, whereas the others all had their own unique styles, yet somehow none looked out of place. This complex was the Academy of Wizardry, the only place in all the realms where wizards gathered and where students could be taught.

Inside the largest tower, the Wizards' High Council was convening to consider the petitions from their two visitors. The council chamber was not overly large and somewhat stuffy, but no petitioner to the council ever failed to be awed. The entrance led down a gently sloping aisle with seating for two dozen on either side. The central aisle ended at a small lectern slightly ahead of the seating from which a petitioner could address the council. Opposite the lectern and the audience seating were eight ornate chairs that were only marginally less than thrones. Each of these chairs had distinctive decoration and symbols, and no two were the same color. Seven of these chairs were spread evenly along the first level, one for the head of each magical discipline and then above those in the center was the seat of the Archmage. This was the ruling seat of the ultimate worldwide leader of all the wizards.

Today, half a dozen men were seated on the right side of the audience. They all had short hair and beards that were carefully cropped and oiled to a perfectly uniform point. They were wearing official-looking green sashes over thicker medium-gray woolen jackets and charcoal-gray pants. On the left side sat two men and one woman, all wearing chain-link armor, decorated metal leg and arm greaves, and blue tabards bearing a stylized yellow emblem of a lion. Their hair was long, but the men were clean-shaven with tanned leathery skin typical of experienced sea captains.

The woman also had an experienced military air about her and gold-leafed engravings on her greaves. Neither group spared a glance for the other, but both were attentive as the wizards entered via doors behind each of their seats. All the wizards who entered were imposing Masters or Adepts of their crafts in their own right, but attention naturally gravitated to the Archmage as the central figure.

The Archmage carried a golden staff with a crystal hourglass at the top, and wore pure-white robes with four rows of golden symbols at the hems. He also wore a long white cape, a large golden ring on his right ring finger, and an ornate shoulder mantle embroidered with golden thread. He was an elderly man with long white hair, a long white beard and light-brown eyes. His default expression seemed to be a knowing half smile, and his gaze gave the unnerving impression he already knew what you were about to say.

After all the wizards were seated and a brief pause to survey the assembled petitioners, the Archmage spoke, "Commander-General Farra, Senior Finance Minister Al'Tyne, it's nice to see you each again and nice that the two of you have arrived at similar times so that we are able to attend both of your petitions in a single session. Also, it's particularly nice that you saw fit to maintain the wizards' peace in our harbor, and I doubt I really need to remind either of you that you must be a day's sail away before engaging in any 'aggressive' negotiations." At this the Archmage raised his bushy white eyebrows and glanced at each side of the room.

Commander Farra on the left nodded her head in acquiescence, and Minister Al'Tyne on the right replied, "Of course, Grand Master Aurcivius, of course."

"Excellent, since you've both been here before, and there have been no changes on the council side, we can dispense with the formal introductions and all that tedium and get straight to business. I'll trust that you've properly briefed your compatriots." Aurcivius paused briefly for affirmation from both parties. "Ok, so it seems that the Talingor delegation has concerns regarding transmutation of silver coins into gold, and Greelin suspects a rogue Mage is aiding pirates. I take it as a sign of progress that your petitions are unrelated this time. The Talingor matter should prove quickest, I expect. We'll start there. Minister Al'Tyne, you may go first."

The eldest of the Talingor delegation, a man in his mid-forties with streaks of gray in his beard and a small bald spot beginning at the top of his head, rose and approached the lectern.

"Thank you, Aurcivius, Archmage of the Wizards Council and Grand Master of Chronomancy. As you say, this matter should be relatively simple. As you certainly must be well aware, there is a wizard living on the outskirts of the empire near the border between our eastern hills and the Skull Sands desert to the south. His name is..." Minister Al'Tyne looked down at his notes at this point, but this was clearly just an excuse for a dramatic pause. "Pulmonan."

"Certainly we are aware of him. He graduated a little over a decade ago. He focused on shapeshifting, and as I recall he took particular interest in spiders and scorpions. He's a bit creepy but harmless, and he has a good reason to live where he does, since it provides him with many examples of his favorite forms," Aurcivius confirmed.

"Yes, that's him, and shapeshifting is a mutamantic talent. We have noticed a shift in the economy of the southern towns in that area. It seems that there are an increased number of gold coins being used to purchase luxury goods from costal cities. These goods are then shipped into his area. Our tax officials keep very meticulous records, and we know for certain that something has

166

changed. The ratio of gold coins to silver coins is most skewed in the towns that Pulmonan is known to frequent." Minister Al'Tyne paused again for dramatic effect. "Alchemical transmutation of silver into gold is mutamantic magic, is it not?"

"So you're worried that Pulmonan is spending gold he didn't earn?" Aurcivius asked with a slightly disdainful lilt.

"Precisely. We believe he is spending gold that he produced via transmutation. This is forbidden by council rule, as I understand it. Creating gold from other materials is disruptive to economies and interferes with the authority of government."

"Ah... well, yes, it *is* technically forbidden, but it's a rule we barely have to write in the first place. I think I'll let Morphosius, our Grand Master of Mutamancy explain why you should be looking elsewhere for the source of the gold coins." Aurcivius gestured to his right, and the wizard at the far end of the lower row nodded. Several other wizards began to look bored or irritated but remained silent.

Morphosius's garb was similar to Aurcivius's but brown with red embroidery, and his staff, now resting on a holder beside his seat, was black and topped with the head of a snake with crystal eyes. The form of the snake head was flattened and flared out similar to a venomous variety found abundantly in the jungles east of Greel city along the southern coast. Morphosius cleared his throat and leaned forward.

"It seems you've wasted several days by sailing out to ask us about this matter, Minister Al'Tyne. I know Talingor's capital has an extensive library, and there are several Mages, Magicians and Wizards retained by the crown and various Talingor nobility. Either the library or any of these wizards could have filled you in on the basic reasons why what you fear is not possible." Morphosius stared straight at the Minister for several seconds. "You are aware that I'm currently the most powerful Mutamancer in the world, right?"

Clearly uncomfortable and embarrassed, Minister Al'Tyne replied simply, "Yes."

"And the coat you wear is magically enhanced to repel all forms of weather, a sign of your position with the Talingor government?"

"Yes."

"Are you aware that I sold those coats to your government? That they were made in my tower?"

"Yes. I had heard that, actually."

"Why do you think I bother putting spells on coats instead of simply exchanging gold for silver and then turning the silver into gold?"

Minister Al'Tyne paused, frowned, and replied, "Because it's prohibited?"

"There is literally no one on the council here who is stronger than I, not even the Archmage, and all of us are the strongest of our fields. Don't you think I couldn't get away with it?"

"Probably, I guess."

"I'll tell you why I don't do it. It's something that every student learns in their very first class on Mutamancy. It is very hard to increase the density of an object. You know what density means?"

"Yes."

"If I put my mind to it, I could turn silver into gold. To cast this spell I would first need to grind one gold coin to fine gold dust, then I would need to heat the silver of two silver coins to melting. While keeping the silver molten, I would then need to spend two entire days slowly adding the gold dust to the molten silver while continuously casting one of the most difficult transmutation spells. After two days of continuous casting and no sleep, I could in fact end up with two pure gold coins, a net gain of eight silver, except it takes a lot of charcoal to keep silver molten for forty-eight hours. I would likely spend three silver worth of charcoal keeping the metal molten, and I'd be exhausted. I probably would need to wait two or three days to try again. So I would earn about one or two silver per day. And for that meager salary, I would also likely die an early death from breathing fumes from the molten metal."

"So it can be done then..."

"Yes, it can, but in the same amount of time, and with a normal sleep schedule, I can rain-repel four coats that sell for a gold piece each. The materials and coat used for that process cost about one silver piece coincidentally. The net profit would be thirty-six silver every day. Only a fool would try to make gold via transmutation for profit. And don't forget the example I gave is for me, a Master of Mutamancy. Anyone with less talent will take much longer, and there are limits to how long anyone can go without sleep, not to mention they will spend more money on charcoal and certainly operate at a net loss."

"I see. One last question. Just for the record, how strong is Pulmonan?"

"Pulmonan progressed from Mage to Magician quickly, but was stuck at Magician rank for a decade after graduation. He has only recently attained the rank of Wizard and has zero hope of progressing to Adept or Master rank. He's reached the maximum capability of his talents. This means it would take him roughly two hundred days to do what I can do in two days. His interest in shapeshifting is somewhat tragic, since it will likely take him most of his natural lifetime to get good enough at a single form to do it quickly. Given his personality, we consider him at risk of exceeding his privileges and setting up a workshop.

"Workshops to facilitate the development of new spells or refinement of existing spells are a privilege reserved for Adepts. Lower ranks attempting such things are mostly a hazard to themselves and their surroundings, so I drop in on him from time to time. I can assure you that there is zero risk of him transmuting silver, or anything else, into gold. After this session, I'll give you list of items your tax officials should worry about for him."

"I understand. My apologies for wasting your time. Talingor will, of course, be happy to assist."

Morphosius nodded solemnly and sat back in his chair. The delegation from Greelin were staring forward, not looking across the aisle in a way that clearly said that they were trying hard not to laugh, and the Talingor delegation was trying hard not to look embarrassed, but several of them were not succeeding very well.

Aurcivius spoke again, "Thank you, Morphosius. Minister Al'Tyne, I see no reason that you or your compatriots need to remain—"

A piercing, loud siren-like sound emanating from Morphosius's direction interrupted the Archmage for about two seconds, startling everyone except Aurcivius, who then said, "Ah, there it is..."

Morphosius then interrupted, "I'm sorry. I must depart. There appears to be a disturbance at my tower that I must investigate immediately."

"I foresaw this, so I asked that the teleportation room be kept clear for you. You are of course excused immediately," Aurcivius said, despite the fact that Morphosius hadn't yet actually asked to be excused.

Irritated, Morphosius asked, "I don't suppose you want to tell me what I'm facing?"

Glancing at the assembled delegations, Aurcivius said, "No, I don't think that would be wise, but I will say that your primary enemy today will be your own temper."

"Thanks," Morphosius said tersely, grabbing his staff and exiting via the door behind his chair.

Aurcivius's knowing half grin seemed slightly more apparent for a second, and then he resumed the session, "Anyway, as I was saying..."

5.4 Morphosius

After waiting and resting for a while to observe anything that might be outside the doorway, Johnny finally crept silently out. There was no text or warning associated with this door, and he found it opened out onto a thirty-foot-wide road made from granite paving stones just like the entrance, also set between walls of a ravine and leading down into a larger open area. Across the open area, Johnny could finally see the tower that should be his destination. It was a massive structure about two hundred feet across at the base and rising as a truncated cone to over one hundred and fifty feet in height. The sight was staggering. Johnny had never even imagined a building of this size. There was a thirty-foot wall around it, evidently enclosing a courtyard off to the left. A large opening near the top of the tower looked like some sort of entrance, but there were no stairs up to it.

The high entrance however was not his most immediate problem. The tower and its courtyard sat on an island of sorts down in the center of a perfectly circular, flat-bottomed basin. The floor of the basin appeared to be made from polished stone. To get to the tower Johnny would need to cross five hundred yards of this surface. Across the stone surface rippled irregularly spaced waves of stone. These waves moved across the polished surface as if the stone were liquid. The waves were not normal waves. Instead of being round on the top, the top edge of the wave projected three to four-foot-high needle-like swords of stone. The stone needles shot up suddenly and without warning as the wave moved with no obvious pattern beyond their association with the waves. When a wave passed nearby, the appearance of the stone needles made a *fttt* sound similar to an arrow passing too close. One would definitely not want to be out on that surface when a wave came by.

When Johnny tossed a rock out onto the stone lake, it bounced just as one would expect of a flat, non-liquid stone surface. When next wave arrived, one of the stone needles shattered the rock into gravel. The waves emanated from the tower outward. There was no safe way across this surface.

Johnny swore softly, "What is the point of inviting me and giving me a pendant when there's nobody for me to show it to?" He turned to leave, but then he remembered that he would have to pass the bear. The sky above was growing pink, and the sun was setting. He fished the amulet out from under his coat, pulled it over his head, and was about to throw it at the tower, but before he could do that he heard a strange sound behind him. He turned and saw that the maze from which he had just exited was transforming. The wall with the exit and the entire maze seemed to melt to the ground, leaving a thirty-foot-wide road straight out to the ravine where he came in. He could see the cliff with the bear's cave off to the right, but there was still a substantial amount of wall surrounding it, keeping the bear contained.

Staring at the amulet, he had the faint impression it was emitting some sort of light or other energy. He tucked it back inside his shirt, and immediately the maze entrance returned.

"I'm an idiot," Johnny sighed and then shuddered, realizing he had risked his life with the bear for absolutely no reason. He took the amulet out again and turned back to the lake of stone. As he walked back toward it, he found that the waves now dissipated when they got within fifty feet of him. A little experimentation showed that shadows mattered, but if he held the amulet up high over his head, he was safe from the waves on all sides.

After testing the surface carefully, Johnny walked out onto the lake, nervously watching the waves, but so long as he held the amulet high the waves of stone needles never came near him. Soon, he had reached the wall around the tower and began to walk around to the left. The sun was almost done setting, painting the top of the tower and the clouds above with a red glow. And a crescent moon was now visible above the western horizon.

As he rounded the left side, he came to a large stone arch that looked like a gate but was filled with solid stone. He waved the amulet at the gate, but nothing happened. He tried again, still nothing. Frustrated, he tried pressing the amulet on the stone. Still nothing. Out of patience, Johnny muttered something extremely impolite regarding the sexual habits of wizards.

The stone filling the archway melted away with almost frightening speed. Just inside the arch was a figure. The figure wore a dark-brown velvet robe with a hood, which was pulled up so that the face could not be seen. The edges of the sleeves and the hood had a coppery satin border embroidered with four rows of red spidery symbols that glowed faintly as if written in molten metal.

"Care to repeat that?" said the figure in a dangerous voice.

"Ah, no. Sorry. It's been a stressful day. I was just frustrated. I apologize. I'm here to accept your invitation to become an apprentice."

The figure responded by removing his hood and fixing Johnny with a baleful stare. The hood revealed the face of a handsome man perhaps fifty years old with a finely styled close-cropped beard. His hair was jet black except for a distinct graying at his temples and some scattered gray in his beard. His hair was parted to one side and made a wave across his forehead. His visage radiated power, authority, and refinement. It was hard not to envy him, just for his appearance.

"Sorry, I thought you were Morphosius"

The figure's steely gray eyes looked up and to the right and then rolled across to the left in an expression of resigned patience. Then suddenly the face melted, transforming within the space of two seconds. Now the figure had a completely bald head, a beak-like nose, big ears that stuck straight out, and a small, pointed beard. His height was also reduced by several inches. Immediately the face transformed back to the regal commanding visage.

"Oh," Johnny said, feeling stupid.

After regaining his original form, Morphosius continued in a stern and demanding voice, "What on earth makes you think you are still invited?"

"You didn't specify how soon I had to accept..." Johnny replied, his voice trailing into a slightly complaining tone.

Morphosius stared daggers at him, eyes drilling into Johnny as if increasingly angry. "It has *nothing* to do with your timing," he said in a tightly controlled voice over emphasizing the word "nothing" viciously.

"Uh... I don't understand. You are upset, but I don't know why. I certainly didn't mean to upset you... Sorry."

"*First,* you show up apparently without your amulet, triggering the alarm in the maze and forcing me to return from a session of the Wizards' Council. *Second,* you injured my bear by baiting it repeatedly. Who knows what it's going to cost me to heal that thing after what you did? *Then* after harming my bear, you put on the most stunning possible display of either stupidity or thrill seeking wherein you decided to traverse the bear pit and find a way across. *That* means I need to go redesign the damn thing. *Then* you pull out the amulet that would have saved you all that effort and saved the time of everyone in this tower who was wasting time watching you for hours instead of doing work. *Finally,* you saunter across my stone lake to stand in front of my gate accusing me of providing sexual favors for various animals and close relatives.

"How could I *possibly* want an apprentice that doesn't follow instructions damages my property, wastes my time, and insults me?"

Johnny listened to this in shocked silence. After a moment he said, "I left my parents' house with the amulet hidden so that nobody would see it and wonder where I got such a precious piece of jewelry. I didn't think I wanted to answer questions about it or where I got it. You told me to show it, and I fully intended to show it to the first guard I met so that they would let me into your tower. I only took it out because I was going to throw it at you. You could have told me I was meant to show it to a stupid wall, not a person. I risked my life to become your apprentice. I'm tired and frustrated, and I already apologized about my inappropriate words at your gate. If you don't want me, fine. I'll leave."

The figure regarded him for a while and then let out an explosive sigh. "I'll accept your explanation this time, but if this sort of thing becomes a regular pattern you're finished."

"Thank you," Johnny said simply.

"In the world of wizards, a person's true name can give opponents a measure of power over that person. You must not use your true name ever from this day forward. Although I'm sorely tempted to give you the Mage name Dumbassius, I'll stick with the one I had prepared. From this day forward, you must use the name Sinprejic. You are now Sinprejic of the tower of Morphosius."

"Sinprejic," Johnny repeated, and smiled. "I like it. It seems to be a portmanteau of Elvish and common speech implying a lack of prejudice. Do you speak Elvish too?"

"Not as well as you. It's good to see you understand your name so quickly. Follow me."

Morphosius turned and led Sinprejic into the tower.

5.5 Tower

The main entry of the tower was a pair of enormous doors that were more than twice his height and wider than a hay wagon. Sinprejic looked up at the monstrous building. It seemed to shimmer in places despite the fading light. As Morphosius approached, he walked through what seemed to be a very faint cobweb. The doors suddenly shimmered and started to open all by themselves.

"Wow," breathed Sinprejic as the doors revealed an interior space that was thirty feet high, and fifty feet on each side. There was a similar set of doors on the far side of the entry. The entry was grand in scale but otherwise plain and seemed like it was rarely used.

"My secrets guard themselves... the doors in this tower open only for people who are meant to use them. If a door is not opening easily, you are not permitted to pass through it. If you try to force any doors, they have built in defenses, and some of them are very dangerous." As he said this, Morphosius's voice echoed in the nearly bare entry room.

"How do I know which ones are dangerous?" Sinprejic said while looking around, distracted by the echo.

"You won't know."

"Ah, I see."

They passed through the second set of doors and came to a space that was just as wide and much longer, but most of it was not visible due to the presence of a large, wide stone column that likely represented the tower's central support. They turned right toward a normal-sized door. Just before they passed through it, a very large hall with a long feast table and a raised platform with a large throne became visible beyond the central column.

The small door opened into a less grandiose and more functional area. This room had a wall to the left, and to the right was a large cistern full of water. The ceilings here were still thirty feet tall, but after about a dozen feet on the left the wall opened into a smaller hallway. They turned into this hallway where the wall to the left radiated coldness. Somewhere along the way into the tower, the script around the hems of Morphosius's robes had ceased its fiery glow. Now the characters were embroidered in a dark red that was much less noticeable against the chocolate brown of his robes.

"Can I ask a question?" Sinprejic said suddenly.

Morphosius stopped, turned, and glared at him. "Go ahead..."

"Something confuses me. The maze isn't much of a maze unless I missed something. Did I miss a path that avoids the bear? I didn't think about the fact you have to care for it. I feel a little bad about hurting it now," Sinprejic said.

Morphosius glared for a moment more and then sighed before answering. "It's not supposed to be a real maze. It says maze on the outside to scare people off. The hope is that the fear of getting lost will convince the more intelligent would-be trespassers to go away. The last thing I want is the liability of someone wandering around outside my tower for who knows how long, or worse yet taking up residence in some corner of it. I especially don't want someone to be there long enough that their friends or relatives wind up petitioning me to dig them out and return them safely. So far, to my knowledge, thirty people have approached my tower. The smartest twenty of them read the signs and left. Ten of them entered. The seven smartest of those left after they saw the bear. Two were so dumb as to stroll into the bear pit without any caution. They paid for their cavalier attitude."

"That's only twenty-nine... oh. I'm number thirty?"

There was an awkward pause and finally Morphosius said, "Yes." He turned abruptly and continued leading Sinprejic down the hallway.

At the end of the short hall, there was another door, and this opened into an enormous but warm kitchen. There were stoves at the far end, shelves with glass windows holding dishes along the right side, and pots, pans, and cooking implements along the left wall. In the middle sat a pair of long tables each with attached benches on either side. Three people sat at these tables eating their evening meal.

On the table on the left, by herself, was a woman also in dark-brown velvet robes. Hers were a darker brown than Morphosius's and bore stitched runes in only three rows, not four like Morphosius. Her hair was steel gray and tied in two small tight buns atop either side of her head. While such a style might have looked girlish, the buns were so tight as to look severe and harsh. Her face, likely of average beauty in her youth, had suffered the severe ravages of middle age. The plumpness of her face and the curve of her eyebrows along with a small hooked nose above a tiny mouth suggested a fierce owl, though her eyes were small, cold, green agates, not large and yellow. She regarded Sinprejic as if he were a distasteful morsel spoiling her appetite. Nearby, in a rack clearly made for the purpose, sat a tall, dark wooden staff. The dark wood was grayish in appearance, and the staff was topped by an owl's head with yellow agate eyes and a perfectly round globe of milky white crystal that appeared to be a moon just above the owl's head.

Two men sat at the right-hand table. On the inner bench was a swarthy man with salt and pepper tightly curled hair and an easy simile that sat comfortably on his thick but not overweight features. He wore a plain, off-white cotton long-sleeve shirt with the sleeves rolled up and ordinary cloth breeches, along with a silky brown cape with three rows of embroidered script along the hem, similar to the woman's robes. He also had a staff at hand that appeared as if it were carved from marble and was topped by the upper body of a man, regarding an upheld multi-faceted crystal.

On the far right sat a fair-skinned, handsome man with blond shoulder-length hair. His features were good-looking but somewhat compromised by a longish face. He also smiled but in a more poised and careful manner. His shirt was pure white, and his tight breeches were bright blue. Nearby sat what appeared to be a four and a half foot tall paintbrush with a ring of multicolored gems around the handle near the bristles at the top.

The man in the white shirt stood up and bowed a formal graceful bow to Sinprejic, saying, "Welcome, my name is Imoed, Wizard of Mutamancy, and you are?"

"Sinprejic," Morphosius answered quickly before Sinprejic could respond.

Imoed smiled, unabashed. "Nice to meet you, Sinprejic!" he said. "My friend here is called Jalsus. I'm the artist around here, and Jalsus... well, he's an artist too, but he focuses on shaping things, whereas I make them colorful and beautiful."

Jalsus responded playfully, "I make things that work, he... well, he just gets paint all over things." He didn't sound the least bit offended.

"Too true," Imoed agreed with a smile. Then glancing at the woman at the other table, he said, "Ah and don't mind Mutara. She's just mad because you didn't manage to feed Boo Boo, and now she's going to have to do it after all. Actually, do mind what she says because she's more or less in charge of anything Morphosius doesn't care about. Morphosius here, he mostly just cares about teaching, studying in his chambers, and oh yeah... our profits."

"Boo Boo?" Sinprejic asked.

"We call the bear Boo Boo," Imoed replied.

"Actually you're the *only one* who calls the bear Boo Boo," Mutara noted acerbically. Then to Morphosius more deferentially, "You'll find your meal on a tray outside your study as usual."

"Thank you, Mutara. I'll let you get Sinprejic settled after he has something to eat." And then he waved his staff and disappeared instantaneously much as he had on the road a week ago.

Mutara looked at Sinprejic and said, "Stew is on the stove, bread in the larder, and bowls in the cupboards. When you're done, wash your own dishes, and I'll show you to your room." After that, she went back to eating her meal.

"The larder is huge. I'll show you where the bread is. Then you can grab some of the stew I made. It's bear stew, in your honor, though they wouldn't let me cook Boo Boo for you," Imoed said.

"You'll find that *bear* stew tastes suspiciously similar to venison stew," Jalsus said.

"Fine, spoil my fun," Imoed complained lightheartedly.

"That's my job," Jalsus said with a straight face.

"Thanks," Sinprejic said to Imoed. After they found some bread and Sinprejic had fetched himself a bowl of stew, he sat down next to Imoed and across from Jalsus. After tasting his stew he said, "This is quite good."

"Thank you, I don't actually confine my art to coloring things. Everything one does is an expression of one's inner self," Imoed said with a significant glance at Jalsus.

"I think he's trying to say that his inner self is quite tasty, though I'm not sure why he wants us all to know that," Jalsus said between bites of stew, a slight smile creeping onto his face.

Unfazed, Imoed continued, "Whatever you do, don't eat anything Mutara cooked. She's the only cook I ever met who burns water."

Mutara exhaled audibly but didn't respond or look up.

"I heard Morphosius say you know how to speak Elvish," Jalsus said interestedly.

"Yes. Um... how did you hear that?"

"Mutara has a small crystal sphere that Morphosius gave her that can scry on almost any part of this tower or the nearby lands. You gave us quite the holiday as we sat around watching your antics with the bear."

"I guess we had to be ready to defend the tower against your unstoppable assault," Imoed added with a laugh.

Mutara spared a sour look for the pair of them. Clearly she

would have preferred that this spying device not be revealed so soon.

"Pretty unusual for a young man around these parts to know Elvish," Jalsus continued, ignoring Imoed for the moment.

"Yes, well, I accidentally met an elf in the forest. It turns out that elves are not the fierce killers that people in my town think they are."

"Heh, no... No, they're not, despite the craziness that your baron inflicts on them. But it's a bit surprising that you got an elf to teach you their language. What did you trade to him?"

"I helped her learn common speech mostly. I think it was mostly a matter of making it easier for us to communicate really."

Jalsus's eyebrows shot up as soon as Sinprejic said the word "her". Mutara looked up, rolled her eyes, and let out a *tsk* sound, but she was now paying attention.

Imoed broke out in a big grin. "Ooooh... he helped her with her... speech. Yes, I'm sure it was mostly about her... uh... language skills."

Sinprejic began to blush and sipped his water, trying to think of how to change the topic. "Really, we mostly just talk or play stones or relax while listening to the forest," Sinprejic said defensively.

"Imoed's just jealous," Jalsus said. "He doesn't get out of the tower enough, and when he does the only place close is your little town."

Imoed nodded. "And it's a serious chore to avoid making fun of folks there. Can't talk to the women either. They're just as crazy as the men. They think their town is a big deal, but it's about the most boring place ever," Imoed complained

"Since when are you interested in talking to women?" Mutara quipped acerbically.

"Hey, I *do* like to talk too."

"You? Talk? Who would have guessed?" Jalsus said with a big grin.

"Hah. Ok, I set myself up for that, didn't I?" Imoed laughed. "Just trying to make Sinprejic here feel welcome. The two of you are dreary serious."

"So you already know how to play wizard stones?" Jalsus asked.

"Yeah, my mother taught me, though nobody calls it wizard stones. It's just stones to people in town. I also learned a lot from Master Percy."

Jalsus smiled. "We should play some time," he said.

Mutara spoke up, suddenly, "Percy the book binder? You called him master. Were you his apprentice?"

"Yes, until recently," Sinprejic said carefully, beginning to realize that he was inadvertently leaking lots of information about himself. He hoped they would think he quit to become an apprentice here.

"Ooops, now you've done it. She'll assign you all the book work," Imoed whispered.

"There's plenty of stuff he won't be allowed to see yet," Mutara said. "But maybe he'll be more competent than *you*."

"So how does a book binder's apprentice wind up with such a fine steel sword and carrying a bow, yet able to sneak so quietly that Boo Boo lets them by? By the way, that was seriously impressive. Boo Boo has magically enhanced hearing," noted Imoed.

Sinprejic paused, not wanting to identify his family. He suddenly worried that Mutara or either of the others might ferret out his true name based on the fact he was Master Percy's apprentice. Eventually, he simply said, "I wasn't always a book binder's apprentice."

Jalsus smiled. "Good answer. We really shouldn't ask such details, lest you ask us about our history," Jalsus said with significant glances at the other two, who each responded with a nod. With that they left him alone and gave him a chance to eat.

"I see you've finished your stew. Wash your dishes and put them in the rack over there to dry," Mutara said somewhat later.

Sinprejic did so and then followed Mutara through the large feast hall and into a door at the far side of it. This door opened into a room of similar size to the cistern room but with a solid stone floor. Against the wall to the left and to the right were two wooden structures built two stories high with room to spare in the high-ceilinged space. These provided four rooms each side, two top and two bottom. There was a stair leading up to the second level at the far end of each structure. Sinprejic's room was the one on the upper right side nearest the feast hall. All the others were empty, and the doors propped open.

At the base of the stairs up to the second level stood Morphosius, evidently waiting for him.

"This is the first of many books you will be reading. The sooner you memorized it, the better. We need to get some basic knowledge in your head before we can teach you actual magic. The doors on the first floor of the tower, except the door to the cellar at the back of the kitchen, should all open for you now. Also, the door to the main library on the third floor will be safe. I'll expect to find you in the library reading this tomorrow morning. Don't touch anything in the workshop on the second floor. All of that stuff is for clients, and you must not delay our work for them. Also, don't touch any books in the library yet. Each shelf has a protective spell to keep students like you from attempting stuff they are not ready for yet. You will be granted expanded access as you progress."

"Understood," Sinprejic said simply.

Morphosius nodded and then walked with Mutara back toward the feast hall, leaving Sinprejic to ascend to his room on his own. It looked like Morphosius wanted to talk to Mutara about something, but not with him around.

5.6 Primer

Johnny opened the door to his room, entered, and shut the door behind himself. He sighed and tossed the tome that Master Morphosius had given him onto his bed. It bounced, landing on one corner, and the pages slid sideways against each other. The binding contorted, and the book came to rest with the pages partly exposed. Alarmed, Johnny rushed over and inspected the binding. Luckily, the book was well bound and unharmed. He softly scolded himself for his carelessness. He straightened the book, lifted it off the bed and set it carefully on the small wooden desk instead. He sat down on the bed facing the desk and sighed again.

He stared morosely at the stupendously thick tome on the desk for several minutes. In another time or place he would have found it fascinating. If he had run across it at Master Percy's bindery, it would have been read multiple times, much as he had done with the book on elf lore. At this time however, Master Morphosius's command that he should not only read it but memorize it made the task of reading such a large book seem like an odious chore. The fact that deep down he didn't actually want to be a wizard also didn't help matters.

As he considered the magnitude of the task assigned to him, he realized that there was an upside to its thickness. He was required to demonstrate an in-depth, detailed memory of its contents before he would be allowed to proceed with the actual study of magic. Taking his time completing the study of this mundane topic seemed like and an excellent way to avoid actually becoming a wizard.

Feigning slow comprehension was a dangerous game, however. If he was too convincing, Master Morphosius would catch on or worse yet, decide he was hopeless and put Johnny back out on the road. Then he would have nowhere to go. He would be forced to go back to his parents and would have the additional trouble of having to explain where he'd been. "Studying with the Wizard of the North" was no better answer to explain a disappearance than "kissing an elf." Johnny had no idea how he would get out of this apprenticeship, but getting tossed out before he had an alternate plan seemed like a bad idea. For now, he would do his best to show no more than adequate progress.

With that plan in mind, he stood up and then sat down at the desk. The chair was plain wood, short backed, and had no cushions. It creaked and flexed when he shifted his weight. Once he was reasonably comfortably seated, he carefully opened the thick tome in front of him. The title page read, "Common and Notable Spells: A primer on the history and use of magic." The authorship was attributed to "Aurcivius Aurelius, Archmage of the Council of Wizards, Grand Master of Time." Johnny pondered what that might mean. Aurcivius was clearly a name, but he had no idea what Grand Master of Time denoted and only a vague obvious guess at what the Wizards' Council might be. One thing was obvious. This was an officially sanctioned textbook for entry-level students.

He turned the page and began to read. The first chapter explained that the present year was not 922 but in fact properly denoted as 20922. Magic had been around and used by all the humanoid races longer than any available recorded history, but the present era and the available history began around 13400. That was the point at which the humanoid races began to throw back the demon Natasha's dark empire. The present day Academy of Wizardry was founded on a remote northern Isle in 13453, shortly after a disastrous earthquake and subsequent massive tidal wave threw Natasha's demonic forces into disarray across much of the western coastline.

Little was known about the time before the reign of Natasha. Only a few artifacts of power and the names and contradictory myths of two legendary wizards were mentioned in the book.

Jackle the trickster, who was also supremely talented at creating magical artifacts, and Lichesis, a figure whose various myths place him as everything from the poor sod who inadvertently unleashed Natasha to the true controlling power behind the demon armies and Natasha's five-hundred-year reign of terror. All the myths agree that he was either very evil or ultimately responsible for unleashing great evil.

As Johnny read through the tome, he found himself drawn in. It was so different from anything he knew from his life in a small border town that it seemed more like fiction than reality. There was a part of him that seemed to be drinking this information in. It was like he had only just realized he was thirsty after being handed a cup of water.

Besides history, the book contained a lot of information about how the wizards were ranked and how students progressed through the Academy. The most shocking bit was when he read that he wouldn't be considered an apprentice until he demonstrated some magical ability. Until then, he was only a "pledge," but even so he was not allowed to switch masters, and if he wanted to quit he had to undergo something called "binding," which would prevent him from being able to cast any spells.

The final section of the book contained a long list of spells from each of the various disciplines of wizardry. There were apparently eight types of magic. Mutamancy, Conjuration, Ergomancy, Chronomancy, Illusion, Enchantment, and Necromancy. These areas apparently dealt with matter, planes, energy, time, sensory inputs, mind, and souls respectively. There also was something called Metamancy, which was the magic of manipulating magic.

The book seemed to go by in the blink of an eye, and yet when he was finished he was exhausted and entirely unsure of anything other than the fact that he needed to sleep now. He closed the book on his desk, and after a momentary pause he muttered to himself, "No idea what roams at night in a wizard's castle..." Then he checked the latch on the window and the lock on the door and fell into bed.

5.7 Night

The thin crescent of the moon had set soon after the sun, and the midnight forest was only lit by the starless sky shining through the still-bare branches of whirly-seed trees. Half a mile south of the tower, a young buck, skinny and hungry after the long winter, nibbled buds that were beginning to swell with spring leaves beside a small stream in the quiet darkness. As the buck nibbled, its ears twitched and swiveled, listening for predators. Nothing else moved or made a sound nearby.

Suddenly, the buck's head raised, and he snorted in alarm. At that moment the silence was broken by the sound of something dropping into the leaves nearby, and a sudden, ominous black mist appeared fifty feet upstream. The buck froze, standing stock still, not wanting to leave the much-needed nourishment behind but afraid of the sudden sound. The black mist shifted around a central point for about ten seconds and then suddenly and silently struck out, enveloping the young buck before it could react. Instantly, the flesh and skin of the buck shriveled and shrank such that bones underneath became pronounced. The buck collapsed, and the black mist seemed thicker and swirled more quickly as it descended on the hapless animal. By the time the mist moved away, bones protruded from its desiccated pelt in many places. A rustling sound in the leaves near where the mist had appeared began to move toward the black mist and the dead deer.

The source of the rustling sound was a disembodied human hand, walking on its fingers and periodically jumping forward to cover ground faster. The hand was calloused and strong, as if it had once belonged to a dockworker, sailor, or perhaps a blacksmith. It appeared to have been violently hacked off whatever arm it was originally connected to. Just above the wrist, desiccated bone and flesh was visible, but it was dry, and there was no blood.

As the hand reached the mist, the mist calmed and circulated more gently. A portion of the mist swirled down just above the hand and then solidified, becoming a shadow of a graceful female hand. The shadow hand made a series of complex gestures, and the disembodied male hand began to levitate beside the mist. The shadow hand disappeared, and a moment later the mist and the now-floating disembodied hand began to head north toward the tower.

Soon, this unusual pair came to a fifty-foot cliff above a small pool of water. North of the water was about five hundred feet of pure, smooth stone. Across this stone surface waves of sharp stone spikes periodically traveled outward from the island at the center. The mist and hand passed unhindered through a simple spell meant to repel forest animals and began to float down from the cliff and then across the stone lake. The stone spikes varied somewhat in height, but the hand floated several feet higher, and the spikes had no effect on the dark mist. Once at the island in the center of the stone lake, the mist flowed over the outer wall and into the tower grounds with ease, bringing the hand with it.

When they reached the tower, the mist began to extend upward toward a window. It paused at the window then shrank back to the ground. At the next window, it paused longer, and the faint suggestion of a female face flickered in the dark mist. After a moment, the feminine hand coalesced again. After a long series of arcane gestures, the latch on the inside of the window rotated silently. Next, the mist levitated the disembodied male hand up to the small sill outside the window. The window was hinged on the sides and split down the middle. The hand slowly, gently pushed open the window about an inch by extending its index finger. The black mist flowed into the room.

Inside the room, a young man lie sleeping on a bed, and a large book sat on a desk nearby. The young man stirred and began to wake, but the female hand appeared in the mist again, and after a few quick gestures the young man became rigidly still, unmoving, staring straight up at the ceiling. The disembodied male hand then entered via the window and was levitated to the desk via a path that avoided the young man's upward gaze. Quickly but quietly, the male hand moved to the book, opened the cover, then began leafing through the book one page at a time. While the pages were turned, a female face formed in the mist and hovered above the book.

Eventually, the hand stopped turning pages, and the face disappeared. The male hand was levitated to the window again, and the female hand gestured some more. The young man's eyes closed slowly, and he returned to a deep, peaceful sleep. Silently, the hand pulled open the window and held it so that the mist could exit. The mist and the hand left to the south, much as they had come. When they were over the pool of water to the south, in the shadows at the base of the cliff they paused. The female hand coalesced again and made several gestures finally ending in five fingers outstretched, palm toward the male hand. The disembodied male hand suddenly stiffened and became lifeless then dropped into the water with a splash and sank to the bottom. After that, the mist dissipated slowly, leaving no sign of its passage.

5.8 Message

Dread, wrongness, menace... lying on a strange bed. Not his usual bed. Unable to move. The room seemed dark, too dark. Something moving. Need to get up.

A banging noise startled Johnny awake. The first thing he noticed was the smell of fresh air. When he went to bed, the room had an old, musty smell, but now the musty smell was mostly gone. Momentarily he pondered the possibility that the room was enchanted and that his presence had triggered an air-freshening spell. This thought was interrupted by a soft thump, and he looked up to see that the window was swinging in the morning breeze.

Sniffing the air again, he noted that it wasn't entirely fresh. A faint stench of rotting flesh also lingered. A chill went through his spine, and his innards tensed as he remembered his dream. He had definitely checked that the window was secure last night. In fact, he remembered thinking that it seemed as if the window hadn't been opened in years. It could not have come open randomly. Something must have entered his room.

He glanced around his room wildly, checked under the desk and under the bed, but that was the extent of the contents of the room, and there really was nowhere else for anything to hide. After a few moments of checking and double-checking, he had to conclude that there was nothing in his room, or if there was it was invisible. More importantly, he realized that whatever it was could have harmed him already if it wished to do so. Then he noticed the book.

The book he read last night was lying open on the desk. He had shut it before going to bed. Whatever had breached the window also opened the book. It was open to a page somewhere in the middle. What would break into a pledge's room via a window two stories off the ground just to read a book as mundane as this? It had no spells and no secrets, and every wizard who ever lived in the last fifty years was required to memorize its contents anyway.

After a moment of reflection, he got up and closed the window.

190

As soon as he shut the latch, there was a small flicker of some sort. He had the sense that something had been activated and quickly discovered that the latch was as immobile and just as securely fastened as the night before. In fact, he was unable to reopen it. He pulled his hand away as if he might be bitten. Clearly the latch was enchanted with a spell to prevent tampering. Yet it *had* been opened. He recalled reading last night that casting even minor spells created a ripple that an experienced Mage could detect if he were close enough, and a Master could often detect from many yards away.

Wouldn't it take a spell to break a spell? Either this was a test by Morphosius or someone was taking risks casting spells to defeat his window lock. But why?

He didn't see a logical answer. The only thing of possible value in the room was himself, and yet he was unharmed. He had not been spirited away in the night. Or had he? Just as he began down that disturbingly paranoid line of thought he noticed the book again... What if the risk-taker wasn't stealing something from the room, but rather putting something in it? Like what? A message perhaps?

Johnny went over to the desk and looked down at the book. It was open to a page with the tail end of the description of Necromancy, and the description of Metamancy. Much less was known about Metamancy than the other disciplines, so the section was short and fit entirely on the two exposed pages.

> *the Wizards High Council. It is also a common occurrence that Necromancers who raise large armies of undead seem to lose control of them at the height of a large battle and fall victim to their own army. This is often referred to as the curse of the Necromancer, or the doom of the Necromancer.*

Metamancy

Of all the disciplines, the most enigmatic, coveted and feared is that of Metamancy. Metamancers have the ability to alter magic itself. A sufficiently talented or experienced Grandmaster Metamancer can ward off any direct attack, deflecting or even reflecting it back at the caster. They can break existing permanent spells and destroy, modify, or create artifacts of almost any power level.

Meta-magic is crucial for artifact construction, yet because of its combat utility it is also highly feared. The paradox of Metamancy is that every Mage wants other Mages to believe that they might have substantial talent in Metamancy and therefore be a dangerous opponent in battle but at the same time avoid any actual confirmation that would lead to real fear and ostracism.

Since Metamancy is unlike the other disciplines and does not give off a detectable aura of power, it does not contribute to the "feel of power" that a spell caster radiates. Therefore, one must always remember that the feel associated with power is imprecise. There is always the possibility that this feel may be off by plus or minus an entire discipline of strength. There is also no known association of Metamancy with any of the other talents, though some have proposed a contrary association with Time. The social pressures around Metamancy make empirical confirmation of this impossible.

Ferreting out metamantic talent is an inevitable pursuit among students given the dangers of the Tournament of the Staff. In the past, rumors about ways to detect talent in Metamancy have lead to major mistakes and a variety of tragedies. To avoid misconceptions and wrong-headed notions, the below list summarizes what actually is known. In order of significance and likelihood from lesser to greater chance that a spell caster is strong in Metamancy:

1. Fast learner - but obviously this could also be reflective of talent in a given type of magic.

2. Spontaneous untrained casting - but also may be simple talent manifesting at times of stress.

3. Variability in the quality of spells - this can be due to experimentation by the Metamancer but may also be lack of talent.

4. Ability to intentionally vary spell output, shape, or focus without changes to the casting procedure. Note that unintentional variation in raw output power is common while learning, and has little to do with Metamancy.

5. Uncanny ability to avoid spells not normally visible i.e. magical wards and traps.

6. Ability to sense meta-magic in others. Possibly only Adept or Master talents have this ability.

7. Ability to defeat attack spells with no explicit counter spell.

The one confirmed attribute of Metamancers that is limited to a Master-level talent is the ability to directly perceive static and active spells of all types in sufficient detail to modify, cancel, or copy them. The few historically confirmed Metamancers were mainly exposed when they appeared to learn a spell "on sight." In one famous case, an apprentice with the talent to become a Master Metamancer looking to impress a female apprentice observed the initial class demonstration of a fireball and followed it up on his first try with a heart-shaped explosion. Shortly after that display of power, this in-

*cautious individual was poisoned. The perpetrator of
the poisoning was never caught, but it was likely another novice or Master of a favored novice who feared
they would face him in the Tournament of the Staff.*

*Thus, it is a serious breach of etiquette to speak
of another Mage's metamantic power, and students
are strongly advised to conceal their true metamantic
aptitude.*

Johnny pondered the open pages a while. Was this a message? He quickly flipped through the other pages, but nothing
had been hidden in the book. What was the point? The necromancer's curse? How to detect a Metamancer? The importance
of not exposing a Metamancer casually? This implied that he
was likely to encounter either a necromancer or a Metamancer.
Or maybe the anecdote about apprentices killing competitors was
the salient point. Meeting a Metamancer or Necromancer seemed
far-fetched, but dangers of preemptive competition from other apprentices or Mages did not.

Johnny stared at the rippled, translucent glass of the window
for a long time. Very quietly, he breathed, more than said, "I saw
the spell on the window handle... and the spell that opened the
doors to the tower." A while later, in a more audible whisper, he
murmured, "What have I gotten myself into?"

5.9 Writing

After calming himself, Sinprejic dressed and left his room. He
purposefully closed the book again and left his door open to air
out his room and get it to smell like the rest of the tower again.
Having others think that he had opened the spell-locked window
would be bad.

The first place he headed was back to the kitchen, which was

194

empty. He found a glass and a pitcher of water and went into the larder. He grabbed a small roll of bread since he knew where that was. He looked around and found potatoes, various vegetables, salt, apples, cheese, dried mushrooms, lard, flour, and various other staples. Of these he grabbed an apple and a small chunk of cheese.

He was about halfway through his breakfast when Mutara entered. She skewered him with a piercing look. "Bread and cheese are for lunch and dinner. Oatmeal is for breakfast, if you wish to waste time on food in the morning. You may add *a few* nuts or dried berries for flavor, and coffee is normally made by the first person down here in the morning. There's probably still one cup in the pot, though late risers are not likely to get much."

"Oh, I don't drink coffee."

"Ok, but here's how the day works around here. From sunrise to noon is your own time. You can study, sleep, or do whatever you like until noon. Work begins at noon and continues until sunset. After dinner, your time is again your own, but most of us go to bed soon after to maximize our morning free time. You will find that magic comes easier when you are not tired, so good sleep and early rising will maximize the quality time you have for study."

"Work?"

"This tower and our supplies cost money, as do some of the rarest spell components. The floor above this one is the workshop where we use magic to craft items of exceptional quality typically for the nobility of the Talingor Empire. Occasionally someone in Pendalir City or Greelin there seems to be able to afford us too, but mostly our customers are from Talingor. You haven't learned enough to help with that yet, so you will earn your keep binding books. I've sent out a letter advertising our new expanded services for binding mundane and apprentice-level books. We have some volumes you can demonstrate your skills on while that work comes in."

"I see," Sinprejic said, not terribly enthused by a return to book binding.

"And I see that you've already forgotten that your first task is to read the book you were given. You should have brought it down to read. You recall being told to read it in the library this morning?"

"Ah, I'm up late because I read it last night."

"What? The whole thing?"

"Yes."

"You can't have absorbed much if you read it that quick" Mutara said doubtfully. "Where does the Wizards' Council meet?" she asked.

"At the Academy."

"Where is that?"

"On the Isle of Wizards off the northwest coast of the Talingor Empire."

"When can you expect to get one of these?" she said, gesturing with her owl-headed staff.

"After graduating from the Academy by defeating two other students in combat."

"What is Metamancy?"

Sinprejic pause a fraction of a second, stunned by the coincidence of the question, but then answered smoothly, "Metamancy is the study of magic that manipulates other magic."

Her eyebrows arched slightly, noting his delay and apparently taking it as a sign that he had trouble remembering the answer to that question. "What is the talent level required for a Directed Mutation spell?"

"That's a druid spell I would never have the opportunity to learn, since druids are renegades," Sinprejic replied confidently, thinking he had spotted a trick question.

"That's not what I asked. You need to know every last detail of that book. You do seem to have read it, but you clearly don't have the habit of precision learning. Get your book and go read it again. Morphosius will ask if you've finished it each day at noon, and if you say yes your day will be spent in testing with him. If you pass the written test, you will be given a magical aptitude test. If you fail, you will have to study another week before trying again. Don't waste Morphosius's time."

"That wasn't mentioned in the book."

"Did you think that book contained everything there is to know?"

"No, of course not."

"Then go get it and learn it cold, every word. Even though it is but a tiny speck of what you need to learn, some things must be learned before others. Memorize the *whole* thing, and answer only the question asked if you are asked about it." And with that she turned and took the stairs to the second floor at the back of the kitchen.

Almost immediately, Imoed came down the same stairs holding up a finger to his mouth with a grin. He paused at the bottom of the stairs and silently put his hand to his ear, and as if on cue Mutara's voice came down from above. "I heard that, Imoed!"

They both shared a barely contained silent laugh, and then Imoed said, "First thing to know about Mutara is that Mutara is always right."

Sinprejic nodded understanding.

"Go get your book, and then I'll show you the workshop very briefly and then the library."

Sinprejic did so, but there was no tour of the workshop since Mutara was there, ostensibly cleaning but clearly waiting to see how soon Sinprejic got up to the library to start reading. Access upward from the workshop was via a spiral stair inside the central support column. Each half rotation around the column led to a door onto the next level.

"The third level is where the library and Mutara's quarters are.

Obviously the only door you should use on that level is the library to the left. Jalsus and I are on the next level up, and above that is Morphosius's private level, and then at the top of the stairs there's no door, so you can go to the sixth floor where the classroom, wizards' meeting room, teleport room, and aerial receiving are, but don't go to any of those until you've been told to by Morphosius. The roof is where we sometimes relax. That's up a stairway from the sixth, but I'm not sure if the door at the top is safe for you or not, so best to wait on that. Really, for now the library, the workshop, and the first floor are the only places you should be."

By the time he finished explaining all that, Imoed was opening the door to the library. In the library there were dozens of long bookshelves all filled with books and the same dusty book smell that had permeated Master Percy's back room. Light filtered in from a few windows, but the entire library was lit quite evenly with no obvious light source. This was true in many other rooms of the castle, and Sinprejic asked Imoed about it.

"Yeah, permanent light spells are key to being able to make a castle like this livable. It's just too big for there to be enough windows, and lamps or torches give off soot and smell. The light is even but not always as bright as you want it. For the rest of us that's not an issue," he said. Then he gestured with his staff and spoke a single syllable.

The jewels around the top began to whirl the shaft of the brush and glow until the many colors blurred into an even white light, which became bright for a moment and then winked out, returning to the original stationary arrangement.

"I suppose we might need to dig up a lamp for you, at least until you learn this spell." He gestured intricately and recited a short poem. A six-inch globe of faintly glowing white light rose from the palm of his left hand. It seemed to float wherever Imoed wanted it to, and when Imoed made it brighter Sinprejic thought he could see some sort of connection from Imoed to the glowing ball. When he concentrated, it seemed clearer, and Sinprejic seemed to see a flow out to the ball and then a complex woven pattern around the surface of the ball of light. The moment he relaxed his focus, all he saw was the glowing ball.

Imoed saw him looking at it intently, and said, "Heh, looks impressive when you're new. I still remember the first time I saw one of these. I immediately wanted nothing more than to be able to do that. Now it's a pedestrian spell that I can cast without hardly thinking about it. Study up. This and much more await," Imoed said with a friendly smile before extinguishing the light ball.

Sinprejic took a seat at the back of the library where there was a table and a fireplace and began to reread the book. Although he had almost finished the book a second time, he decided not to admit he was finished to Morphosius, just to be safe and also in the hope that the delay would mollify Mutara somewhat.

For several mornings Sinprejic read and reread the book. In the afternoon, he rebound several books and was asked to prepare some paper and bindings for half a dozen books yet to be written.

On the third day after lunch, at noon, Morphosius asked him. "Have you finished studying the primer?" He answered that he had.

"Very well. Follow me," Morphosius instructed, and together they ascended the stairs from the kitchen. They went all the way up to the sixth floor. As they left the stairs, Sinprejic found that the ceilings on this level had become taller again, approximately thirty feet high, and to his left was the large archway he had seen in the side of the tower when he approached. It was apparently open to the air outside, and Sinprejic could see the circular stone lake with its waves of spikes, the block of stone through which the maze wandered, and the tops of the forest trees beyond. Sinprejic wanted to go look out across the landscape, but Morphosius didn't pause.

To the right, opposite the open arch was a solid wall, and

Morphosius followed this past a pair of double doors to a single door. The door was shortly before a set of stairs that, according to Imoed's prior description, likely lead to the roof. The door opened into a long room. Inside was mostly open space, but in the center was a table and a chair. A sheaf of blank paper, a bottle of standard copying ink, and a quill pen were on the table.

"Have a seat," Morphosius said.

Sinprejic sat down in the chair on the far side of the table.

"When I leave, the door behind me will lock for eight hours. There's a chamber pot back there, and don't touch anything else. Some of the implements in this room are very dangerous. This room is protected from all communication in or out to prevent cheating, but this also means that if you injure yourself playing with something you shouldn't, we won't know and won't come to help you. When the door opens, if you hand me a full faithful copy of the primer ready to be bound, you pass. If there are any errors or omissions, you fail."

"Don't I need a copy to work from?" Sinprejic asked reflexively but even as he did so he knew what answer he would get.

"You claimed to have studied the primer. You should not need a copy anymore," Morphosius said with a tone of finality. Then he turned and left, closing the door behind him.

Sinprejic sighed and began his best but within a few minutes he was pretty sure he was forgetting something, and then he realized for sure that he had skipped a paragraph. He was prepared for questions about the book, but he hadn't actually committed every word of it to memory.

Hopelessly, Sinprejic said out loud, "Well I'm going to fail this test. That's for sure, so I suppose I should stop wasting paper.... but what will I do for the next seven hours?"

He sat back and thought about the passage regarding Meta-mancy. He had reread it many times and could recite that by heart for sure, but without the rest of the book copying it here would only draw attention to the possibility of him having that kind of talent.

Vaguely, he wondered if there were any spells in the room, and he remembered what he saw when Imoed cast the light ball spell. "When I concentrated I could see more," he mused. Absently, without really meaning to, he started to concentrate again. As he did so, he noticed a number of things in the room shimmered faintly, the door, the window, and a number of items on the table along the wall. For an hour he practiced going in and out of that concentration mode, and it got easier. Soon it took very little concentration, and he began to see more detail. In some places, the magic was arrayed in sheets, others lines or nets, and he could see that there were differences other than shape. The various structures had subtle differences that were like colors but without actually being colorful.

"I bet those are different types of magic," he mused quietly.

He was increasingly tempted to pick up items on the desk so he could examine them better. Most of them were foot-long sticks of various materials, some wood, some glass, some metal, many with symbols and gilding or gemstones set in them. His hand was hovering over one when he came to his senses.

"Ok, this is dangerous. I have to stop," he said after a loud sigh. He returned to the table and sat in the chair, but the boredom was overwhelming. He began looking at magic again and realized that all the walls had a faint silvery sheen across them. "That must be the protection that Morphosius mentioned that prevents folks from cheating."

He sighed again and began running through everything that had happened since he joined the tower. His memory of Imoed's light globe stuck in his mind, and he pondered the spell he had seen lacing itself through the glow. He tried to remember exactly what it had looked like. The pattern seemed to be a regular repeating pattern of triangles, and he tried to imagine it fully in three dimensions. There had also been a thread flowing power out from Imoed's hand...

Suddenly there was an odd tingling sensation in his finger, and he realized he wasn't just imagining the spell—he was actually constructing it. The tingle changed to a flowing feeling, and suddenly the air inside his globe began to glow faintly.

Sinprejic was so shocked by this he lost his concentration, and the far side of the spell came apart. The light suddenly changed to a three-foot gout of blue flame as the net tore apart and shriveled. Luckily the flame was directed up and away from him and disappeared as quickly as it had appeared, but clearly he could have harmed himself or burned the papers on the desk, which would have been very hard to explain. As it was, there was a very faint acrid smell in the air, which he hoped nobody would notice. Luckily, he still had almost five hours for it to dissipate.

"Well, I just displayed untrained casting. I can see spells, and I learned a spell just by seeing it performed once. That pretty much fits the definition of Master-level talent in Metamancy." He sighed loudly. For a while, he stared at the window thinking.

Sinprejic resisted the temptation to try again for almost ten minutes, but this time he made sure he was in the middle of the room away from anything inflammable, and he formed the net part of the spell significantly further away this time and made it smaller. Soon he had a wavering but stable glowing ball floating four feet in front of him. He found he could vary the brightness and releasing it once it was almost too dim to see didn't produce a flame. For several hours he practiced the spell and played with the size and density of the net, being very careful to dim it down before releasing it. Eventually, he was able to call it up in a matter of seconds any size or brightness he wanted. Eventually he began to become tired, and he almost lost control of it while it was dazzlingly bright.

"Ok, I think that's enough for today" he said to himself, wondering how much longer he had to wait. Besides being tired, he realized that he really had to stop because it would not be good to have Morphosius walk in to see him casting a spell when he wasn't even tested for talent yet. He didn't realize how tired he was until he sat down in the chair again. He leaned on the desk and soon put his head down.

"AHEM!"

Sinprejic stirred groggily from where he had fallen asleep with his head on the desk. The few pages he had attempted to write were now soaked with drool. As he looked up to see Morphosius staring down at him. He was unaware of a large amount of text that had transferred itself onto his right cheek.

"Surely you can write faster than that," Morphosius said, looking at the few sheets of paper that Sinprejic had written on.

Sinprejic yawned and blinked. "Sorry, I realized that I was not remembering it right and figured that to continue was just a waste of paper."

"Hmmph. Next time you write everything you can remember, or it will be a month between tests. Try to be better prepared before claiming to be prepared. This is not just an idle exercise. If you try casting spells before you have exactly memorized them, you'll likely kill yourself. You now have a week before I'll let you try again. Use it well."

"Understood," Sinprejic replied quietly.

Morphosius nodded and said, "Clean this mess up. Put the unused paper and supplies back on the binding table in the workshop."

"Will do," Sinprejic replied.

For the remainder of the week, Sinprejic spent mornings rereading the primer and then practicing writing out sections of the book. He broke it into sections and focused on one section at a time. In every spare moment available he recited passages from memory. When the end of the week came, and it was time to meet Alfyra again, he was especially glad to take a day off.

5.10 Scrying

Sinprejic took the stable door out of the tower and approached the main gates of the tower courtyard on foot. The pre-dawn morning was chilly, but for once, there had been no frost, a sure sign that spring was progressing. He retrieved the silver caw bird amulet from one of his pouches. Now it was dangling from a short metal tube instead of a neck chain. The tube had an oval cross-section and was slightly flared on one end. He recalled convincing Jalsus to make it for him.

"Won't it be super obvious to any observer that I'm holding the key to crossing the lake if I leave dangling something over my head. It will catch everyone's attention. I'd really not want to have to face down whichever enemies these defenses are meant to dissuade if they happened to be watching from the cliffs above when I left."

Jalsus nodded. "Well scrying is more likely than standing on the cliffs above, but perhaps you're right. Though, honestly, I think the risk is low."

"Could we mount it on a walking stick?"

"Fitting it to a walking stick would make sense from a practical standpoint, but if I make you something that looks like a staff with enchanted jewels on top of it to carry, we'll both be in trouble. Carrying any magic staff of any sort before you are a graduated Mage and properly sanctioned by the Academy is a fast way to get in big trouble. Even if it isn't a real staff, it would sure look like an imitation, and that's very strictly forbidden."

"Oh. Well...My bow sticks up above my head when I wear it. Something that fits up there?"

"Ah, about that... I saw you using study time to practice with your sword and your bow. These are things you should be giving up. Mages have much more effective means of defense."

"When someone actually teaches me some magic, I'll consider it. Until then, I don't care to walk around the woods defenseless," Sinprejic replied flatly.

"I suppose that's reasonable. Most apprentices don't spend time in the woods either, but I suppose everyone is different. Let me see the amulet and your bow. I'll see what I can do."

A day later, Jalsus had returned it to him attached to the tubing. It was designed so he could thread the neck chain attached to the amulet through a hole in the tube where the chain could be secured with a small pin. The tube could then be slipped onto the tip of his bow. One side of the tube had a slot to accommodate his bow string. When his bow was slung over his shoulder with the tube mounted on it, the amulet was held above him so that it could suppress spikes on the stone lake in all directions at once. A casual observer might notice it, but it would just appear as if it were a decoration.

Standing before the gate in the morning air, Sinprejic fitted the amulet on its tube to the top of his bow and approached the gate. The gate area melted away, leaving an aperture about the size of a normal door as he approached. Once he was through and moved away, it resealed itself. He edged around the thin strip of stone along the outer wall, avoiding the lake with its spikes until he was directly across from the structure that held the maze. Everything worked as designed. The waves on the lake dissipated as they approached him, and as he neared the maze it transformed itself into the wide exit road shortly before he reached the edge of the lake.

As he left and the road faded into a hunters trail, he removed the amulet from his bow. The sun was just beginning to peek over the horizon, lighting the tips of the tallest branches with a golden glow. The leaves were not yet on the trees, but as he followed the trails they passed through a swampy area, and he could see that the whirly seed trees now had reddish tips on all their branches. Soon there would be leaves and spring would truly begin.

The route he followed through the trails was far from direct. He was sure there was a faster set of trails to follow, but he had not explored them, and getting lost was not something he wanted to risk today. In a day or two, he'd spend a morning learning the nearby trails and finding a route that was more direct. As he walked, he began to smile, and his step became lighter. The birds were singing in a full dawn chorus now, as only spring time birds can at sunrise.

After carefully hiding his departure from the main trails again, he soon approached the needle tree grove and noted that he was first to arrive again, and this time he adjusted the signal rock and found a spot to hide near the spring. The sun crept higher, and the day began to warm quickly.

It was over an hour before Alfyra tapped him on the shoulder, almost startling him. He smiled at her, and they hugged. Holding hands, they went to sit in the morning sun where it was warmer. Before they sat down however, he pulled her close for a brief kiss, and then rather than letting her pull away he whispered in her ear.

"Morphosius spies on this grove. He knew about it when I arrived at his tower." He released her, and she spoke softly in Elvish.

"Well, he is a wizard. I suppose it's not likely he would offer apprenticeship to someone without learning all he could."

He leaned close and whispered, "He also speaks some Elvish, though he claims I'm better at it than he is."

"Then Elvish it is for now," she said with a sly wink.

Sinprejic laughed. "I suppose so," he replied in Elvish.

Alfyra seemed to hesitate and whispered, "I also have a trick we can play on anyone trying to spy on us. Follow me." Alfyra stood and walked silently back under the trees, and then fell into a stealthy stalk, slipping into an area of relatively thick under-growth where some small pines had taken advantage of a break in the trees.

In among the pines she smiled and said, "We can talk freely for a few moments at least, or we can sneak away."

"Why is it safe in here?" Sinprejic asked.

"Because all elven scouts carry one of these." Holding out her hand, she displayed a thin rod of reddish wood with a complex pattern carved along its length.

Puzzled, Sinprejic said, "What's that?"

"A scramble stick. It's a magic talisman that radiates a field of planar magic that is guaranteed to disrupt any scrying within a couple of hundred feet."

Sinprejic, realizing it was magical, immediately concentrated and could see significant magic webbing its way through and around the rod.

"I see. But won't they just come back?"

"Yes, but unless they have spent time here physically familiariz-ing themselves with this spot or carefully prepared an aerial route, they will have to retrace your steps to bring the scrying spell back here. If we leave, they won't know where we've gone. Even an aerial route should take several minutes from the tower unless the device is exceptional or the caster is a true Master."

"Let's go then. I have lots to tell you."

She nodded, and they quickly but lightly stalked out the back of the grove along a deer track that split and they headed north and east. Alfyra seemed to know where she was going. Eventually they came to a wooded hollow thick with flat-needle trees. It was smaller than the grove with the spring, and it was much cooler in the shade than sitting in the sun, but they would not be visi-ble from above, and the thick trees muffled much of the outside sound.

"This is just west of the trail along the river. I wouldn't go back to the grove today," Alfyra said after they were safely under the flat-needle trees.

Sinprejic focused his attention on magic and looked around carefully. He saw nothing in the surroundings but noticed that her thin leather moccasins and a knife on her belt were magical.

"So I think I may have made a mistake."

Alfyra listened patiently, waiting for him to explain.

"Becoming an apprentice is much more serious than I had imagined."

"You found out about the test at the Academy," she guessed.

"Yeah, I don't want to kill anyone. That's one problem."

"It's a barbaric practice, for sure, and most elves don't participate. Technically that makes us renegades, but there's an informal agreement that so long as we stick to simple things like magic detection and silence for stealth we won't be bothered. The Academy really can't handle training twenty percent of all the elves in the world, nor does it want to waste time on a host of very low-talent students. Their whole system would fall apart if everyone like me tried to attend. Our rare individuals with true talent however must attend like any human would."

"So every wizard is a murderer," Sinprejic sighed.

"From a certain perspective, and while the practice is repulsive to elves and beautiful snowflakes like you, it does give the Academy ample excuse to weed out bad apples. With the long perspective of the elves, we have come to suspect that a great many of the students who fail at that stage are ones deemed to not hold the principles of the Academy dear to their hearts. Individuals who seem likely to disregard the regulations set forth by the council or harm the general populace rarely graduate. Most elves that attend have graduated successfully since our leaders figured this out and began forewarning the students sent to the Academy."

"I see."

"But there's something else? I can see you're still tense."

"I'm afraid to tell you," Sinprejic said simply.

"I can see, but there's nothing you could tell me that would change the things I know and love about you. I know already that you have a good and kind heart, very little else matters to me."

Sinprejic looked around, checking for magic again, and listening for motion. Then softly he said, "I think I'm a Metamancer."

"Oh, I see," she said with concern and then immediately moved over to hug him. "Please be very careful," she said.

Sinprejic stared at her with wonder, and then hugged her back fiercely. After a long moment he said, "You're not afraid of me? Based on what I've read, Metamancers are the most feared and often are killed for fear of their power."

"Silly snowflake," she said, playfully bumping his nose with hers. "Magic is a tool. What's important is how you use it. Magic talent is no different from physical strength or brilliant intellect. I might as well fear you for being left or right-handed as fear what type of magic talent you have. This is a problem humans always seem to have. They always want to categorize each other and then fear anyone not like themselves. The only legitimate fear is the fear that other students will have if they think they might have to face you in combat trials."

"You have no idea how good it is to hear you say that. It's so stressful worrying that I'll give myself away. I always have to be thinking about anything I do."

"How did you discover your talent?" she asked, releasing him and sitting back.

"I can see spells. All I have to do is decide I want to, and they are as clear and obvious as the needles on these trees. Your shoes and your dagger are magical."

"That's good. Wonderful. It means your talent is strong, and you are virtually guaranteed to pass the combat trials. I've been worried that this path of apprenticeship might take you from me if you were not talented enough. Also, I'm relieved to hear you didn't discover it by casting spells. That can be a very dangerous way to discover talent."

Sinprejic concentrated briefly, and a very small version of the glowing globe he had practiced while failing to copy the primer for Morphosius appeared before him. He held it for about five seconds and then carefully released it.

Alfyra stared at the air where the glowing ball of light had been and sighed. Then she started to speak. "Joh..." She paused and asked, "So what is your Mage name?"

"Sinprejic," he said.

She smiled, cocked her head, and said "I like it. It fits." Then more seriously, she said, "Promise me you'll not try any more spells without training. It's a huge risk if you get caught and very dangerous."

"I understand. I couldn't help it though." And then he told her about the book writing test he was given and how bored he was trapped in that room, about how Jalsus and Imoed were friendly and Mutara was all sour and stern. Then Alfyra related her conversation with her brother and their plan for how to tell her father about him. She admitted that the timing was sensitive due to internal politics.

"This situation is really unusual for elves," she said. "I fear your baron's continual nettling and pestering of us and his capture of Sylian threatens our harmony. Elves are never war-like, but some are asking how long we should suffer when we are continually being attacked without provocation. War is not the elven way, and my father is patient, but some of the younger elves and some of the families who have lost members or ancestor trees are understandably less patient."

"You've lost ancestor trees?" Sinprejic asked, surprised.

"Yes, two of them, and another was damaged." Those were the only times we killed humans. We cannot tolerate those losses.

"Oh. I think I know when each of those was. It's been rare for guardsmen to die. Arrow in the foot or grazing the arm happens a lot, but you're right. I only remember funerals a couple of times."

"If there is a change in my father's policies, not a single guardsman will return from the forest."

Sinprejic nodded. "I've seen you shoot. I see now that elves have been intentionally wounding to avoid killing. Unfortunately, I'm the last person who could possibly help you."

"I know. It's sad because I know you would try, but it seems your fate lies elsewhere."

"Maybe if I go back and talk to my father..."

"No," Alfyra said firmly.

"But my father is well respected in the town, and he knows leaders in Mountain Gate."

"Perhaps, but the path you contemplate leads to revolt and war among the humans. We do not hate the humans. It's only their leader who is driving them at us. Far less will die, and only those prepared to die in battle will pay the cost if we defend ourselves for real. Your way would likely ruin the lives of many innocents as they were forced to choose a side or provide soldiers to one faction or the other."

"In a way the impatient elves are right," Sinprejic said solemnly.

"What do you mean? How can you want your own people to die?" Alfyra said.

"I don't, but there is an urgency. Letting this problem fester is a mistake. Until I met you, all I knew about elves was that they hunted humans and denied our rightful access to timber and furs in the forests. It was a lie, but I grew up believing it. In another ten years, only old people will remember a time when the elves didn't bother the town. 'Evil elves' will be a fact beyond question for the townsfolk by then."

"There it is."

"There what is?"

"The reason my father needs to meet you. He needs a better window into the minds of people in your town. This is how you can help. We do not understand what's going on well enough."

"I don't know everything about our town. Living in my father's manor, I didn't get into town as much as might be ideal for such a purpose, but if I can help I will."

"Next week, I think we can introduce you to my father. We'll meet here."

"But what if I'm being scried?"

"Take this. You activate it by squeezing the end. You should disappear into cover before using it so it's not obvious what it is you did that disrupted the spell that was following you. Then, you need to move before you can be relocated by the person who was watching you. The further you have traveled from where they are, the more time you have before they can find you again."

"Got it."

"Don't lose it. They are very expensive. We have no wizards among us who can produce them. We have to buy them from the Academy. I'm not really supposed to give it to you."

"I understand," Sinprejic said, turning the intricately carved rod over in his hand. Already he felt a temptation to examine it and figure out how it was made, but he resisted for now.

"Ok, enough serious stuff," Alfyra declared. "Let's go back to the needle tree grove and play stones. I want to see if you've improved over the winter."

Sinprejic smiled and agreed. They returned and played, but when she tried to give him the usual two stone handicap he won convincingly. They agreed that they should play without handicap next. After that it was time to leave. They parted with a long hug and a passionate kiss. Both of them smiled all the way home.

6 Control

6.1 Jalsus

"And remember that I want as much as you can recall on paper. I need to see that you are making progress," Morphosius said. Sinprejic was seated at the desk in the testing room on the top floor again, paper, ink and quills at hand.

"Understood," Sinprejic replied solemnly.

Morphosius glared at him briefly and then turned briskly and left, closing the door behind him. Sinprejic looked at the stack of papers and sighed. The room was quiet, and virtually nothing had changed since his last attempt to write out the basic primer from memory. In fact the only thing new was a funny-looking set of candles in a candelabra. The design was strange and unwieldy looking, with two rows of six candles in paired colors. A moment's concentration told him there was something faintly magical about the candles, but the candelabra was perfectly mundane. It wasn't clear what the purpose of the candles were, but there was a sense that each twin pair that shared a color also shared some sort of opposition or opposite function.

After staring at the candles for a minute, Sinprejic looked again at the door as if to check that it was still closed and pulled the wooden rod Alfyra had given him from a pocket in his pants. In here was the only place he could study it without fear of Mutara spying on him. He studied it for many minutes and pulled another wooden dowel out of his pocket. He laid them on the table next to each other, mentally comparing them. After another couple minutes, he shook his head and softly said, "Better not. I think I can duplicate it—the magic isn't very strong—but it's planar magic, and to be honest I have no idea what could go wrong if I try."

With that he put both back in his pocket and sighed again before pulling a sheet of paper off the stack to his right, opening the bottle of ink, and dipping a quill in it. "The modern practice of magic endeavors to make magic safe for the practitioner and for the common-folk of all the realms," he muttered, and then transcribed the line, and then continued writing in silence.

After three hours, his hand began to ache too much, and he had to take a short break. He wandered the room gazing at the various implements and studying the fine layer of spells that coated the walls of the room.

"This shares some similarity with Alfyra's rod," he mumbled at one point, looking at one of the decorated sticks. Soon however, he returned to his writing, discarding the worn quill he had been using for a fresh one. He finished with an hour to spare but was exhausted. He carefully set aside his work, closed the ink, and cleaned the quill before putting his head down to rest.

This time he woke to the sound of footsteps approaching. By the time the door opened, he was sitting upright with his hands folded, though the red mark of his hand across his forehead betrayed his nap nonetheless.

Morphosius opened the door, looked at him, a slight smirk quickly passing across his face. Then he inspected the pile of carefully written sheets sitting on the desk. As he picked the pages up, his eyebrows raised slightly, and he made a soft humming sound.

"Much better, it seems. I'll give this to Jalsus to check. Dinner is underway downstairs. You may go now."

Sinprejic nodded and hurried down to the kitchen. Imoed had prepared a savory meat-filled pastry and some vegetables. Sinprejic hurried to get his and sat down with Jalsus and Imoed. "He seems hungry," Imoed noted.

"Imoed, if you sat writing for eight hours you'd be hungry too," Jalsus said.

"Only took six hours, but my hand still hurts," Sinprejic said.

"Only six hours?" Imoed queried in a faintly mocking voice. He seemed impressed and faintly jealous.

"That's impressive. Sounds like you might have got it right," Jalsus said approvingly.

"Morphosius said you get to check it, so you'll know first."

"Ah..." Jalsus sighed. "I suppose I should have seen that coming."

They ate in silence for a while, Sinprejic wolfing down his food as only a young man in his late teens can. He finished at the same time as everyone else.

"So you mentioned that you play stones..." Jalsus began.

"Uh oh, watch out. Jalsus here is a shark. Don't play for money, He'll clean you out. He competes at the Academy several times a year too," Imoed warned.

"Friendly games only, no money," Jalsus said solicitously.

"First one's always free," Imoed quipped.

"If you're interested..." Jalsus said, gathering his plate and heading for the sink.

"Of course I'm interested," Sinprejic said with a smile. "Sounds like Imoed here's had a bad experience or two."

"Just trying to save you some pain, kid. Suit yourself. Show me the game afterward?"

"Show it to you?"

"Yeah, replay it from memory... you can replay a full game from memory, can't you?"

"I don't know. Never tried really. I suppose it wouldn't be too hard."

"Ha! Never mind. Have fun. I don't need to see the game. I know the result already," Imoed said as he left the kitchen.

"Don't listen to him," Jalsus said. "He just likes to hear himself talk. I have a board in my study. We can play there, so he doesn't come watch and distract us."

"Sure, that sounds good," said Sinprejic eagerly. He had not seen any wizard's study before. He followed Jalsus up to the fourth floor.

As they exited the spiral stairs, Jalsus said "The door to this floor is unfriendly to all but Imoed and I. Don't ever test it. I like you so far, and I don't want to have to clean what's left of you off the walls."

Sinprejic nodded. "I understand. Morphosius was quite clear about not trying random doors. First floor, workshop, library, and testing room only." As they exited the stairs, the door opened onto a long hallway with two doors on either side at the near end and a window at the far end for light.

"To the left are my rooms, and to the right is Imoed's area," he said and opened the door to the left. As they entered, Sinprejic looked around. To the right of the door were several rows of shelves, which were about half full of books and half full of boxes. Ahead and slightly to the left was a large wooden table with massive sturdy, round legs. The corners of the table were carved with gargoyle heads, and arcane script covered the outer edge. The top seemed to be a solid slab of granite. On top of this monstrosity of a table were a variety of chisels, and gouges, a lamp, and a large book. The book was unidentifiable because it was closed, face down, and had the binding facing away. To the left of that was an area that contained various sculptures and an assortment of mechanical devices. Between the table and the sculpture area along the back wall sat a large solid block of wood, the top of which bore the nineteen by nineteen grid used for playing stones.

"Wow, this is all yours?"

"Benefits of being recognized by the Academy as an Adept. I am allowed to have a laboratory in which to attempt to develop new spells or produce items of power."

"Wait, are you more powerful than Mutara? I thought since she wears robes any time she's not going into town to get supplies she must be stronger."

"Well, we're more or less equal in Mutamancy, though she's probably slightly stronger overall. My talent is more narrowly focused to the shaping and crafting of objects, whereas she has a little more general talent for other types of magic, especially scrying. She's very fond of watching people. As for robes, I've got robes, but in my opinion they're not very comfortable. Also, I tend to get dirty when I work, so I stick to the cape and staff most of the time. You know about the symbols of rank from the book you just copied, right?"

"Yeah, staff for Mages, cape for Magicians, robes for Wizards, ring for Adepts, shoulders for Masters, and a stole for a seat on the council. But I guess I never noticed your ring before."

"Yeah, Mutara is the second-strongest living Mutamancer. She wore the stole and had a seat on the council for over a decade. When Morphosius arrived at the Academy, she recognized his talent and took him under her wing. She knew he would outstrip her and take her place, but I guess she also knew he would have enough talent to eventually help her improve her shapeshifting and that he would be allowed to build a tower.

"Shapeshifting is very hard and dangerous too. It takes time and repetition to get fast at a transformation. There are only four individuals known to be seriously studying it right now, Morphosius, Mutara, Dracolus the renegade, and Pulmonan who is too weak to ever have much hope of Mastering even a single form. I also suspect she was tired of the distractions associated with being on the council. I'm sure she gets more opportunity to practice now that Morphosius has that job."

"So you're strong enough to shapeshift too?"

"Certainly I have the strength, but I just don't care to spend time dissecting animals and learning their anatomy and then risking my life and my sanity imitating them. Sculpting and making beautiful and useful objects is much more satisfying, safer, and not as gross."

"I see."

Jalsus nodded toward the large block of wood and said, "Have a seat." As Sinprejic approached, he noticed that the board was set apart in its own dedicated area, and the eight-inch thick block of wood sat on four small feet. It seemed very old but well-preserved, except for a faint stain in one corner. On right and left of the board were two dark wooden bowls carved with some sort of stylized flower pattern, presumably containing the stones. The near and far sides of the board had low, cushioned chairs with no legs clearly meant to support the players in comfort while they contemplated the game. All of this sat on a woven straw mat.

"Wow. I've never seen a stones board like that. Really impressive."

"Yeah, I picked it up in a pawn shop in Pendalir of all places. Guy who sold it to me said the prior owner claimed it was an ancient board. According to him, it was a relic of the first age, which of course is preposterous, though I must admit I've never seen anything like it, nor have I ever seen wood quite like this. It's a shame about the stain, but it's clearly been there since long before I got it."

On a whim, Sinprejic focused his attention for a moment and found that while the board was not magical, the table, tools, and some of the mechanisms around the room were magical. Strangely however he seemed to sense something else about the board, especially the stain. It was a nameless feeling that made him think of the faint lingering shadow of a soul long departed, but that notion seemed crazy and odd and made no sense to him.

Yet somehow it also seemed to suggest the board was indeed of extremely ancient origins.

"Well it's... amazing. Seems like it would be a shame not to use it."

Jalsus grinned broadly, showing his bright white teeth, which contrasted sharply with his dark skin. "Yes, that's mostly why I bought it. I paid way too much, but standing there in the shop looking at it, I just wanted to play a game on it. It seems to have that effect on people, though I've not seen any sign that it's enchanted. Maybe it's just such a magnificent work of art that it inspires the soul to a degree that compels one to play the game."

And with that they sat down and prepared to play. "Since there's really no good way to know our relative levels, let's just try one without handicap and see how it goes."

Sinprejic agreed, and they drew stones to choose colors. Sinprejic got white, and so Jalsus moved first. They played quickly, and Jalsus's play and his desire to chat as the game progressed set a tone of just playing for fun rather than for serious competition.

"So what do you think of life in the tower so far?" Jalsus asked.

"I can't say I'm thrilled to be spending half my time binding books, especially since ninety percent of them are copies of the same book I've been memorizing."

"Ha, we all earn our keep here. There's no free ride anywhere in life. The sooner you develop some more useful skills, the sooner you can stop mixing binding paste."

"Seems fair, but I'm not getting to learn any magic in return. I understand this primer is important, but memorizing it to the point of recitation seems extreme."

Jalsus placed a stone in the center of one of Sinprejic's groups on the board and said "It is extreme. I, for one, am glad I didn't have Morphosius as a master. Though I think this task likely just reflects what his master probably had him do. As inane as it seems, there's a certain logic to it too. To perform spells, you must memorize the words and even the last little detail of the pronunciation, along with any hand or body motions, and any physical components that are used as well. It all has to be very precise, or your results will vary in ways that are usually undesirable. That said, there's no spell even one hundredth as long as a whole book."

Sinprejic regarded the stone Jalsus had placed inside his group as if it were a worm suddenly protruding from an apple he was eating. Absently he said, "I see. So if I can do this, spells should be cake."

"Something like that, except if you get a spell wrong it might blow you into tiny bits, erase your brain, or leave you falling through a wormhole into a plane of fire. These things don't happen quite as often with books."

"Hmm," Sinprejic responded and resumed concentrating on trying to find a move to save his group. Several moves later he said, "I resign."

"You play quite well. I think you're almost a match for Imoed, but probably we should try giving you a three stone handicap next. You tend to get too focused on one area of the board and don't take care of your weak groups very well."

Sinprejic nodded and changed the topic. "Why did you become a Mage, Jalsus?"

Jalsus studied Sinprejic for a while and said, "It's not polite to ask a Mage about his past."

"I know, and I don't want to know where you're from or anything like that. I just wonder how it happens to others, if it's anything like me."

"Mmm... Well, in my case it was pretty simple. I discovered my talent on my own, and I began using it to shape pebbles from a nearby stream. One of the first things I made was a set of stones, actually. Did you cast any spells before you came here?"

"No, I mostly came here because Morphosius invited me and things kept going wrong in the rest of my life."

"Running away from your life is not a good way to live."

"I've even thought that myself, but so far people dying, false accusations with no apparent motive, and the strange prejudicial war of the town I grew up in really aren't things I can do anything about."

"I see. The seas of life do throw storms at us. It is up to us to build a boat strong enough to ride them out. Again the solution to your problems is to learn enough to take charge of your own life."

"Yeah, I hope that works out better on the third try. I was quite good with the sword, and bookbinding was a piece of cake, but the wheels came off of each of those wagons in turn."

"I'm sure you will do fine."

"Yeah, if I can get past this stupid book writing."

"You will. I think you will do better with magic. In fact, I'm sure of it."

"Why?"

"You're only an average-sized guy, and sword fighting is a physical skill. You were chasing a dream that relied on your mediocrity. Book binding is a boring, stable, hard-working occupation, something for those with few talents but a lot of grit. Again, not playing to your strength. What I see from your stones play and the way you pick up on details in things people say is that you are quite smart. You are now moving toward becoming a Mage, and this is a place where you can use your superior intellect to your advantage. Now you are playing to your strengths. Also, I can tell you exactly why Morphosius picked you."

"He claimed it was for my brains."

"Nope, though that helps of course. The real reason is that you radiate immense raw talent. As you know from the book you are studying, with practice it's possible to sense the strength of another Wizard in a sort of vague way. I can sense quite easily that you have more raw talent than I do and possibly more than Morphosius. If you are careful and don't kill yourself with the sort of experimentation that tempts every young Mage, you'll likely become the strongest Wizard of our age. I think great things await you. Once you are trained, this tower will be home to more than twice the raw talent of any tower. More than anywhere but the Academy itself.

"That said, a sense of raw talent only gives you a general idea of net strength but not any clue as to what type of magic they are best at. You will need to be tested to discover your affinities, but whatever they are you're almost certain to be a Master of something."

"That's hard to believe."

"You probably have no idea how hard it is to believe, actually. Entire generations go by without seeing someone of your talent level. That's why I'm sure you'll do well so long as you keep your wits about you and work hard. I'll check your writing first thing tomorrow."

"I really appreciate your encouragement, and it's nice to find someone to play stones with."

"No problem. You've got a few interesting ways of playing. Let's play every other evening or so."

"Deal," Sinprejic said with a smile. "Time for bed now, I guess."

"Yes. Ah, I should help you with the doors."

"Yeah, less mess to clean up that way," Sinprejic said, and they both laughed.

6.2 King

Sinprejic slipped into the dry interior of the flat-needle tree grove, glad to be out of the fine, cool drizzle that persisted after the rain the previous night, and found Alfyra waiting for him. She smiled as he entered and rose to greet him with a hug.

"How did you avoid scrying? I think if there's one thing we want to hide it's your meeting with my father."

"I triggered the rod you gave me in exactly the same place you did it before and came here by the same route. I wasn't sure I'd find it any other way."

"Ok, that's probably good. If anyone's been watching they may think that the effect is location-based rather than something you carry. In any case, it's a risk for you to keep the rod I gave you in the tower. They might search you and take it from you now that you disappeared without me. Are you sure you triggered it correctly?"

Sinprejic handed the small rosewood rod to her and replied, "Oh yes, I could see the magic emanate from it, and furthermore I know I was being watched. On the way here I stayed alert to magic and noted that there was some sort of magic presence following a few paces behind me almost from the moment I left the tower. It disappeared as soon as I triggered the rod."

"Excellent. Not good that we are watched, but fabulous that you can detect it. We should be gone from here, just in case your watcher is smart enough to pre-research locations we might hide. It's unfortunate we had to use this twice in a row."

Sinprejic nodded. "Yeah, makes sense, You lead."

With that they exited the far side of the flat-needle tree grove heading almost due east at a steady but silent pace. Soon, the animal run they followed led them to the river trail. They turned north, and then soon they took advantage of a fallen tree that provided a natural bridge over the river. The river was really more of a large fast flowing stream here, but it widened out just before it passed to the east of town on its way south.

On the far side, Alfyra stopped. "Let's listen to make sure we're not followed."

Taking the hint, Sinprejic opened his mind to the presence of magic. After a few moments and carefully turning all the way around and then looking straight up, he said, "Nothing."

"That's good. Then we can talk freely. Though be mindful that we may pass elven scouts as we get near the field where we are going," she said and shook some of the water out of her hair. Sinprejic's coat had started to soak through in the back, and he shivered.

"Aren't you cold?"

"The tips of my ears and my nose and chin are a little bit, but these fur-lined leathers are well treated to shed water, so other than that a light drizzle like this isn't a problem."

Sinprejic looked around and sighed. "I hope this doesn't get worse."

"Oh, can't you tell? It's ending and will probably stop any minute now. Look at the direction the clouds are moving, and over there the sky is lighter. The wind changed direction just recently too."

"Ah, you're right of course. That's good. What do I need to do and not do when I meet your father?"

She turned and continued down the path answering over her shoulder as they walked. "For you there are no expectations, other than a civil tone and not drawing weapons, that sort of thing. You are not an elf, so we really can't expect you to know any of our rituals. My dad will make a formal entrance and begin the conversation. From there, just be yourself. How was your week? Did you succeed in writing out the book?"

"No, I missed a couple sentences, didn't write the title page that he wanted, and it turns out I'm also supposed to write exactly the same words per page, and I used three extra sheets of paper."

"Seriously? That's ridiculous!" she exclaimed.

"I know, but I guess his point is that I understand that he doesn't want me to miss any detail no matter how small. I'm also going to make sure I mimic Aurcivius's penmanship, which is quite good practice anyway."

"Certainly I've been given passages to memorize. It's a skill, but this is so extreme. The magnitude and length is unreasonable. There aren't many elves who could do this in their lifetime," Alfyra commented.

"It's not that hard..."

"Sometimes I think you have no idea how talented you are," she said and smiled warmly at him. Sinprejic didn't know what to say to that, but then she continued, "One problem you will face eventually is the problem of anticipating when people will do really dumb things. They may do things that make no sense to you but make perfect sense to them from their illogical or emotional perspective."

"Dillon," he said softly.

"What?" she asked.

Louder, Sinprejic continued, "There was this guy my age named Dillon. I barely knew him, but his dad died, and I said something I thought would comfort him at the funeral, but he took it wrong and didn't understand. It was a dumb thing to say, I now realize, but years later I found that he had turned me into a monster in his head, and it was like he had converted his grief for his dad into hatred of me and my family. I never anticipated that. It baffled me. It still doesn't make any sense, but clearly it was the core of his thinking whenever he interacted with me."

"Yes, that's the sort of thing I mean. Everyone has their own experiences and emotions, and that's the lens through which they see the world. Some lenses are foggy or warped in strange ways. Those people do things that make sense to them but seem incomprehensible to others."

"That's an excellent point. I never thought about it like that."

"It takes most people, elves and humans alike, somewhere between twenty-five and fifty years to realize this. Elves have the good fortune to benefit from this understanding for over half a millennium. Sadly, from the stories I hear it seems that many humans don't realize this until late in life, with no time to undo the tragic consequences of their misunderstandings."

Sinprejic thought about that as he walked silently behind Alfyra. About a half an hour later, they came to a wide clearing in the middle of the woods. The rain had stopped, and the raw, chilly wind had begun to dry things out.

"This is where we will meet him?" Sinprejic asked.

"Yes."

"How soon?"

"Momentarily. I expect he's already seen us. He'll probably come from that direction." Just as she pointed, a majestic white horse with long white wings flew over the treetops and landed gracefully in the center of the clearing. Atop this magical beast was a lean elf with white hair dressed in violet-colored robes wielding a tall wooden staff, the top of which appeared to be a tangle of roots enclosing a purple amethyst gem. Both he and his steed appeared bathed in golden light despite the cloudy skies above. Upon landing, the regal elven Wizard leaped gracefully off his steed and stepped forward far enough to be out of the way as the beast folded its wings.

Sinprejic just stood there gaping in amazement until Alfyra took his hand gently and pulled him forward. Once he was moving she let go almost immediately. As they approached, Sinprejic wondered if he should bow or something, but Alfyra had said to just be himself, so he just waited.

After a brief pause, the elven king spoke. "Greetings, I am Telperios, Steward of the Trees, Protector of the Forests, and Wizard of Illusion. My daughter informs me that you are called Sinprejic, the pledge-apprentice of Morphosius, the Grand Master of Matter. I welcome you to our forest. May you find peace and harmony here."

"Thanks, um... glad to meet you," Sinprejic said, feeling like he really should have a formal response but not having a clue what it should be.

Telperios smiled kindly. "Pardon the formal entry and greeting. We elves love our rituals. Greeting you this way lets all the watching elves know that you are accepted as a friend, and that you should not be pestered, tricked, or needlessly followed."

"Watching? Oh, yes, I guess I should have expected that," Sinprejic said.

"Be at ease. The formality is over. Would you like to meet my pegasus? His name is Archaeron, he too is a leader of his kind. We cooperate. We help each other impress our followers and guests from time to time."

"Of course," Sinprejic said, again staring at the magnificent steed. As he approached, the pegasus watched him much like any horse would, and when he was close enough he lifted his hand to where it could be sniffed. The pegasus sniffed, snorted, and danced, looking at Telperios. Something seemed to pass between the elven king and the pegasus, and it returned, pushing its nose into Sinprejic's hand.

"My friend apologizes. He's had a bad impression of humans, and your scent brought back memories he'd rather forget. He's glad to hear that there's at least one human who prefers to speak with elves instead of fight with them."

"Apologies accepted. I am all too aware that some of my kind can be unpleasant at times."

The pegasus whinnied, seemingly laughing, and then bobbed his head a few times. Again he and the elven king stared at each other, and the pegasus resettled its wings and moved off to graze nearby.

"He likes your answer. He approves of you, which is quite important. Pegasi are very sensitive to malicious intent, and if he's comfortable with you that says a lot."

"It must be amazing to ride him."

"Certainly." The king smiled and added, "But that is a privilege that has to be earned, usually over a period of several decades."

"I'm not surprised. He's amazing. I never thought I'd actually see one. I've only read about them in stories."

"I'm sure not too long ago you'd only read about elves too."

"Actually, I realize now that you say it I never saw anything written down about elves. The only knowledge I had was based on what people told me. Unfortunately people told me a lot of things that were badly skewed or completely wrong."

"And yet here you stand. Tell me, how is it that your first meeting with my daughter did not end in tragedy?"

Sinprejic paused and gathered his thoughts. This was not a time to misspeak. The elven king waited patiently, if anything seeming pleased that Sinprejic did not answer in haste.

"As much as I would like to say I knew better despite the lies of my friends, that would be untrue. It's actually entirely Alfyra's doing that things went well. She took control of the situation instantly with her quick reflexes. It's not hard to act peaceful while staring at the pointy end of an elven bow."

Telperios smiled at his daughter approvingly, and she smiled back. Then he said, "So her beauty had nothing to do with it?"

"Ah, um... well that certainly helped too. I'd never seen a drawing of an elf, and while I don't think anyone actually said elves had fangs, the way they talked I had somehow created that image in my mind. It's one of only a few times I've been so very pleased to be wrong."

The elven king looked at him gravely for a moment. "Well spoken, and your manner and tone rings true, but I'm horribly saddened to learn that humans are viewing us this way. I can't imagine what we've done to inspire such fear. I do my best to use my illusions and enchantments to turn humans away without conflict, usually without them ever realizing they've been led, but this doesn't always work. Honestly, I've done my best to kill and injure as few of them as possible. We want nothing but peace and harmony, but you're the first human in two decades we've been able to speak with."

"This has worried me too, but sadly I think I know what's going on, and it's not your fault at all. What I'm about to say is conjecture, but it fits well with the things I do know, and the things I heard before I left for Morphosius's tower.

"I believe the problem lies almost entirely with our baron. I think he is demonizing and spreading fear of the elves to motivate people in the town to work hard and build up military strength. I'm not sure why, but I do recall that every time something bad happened, and a guardsman got hurt there would be a collection taken up. It became so standard that some who were tired of paying it called it the vengeance tax. It was never required by law, but if you weren't seen contributing people whispered about those folks and treated them poorly. The bartender would serve them three-quarter full mugs, and once or twice I heard of folks who didn't contribute getting windows broken, even in mid-winter."

"Ah, this is sad news indeed. It's a little different, but I remember some other human leaders like this. Once they gain some amount of military power, they typically try to take over one or more of their neighbors, leading to war and bloodshed. It's a human cycle that's sad but seemingly inevitable. This is the first time in my life that I've seen elves being used as the foil to such plans, however." The elven king sighed and continued, "Unfortunately, this is good and bad news. The good news is that now that I recognize the cycle, I know it will pass in time, but the bad news is that the winds of the storm are just starting to blow. If we are very unlucky, your baron will become rich enough to afford the services of a Wizard before he turns his focus elsewhere."

"Well if it's not too soon, and I'm a Wizard by then, I'll stand with you, of that I am sure."

The elven king smiled gently. "A noble sentiment, but your life is in flux. I'll not take that as a promise, because I know what it is to attend the Academy on the Isle of Wizards. There is no experience that has greater potential to change the course of a person's life. Nonetheless, we should discuss the future soon, but I have one more curiosity. How is it you chose to become an apprentice to Morphosius?"

"I didn't really choose him. He just seemed to be the only option. I had to stop living in a town full of lies, and someone there had caused some trouble for me. That got a lot of folks talking about me. As I'm sure you can understand, nothing was scarier to me than people paying attention to me. If someone had suspected I was talking to elves, I would have been in serious, possibly fatal trouble. Morphosius apparently had been intending to recruit me already, and his offer to me was the only option I could find that kept me near here but got me out of town. Honestly, I never wanted to be a Mage in the first place. Even now I'm not sure of it, but it does seem like a way I could gain some control of my life and still keep my friendship with Alfyra."

"Friendship?"

"Well certainly that, but love too. She's the only person in the world I feel I can really trust wholeheartedly. We both enjoy the woods and playing stones and discussing whatever comes to mind or just sitting together. All I know is I'd be sad for a very long time if she left my life. Possibly sad forever."

Alfyra spoke up suddenly, "I trust him too, Dad. He's truly got a peaceful heart, and I know from what I've learned of him that he would rather completely abandon his hopes and dreams before he would hurt innocent people around him."

"This is good," the elven king said, then his manner became more formal. "Trust and friendship to the elves has been established, but this is not all that is required. My daughter is a princess of the elves and a possible future leader. She must not waste, time however sweet it is, with a person of no accomplishment. I would no more allow her to spend decades with a wagon driver or farmhand than I would with a young man who repeatedly takes on professions and gives them up.

"You will have my blessing only if you are able to do two things. First, you must earn your amulet and accept attendance at the Academy on the Isle of Wizards, and secondly if you wish my blessing *before* you have earned your staff, you must bind each other with a mutual trust pact sealed upon the jade ring. This ring makes all promises magically binding. The required pact will be spoken by each of you to the other as follows. 'I swear to protect and defend you with my life if necessary until by death or by mutual oath do we part.' This is a necessary precaution, because many things can happen in the Academy, including forbidden magics cast by students who think they can get away with it. You must not be turned against my daughter by any means.

"I revealed that I am a Wizard of Illusion at the start, but my other less well-known accolade is as a Wizard of time. I've cast several auguries regarding you, and they seem to come up good and bad in equal numbers. That generally means that your future is in flux. You will have an effect on us, and there is no avoiding that. Therefore, I must do what I can to try to push that effect into a positive one if I can. I hope you understand."

"I understand, and it seems reasonable. I would gladly speak such an oath the moment I am qualified to do so."

"Good, and one final condition. Although our lives are long, yours is not. If you are of a mind to dawdle and waste time and then fail to enter the Academy, this delay will only deepen the pain of separation for my daughter. I sense fantastic talent in you, and I've heard nothing but praise for your intellect from Alfyra, so I feel it is reasonable that you should achieve this before the summer solstice. If the sun rises on a day when the daylight is shorter than the day before, and you are not possessed of an apprentice's amulet, you must each cease your meetings with my daughter. To ensure this, if I fail, I will send Alfyra across the mountains to the east to learn of our kindred the Winter Elves and build relationships there. This is something she will have to do someday, and if she is old enough to love you she is also old enough for that too."

"I understand, and I will earn your blessing. I promise."

"Good, I genuinely hope so," the king said with a mischievous smile. "Because I know I'll have to weather an epic temper tantrum if you don't."

"Dad!" Alfyra gasped indignantly.

The elven king winked and smiled and then said formally, "Sinprejic, pledge-apprentice of Morphosius, it has been a pleasure to meet you."

Sinprejic replied, "Telperios, Steward of the Trees, Protector of the Forests, and Duo-Wizard of Illusion and Time, I've really enjoyed meeting you. I look forward to our next meeting."

The elven king smiled, and the Pegasus, which had trotted up behind him, whinnied. Then, just as the elven king mounted the pegasus, the clouds finally broke and bathed the field in sunlight as they flew away.

6.3 Lunch

"So how did I do?" Sinprejic asked Jalsus at lunch two days after his meeting with the elven king. He had made a third attempt to copy the book yesterday.

"I couldn't find any difference. I gave it all to Morphosius, so assuming he doesn't find something I missed you should be good. I notice you even mimicked the handwriting style this time too. I think he'll like that."

"Yeah, actually it was mostly a matter of cleaning up my own bad habits. Aurcivius writes entirely conventionally. It is the way

I was taught I should write, which is to say better than I normally write."

"Seriously impressive, kid," Imoed agreed and looked at Mutara. "Come on, Mutara. Tell me you didn't expect him to take six months to get it down."

"I didn't expect six months, but certainly he's exceeded expectations," Mutara replied grudgingly.

"You need to watch out, Mutara. I think tonight he's going to earn the right to play even stones with me. Soon he'll be coming for you."

Mutara raised her eyebrows in surprise. "Really? I might just have to play him if he improves another stone or two."

"She's better than you?" Sinprejic asked.

"Yeah, by about a two stone handicap, and Morphosius is another stone beyond that, but she's probably rusty, so I think it could get interesting if you played her."

The lunchtime banter was interrupted by Morphosius's arrival.

"Enough about stones. Sinprejic when you finish your lunch, meet me in the examination room. It's time for your aptitude test. You've passed the written test," Morphosius said as he entered.

"Thank you! I'll be there as soon as I can." Sinprejic beamed.

6.4 Aptitude

Fifteen minutes later, Sinprejic entered the testing room and found Morphosius fussing with the strange candelabra that Sinprejic had noted during his second attempt. Morphosius seemed to get things set up the way he wanted just as he noticed Sinprejic.

"Ah there you are, good. Let me explain the process. These candles are of two types. One type will ignite in the presence of any magic of a given type, and the other type of candle extinguishes in proximity to a person with talent in its corresponding type. You can see that each pair is a different color. Black for Necromancy, green for Thought, violet for Illusion, blue for Energy, red for Planar magic, and brown for Mutamancy. Today we will start with the second type. I will light one of each color, and then you will slowly approach them. The more talent you have for each type of magic, the greater the distance at which each candle will extinguish."

"The tricky part of this is lighting the candles without triggering the energy candles nearby. At the Academy they have a mundane cleaning staff or helper light these things with a normal flame. With my talents, I'll put out half of them just by standing close, so I've had to get a bit creative here. I *think* I've to come up with a small enough spell to avoid ruining the energy candles. At the Academy they have a somewhat bigger room for this. We'll need to start outside the room since I'm a Master of Mutamancy..."

Once they were positioned outside the room looking in where they could still see the candelabra on a table at the far end of the room, almost eighty feet away, Morphosius cast a small spell that used a verbal incantation sounding, almost like a buzzing bee. The result was a very tiny point of flame that wavered and wandered through the air like some sort of drunken mosquito. As it neared the candles it became steadier and then momentarily darted in to each candle, lighting it and withdrawing in the blink of an eye. After all six of the front candles were lit, the *firebug* spell winked out. The flame of each candle matched the color of the candle, which was particularly strange and eerie for the black candle.

"Ah good, it worked," said Morphosius. "Now what you need to do for me is to walk very slowly one step at a time until you get within arms reach of the candles and then stop. Once you are there, I'll give you further instruction. Call out as soon as you see any candle flame extinguish.

Sinprejic did as he was told, and just inside the door to the room, about fifty feet from the candles, the black candle on the left sputtered and winked out. Sinprejic gaped, and turned back asking, "Wait, the black one went out already. Do you need to relight it?"

Smiling in satisfaction, Morphosius said, "Did I say you could stop walking? Keep going."

"But, that can't be true. I mean, that's the Necromancy candle. It can't mean anything."

"Of course, it does. Now move and remember to stop when you get to arm's length."

Sinprejic kept walking, a look of pure horror on his face. He was staring at the black candle as if willing it to relight itself, but to no avail. For a while, nothing happened, and he stopped at arms length as requested, still staring at the traitorous black candle in disbelief.

Morphosius spoke from behind him saying, "Now carefully take your left arm and extend it straight out to the side. Good, just like that, and now when I say go slowly move your arm in an arc toward the candles, but stop the moment any candles go out. Understood?"

"Yes."

"Go."

Sinprejic slowly moved his arm inward, dread on his face, his fear that his only talent would be Necromancy laid bare by his expression. When he got within five inches of the black candle, the green candle also went out, and he sighed in relief. "Green," he called out.

"Very good," Morphosius said. "Resume slowly."

An inch closer and the purple candle also went out. "Purple," he called out.

"Excellent, excellent. Again, still slowly," Morphosius said, sounding almost greedy.

"Blue," Sinprejic called out almost immediately.

"Good," Morphosius said, suddenly sounding doubtful. More quietly he mumbled something that sounded like "joke" at the end.

Sinprejic continued, but nothing happened to the remaining two candles before he touched the black candle.

"I'm touching the black candle now," Sinprejic called out.

"Good, now slowly, from left to right, continue to touch each candle. Let me know if either of the remaining two go out."

Sinprejic proceeded from candle to candle with nothing happening until finally it was time to touch the red candle. The red candle winked out nearly instantly when his finger was less than an inch away."

"Red."

"How close was your finger when it went out?"

"Less than an inch, maybe half an inch or slightly more."

"Ok, proceed," Morphosius said.

The final brown candle didn't go out until just about the time Sinprejic touched it.

"Brown."

"How far?"

"Maybe just a small fraction before I touched it? Hard to say."

"Ok, you did well, very well." Morphosius delivered a monologue as he walked into the room to stand by Sinprejic's side. "Almost too well to be believed. Your talents appear to be, Master of Necromancy, Wizard of Enchantment/Thought, Wizard of Illusion, Wizard of Energy, Magician of Planar and Conjuring magic, and Mage of Matter and mutation. I will double-check these candles against myself and by other means later. If there are no defects, and Micropolis hasn't played a joke on us, this would make you more talented than any living Mage and possibly on par with some of the legendary names in the past.

"This candle test is a recent development in the last hundred years. Unfortunately, given this much talent in the primary types of magic it's very unlikely for you to have any talent in either Time or Metamancy, but if you work hard and are extremely careful you will have a good chance of earning a seat on the council someday. Bear in mind, however, what we discovered today is only potential. You are not even a Mage or even a full apprentice just yet. Next you have to demonstrate you can learn. The practical test is for you to learn to evoke power in each of your talents and then learn at least three cantrips. Given your results, any of *disturb*, *blink*, *remote knock*, or *light candle* would make sense as your first spell. Once you demonstrate three of those, I can give you your amulet."

"Ok, when can I start?"

"Right now of course. Have a seat at the desk."

Sinprejic noticed that the desk had been moved to the center of the room again along with the chair. Morphosius picked up the candelabra, which now had one candle of each color with a black, burnt wick and a matching one with an unburnt wick. Sinprejic sat down, and Morphosius set the candles down in front of him with the unburnt side toward him.

"This next bit was the old test for many centuries, and while it can confirm talent it's not very good at judging relative strength, and it's easy to miss talents. These days, it's used as a training exercise to kindle the first spark of sorcery that will become the seed for all your subsequent wizardry."

"Ok, what do I do?" Sinprejic said eagerly, sensing that his goal of becoming an apprentice was near.

"First, close your eyes and breathe deeply ten times in a row. As you do this clear your mind then open your eyes and focus on the black candle. While remaining calm, try to think of a loved one who died or something having to do with death."

Sinprejic did as he was told, and when he opened his eyes he saw all the spells in the room, but he had expected that and was not surprised. He stared at the black candle with a baleful stare and suddenly the green candle burst into flame, burning almost a quarter of its length immediately.

Morphosius sighed loudly, brought his hand up to his face, and massaged his temples briefly. When he brought his hand down, he looked straight at Sinprejic with a penetrating gaze. "Did I or did I not tell you to clear your mind?"

"Yes, and I did." Sinprejic said defensively.

"And then what?" Morphosius said with exaggerated patience that implied the exact opposite.

"I looked at the black candle, and I just felt disgusted. I hate death and want nothing to do with skeletons and zombies or anything like that."

"Ok. The only time when emotions can be involved in casting is for certain types of Enchantment, but for all else you need a clear head and a calm mind. Focusing on strong emotion is how the thought candle is lit. Try again."

Sinprejic tried again, but the green candle flashed into brilliant flame and melted entirely, puddling wax all over the desk.

"Ok, let's come back to Necromancy. It seems you have issues. I have a book in the library that maybe will help you adjust your thinking to something less... embarrassing. Next, we'll want to work on illusion. Morphosius drew a piece of paper out of his pocket and placed it on the desk. "What do you see?"

"A vase."

"You don't see two faces?"

"Oh, sorry. I see it now, but the space between them also looks like a vase."

"Precisely, it's an optical illusion caused by a shift in perception. Shifting perceptions is the fundamental work of illusions, so think about that moment when your perception changed. Carefully remember how you felt in that exact instant when the vase turned into faces. Now relax and concentrate on that feeling."

Sinprejic did so, and the purple candle smoldered and then sprouted a perfectly normal-looking flame.

"Good. Much better. Now for energy, the easiest thing for most folks is to simply think of a candle flame. Almost everyone gets this on their first try if they have even a little talent." Morphosius blinked in surprise as the blue candle promptly sprouted a flame on its wick.

They tried the two remaining candles, but with no success. "Well three out of six candles on your first day is way above average anyway," Morphosius said. "I have about half a dozen candles of each type. You are free to experiment with them, but I caution you to not use them all up, because I need to see you light all six in sequence. Also, you can now have your first spell manual. This contains five cantrips, any three of which you must master to earn your amulet."

"Only five?"

"Planar magic and Conjuration is too dangerous. Be cautious when attempting to light that candle. If you try too hard and then suddenly succeed, you could open a peephole to another location, which if it is badly placed could easily injure or kill you. So take it slow, steady, and careful with that one. Once you do that, don't touch planar magic until you've been certified to train with it at the Academy. Many things can go badly wrong when you bend or warp reality. Few mistakes with planar magic end well unless you are extremely lucky."

"Ok, I'll be careful."

"Now that you are evoking magical essences, there is one final thing I am required by council law to do, and that's to bind you to my service. From the point at which you lit the first candle forward, there are only two options. Be bound by a spell that commits you to my service until your graduation as a certified Mage, or to escape that you may accept a different binding that will prevent you from invoking any magic for the rest of your life.

The latter choice is permanent and cannot be undone. You will, of course, recall this from the primer."

"Yes, I choose to be an apprentice."

"Good, those are the exact words you are required to say. Now, hold still and don't try to light any candles or anything while I do this."

Sinprejic nodded, and Morphosius recited a series of rhythmic phrases and made some intricate hand gestures. He repeated them three times. Each time ending with "Johnathan D'Abrac." The first two incantations were successively louder, but the third one trailed off. Sinprejic could see some magic being layered onto him, and then when his name was said each time it seemed to dissipate, After the third time, Morphosius stared at him for several seconds, during which the corner of his mouth twitched once.

Suddenly he said, "Ok, that takes care of that. Let's recap your assignments. First, light the red candle, carefully. Second, light the brown candle, also carefully, but it's fundamentally less dangerous. Then light the green candle normally, without melting or exploding it. Finally, you must place a green candle next to the black candle and light only the black candle. For extra credit or as a break, you may begin to work on the *remote knock* cantrip for illusion and *light candle* cantrip for energy. Under no circumstances should you attempt any cantrip for which I have not approved your candle. Understood?"

"Aren't I already lighting candles?"

"These candles are specially prepared and magically sensitive to specific types of magic. The energy cantrip will be for lighting a normal non-magical candle."

"Oh, I see. Thank you."

"Ok, you may take the remainder of the day off to begin work on this. No book binding today. And you now have access to this room. The door should open and shut for you without incident. This is the only safe room for apprentices to experiment with completely new spells, so you must do your work here."

"Ok, understood. Can I try the green candle by itself right now?"

"Yes."

Sinprejic set up a new green candle and smoothly lit it with no trouble.

"Ok, you are approved to work on the *blink* cantrip for thought magic too, but you have three more candles to go, and those are your priority. I don't want to be pestered, so if you have progress to show, tell me at lunchtime. If you need help or explanation, Jalsus can assist you since the two of you seem to get along well." And with that Morphosius turned and left him with his box of candles and the manual of basic cantrips.

6.5 Problem

"You wanted me?" Mutara said as she closed the door behind her. Morphosius looked up from the book he had laid open on the stone table in front of him and looked directly at her, his eyes conveying a smoldering anger.

In a cage to Morphosius's left, a man wearing tattered black rags with an unkempt beard and matted black hair cackled and said, "Nobody wants you, you hag!" And then he broke into an incongruous stream of giggles. "Crizane made a funny."

Morphosius and Mutara didn't acknowledge the comment or even seem to have heard it. Clearly, they were very used to such ravings. Morphosius nodded toward a door, and they headed to another room to talk.

Crizane stopped giggling, frowned, and then shouted triumphantly, "Hah, don't want Crizane to hear do you? You know I'll escape some day! Leaving won't help! I already know all your sins! All of them, I say, all! And when I tell Aurcivius, he'll give your pretty little stole to someone else. I can't wait to see what seemingly random freak accident you encounter... that's right! Hide in the summoning room—it doesn't matter! Crizane will have his day. Have his day in the sun. Sunny day. Sunny side up! Ah, the best way to eat eggs..."

And then, staring into space and contemplating eggs, he began to drool. His threats were useless anyway. The underground walls absorbed all sound, and Mutara had shut the door to the summoning room halfway through his speech.

The summoning room was a set-up with braziers, incense, candles, and fine black granite flooring. The granite was finely veined with red, and at opposite ends of the room were two inlaid summoning circles. The circles were inlaid with slightly raised rose quartz in the shape of pentagrams within a double circle, and spidery script between the inner and outer circles.

Once safely away from the distraction of Crizane's ravings, Morphosius turned to Mutara and said, "Damn kid didn't give us his true name."

"His name is definitely Johnathan D'Abrac. I've watched both his mother and that book binder call him by that name. I saw it early on, back when you first had me start watching him. He wouldn't even have known there was anyone to hide from."

"Yes, but it seems he doesn't know his own true name, because the binding spell wouldn't take. It just fizzled three times in a row. I had to pretend it worked."

"That's not good."

"No, it's not"

"What will you do? Am I here to assist in conjuring our dark little friend again?"

"No, although that might be the easiest way, it would mean that Sinprejic's true name would be floating around in the plane of chaos where someone else might get hold of it. That could be used against him or in the worst case could allow someone to use him against us. Too big of a risk."

"Ok, what then? Do you think his parents know?"

"Certainly, it's the next logical step, but I suppose I'll have to handle it myself."

"What do you need from me?"

"I'll need you to skip your practice flying as an owl for a couple nights and focus on preparations. I need you to secure the teleport room and add a temporary cage and silence spells. If I return with one or more prisoners or bodies, we'll need to stash them till everyone is asleep."

"You plan to obliterate any knowledge of his true name?"

"Might as well kill two birds with one stone. On the plus side, there will be no need to sanitize an entire town now. Ready a cage down here too, just in case we have to give Crizane some company."

"We should really think about making a muzzle for him."

"Tempting, but what little utility he has as a puppet necromancer is sure to evaporate if we treat him any worse. His sanity is not improving. I assume you'll feed him and the pets since you are already down here?"

"Of course."

"Good, I'll be in my study preparing."

6.6 Sir D'Abrac

"I wonder what has become of him," Sir D'Abrac sighed, staring at the worn scrap of paper-bark that had served to introduce Johnny to them so many years ago. He looked at it often now that Johnny was gone. The disappearance of his adopted son bothered him greatly. Though he could think of nothing he would have done differently, he wished somehow things had turned out better.

He and Madeline had spoken with every trader and tradesman in town and ridden west and south for over a week. They had talked to everyone they met along the road but found no trace of Johnny. It puzzled him that a youth so young and inexperienced could disappear so thoroughly, but somehow he was convinced that Johnny was still out there.

Sighing, he placed the scrap of bark back under the blotter on his desk and took a ledger from the bookshelf behind him. After sharpening a quill and opening a bottle of ink, he got to work.

The scratching of a feathered quill pen, the ticking of a clock, and the occasional muffled bird call filtering in through the paper window lit by the noonday sun were the only sounds in the dusty old study for many minutes. Some might have found it odd to see the large weather-beaten old warrior studiously entering figures in neat, precise columns. Accounting for income and expenses was hardly warrior's work, but then he hadn't fought in a real battle in over ten years. Today, his only occasional battles were with his ledger. A few years ago he'd come to the conclusion that it would be necessary to produce at least some crops from this land to avoid spending down his entire wealth, and thus the ledger wars had begun.

Chasing away the occasional goblin raiding party hardly counted as battle, though it did at least keep him from getting too rusty and force him to oil his sword. Right now his sword was propped against a bookshelf ten feet away. In his youth, he would have never allowed the sword out of reach. It was a simple rule of survival for a warrior. Certainly it was not true that one needed a sword at all times, but if ever it was needed and out of reach, the countless hours of honing reflexes and drilling precise cuts, strokes, feints, parries and stabs were useless. A warrior such as Jared D'Abrac lived and died by his skill with the sword.

He was not helpless without the sword, but there were plenty

244

of folk who could present a serious threat when he was unarmed. Armed with his sword, on the other hand, even at his age and with his lack of practice, precious few could best him, and even those would find the fight to be nontrivial. At least it would be non-trivial without magic.

Magic, of course, was another matter. He had fought and won against wizards, including dispatching the Necromancer Nazh Al' Farren when he turned on the kingdom and attempted to raise an army of the dead. The number one rule for fighting wizards was... don't. When that rule failed, the second rule was to make sure they were fighting someone else before you started fighting them. Preferably, they should be battling another wizard, who they would almost always see as a much greater threat.

That was the way of it when Jared had dispatched Nazh. Madeline had planted the fear of an attack by the Archmage himself in the Necromancer's dreams and then created a diversion. In rushing to meet the challenge of a great wizard who hadn't actually come to fight him, Nazh failed to pay attention to the more mundane threats. A simple *detect metals* spell or *sense life* spell would have forewarned him, but instead he took the predictable path to his adversary, eschewing magic to avoid detection himself. He never made it past the intersection of two narrow hallways where Jared had lain in wait. A single well-placed stroke too fast for a spell or ward to be raised separated Nazh's head from his body. It was precisely the same strike that green recruits were forced to drill repeatedly but delivered with the power, speed, and accuracy of a veteran.

Rule number three of fighting wizards was the same as rule number one but with an entirely different meaning. If the wizard was alert, focused on you, and prepared for battle, the game was already over. Don't fight... bargain. This rule came to mind immediately when Jared looked up to see a figure wearing a chocolate-brown velvet robe with a hood that was pulled up so that the face could not be seen. The edges of the sleeves and the hood had a satin border, which was embroidered with spidery symbols that seemed to be made of fire.

The instant he saw the figure, his blood turned to ice, and his legs turned to jelly. He wanted to yell for help, but his finely honed warrior instincts prevented that reaction. Instinctively, he knew that an entrance such as this spoke of a truly powerful wizard. Shouting would do nothing but ensure the involvement of his family in what might be a dark or dangerous dealing.

The figure stood silently, holding an ornately carved staff, the top of which formed the likeness of a snake with a flattened head. The jewel eyes of the snake-staff were glowing fiercely. Seconds ticked away, marked only by the sound of the mechanical clock. Seconds turned into a minute, one minute into two and then four. Neither of them moved. Jared used the time to study the man, searching for a sign that this was illusion or for some trace of information that might give him a handle on who he was dealing with and what arguments might be persuasive to them. The longer the silence stretched, the surer Jared was that he wasn't going to like the conversation when it came.

Eventually, Jared began to worry that this might drag on until Madeline or one of the children barged in. He decided that for their sakes he must begin the conversation with the dark figure. Just as he began to clear his throat, the eyes on the snake head staff stopped glowing, and the figure slowly came forward, extending the staff such that it pointed diagonally across toward Jared's sword arm. The staff was within easy reach, and the figure stopped and appeared to wait.

Despite the closeness of the figure now, the view inside the hood revealed nothing but a vague sense that there was a head inside. Clearly, the wizard was hiding his face with a simple but effective illusion. Nothing complicated would be needed to fool a warrior like Jared.

Again, there was a long, quiet pause, and the staff remained extended. Jared realized that the clear intent was for him to grab the staff. Madeline had told him that some of the greatest wizards had spells or artifacts that allowed them to transport themselves and others across distances instantly. According to Madeline, a person could not be transported against their will, and voluntary physical contact was required. It seemed clear to him that he was to grab the staff and then the figure would transport him to a location where they could talk safely.

Slowly, non-threateningly, Jared raised his hand from the desk and took hold of the staff. The figure did not move, speak, or shift the staff, so Jared closed his fingers around it. The section he was holding was just below the serpent's head. The staff was smooth and textured like scales. Much like a snake, it was cool to the touch. For about three seconds nothing happened.

The figure spoke a single word that Jared didn't recognize, but its tone and sound were sibilant and breathy. Instantly, the head of the staff curled over and struck Jared on the back of the hand, too fast for the eye to follow. The strike left just a tiny pin prick, but instantly Jared was paralyzed. The instantaneous nature of the paralysis clearly indicated magic and not poison from the bite, but the snake was now all too real, looking nothing like any sort of staff.

In lazy fashion, the snake draped its body over either side of Jared's frozen, outstretched arm, as if his arm were a tree limb. In that steady, slow manner unique to serpentine reptiles, the snake began to advance toward Jared's body. The motion was never fast, but it was continuous, and a surprising distance could be covered during a just a moment of inattention.

Jared's attention however never wavered. His face could not move, and his expression never changed, but his eyes shown fear and revulsion, along with a certain sad knowing feeling. Jared could no longer see the snake's head as it crossed onto his shoulder and around behind his neck. He felt the cold reptilian nose tuck under the opposite side of his collar as the snake flowed into his shirt and then back out onto his lap. After gathering its coils in Jared's lap, the snake began to descend, following the curve at the back of Jared's left calf and then spiraling down to the floor.

An instant of hope crept into Jared's eyes as the tail of the snake unwrapped itself and the snake coiled itself like a scaly rope on the floor near Jared's leg. Perhaps this was just a show of power, an intimidation tactic. Then, without warning, the snake flared the skin around its head, showing a skull-like pattern on its back and struck the side of Jared's left calf. This was no pinprick. Had he been able, Jared would have cried out in agony as the snake latched onto his leg and sank its fangs deep through skin, veins, and muscle. The snake did not let go instantly, holding on with a chewing motion that pumped even more venom into its prey. Jared's calf went numb instantly, and within seconds none of his leg had any feeling. His breathing became shallow and slowed as his eyes lost focus. The original paralysis spell faded. But by now, the venom had nearly completed its work, and Jared managed no more than a single weak, breathy word as his world sank into permanent darkness.

"Why?"

After Sir D'Abrac's body slumped into stillness, Morphosius leafed through a couple pages of the ledger and sniffed disdainfully. He then wandered around the bookshelves in the study, pulling books, leafing through some pages, and replacing each book until he came to a series of personal journals written in handwriting matching what he had seen in the ledger.

"Ah good, I was hoping you were the methodical sort to keep journals," Morphosius murmured as he pulled and replaced each journal quickly after checking the dates of the entries until he found ones marked as year 903, the colloquial numbering for the year 20903. He began to leaf through these volumes more carefully.

"Here it is," he said as he came to an entry dated as the 28th day of the 11th month of 903. He read intently for a bit then swore softly. "Shit, well that explains it. Johnathan D'Abrac is not his true name, but no lie was detected because he's a basket baby and doesn't know that his parents replaced his true name. Figures that this oaf of a warrior wouldn't bother to record his true name."

Morphosius sighed and squinted. "It was that chit Madeline's idea no doubt. She trained at the Academy and would likely have sensed his ability. She probably wanted to protect his name. Strange that she then let him train as a warrior though. As I recall, she was so weak no one could figure out how she made it through the final combat trial. Rumor was both her opponents were both conjurers who attempted to conjure beings beyond their own abilities, and all she had to do was watch them get eaten by their own summons. Then, embarrassingly, first thing after graduation she went off to the capital then gallivanting around with this lout, and somehow she helped slay Nazh. Probably she was the bait or something stupid like that... Nazh always did have that weakness." He paused, and his expression became stony. "Time to talk to her. That makes twice now she's gotten in my way."

7 Apprentice

7.1 Culture

The cool morning was warming quickly as Sinprejic reached the needle tree grove. The day promised to be the first truly warm day of the year. The leaves were just beginning to spread from the tree branches, hinting at the possibility of shade, but not yet really providing it. When he arrived, the signal rock was already shifted, and Alfyra soon revealed herself.

"You did marvelously with my dad last time. He's mentioned you several times. I think he wants you to succeed. Did you manage to write out the book?" she said in Elvish. They spoke Elvish almost exclusively now that they knew someone from the tower was likely to be watching them. Sinprejic suspected it was probably Mutara. Hopefully, she didn't know Elvish.

"Yes, and I passed this time. I was worried that he was just finding excuses to put me off, but perhaps I didn't manage to give him an excuse. I think Jalsus would have complained to him if he hadn't passed me anyway."

"Awesome, so did you get tested? What are your talents?"

Sinprejic's face became serious. "I'm strong, very strong, apparently."

Alfyra sensed his tension. "But something's wrong? You don't like the result?"

"I'm a Master quality talent in Necromancy."

"And what don't you like about that?"

"It's Necromancy. I don't want anything to do with the dead, death, or undeath. The idea is repulsive to me."

"What did I tell you about Metamancy?"

"It's a matter of how I use it, yes, but this is different. It's messing with people's life force, their very souls. That's wrong. Necromancers are hunted. I don't want to be hunted."

Alfyra looked at him seriously, and asked, "You don't want to cure diseases? You don't want to heal people who have been wounded? You don't want to provide enhanced crop yields or fertility for those who are having trouble having conceiving? These are all Necromancy too..."

"I know that in my brain, but in my heart I just can't like anything associated with manipulating people's souls."

"Think on what I said, think of birth and growth of new life rather than death. That's Necromancy too. What were your other results?" she asked, and when he told her she smiled. "Wow, that's wonderful. You've got talent in everything."

"Not so much in Mutamancy which is slightly awkward given that I'm in the tower belonging to the head of that discipline."

"Well true, but that's why the Academy exists. The sponsor doesn't always fit well with the apprentice."

"How did the other elves react to me?" Sinprejic asked.

Alfyra pursed her lips and looked at him for a moment, clearly noticing the change of topic, then she brightened and said, "They're all impressed, but that's a natural outcome of the fact that you impressed my father. He has a huge influence on the opinions of other elves. That's part of why I introduced you to him first. He's been their leader for over three hundred and fifty mostly prosperous years. My father's opinion is everything. He could see you were careful with your words. Other humans he has met have been more hasty. By the way, most of my friends are jealous because my father complimented your intelligence."

"That's wonderful news."

"Yes, and it's an absolutely fabulous day today. What do you say we go have a deer-touching contest?"

"Deer-touching contest?"

"Deer touching is an elven game. The idea is to sneak up so silently or so peacefully that the deer allows you to touch it without fleeing in fear. It's really just an excuse to practice our stalking but with an added spice of competition."

"Ok, sure, stalking is always a good skill to keep fresh. Let's go, but you can't use your magic moccasins. That's not fair."

"Haha, I was hoping you'd forget about that, but you're right. I'll take them off."

Two hours later, they had located six deer, and Alfyra had touched five and Sinprejic three, including the one she spooked. The sun was now high, and the work of stalking had both of them sweating.

"It's too hot," Alfyra said suddenly and stripped off her shirt. "First shirtless day," she said with a joyful smile before noticing the look on his face. "What? Why are you looking away? You're all red! Are you that hot? Take off your shirt too. I didn't realize you were so hot. We should go back and swim in the spring. What's wrong?"

"You took your shirt off!"

"So? It's hot. The breeze feels soooo good."

"But your breasts are exposed..."

"So? There's nothing wrong with them. They're normal. All my friends think they're prettier than average. You don't like them?"

"Um, ok. Clearly this is a cultural thing. Human women never show their breasts to men... except maybe their husbands when they... um... well... you know..."

"Oh my, you're blushing, not hot. Oh dear. You'll need to get over this if you're going to visit our home settlement during the summer months. We only wear what we need to keep warm, plus belts or harnesses to carry useful items."

"Oh dear."

"What?"

"That's going to be very difficult."

"But I thought you must know this from the first day we met."

"I thought I had stumbled on you in a private moment. At the very start, I worried you might shoot me because I had seen you naked."

Alfyra giggled. "This is the funniest conversation. Well, we elves are practical. We don't waste time dirtying cloths with copious sweat while being entirely uncomfortable at the same time. Who likes laundry anyway, especially sweaty laundry."

"I mean it makes sense when you say it that way, but my whole life I've always been told I shouldn't be naked and that it's wrong to look at someone who is naked."

"I suppose for a human who doesn't want to be seen it wouldn't be nice to look if it made them uncomfortable. In any case, I see you sweating. If I heard what you said correctly, it's ok for men to take off their shirts because they don't have breasts?"

"Yeah."

"That's so weird. Anyway, go ahead and be comfortable."

"What about mosquitoes and deer flies? Three of those bit me already."

"I should get you one of these charms." She indicated a small wooden pendant on a thin string around her neck. "It's a super simple enchantment, and we can make these ourselves, so they are not very valuable. Soon, you'll be able to cast the associated spell, I'm sure. That spell is so simple I've even managed to cast it a few times, but my talent is so low that it takes me almost fifteen minutes. Once you master it, the casting should be nearly instantaneous for you. Here, let me take a few minutes and see if I can cast it properly on you."

Sinprejic watched, and it did indeed seem simple though he

wasn't quite sure what the consequences of messing it up would be given that it was applied directly to him.

When she finished, he asked her about the risk of miscasting, and she said, "Usually it just doesn't work, and you just get a lot of bug bites if you mess it up. Once I heard of a guy smelling like a candle for a day, but I don't think it will harm you. The spell wears off in a few hours anyway. But in any case, now you can take your shirt off," she said with a sly smile, and he obliged.

She looked him over, smiled, winked, and said, "Let's go find some more deer."

A few hours later they returned to the glade, and after a quick dip in the icy water of the spring they dressed again and played a stones game. At the end, she sighed and said, "I knew this day would come. You've finally beaten me without a handicap. You're probably practicing with wizards now."

"Jalsus and I play every other night," he admitted.

"How strong is he?"

"He beat me after giving me three stones a few times, but recently we've moved to a two-stone handicap."

"I'll have to get Oyonaril to give me lessons again" she said.

"I think it's getting late."

"Yeah, good luck this week. I'm sure you can get the remaining candles soon. Remember, I expect you to become the best healer in the world. No slacking on Necromancy."

Sinprejic nodded. They kissed each other goodbye and headed toward their respective homes.

7.2 Flavors

The next morning, Sinprejic rose early, grabbed a quick breakfast, and headed straight to the testing room. He immediately got out a red candle and began the exercise to try to learn to light it. Supposedly the trick was to think of two places far apart and imagine that they were getting closer together. This apparently was an element of how one created a portal between two locations, but the idea was to pick two locations far enough apart that you would not accidentally succeed and have to control a planar rift. The examples he had read about in one of the new books he now had access to in the library all spoke of locations in separate cities. Sinprejic had never been more than a few miles from his home.

The furthest two places he knew of were the bridge over the river east of town and his room in the tower, but he frequently had the impression that he might be actually going to make a connection. The red candle actually gave off a wisp of smoke once, but that was the time with the scariest feeling of all.

Then he got out a blue candle and a green candle and lit them easily, which only frustrated him more. "There has to be a better way," he muttered to himself, exasperated. Then he sighed. "I need a break." He took out the manual of cantrips and read through the instructions for the *light candle* cantrip. As instructed, he practiced the short incantation without focusing on magic, and then he got out the plain white wax candle he had been given for this and set it in a holder.

On the third try he got a little bit of smoke, and there was a feel of something almost falling into place. A few attempts later, he finally got the inflection and rhythm right, and suddenly magic flowed into the candle tip almost effortlessly, and it instantly sprouted a flame. Startlingly the blue candle nearby also flared up.

Some experimentation revealed that if the blue candle were within half a dozen feet, it would light too. Then he had idea. He put out both candles and created a light ball via the spell he had copied from Imoed. He immediately noticed two things. The light ball required somewhat more effort to initiate, and it also caused the blue candle to spring to light itself.

"Ah, now I see why these candles must stay in this room only. It would be easy for someone to start a fire accidentally," he noted to himself.

He cast both spells again and then tried lighting the plain wax candle without the incantation. That turned out to be twice as hard as with the incantation, and harder to control at first. Something about the rhythm and sound of the incantation seemed to ease his mind into the right state. The difference was like the difference between walking on solid ground and walking across ice. Both were possible, but one was more difficult and less predictable. It did get easier with practice though.

Encouraged, he looked at the cantrip for illusion. The name of the spell was *remote knock* and it was intended to fool a person into believing they heard a knocking sound come from a particular direction. He brought over a purple candle and went through a similar process with *remote knock*, and it too could light the purple candle. Once he could easily cause a faint knocking sound from any location nearby, he realized that the magic for *remote knock* seemed different from the candle lighting and the light ball, and they reminded him of the spell to chase away mosquitoes as well.

Suddenly he paused, his mouth coming half open, and then said, "Oh, I'm an idiot. Of course. The different types of magic I see correspond to the different disciplines." He thought for a moment and then said, "Alfyra's rosewood rod for preventing scrying must have been mostly planar magic."

He brought the red candle back and concentrated, but this time he tried to recall what he had observed particularly the way the magic in it looked. The types of magic differed when he perceived them in a strange sort of way that was halfway between a color and a flavor, yet was neither visual nor tasteful either. He decided to think of them as flavors.

When he ignored Morphosius's original instructions to think about distant places and focused on the flavor he recalled from the rosewood rod, a cheerful flame popped into existence atop the red candle easily.

"Yes," he cheered quietly with a small fist pump.

"All I need to do is find an example spell that uses each type, and then I can solve all of these candles." Thinking for a moment, he realized that one flavor of magic was by far the most common around the tower. Soon, concentrating on the flavor of magic associated with the spells that powered the waves in the stone lake allowed him to light the brown mutamantic candle.

Just after this triumph, he was startled by a knock on the door, and for a brief instant he thought someone else had cast a *remote knock* spell, but then he realized that it was an actual knock on the door, so he stood up and opened it.

Imoed looked past him and observed the clutter of candles on the desk and said. "Looks like fun, but I thought you might want to know that lunch is half over. If you don't hurry, you'll be working hungry all afternoon. Seems the Academy is now sending over copies of the cantrip manual for binding work as well now."

"Lovely," Sinprejic said sarcastically. "Thanks for reminding me though. I'll be down in a moment."

Imoed nodded and left. Sinprejic cleaned up and got down there with barely time to grab an apple, some cheese, and a hunk of bread. It was a light lunch, and he was hungry well before dinner, but he didn't care. He only had one candle and one cantrip to go.

7.3 Fear

"So good to see you again," Alfyra said.

"Yeah, I hate it when it rains that hard."

"Don't hate it. It's good for the trees. I missed you, but the forest needs to drink."

"I hate anything that keeps us apart."

"Even your studies?"

"Kinda, but at least that's interesting. Rain is just wet."

"Nonsense! Rain makes the most wonderful sound on the leaves, and it's cool on your face. It's like bathing in the life of the forest. How can you say it's boring?"

"True, I suppose it's not actually boring, but it is wet, and makes it hard for us to meet since we would catch a chill and probably get sick."

"Soon you can cure us if we do," she teased.

"Not soon. I still can't light that candle."

"Did you light the others?" Alfyra asked, worry creeping into her voice.

"Yes, I got red and brown on the morning of the first day after our last meeting. I figured out that I only need to think about how each type of magic looks or maybe feels. I'm not sure how to describe it, but each type is different. It's a sixth sense really. I've actually learned quite a lot. I mastered all the other cantrips, even the *bend rod* one. That was the hardest. I'm not very good with Mutamancy. Somehow that type of magic seems... well, slippery in a way. I have more trouble controlling it than the others."

To demonstrate, he picked up a twig and lit the end of it as if it were a candle. That spell was already almost effortless unless he mispronounced something in the incantation.

"But you still can't light the Necromancy candle?" she asked, still worried.

"No, I can't find any examples of spells using necromancy any-where in the tower. There's something that might be it buried in the traps on the doors, but it's covered by too many other layers. I suspect that this is how it recognizes who is and isn't allowed, but it's all hidden, probably by design. I tried the other way, think-ing about death, but I don't seem to be able to remain calm. My emotions always get in the way. Sometimes I feel disgust or hate or occasionally disdain for that candle, but more and more often now it seems to be fear."

"Fear of what?"

"I don't know. I never thought about it, just fear."

"You must fear something. Think about it. What do you fear?"

"I don't know... hmm... it's like I'm afraid of succeeding, but that can't be, because I absolutely want to succeed. I *need* to succeed to keep seeing you. Sometimes it's fear that I won't succeed too, I think."

"Your parents," she stated.

"What?"

"It's just a guess, but tell me if it sounds right... I think you are afraid that if you succeed, your parents will be lost to you forever."

Sinprejic sat staring into space for a moment with his mouth half open, stunned. "I think you're right. I miss them so much. And my brother. I think I need to see them again. I need to know that they won't hate me for what I am. Or if they do, I need to know that too so I can accept it, I think. I should visit them."

"No."

"What?"

"Absolutely not. If you visit them, then the fact you became a Mage will be known by many. Your brother especially can't know. He is too young to keep that secret. Also imagine what would happen if the famous knight Jared D'Abrac declared that the Wizard of the North had stolen away his son. He could raise an army for that. He could fight the baron for control of the guards, or maybe even get the duke to send a force to assault the wizards' tower. Or maybe give your true name to another wizard so that you could be captured and returned.

"There's a very good reason that wizards hide their true names. Only a few have ever been caught, but there are cases where wizards have wiped out entire villages or families to ensure nobody knew their true name. Some think that the great plague two hundred years ago was started by such a thing. You have escaped your village at a time when you were facing public humiliation. Everyone will assume you just ran away, and only I know what became of you. Do not give the world easy access to your name."

"What about your father? Don't you know his true name?"

"No, before any of us who are strong enough are sent to the Academy, we perform a month-long ritual of forgetting. All who know him feast and party and drink elven wine that has been enchanted, and the memory of the name is slowly but surely erased. Nobody knows my father's true name but him now."

"Wow. How do you guarantee everyone attends and no one cheats?"

"Why would we want to? It's a protection for us. Nobody can capture us and torture us for his name, nobody can suffer the guilt of accidentally speaking his name where it might be heard. There is nothing good about knowing a wizard's name."

"What about my name?"

"Tindaliur and I have been trying to figure out what to do about that. We haven't told anyone else or spoken your name. We don't want to tell your name to Oranyil or our father, either of whom could prepare the wine. Our best idea is to have Oranyil teach you how so you can prepare it for us, though that means waiting until after you graduate."

"I see. That seems like an answer, I guess, assuming I can light this candle and be welcomed by the elves as your... hmm, what would the elves call me actually? Is what we're doing considered marriage among the elves?"

Alfyra thought for a moment. "I'm not sure that I know how to answer that or what the word marriage *really* means to humans."

"It's a lifelong commitment to love each other and never fall in love with anyone else. Usually the woman takes care of the man, cooks, and cleans the house, and the man protects the woman and earns the money."

Alfyra's eyes went wide. "You think I'm going to cook and clean for you?"

"Of course not. Frankly, I can't even imagine that."

"Do you think you need to protect *me*?" she asked incredulously.

"Certainly not. You're probably more dangerous than I."

"Probably?"

"Ok, certainly, especially if you have your bow."

"I'm better with my knife."

"That's kind of scary."

"Silly snowflake, I'd never use it on you."

"I know, but you're better than anyone I've met with your bow."

"How many archers do you know who have been practicing for over two hundred seasons?"

"Good point. It's hard to remember that you're older than anyone else I know. To my eyes, you look like you are my age."

"Yeah, and I have to remind myself how young you are. You do much more at sixty-eight seasons than I did. But I guess as a human you can't waste time. In any case if that's what marriage means to you, then it's not the right word."

"Yeah, I just want to spend time with you and remove barriers that separate us. I want to be free from needing to hide all the time."

"Elves will call you my dedicated. And I yours. It means we have the commitment and love you described but none of those strange ideas about who does what."

"That sounds just great to me. You mentioned wasting time, and I feel like I've wasted two weeks trying to light that candle."

"You need to let go of your past. I'm sure that's terribly painful, but unless you think you can get your entire town to party for a month, it's your only option."

"I suppose, but I love my parents. They haven't done anything wrong. I'm sure I've hurt them terribly by running away."

"A choice already made, and one I think you had to make. With your talent, you would have eventually discovered magic on your own and been forced to the Academy one way or another. This way, you're more in control. The elves don't trust Morphosius at all, but I do feel thankful that he took you in. This way you will be properly prepared before arriving at the Academy."

"You're right of course, but I didn't know that at the time. I still feel like I chose to abandon them, like I owe them an explanation."

"Do you owe them the danger of knowing who you became? Would you hurt them just to make yourself feel better? I can see you're thinking about visiting them. I know you that well."

"Of course I am. I've thought about it many times before too. My mom is pretty smart. I think she could keep the secret. If nobody knows I visited them, and they don't tell, that might be ok."

"That's a risk. A big risk. Please try to solve this on your own. It's also a big risk to you, and I would be so sad if this came back to ruin you and took you from me."

"I know. I know. You are not wrong."

"Good. The clouds tell me it might storm later. Let's calm ourselves and listen."

"Yes, that would be good I need to relax."

For over an hour, they sat back to back, leaning on each other, listening to the forest, and enjoying each other's presence. It had a meditative effect, and Sinprejic felt his worries fade. They tried to play stones, but halfway through the wind began to blow and thunder sounded. The weather forced them to put everything away before it rained. They sheltered under the pines and were startled when the wind snapped a branch above them, but the wind took it beyond them. Despite the pines, they were both soaked.

"Early storm," Alfyra said when it calmed to a steady rain a few minutes later.

"Yeah, storms are always exciting, almost fun except for the danger from things like that branch."

"Yeah, makes you feel alive. But now we're soaked, and the wind has shifted to the north... Soon we will be chilled."

"Yeah, time to go. I hope I can tell you I lit that candle next week."

"I'm sure you will. I don't think anything will be able to stop you from earning your staff."

"Thanks, I love you."

"I love you too."

They hugged each other quickly and then headed for their homes and dry clothes.

7.4 Early

Sinprejic made his way quietly down the stairs from his room and across the feast hall into the kitchen. He grabbed two apples, some cheese, and half a loaf of bread for lunch. Mutara would scold him, but he didn't care. It wouldn't hurt for the people in the tower to be thinking about something trivial like that today. He settled the food into his bag, and adjusted his bow and sword, and then left via the door to the stable.

The horses whickered as he passed their stalls in the darkness, but he was moving quietly, and they didn't react any more than that. When he left the stable, he was greeted by a starlit sky that was only just barely showing signs of morning. He installed the raven medallion on the tip of his bow, and the outer gate let him pass into the darkness outside.

In the dark, the stone lake seemed much more ominous. There was no moon, so the waves of spikes were impressions in the distance, seemingly always lurking just out of sight. It suddenly occurred to him how dangerous it would be to slip. Even though there was nothing to trip over, and he had crossed the lake many times, now he found himself slowing and walking more carefully than usual.

When he got off the stone lake, he began to move faster. The "Maze of Morphosius" recognized the amulet and melted away leaving a wide stone path. This was how it should have been the first time he encountered it if he had used the amulet properly. Once he was on the trail, he took up a brisk jog.

Soon he reached the needle tree grove, and the sun was just peeking over the horizon. Only the very tips of the tallest pines showed some light. He quickly adjusted the signal rock so that it pointed toward the tree where they stashed the stones board and then went to the tree and left a note in the tree hole next to the board.

Next, he moved into the bushes where Alfyra always triggered her rod. He had given the rod back to Alfyra, but it was critical that he not be followed. He didn't sense any scrying, but he needed to be sure. Planar magic was risky, but if he was followed today it would be an enormous problem. He had to take a risk.

He breathed deeply and concentrated, remembering what he had seen when the rod was activated, and then with a short wish that he wouldn't mess it up he did his best to duplicate the effect via sorcery. The result was somewhat haphazard and rather stronger than he had intended. He felt a wrenching in his gut and some lightheadedness, but he also achieved the planar vibration he remembered, and when he relaxed it subsided. A moment later he nearly threw up, but after the nausea subsided he disappeared into the early dawn forest.

7.5 Note

The birds were calling, and the trees were in full leaf, shading the path as Alfyra made her way along it in silent grace. At one point the breeze gusted, and whirly seed trees dropped a flurry of seeds, all spinning gleefully in search of a place to begin their new lives. She danced and spun with them briefly and then continued. Just before she got to the log across the stream that she always used on her way to the needle tree grove, she paused to observe the nest of dee-dee birds she had been watching for the last couple of weeks. Joy filled her as she realized that today the young birds were fledging. New young birds peeped their heads out of the nest hole, and the parents were nearby with food, tempting them out. The renewal of life every spring was so precious and special.

At the same time, she found that the fledging gave her a faint sense of dread. Fledging birds meant the solstice was nearing. Sinprejic only had a few more weeks to complete his apprenticeship. She trusted her father's judgment in giving Sinprejic this task, and he had said that he hoped Sinprejic would succeed, but she also knew her father's word was less flexible than iron. If he said he would do something, that was what he would do.

She crept away from the nest and crossed the log. As she reached the other side she said, "Surely today he'll have good news. Now that he understands his fear, he should be able to conquer it." After that she was quiet all the way to the needle tree grove. As she approached in the early morning light, she noticed the signal stone was in a wrong position. She stopped, hid, and watched for almost an hour. While she watched, she pondered if maybe a squirrel or some animal had bumped it, but she also realized it pointed at the tree with the stones board.

When the morning sun was halfway to its zenith, she realized that Sinprejic was late, and she was sure she was alone, so she adjusted the signal stone to show she was here and went to check the tree with the stones board. When she found the note, her heart sank.

"Oh, no, please tell me you didn't..." she murmured. She opened the note and scanned it. It was written in human common tongue, and she had a little trouble reading it, but the message got through, and she sat down sighing heavily.

"What have I done wrong? Why didn't he listen to me?" Then she sighed and breathed. "May the blessings of the forest follow him."

7.6 Staff

In the early morning light, Johnny looked up at the wall, remembering a time when he had stood on top and watched his father fight goblins. The inside had crumbled in a few places, but the outside remained intact. Initially he wondered if he shouldn't just go around to the front gate, but as he looked closer he saw that there were several places with cracks or missing stones. Soon he found a combination of these that allowed him to climb up to the top of the wall. From there he could see across the fields to the house.

The first thing he noticed was how quiet everything was. Next, he realized that only a small patch of the fields was planted with crops. It seemed strange that his father would have stopped trying to grow crops. He worried that his disappearance had disrupted the planting. The answers would be inside, so he found a way down the inside of the wall and made his way to the back door.

His next surprise was finding this door locked. Normally, it was never locked during the day. After a moment, he fished his key out of his pouches. He still carried it. He had never quite been willing to admit he was never going home.

Inside, the kitchen was quiet. Something was wrong. Very wrong. There was a plate of food on the table long since taken by flies and other insects. The floor had mouse droppings. The water barrel was dry, and there was a layer of dust over everything.

Only one word came to his mouth. "Mom..."

He looked at the table with the abandoned food and said, "Not good."

Carefully, he checked through the entire main wing of the house, and there was no sign of any recent disturbance. He did note that when he got to Zach's room something was different. Almost none of his brother's stuff was there. The room still had a fine layer of dust everywhere, but it was completely empty.

His room was as he had left it more or less, and his parents' room looked undisturbed. He looked in drawers, and all their stuff was still there. They had not packed up. Something was very wrong. Finally, he came to his mother's locked closet. As a kid he'd always been curious about it, but the one time he tried to open it his mother caught him, and he still remembered her scathing words. But now with his parents seemingly having abandoned everything, he felt no guilt about forcing the lock on the closet.

Inside he found several dresses and some shirts, but then his eyes fell on a long thin staff at the back of the closet. The staff was about four feet long, and most of it was a single shaft of wood that had a texture and appearance of driftwood that had been oiled and stained. The top however had an enameled metal section that was about six inches of inky blue with stars that seemed to almost twinkle as much as stars in the night sky. Above and below this were purple and green bands, and set in the top was a small, milky white crystal of a diameter slightly larger than the staff. There could be no doubt what it was, a Mage's staff.

"Why does Mom have a Mage staff in her closet? No... but how... how is it possible?" He sat down heavily on the bed opposite her closet and stared at the impossible staff. As he sat there, he remembered.

"My shirts never stained..."

"The horses calming when Karl died..."

"We always had rats and mice in the barn, but somehow never in the house..."

A flurry of other oddities he'd always wondered about ran through his head and began to make sense. He knew it was true. Madeline D'Abrac was an Academy-trained Mage. He'd always felt an affinity for her that didn't exist with his dad. Now he understood. It was her talent interacting with his.

He sat for several minutes trying to get hold of his thoughts. It was the sort of discovery that changed nothing and everything at the same time. He thought of the conversation he had over-heard so many years ago outside their door... and something that never made sense was suddenly so obvious. He'd never under-stood how it was his mother had come to participate in the killing of a Necromancer. That unsolvable mystery was suddenly solved.

Slowly, he stood and withdrew the staff from the closet. There was no surprise at all when he focused on the magic and saw it was heavily woven with illusion and thought. He had no idea what the staff did, but he had already guessed that these were likely talents for his mother to have had. But as he looked, he realized there was a third type, finely woven in as well... a type he had never seen before.

A chill ran down his spine, and goosebumps pebbled his arms. There was only one type of magic he had never seen, and it was inside his *mother's* staff. His mother, who helped kill a Necro-mancer, used Necromancy.

"I've been a child, and a fool," he said quietly. "It's what Jalsus and Alfyra have been trying to tell me. It's not the magic but how you use it. Why couldn't I hear them? Even my mother uses Necromancy..."

Again, he sat for a while, reorganizing his thoughts around what he just learned. A while later he said, "And if I want to find out what happened to her, I have to use Necromancy too."

He studied the new type of spell essence he saw carefully, but almost immediately it seemed to him like somehow he had always known of it. It almost called out to him, and he was tempted to try to manipulate it, but he knew that staves were very powerful, and so he resisted that temptation. After about five minutes he carefully replaced the staff at the back of the closet and closed it.

"I don't have anywhere else to store it. This will have to do for now," he said with a sigh.

7.7 Study

There was only one more room to check in the house, his father's study. He almost skipped it, but in the end he decided to check it out since he wouldn't likely be back soon.

As he entered the room, his eyes filled with tears. The room had a distinctive uncomfortable and oppressive feel. He had felt this feeling once before when he was young, but at that time he had not realized what it meant. It had been strongest at the exact location where the coach had capsized, killing Karl and had persisted for almost a year. Now he felt that same feeling again, but much more strongly than ever.

"This feeling, it must be from my Necromancy talent. Someone died here," he whispered despondently.

He knew no way of verifying who had died, but he knew his mother rarely came here, and his dad did so frequently. Eyes blurred with tears, he sat in the chair at his father's desk. He had sat there sometimes as a kid. His dad knew this and occasionally left him a joke or funny story written on a slip of paper under the blotter. Hopelessly, he lifted the corner and was shocked to see something actually underneath.

Carefully, he withdrew a tattered piece of paper-bark. It appeared to be quite old, and the writing was somewhat faded, but still legible. It read, "Please, if you have kindness in your heart, give him the love and life I cannot. His name is Sal Lehan."

270

His parents only had two children, and he remembered his mother being pregnant with Zach. There was only one possible meaning... his parents were not actually his parents. His vision blurred again, and he sobbed uncontrollably for several minutes.

Slowly, he got control of himself and sighed. "I don't care. I still love you both. You cared about me and for me. I don't care." Then the tears came again but not as bad.

"I *will* find out what happened here. I need to become a Mage first, but I'll be back. I will return, and the person who has hurt you will pay."

With that oath, the tears disappeared, and a new clarity settled upon him. He looked around carefully, looking for clues. He found no blood and no sign of cleanup that he could identify. The desk was untouched, A few silver coins and two gold coins remained in the drawer, and he noticed that his dad's sword still rested in the corner."

"No violence then, and either my dad was taken by surprise, poisoned, or it wasn't my dad who died here."

Next, he studied the rest of the room. He noticed several books slightly pulled out as if they had been replaced carelessly. That was very unlike his dad, who was extremely fastidious and orderly. The books that were disturbed didn't seem to have any pattern. Someone looked for something, it seemed, but there was no telling if they found what they were looking for.

"This must be related to whatever caused them to leave Pendalir City. That's where I'll start once I graduate. But first I should check the barn and servant quarters. I hope Al and Cindy are OK."

7.8 Al

To Johnny's surprise, the barn seemed to have fresh hay, and there were two horses, his father's Stallion named Storm and his mother's mare named Feather, both in good condition. He walked over and greeted Storm, who nosed him enthusiastically. Feather whickered jealously from her stall. It seemed as if they were glad to see him.

"Can I help you?" a familiar gravelly voice called from the door where he had entered. Johnny turned around smiling.

"Al! You're ok!" he said happily.

"Johnny, oh, thank heavens. Did your parents find you? Did they come back with you?"

"No. I came back to see them, let them know I was ok, but the house..." He saw Al's face droop wearily. "Did they go off in search of me? Why would Mom leave the kitchen in such a state? And my dad left his sword in his study?"

"His sword? I didn't know that. Honestly, Johnny I don't know what caused your parents to leave. I just assumed they had gone off looking for you. I was out teaching Zach how to trot a horse, and Cindy was in town shopping. When we found the house empty and abandoned, we just locked it up. We didn't know what else to do. It was so strange. I don't understand how they could have left without making plans for Zach. After a couple of weeks, Rhielda took in Zach. I didn't have money to hire hands, so the fields never got planted beyond what Cindy and I could manage on our own. I'm afraid that at our age that's not very much."

"I see. Hmm. Why Rhielda? Dillon won't be a good influence."

"Dillon is top of his class in the guard and rarely comes home now. I don't reckon he'll have that much contact with Zach. Rhielda's a good woman, and I think she's not proud of Dillon's attitude toward you. Dillon's been a troublesome child. One can hope that the sergeant and guard life can straighten him out. I get the feeling Rhielda thinks your leaving the guard had something to do with Dillon, and to her that means she owes something to the D'Abracs.

"I figure that's why she went out of her way to offer to care for Zach. She's from the eastern kingdoms. They've got a funny sense of honor out there. In any case, with nobody but Cindy to help with the crops and stable work and other upkeep, we hardly have time to watch Zach. He's only ten, and he's been fairly pampered. He needs a watchful eye that Cindy and I are too busy for. Also, she's a lot younger than either of us. I'm only a couple of years from seventy and Cindy's only five years younger than I. Keeping up with a ten-year-old boy is not as easy as it used to be. Anyway, since you've been in the house, and you didn't leave your sword and bow in your room, I'm guessing you're not staying..."

"I can't stay. That's true."

"So what future have you made for yourself? Most folks believe that you ran off down to Pendalir City."

"Ah, well. I guess I kinda want to tell Mom and Dad myself first. It's a little complicated, and I don't want them to think the wrong thing if they hear only half of it. You wouldn't want to lie to Cindy, and we both know she's going to gossip... right?"

"Ah. I can't say you're wrong, though I'm sad you can't tell me. It sounds like maybe you haven't fallen in with the best sort of folks."

"No, so far as I know they're all just fine. That's not the problem, but I really can't say more just now."

"Ok, I'll take your word for that then. Sure is good to see you again though. It's been down right lonely here. I worry a lot about what could happen if goblins or some unsavory folks showed up with us being so far from town."

"I see. Yes, that would be bad. Eventually word will spread of my father's absence. I can't stay to help either, but I think there's definitely nobody better than you to take care of things until my parents return. I'll show you dad's treasury, and you have my permission to use it to keep the grounds and the horses. It's too late for summer crops, and a year fallow probably won't hurt, but if it should go so far as next year before they return you should hire folks to help you plant and try to make profit to replace what you've used. If you make more than you use, the balance is yours. Also, talk to Corporal Zandar. I think he's pretty good friends with my dad. He can probably shift some ranger patrols over this way. Is that all ok with you?"

Al shook his head. "Johnny, I'm just a merchant guard who settled down as a stable keeper so he could stay with the woman he loved. I'm certainly not a noble. I don't know if I should do this."

"I've known you all my life. You are someone I would trust entirely, and I know you're not a fool either. I trust you wouldn't squander Zach's inheritance, and I'm sure you are capable. My parents wouldn't want their horses to starve or their roof to leak. I think it's fine to clean up and keep an eye on most of the house. Just leave their room and my father's study as is. In fact just lock them. If they are not back the next time I come back, I suspect the clues on where they went will be found in one of those two rooms, so I don't want them disturbed. We'll fetch the latest ledger and a blank one too so you can work from that."

"I'm humbled beyond belief, Johnny. I don't know what to say."

"If you think it's something you would want to do, say yes," and gave Al an encouraging smile.

"Oh, certainly. I've been lamenting what would happen when we ran out of horse feed and where we would go. I'm awfully used to living here. It's hard to change everything at my age."

"Good. Thanks, Al. This is a huge service to my parents."

"What should I tell Zach?"

"Ah, hmm. I wouldn't want you to have to lie to him, and I really wouldn't want him to go chasing after me. I guess I need you not to mention this visit to him at all. It's sad to say that, but he caught me leaving, so at least I got to say goodbye to him. Also, be sure he knows that when he's of age, the manor and the treasury are still his. He shouldn't be allowed to think that he's lost his inheritance. Keep good ledgers so there's no questions later."

"Yeah, hard enough on him to have your parents disappear. Running off chasing you won't make his life any better. You're right about that. Ok, I'll not tell him you were here, and I already planned to keep careful records anyway."

"Thanks."

After Al had access to the treasury, they said their goodbyes, and Johnny left through the front gate. The gate squealed as he opened it, and the familiarity of that sound and the memories of his dad opening that gate so many times in the past almost choked him up. But then he was on the tree-lined lane, and at the end he suddenly stopped and stared at the griffon statues.

The moment he focused on magic, they revealed a myriad of extremely strong and complex magic. He sensed large amounts of Mutamancy, some planar magic and projecting out ahead of them, toward town and away from him, was a fine skein of thought magic twined with a little bit of Necromancy. The sheer power of the magic involved was frightening, and he recalled his past fear when passing between them.

Leaving the road and avoiding the statues, he climbed up the hillock with the rotting stump. From there he kept low and out of sight but gazed across at his father's manor and the cap nut tree path and the griffon statues for several minutes as the sun crept to its zenith in the sky. Soon he saw a plump, older lady approaching from the direction of town. Almost certainly it was Cindy, and he didn't want to have to talk to her, so he crept down the back of the hillock and made his way back into the woods.

As Sinprejic approached the needle tree grove, he was relieved to see that the signal rock was set, indicating that Alfyra was waiting. When she revealed herself, she said in Elvish, "You don't listen to me, and you make we wait for you half the day?"

"I'm sorry I—"

"Never mind. Let's get going," she said and headed for the bushes where they used the anti-scrying rosewood rod.

Sinprejic almost missed the hint and started to argue but then caught on and followed her. They used the rosewood rod and departed for the hemlocks. They traveled in silence. When they got to the center of the hemlocks, she said, "Seems quiet enough in here," which was their agreed on signal for him to look around for evidence of scrying.

After a moment he replied, "Yes, it does seem quiet." That indicated it should be safe to talk.

She sighed, and asked, "Why, why don't you believe me?"

"I do, but I also believed that if I didn't take a risk I would be certain to lose you. I don't know if Morphosius is going to throw some new criteria at me at the last second. He did that twice with the book-writing exercise. If I complete what he's assigned on the last possible day, I might still fail, and that seemed like a bigger, more important risk to me."

Alfyra sighed. "Did you at least try to think of life and birth instead of death?"

"Yes, every day, but the problem I found is that it wasn't the thought of death that was scaring me. It was the candle itself and the implications of success. I knew that if I confronted my parents either outcome would free me from the uncertainty. What I really feared was that I would lose a chance to still be their son. If I had lit the candle without going to see them, I would forever wonder what I might have lost. So if they accepted me and kept my secret, I wouldn't lose that chance, and if they reacted badly then the chance to maintain a relationship with them was never there. Then I wouldn't need to worry about losing it. Really, it was fear of the unknown. Having an answer, any answer, should unlock it for me."

She sighed. "So what answer did you find?"

"I found a mystery instead but also an answer of sorts."

He told her about his day, his discovery about his mother and her staff, and also his father's likely death. Partway through, he choked up and couldn't continue, and she held him for a while. He noticed her cheeks were not dry when he finished either.

"I'm so sorry for your loss. While I think the conclusion you leapt to might be the most likely one, there is another less likely but more hopeful possibility. It could be that the would-be assassin got the short end and that's who died in your father's office."

"No. I thought about that, but then my father would have taken his sword with him. The only thing that would separate him from his sword is death."

"Oh. Darn, you're probably right," she said, and she hugged him, and he hugged her back. They kissed, and their kiss started to become passionate, but then he pulled away.

"I should return to the tower as soon as possible. I need to prepare to demonstrate all the candles and cantrips to Morphosius. It would be so easy to lose myself in you for the rest of the day, and it would be a welcome solace, but I can't bear any delay. I must earn your father's approval as soon as possible."

She smiled and asked, "You are confident you can light the black candle now?"

"On the first try, I'm sure of it. The candle is no longer threatening to separate me from my parents. It's now the thing that is separating me from the knowledge and skills I need to find and maybe rescue my mother and learn who killed my father."

"Good, then go. You are right. The most important thing is getting that apprentice's amulet."

7.9 Amulet

The next day at lunch, the moment Morphosius entered, Sinprejic said, "I'm ready to demonstrate all the candles."

Imoed raised his eyebrows, and Jalsus smiled. Mutara snorted, as if she doubted it.

Morphosius however looked at him intently and asked, "Any cantrips?"

"Four out of five of them, all the ones you've authorized."

"Good, you are authorized for the fifth. Let me know when you've mastered all of them."

"So you can test me tomorrow?"

Morphosius said, "Don't waste my time, boy. Just tell me when you've mastered it, and don't bother me before then."

"Ok, but once I discovered how to do it, lighting the Necromancy candle was the easiest of all. I'm sure it won't take long to master the *disturb* cantrip. I already have a mouse to practice with. Mutara gave me one for the *blink* cantrip."

"Don't boast. Just do it."

"Understood," Sinprejic said knowing that he had already mastered it last night but also knowing it was important not to say that.

After lunch the next day, he was in the testing room with Morphosius, who looked as if he expected a debacle.

Sinprejic set up one candle of each color and said, "Name a color and I'll light it."

Morphosius squinted at him and said, "Blue."

Instantly a flame appeared above the blue candle. Then in quick succession Morphosius named brown, then black, then violet, then red, and finally green. At each of Morphosius's commands, Sinprejic lit the corresponding candle instantly.

At the end Morphosius raised his eyebrows, pursed his lips, and nodded. "Very good. That's how it should be done. Now for cantrips."

They ran through the cantrips, and the only one Morphosius could find fault with was the *bend rod* cantrip.

"Well, your bend is not pretty, but it was distinct and without hesitation. I've certainly passed students at the Academy for less, and technically only three cantrips are required, so I guess you have indeed earned this."

He reached into the folds of his robe and brought out a white ivory pendant with an engraved seven pointed-star containing an hourglass. Around the edges, the words "Magic, Education, and Service" were inscribed. The points had varying numbers of gemstones of various colors. The top point was empty, and the upper right had a single large triangular onyx stone set in it. Continuing clockwise he found that the next point had two emeralds, one in each corner nearest the center. Two purple amethysts were placed similarly within the next. After that came two sapphires and then a single red ruby. The final had no gemstones. Each of the six lower points were also enameled with a background color matching their gemstones. Only the top most point had no color or gems.

"Unlike the last amulet I gave you, this amulet confers only privileges, not any power or ability, nor is it a magical key. It grants you access to the Academy if presented to a guard at the gate, and access to the library of the Academy when presented to a librarian. It will only allow you access to the general section however, so don't even think of presenting it for the Wizard stacks or restricted section. Also, it gets you free meals if you show up at meal time in the apprentice's cafeteria."

"Thank you," Sinprejic studied the amulet and noted that the empty point. "Why is the top point empty?"

"That point represents your ability in Chronomancy. Only Aurcivius can test for that, and so it remains unmarked, since your talent is unknown. Most students will have several blank, uncolored points indicating a lack of talent. Your amulet will make you the envy of others and also place a target on your back. I wouldn't flaunt it."

"Ok, that makes sense."

"I was not anticipating that you would succeed this quickly. There are a couple of things that need to be taken care of here before I can take you to the Academy in two to three weeks' time. I suspect you'll want to say goodbye to your elven friend anyway, but you should not sit idle. I want you to perfect your *bend rod* cantrip. Before we leave, you must make your bend a perfect semicircle in one plane, like this..." He promptly demonstrated by first straightening Sinprejic's rod and then re-bending it.

"Got it. Will do."

"Mutara can get you a box of rods to work with, and you will practice each morning. I'll evaluate your progress briefly each day after lunch."

Sinprejic smiled. "Great, thanks!" He put the amulet over his head and couldn't stop grinning with relief and joy for the rest of the day.

7.10 Elves

The next week rained, but Sinprejic went out to the needle tree grove anyway and was pleased to find that Alfyra had come too. They didn't stay long because of the rain, but for the first time ever she forgot to be quiet and squealed with joy when he showed her the amulet.

"Don't tell my dad I squealed like that. He might disown me," she said.

"I won't," Sinprejic said, and then they kissed, hugged, and did a small, impromptu dance.

Soon after, they agreed to meet rain or shine the next week to take him to the elven home for the dedication and its celebration. Then they parted with a kiss and returned to their respective homes.

The following week, the weather was sunny and warm, the first day of the year that truly felt like summer. They met at the needle tree grove, as usual, and of course Alfyra was dressed for the weather and teased him about wearing too much despite the fact he was only in a thin short-sleeved shirt and shortened summer pants. He had asked twice what he should wear, and she always replied, "Whatever the weather requires." It seemed the elves had no concept of a dress code for special events. The idea that someone might tell someone else what to wear completely shocked her when he mentioned it.

They used the rosewood rod in the usual way and then twice more just to be safe as their course meandered northeast. They passed through the hemlocks and across the log over the stream. Soon they passed the field where Sinprejic had met the elven king and the pegasus. From there the forest began to change, the trees were older and more majestic, and it had the feel of a forest that had never been logged or burned. It was somehow quieter and yet felt more alive. After a while, they came upon a place among the trees that was open underneath but still shaded by the canopy, and in the middle there was a large flat rock about twenty feet in diameter. They climbed up on it, and Alfyra made a startlingly loud whistle.

All around, similar whistles responded, and soon various elves appeared from behind trees and rocks and in the branches of some trees. They all had lightly tanned skin and red, brown, or yellow hair, and Sinprejic noticed that all of them were athletic looking and fit. Even those who were elderly still seemed more like old, tough vines than frail dead twigs.

As Alfyra had promised, there was no consistent theme to what they wore. A few wore thin diaphanous silk, others, just a belt with a dagger and some just a bow across their shoulders. It was humid and muggy, and Sinprejic's shirt was clinging to his back. He certainly wore more than anyone except the elven king, who was now approaching in a thin silk version of Wizard robes, carrying his staff. Alongside him was a younger female elf who nonetheless seemed significantly older than Alfyra. The female elf was also in similar silken robes, green instead of purple, and carrying a short ivory staff with a faceted crystal at the top in one hand and a large circular ring made of jade in the other.

As these two approached, the other elves gathered around the rock in groups of two to six, chatting casually among themselves in Elvish. This chatting and socializing continued through the entire short ceremony. There was never a call for silence, and it seemed the elves who were interested listened, and those who were not listening did as they pleased.

When he arrived, the elven king spoke in a voice loud enough for all to hear. "Welcome to our home, Sinprejic, Academy Apprentice of Grand Master Morphosius. My daughter Alfyra has requested that you be accepted among us and welcomed in celebration and recognition of your mutual dedication to each other and the heart pledge you are both about to make. Please hold your apprentice medallion up for all to see."

Sinprejic obliged, and the king continued, "Alfyra has chosen well. Sinprejic has demonstrated purity of heart and good will to all, and furthermore he is expected to become a Mage in all disciplines of magic, Magician of conjuring, *Master* of healing, and Wizard in all else."

There was a brief silence, a few gasps in the crowd, the sound of several folks being told what it was they hadn't been listening to, and then suddenly they all let loose with a jubilant cacophony of cheers, most of which sounded like imitations of various bird songs. It was clear that the idea was that the elves had gained a strong and important ally in the world of men, or perhaps in the world of magic, or both. Sinprejic was stunned and did not know what to say. Nobody had ever treated him as if he were an important person before. He had no idea how to react.

The elven king saved him from his awkwardness however, by turning to him and saying, "And now for the oath, Oranyil..."

At that cue, the elven Wizardess in green stepped forward and held out the green jade ring between Sinprejic and Alfyra. Sinprejic could see that it was powerfully laced with thought magic. The elves nearby cheered again, though it was not as loud this time because some had resumed their conversations. Previously, Alfyra had told him what to do at this point, and the two of them each grasped opposite sides of the ring. Oranyil energized the ring with additional thought magic and nodded, indicating that they should now proceed. In unison, he and Alfyra spoke their oath to each other.

"I swear to protect and defend you with my life if necessary until by death or by mutual oath upon this same ring do we part."

Sinprejic could feel the magic in the ring flow into him, and he noticed that there was a whisp of Necromancy in it as well as thought. When it finished, he had a new sense of connection to Alfyra. He now had a vague sense of what direction she was even if he couldn't see her.

"The magic of this oath ring now binds you and aids you in your oath. May this day be joyful and beneficial for each of you and for all elves in the forests west of the mountains."

And that was the extent of the formalities. Instruments appeared, and soon an assortment of wooden flutes, harps somewhat larger than a storyteller's harp, drums, and rows of different-sized wooden bars struck with small mallets were playing in a strange sort of cooperative fashion where they seemed to both do their own thing and also cooperate and harmonize. Sinprejic was entirely unsurprised to find that many of the motifs resembled bird song or called to mind the sound of raindrops and other such natural sounds. The effect was pleasant and entertaining but did not drown out conversation either. Elven bread similar to what Alfyra had fed him on that first day was also being passed out. Guests had apparently all brought their own water or wine.

Alfyra came over and kissed Sinprejic openly, and a few cheers went up, but mostly the elves were now just socializing with each other. A few moments later the king began to talk with Sinprejic.

"Your fate and ours are bound now, and as you may now realize the elves hope that your friendship will benefit us. Nothing specific is asked of you, of course, but we encourage our youngsters to find a connection to humans of some importance so that we can remain aware of the human world, and humans can continue to understand us. Your news about how the baron of your former town is using fear and loathing of elves for political gain strikes at the heart of one of our deepest fears.

There are perhaps ten thousand elves in the forests of the north on this side of the mountains, but the kingdoms of men, Pendalir, Talingor, Greelin and the three Jewels to the south may contain as many as ten or twenty million humans. Elves are fierce and capable warriors, easily worth ten or twenty human warriors, but no force can ever overcome a deficit of numbers like that which exists between the world of man and the elves of the forest.

"There are three groups of elves, the western forest elves you see here, the eastern forest elves on the other side of the mountains, and the sea elves along the southeastern coast, also east of the mountains. There used to be elves who dwelt on the plains along the west of the southern continent across the inner sea. They had dark skin and white hair and eyes that glowed faintly. They favored the night and reveled in the starlight and moonlight and were known as the star elves, but they made the mistake of becoming too isolated, too oblivious to the world around them. The tribes of men on those plains became united under a single chieftain about two thousand years ago, and without warning the united tribes attacked and eliminated the star elves from the plains entirely. The terrible cost of that war in terms of human lives caused the tribes to behead their leader, and they have never united again, but the star elves were shattered. A few survivors wandered, spreading the tale, but now none of their kind remain.

284

Thanks to you, we have now learned of a similar danger brewing on our doorstep, and so we have already been enriched by your friendship. We will aid you when we can, and you will always be welcome here. We have one apprentice at the Academy and I will send word to him to contact you and help you get settled. How soon do you expect to leave?"

"Perhaps some time this week, next week at the latest. I'm happy to have helped you already. I'm a bit shocked that so much importance has been attached to me, but more than ever the idea that people such as you should come to harm upsets me, and I'll do what I can."

The elven king nodded. "Then time is short. You and Alfyra should mingle and meet some of the others and of course find some time together since you may be apart for a while."

And that was what they did. The other elves were happy to meet him, asked him about his town, and teased him about the fact that he had sweat through his shirt. He didn't tell them that half the sweat was from nervousness at being the center of so much attention. After an hour or so, Alfyra led him out into the forest. He glanced back, and the elves watching them go all had knowing smiles. Indeed, Sinprejic would never forget their time alone in the forest, and this day was far and away the happiest he had ever been in his life.

7.11 Carpet

Three days later, Sinprejic was in his room in the tower packing his things into his sack. The upper corner of the sack still had a hole in it, and when he finished the corner of one of his shirts peeked through. "I'll have to find someone to fix this at the Academy," he said, tucking the shirt back in.

He lifted his sword and dagger off of the back of his desk and threaded his belt through each of the scabbard loops. After rebuckling his belt, he shouldered his pack and left his room just as empty as the day he found it. The outline of the cantrip manual and the primer could be seen pressed against the fabric. All his worldly possessions fit into one sack.

He left his room and was about to close and lock the door but then stopped, looking into the empty room. After a brief pause, he left the room door open and unlocked, just like all the other guest rooms, since there was nothing to protect. From the guest rooms, he passed through the feast hall. Mutara entered from the other side heading for the store rooms most likely.

"Say, Mutara, why does this place have a feast hall? Does it ever get used?"

Mutara paused, looked him over, then impatiently replied, "It's there in case it's needed. It did get used once. We invited Baron D'Arnor here just after he arrived in the area. It hasn't been used since, but if one needs a hall it's much harder to add one after the fact. So when Morphosius and I drew the plans, we included a feast hall."

"Ah, that makes sense, I guess. Anyway, I'm leaving in a few moments. See you in a month or so."

"Hmmph. Try not to get yourself in trouble. I'll have lots of binding work ready for you when you get back."

"Of course, I don't plan to get in trouble. Later..." Sinprejic waved, unfazed. Getting a cheerful response out of Mutara was about as likely as getting a fish to sing a song.

Sinprejic passed into the kitchen then up the stairs all the way to the sixth floor. When he got there, Jalsus, Imoed, and Morphosius were waiting for him. Jalsus looked at his sword and dagger. "Not sure if you should be taking those to the Academy," Jalsus remarked.

Imoed spoke up, "Nonsense. I arrived with a rapier. It's definitely allowed."

"Yes, but someday he needs to learn to defend himself with magic, not swordplay," Jalsus countered.

"For now, any defense is good. The goal is to survive and learn," Morphosius said, ending the discussion.

"What happened to your rapier?" Sinprejic asked.

"The day I realized that I should stick to imagery and magical painting was the day I tried to 'improve' my sword. I'm fantastic with perspective, shape and color, but when it comes to things with three actual dimensions I am all thumbs."

"I see."

"Enough chitchat, I don't want to be flying after dark," Morphosius said. He motioned to a carpet stretched across a wooden frame. There were several bundles strapped to each of the corners and one in the center. "You should sit here with your back to the center bundle so that you are facing out. Tuck your legs under the rope here..."

"Won't I be facing backward?"

"Yes, if you prefer you can face forward, but you'll probably fall off as soon as I accelerate," Morphosius said.

"Ah, backward it is then," Sinprejic said and climbed aboard as instructed.

Morphosius settled himself on the opposite end in similar fashion and then recited an incantation that caused the carpet to levitate a foot above the ground. As they floated forward out of the aerial entrance to the tower, Sinprejic waved at Jalsus and Imoed, and they waved back. The carpet began to rise and pick up speed quickly, the land below looking small and far away. The wind was strong in Sinprejic's hair, and he was glad he had worn a thick coat as instructed.

When the clouds were closer than the land, they began to move northwest toward the Island of Wizards and the Academy.

8 Appendix

This story is imagined to take place in the extreme far future on Earth, many eons after multiple incidents each of which nearly annihilated the human race. These incidents had various effects such as, the destruction of all prior scientific knowledge, the discovery of magic, the reshaping of major continents, and divergence of new humanoid races from the original human ancestors. All but the most recent of these calamities is now fully forgotten by all the remaining inhabitants, and even that is more legend and myth since only selected histories and information was retained from the prior era when the catalyst of that particular disaster relented. It should be noted that although this book contains a reference to the year 20922 this in no way provides an actual future date. It is merely a lower bound, since it's entirely possible that several eras precede that numbering system.

The primary language spoken by humans in and around 20922 is known as "common speech," which is a much more advanced derivative of English. Common speech has substantially more complicated and hard-to-predict punctuation, liberal use of capitalization, variable spellings, more freedom with placement of adverbs, liberal use of adjectives, and a grammar that encourages very long run-on sentences. Luckily, I was able to find a translator to help me render this advanced form into the present day archaic form.

As part of the translation, the names of things humans create, farm, hunt, or otherwise interact with frequently are retained as their standard English-language names. However, our present names for things that grow in the wilds and mostly exist outside human settlements are lost in the sands of time. Naturally new names have been given by the survivors. All notions of scientific, taxonomic classifications and even a solid definition of what a species is have been lost.

The names for animals and plants in the future are purely descriptive. To retain the future sensibilities, these were left untranslated, but below are some translations of names used in the future era of the book to names that are used in the present day. Despite the lack of a clear notion of a species, these names are capitalized in accordance with American Ornithological Union conventions since they designate the character's (or the narrator's) recognition of a specific type of bird, not a group or class of birds. Thus, a Red Bird is a specific type of bird that the character recognizes but a red bird is an unrecognized bird that happens to be (more or less) red in coloration. Other plants and animals are treated similarly.

8.1 Birds

Dee Dee Bird
> Chickadee, named for the end or its call that sounds like *chick-a-dee-dee-dee*.

Pee Bee Bird
> Also, Chickadees, but many humans would not realize this is indeed the same bird, singing its spring territorial song which sounds like *Pheeeee Beeeee*.

Peter Peter Bird
> Titmouse, which has a spring territorial song sounding much like *Peter! Peter! ... Peter! Peter!*

Cheer-Up Bird

American Robin, which has a song that sounds a bit like *Cheer-up, Cheer-a-lee, Cheer-up.*

Needer bird

Nuthatch, a small bird most often seen foraging along the trunks of trees, with a call that sounds like *Needur, Needur* or sometimes *NahNahNahNahNa-nee.*

Question Bird

Red-eyed Vireo, a common bird not often seen that tends to stay in forest tree tops. Its song is reminiscent of *Here I am ... Where are You?* Though those phrases might be repeated in any order.

Red Bird

Northern Cardinal, which of course have males that are bright red. Most humans in this book would fail to understand that the brownish female was the same type of bird, but of course this would be basic knowledge to elves.

Red Badge

Red-Wing Blackbirds, which have a patch of bright red and yellow on their wings, but are otherwise black. This looks something like they are wearing a badge on their shoulder.

8.2 Trees

Trees are typically treated with the human perspective. Elves would have much more specific names for subtypes in most of these categories.

Cap Nut Tree

Oaks of various sorts, "cap nuts" of course being acorns.

Needle Tree

Pine trees in general, for obvious reason.

Blue Needle Tree

A type of pine tree known today as a Blue Spruce tree.

Flat-Needle Tree

Hemlock, a type of pine with small, softer, broader needles arrayed in flat planes.

Whirly Seed Tree

Maple trees in general.

Gray Bark Tree

Beech trees which tend to have smooth gray bark.

Paper Bark Tree

Birch trees in general.

Wrinkle Nut Tree

Walnut trees, which have a large seed with a wrinkly hard outer shell.

9 Acknowledgements

I would like to thank my wife, friends and family for their patience and feedback on early drafts. Additional thanks to my editor Jason Letts who was very professional and responsive. I would also like to thank my cover artist Matthew Stawicki who was a joy to work with. You can find his fabulous work online at https://www.mattstawicki.com/

This book has taken several decades for me to write. There have been innumerable inspirations and influences, far too many to list, but I certainly should thank my friend Keith. His gift of *Pawn of Prophecy* by David Eddings for my twelfth(?) birthday introduced me to the world of fantasy fiction. Perhaps that introduction is why I am especially drawn to stories involving wizards. I certainly read non-wizard fantasy and love science fiction too, but wizards are the characters I enjoy most.

My childhood D&D gaming groups of course deserve thanks, as do authors who wrote wizard characters I enjoyed including Margret Weis and Tracy Hickman (Raistlin, Fizban), Ursula LeGuin (Ged), Glen Cook (Goblin, One-eye, Silent, Lady, etc) Robert Jordan (Rand, Egwene, etc.), Barbra Hambly (Ingold Inglorion), and of course many more including the ultimate father of modern fantasy fiction J. R. R. Tolkien without whom this entire genre might not exist as it does today. These inspirations, along with forays into writing zones for text MUDs (M.U.M.E. and WoTMud) definitely made me want to invent and write my own fantasy world.

10 About the Author

William I. Zard is the pen name for Patrick G. Heck's fantasy fiction writing. He was born in Ohio, but moved to Massachusetts at the age of ten. His originally intended career was Biology, and he earned a Bachelors and a Masters in Biology at Clark University and S. U. N. Y. Buffalo. However, he soon found that his hobby of computer programming offered substantially more lucrative opportunities. He spent most of a decade writing Java Web applications and then transitioned to enterprise search systems. Since 2012 he has been a successful independent consultant is a committer and PMC member for Apache Solr and Apache Lucene.

Despite his distinctly non-literary career thus far, he has always been an avid reader of fantasy and science fiction. This story started as the final project for his creative writing class at Clark University. Since the assignment was to write a "short story" and his writing quickly expanded to twenty-seven pages, with a lame tacked on ending, it wasn't much of a success as a final project. However, the story wouldn't leave his head and as new ideas arose he kept writing them down and sometimes adding to the text. After many years bursting with ideas and repeatedly having to re-read his own half written novel to get going again, he finally resolved to push forward and finish it. Nine months later it was ready for publication.

In addition to science, computers, and fiction he also enjoys autocross racing, computer games, the game of go, and flying airplanes. Only time (and sales numbers) will tell if he can turn his

writing hobby into a third career. He certainly hopes to find time
for at least three more books in the series.

10.1 Style Notes

So that folks can correctly point out my mistakes and are not confused by intentional choices, I will list some conventions used in
producing this work:

1) The naming and capitalization of wild animals and plants is
as noted in the Appendix.

2) Spell names such as *remote knock* are italicized for clarity.

3) The names of magical ranks awarded by the Wizards' Council
are capitalized, but wizard is also a popular colloquial among the
general populous, so that meaning is not capitalized. Scholars of
magic may use the term "spell caster" to avoid such confusion.

4) The author finds ellipses that...don't have a space incred-
ibly...distracting and has therefore mandated a trailing... space
despite the suggestions of his editor who prefers...no spaces.

5) The elves in my books are similar in form to those in Tolkien's
works. They are similar height to humans, have similar body pro-
portions as humans and do not hide from humans. Thus, I adhere to his spelling of "elven", for adjectives relating objects to
elves and use the word "Elvish" for the name of the language they
speak. Elvish is a single, unified language common to all elves,
and thus capitalized. There are at least three types of elves described in this book so elven is an adjective similar to avian for
things relating to birds, so it is not capitalized.

If I someday write a fairy tale with a tiny elf that hides and
secretly helps folk with their shoes or bakes cookies I'll use elfin
and Elfish.